D0364470

# THE GOOD GROUND

After the Crash of 1929 Gregor leaves the wreck of his father's business empire behind him and settles in California. He is no longer the heir to a massive fortune, just the humble owner of orange orchards. The Craigallan wealth was founded on the land's riches – can Greg reap them again? His daughter, Clare, is lured away by the glamour of Hollywood. His son, Lewis, a fiery radical, takes up the cause of the dirt-poor Spanish fruit-pickers, clashing with his aristocratic Spanish mother and sparking off a war that brings violence and tragedy into Greg's family...

# THE GOOD GROUND

# THE GOOD GROUND

*by*

Tessa Barclay

**Magna Large Print Books**
Long Preston, North Yorkshire,
BD23 4ND, England.

British Library Cataloguing in Publication Data.

Barclay, Tessa
        The good ground.

        A catalogue record of this book is
        available from the British Library

        ISBN   0-7505-1828-6


First published in Great Britain by W. H. Allen & Co. PLC 1984

Copyright © Tessa Barclay, 1984

Cover illustration © John Hancock by arrangement with
P.W.A. International Ltd.

The moral right of the author has been asserted

Published in Large Print 2002 by arrangement with
Tessa Barclay, care of Darley Anderson

Magna Large Print is an imprint of Library Magna Books Ltd.

Printed and bound in Great Britain by
T.J. (International) Ltd., Cornwall, PL28 8RW

# Chapter One

The inhabitants of San Francisco waited with some interest to see how Gregor McGarth would deal with the wreck of his family fortunes on the East Coast.

Those who liked him viewed the situation as one of sad irony. His enemies – and he had more than a few – found it a source of glee. 'This'll cut the bastard down to size!' they crowed. 'Looking down his nose at us because he had a fortune waiting for him…!'

There had always been argument about Gregor McGarth's supposed inheritance. 'I tell you, Old Craigallan won't leave it to McGarth! He wants his name carried on. He'll leave it to the legal heir.'

'Naw, how can a deaf man handle Craigallan Agriculture?'

'Oh, they can do wonders these days with hearing aids. 'Sides, Cornelius Craigallan's got a wife who helps him handle–'

'You think Craigallan's going to leave all his money to a guy who needs his wife at his elbow all the time? He'll leave it to Mc-Garth. McGarth's always been his favourite, even if he was born the wrong side of the blanket.'

'If he means to leave it to McGarth he'd have taken out legal adoption papers on him years ago – or had his name changed by deed poll. Stands to reason, the company'll go to Cornelius when the old man snuffs. How much is it quoted at now? Forty-one million dollars?'

'And then some. I wish I had a piece of it.'

There was no doubt that it had influenced the people Gregor dealt with when they believed he would inherit the Craigallan fortune. For instance, though the rich owners of the fruit estates used bribery on a large scale to gain their ends, Gregor had never been offered money. 'I wouldn't mind so much,' groaned Lester Fidieu, fixer and trouble-shooter for the Fruit Growers Association, 'if he'd take something else. Most guys who say they never take money can be bought with a girl or a piece of real estate. But McGarth doesn't even hear you when you drop a hint.'

His detractors declared it couldn't have anything to do with upright Scottish parents. For though his father and mother were of Scottish descent, they certainly weren't upright. Old Robert Craigallan had come by his money as dishonestly as most in the rough and tumble of the turn of the century. As for Gregor's mother, Morag... That was a strange business. When she paid her occasional visits to her son in San Francisco, the society columns faithfully reported it.

'Mrs Gregor McGarth gave a dinner party to welcome her mother-in-law, Mrs Morag McGarth, to her lovely Pacific Heights home...'

In the strict social etiquette of 1930, those titles told their tale. Mrs Gregor McGarth was the wife of Gregor, distinguished citizen of San Francisco, Director of the Bureau of Hispano-American Relations. Mrs Morag McGarth was the wife of nobody, despite the handsome engraved gold band she wore on her third finger left hand.

It was known – because the New York papers sometimes referred to it – that Rob Craigallan spent long periods at the home of Mrs McGarth near Pike's Peak. It was acknowledged that Mrs McGarth's son was Robert Craigallan's child. Yet old Rob Craigallan had never got a divorce from his wife to marry Morag and legalize the position of this favourite son.

When Craigallan died suddenly during the Wall Street crash, his will was eagerly awaited. Who would be named as heir? Who'd get the millions?

In the event, there was nothing to inherit except debts. Unwise faith in the recovery of the Stock Market, unwise and massive dealings in wheat futures, left the legal Mrs Craigallan, two sons and one daughter without a penny. For those interested in such things, Craigallan Agricultural Products had been assigned in the will to the care of Cornelius, the eldest child, the legal son. But his only role had been to pay off as much as possible of what was owing and sell the company for what he could get.

Craigallan's widow, Luisa, had removed herself to live out her days in the sunshine of Naples and the reign of Benito Mussolini, of whom she heartily and vocally approved.

The San Franciscans waited to see which members of the Craigallan family Gregor would bring west. Not, presumably, his half-sister Ellie-Rose, married to a New York radio journalist who never let any opportunity go by for a slap at the fascist regime so much admired by his mother-in-law. Some said John Martin was a pinko: most

10

thought him a strange marriage partner for the widow of a Republican Congressman and daughter of a tycoon. But he appeared to be the kind of man who could provide for his wife even if she were not cushioned with her father's millions.

Nor was it likely Ellie-Rose's son would leave the East Coast. He, without much talent for anything except sport, had been lucky enough to land a job at a prep school for the sons of the rich.

In the event the group that stepped off the train after the three day trip from New York numbered Gregor himself, his mother and his niece Gina. It was later learned that his half-brother Cornelius was to have a job on Gregor's orange orchard in the San Joacquin Valley where he would live with his wife Bess. Unkind critics thought it a clever move to keep 'the deaf one' hidden away in the fruit-growing backlands; he certainly wouldn't be a social asset.

For now, it was generally agreed, times would be a bit harder for Gregor McGarth. 'He's got that bunch to provide for now as well as his own two kids,' people said.

'But he's not exactly on Skid Road, is he?' Skid Road was the district in San Francisco where the derelicts gathered. 'He's got real

estate in the San Joacquin and in Oakland.
And they don't pay him peanuts for that job
with the Federal Government.'

'All the same... All that gang have been
used to living high on the hog. He'll have to
pull his horns in a bit.'

Gregor was aware that the eyes of San
Francisco were upon him. What was needed
was a grand entry, and the city provided him
with that.

Each fall 'the season' began with two big
events, the opening of the horse-racing and
the resumption of the opera performances.
It had been the custom for Gregor and
Francesca to take part, even though they
never put a bet on a horse any other day of
the year. This autumn they went as usual to
the Turf Club at midday to lunch and be
seen, Gregor in the traditional grey frock
coat and top hat, Francesca in a slender
frock of lilac voile under a blue fox wrap.

Having eaten smoked salmon and drunk
champagne, they wandered to the betting
windows and were photographed making
their bets. Their horses weren't even placed.

Around five o'clock the crowd hurried to
get into their cars for the return to town,
leaving a trail of torn ticket stubs in their
wake. They had to rush; they were due in

the smart restaurants to eat dinner before the opera house opened its doors to the first-nighters. Then they must all stroll to and fro in the foyer, or drop in on the basement bar, or be seen in the Golden Horseshoe Lounge, to be duly scribbled about by the columnists and photographed for the magazines.

When Gregor and Francesca arrived at the Mural Room of the St Francis Hotel for dinner, they were met by the maitre d'hotel who conducted them to a table for four. A moment later a handsome grey-haired lady appeared, escorted by a tall young woman in a dress of layered black lace by Patou. Heads turned and tongues wagged as they sat down with Gregor and Francesca.

'I feel as if I were being put under a microscope,' Gina muttered, as she accepted the great stiff menu from the waiter.

'My dear, they'll soon find something else to stare at,' Morag comforted. Morag was accustomed to scrutiny. She had had to meet it many a time in her life when she was in company with Rob.

'What amazes me is that they're so interested! What can it matter to them whether we come to the Opera Ball or not?'

Gregor shrugged but made no response.

13

He knew why the San Franciscans were interested. There were always men who wanted to reach him, to get at him. Oftentimes he was involved in negotiations which concerned the Spanish-speaking section of the population. Sometimes he helped over court cases to do with land rights: many of the old Spanish families considered they had been heartlessly swindled by the *foresteros*, the newcomers, in deals concerning their ancient estates. Sometimes he advised over labour problems concerning the Mexicans who flocked in to pick the fruit crops at harvest time. When people kept him under observation, it was to see whether these new arrivals in his family could give them any leverage.

A group newly entering attracted attention away from the McGarth table. They ordered and were beginning the cold consommé when a short, dumpy lady arrived table-hopping at the table next door. She was dressed in a grey taffeta frock with godets at the hips which made her look even plumper than she was. Her voice, however, redeemed her – slightly husky, and with a tinge of vagueness in the style.

After a moment it became clear that though she was talking to the Mandersens at the next table, her eyes were on the McGarths.

'Who is she?' whispered Gina.

'Louella Parsons, the Hollywood columnist. She usually gets north for the opening.'

Gina applied herself to her soup. Francesca carried on a near-normal conversation with Morag under the gaze of the journalist. It was difficult to tell whether she was watching them or whether sheer absence of mind directed her eyes towards them.

'She can't be interested in us,' Francesca said. 'She only writes about Hollywood.'

Thus comforted, Gina managed to disregard Miss Parsons' glance so that when, a little later she turned her head, she found the journalist had gone.

The opera, *Tosca*, had suffered from economy cuts brought on by the Depression. There were fewer soldiers marching about under the orders of Scarpia, and the choir of children had clearly been brought in at the last minute. But the audience applauded politely, the diva received the requisite number of bouquets, Maestro Merola was complimented, and the audience hurried off to the main event of the evening – the Opera Ball at the Palace Hotel.

Here the McGarth party rejoined the

group they had met at the Opera House. Gregor had carefully arranged sufficient unattached males to make escorts for his mother and his niece. Once seated at the supper table, Gina was courted by partners for the dance floor. 'You Were Meant For Me' was the hit song of the year, from the first big Hollywood musical *Broadway Melody*, but the band had a seemingly unending repertoire of tunes from the films – more to the taste of the ball-goers than the opera they were honouring, if truth were told.

When she returned to the table after foxtrotting energetically to 'Tiptoe Through the Tulips', Gina was startled to find Louella Parsons seated at ease at their table. 'Oh, Mrs Gramm, I do hope you don't mind my introducing myself to your aunt and uncle? I so much wanted to meet you.'

'Really?' Gina replied, not troubling to disguise her surprise.

'May I speak to you a moment? I won't keep you from the dance floor, I promise.'

Gina's dance partner, taking this for dismissal – which it was – bowed and removed himself. Miss Parsons arranged her chair so that her back was to the rest of the table. 'My dear, you really are a delicious looking creature. I couldn't help noticing you in the St Francis.'

'It's very kind of you to say so,' said Gina, trying not to sound offended. She was wondering exactly what was being done – was she being propositioned by someone of odd sexual taste? Or was the columnist hoping for some tattle for her newspaper? But no, Francesca had said she only reported film gossip.

'You're new out here on the West Coast, right?'

'Yes, we only arrived two days ago.' Deciding to give her the news she perhaps wanted, Gina went on: 'I expect you saw in the papers that my grandfather, Robert Craigallan, died earlier in the year. You know how things are at the moment – the Craigallan fortunes are at a low ebb so for the time being Uncle Greg is making a home for me here.'

'Darling, I adore that lovely British accent of yours! You were born in England, I take it?'

'No indeed! In New York.'

'But you were educated abroad?'

'Not at all. I did spend some time in London, however.'

'"However"!' Miss Parsons threw up her

hands in delight. 'No one I know in Holly-wood ever says "however"! Listen, dear, you know that since the coming of the talkies a heap of actors and actresses have been closed out of the sound stages because their voices are so awful. Gaynor now – have you seen *Broadway Melody*? Gaynor sounds like a grasshopper with a sore throat!'

'I've only heard about the film, Miss Parsons. But in any case I hardly see–'

'Mrs Gramm, how would you like to have a screen test for Thalberg?'

'Thalberg? Who is Thalberg?' Gina asked, perplexed.

'You don't know who Thalberg is? Oh, come now, Mrs Gramm, everybody knows Irving Thalberg is married to Norma Shearer–'

'Really, I know nothing about the film industry, Miss Parsons. I've heard of Norma Shearer, of course–'

'But even if you know nothing about films, you'd like a screen test.'

'Well … no, thank you. I had a very short career on the stage and I really don't think–'

'You have stage experience? But darling, that's terrific! That gives you better than a fifty per cent chance of making it in Holly-wood! Producers and directors are sending out distress signals to Broadway for actors who can actually speak the lines and be understood. Dear Mrs Gramm – Gina, may I call you Gina? Gina, Thalberg will be thrilled to have you test for him. He truly values good technique–'

'No, really, thank you very much, Miss Parsons, but I couldn't really–'

'Call me Lollie, dear, everyone does. Now don't be coy about this. People would climb the Ferry Building in the dark without an alpenstock for the chance I'm offering you. I *know* you'd make–'

'But I'm too old,' Gina protested. 'Hollywood wants girls, surely–'

'Oh, I'm not saying you could be a star – nothing like that. But Gina, I think you'd be a hit in supporting roles–'

'It's very kind of you, Miss Parsons, but I honestly don't think–'

'I'll have them call you, dear. It'll take a day or two, but you'll hear – rely on it, you'll get a call. Well, 'bye now, Gina, lovely to have this opportunity to do you a favour.'

With this the journalist pushed herself painfully to her tired feet and trotted away towards the bar. Gina, bewildered, looked at her aunt.

'What was all that about?' Francesca inquired.

'I really don't know, Aunt Fran. She seemed to think I wanted to be in pictures.'

'*Dios impedi*!' said her aunt. 'Those people in Hollywood are not respectable. Always marrying and divorcing – and some of the films they make are in such bad taste. I hope, Gina, you don't think of going to Hollywood?'

'Certainly not. I enjoyed my stage career but I was younger then...' And more carefree, she thought. Widowhood and the events of the past year had changed her greatly. When as a girl she first forced her grandfather to pay for drama school, she would have leapt at the chance to go into film-making, then a new and amusing entertainment. Anything to shock her relations.

But she had had enough drama in real life to make her turn away from even the pretence of it. Besides, her talent had always been slight. A beautiful face, a slender body, a certain confidence in her own vitality, a few special lessons in dancing and voice production while she was appearing in a London musical comedy – those had been her assets as an actress.

She had come rushing home from England when her grandfather was nearly killed in a bomb attack on the New York Stock Exchange. After that, her acting career seemed to recede. She had no wish to resume it.

And certainly not in Hollywood, famous for a vast avalanche of mediocre films which overwhelmed the few precious gems by the great directors. Not in the Hollywood of the gossip columns, the centre of intrigue, infidelity and vulgarity.

Miss Parsons' conversation was tucked away with the other events of her introduction to San Francisco society. For the next few days the telephone at Montemoreno, 'the McGarths' lovely home in Pacific Heights', was busy with invitations to Mrs Gramm to come picnicking, to play tennis, to drink cocktails at someone else's poolside, in short to join the social scene.

Men spoken of as 'eligible bachelors' took a special interest. They were mostly not bachelors, but divorcés. Francesca disapproved of them in theory, divorce being against the teachings of her church, but of course encouraged her niece to date them. She had a secret wish to see her niece happily remarried, preferably to someone

21

from an honourable, secure and wealthy family. But this was a longing cherished by many a mother and aunt in these unstable times, when the very fabric of society seemed to be shaking after the Wall Street disaster.

At the end of the following week they all went to help Cornelius and Bess settle into Regalo, the orange orchard in the San Joacquin Valley which Cornelius was to manage. The house on the rise overlooking the vast orchard estate, the *casa del patron*, had most recently been in use as a store-house. Jose Entonches, the ranch manager, had never even dreamed of taking it over. He was the foreman, he lived with his family in a comfortable cabana half a mile away from the main house, as was proper.

'It seems strange to me that he doesn't resent my arrival,' Cornelius said to Gregor.

'Oh, Jose understands the situation perfectly,' his half-brother reassured him.

'If he doesn't, so much the worse for him,' remarked Lewis, Gregor's son.

'What was that?' Half-turned away from his uncle, Lewis had spoken knowing Cornelius couldn't hear him or read his lips.

'Don't bother – it's just Lew showing off his social conscience again,' Lewis's sister

Clare said, with some asperity. 'It's his hobby at the moment – to wear his bleeding heart on his sleeve whenever he senses injustice to the Hispanos.'

'I don't want to be unjust to Jose–'

'Of course not, Neil. And Jose feels no inustice, I assure you. The technical changes in harvesting and packing are going to be beyond his grasp and he knows it. Jose is content to run the working side of the orchard and leave the management to you.'

'How can you be so sure he feels no injustice?' Lewis challenged. 'Have you asked him?'

'As a matter of fact, I have. Did you, before you rushed in to pick up the cudgels on his behalf?' asked Greg.

'*Mi querido*, this is to be a welcoming party, not a political debate,' Francesca reproved. 'Come, let's look at the furniture and see where it will fit best.'

It gave Gina a strange feeling of dislocation to see the items from Castle Craigallan in New York parked under a tarpaulin on the grass under the November sun of California. Cornelius had been able to retain only a few things, but he had brought his father's old desk from the office of Craigallan Agricultural in Chicago, and some of his own laboratory equipment.

'What's that for?' Lewis asked with some surprise. It had not occurred to him that his Uncle Cornelius would actually carry out any scientific work – or much work at all. He had taken it for granted this was a case of family favouritism.

'I'm hoping to investigate the medicinal properties of the citrus leaves,' said Cornelius.

'The what? Oh, medicinal properties...' Lewis looked embarrassed. He was in an awkward position with regard to Uncle Cornelius. His social conscience dictated he should feel indignant on behalf of Jose Entonches, who was being dismissed by having Cornelius installed over his head. But on the other hand, Uncle Cornelius deserved special consideration because he had this terrible disability of deafness; and moreover he had suddenly been rendered penniless and out of work by the demise of Craigallan Agricultural Products.

His sister, senior to Lewis by just over a year, regarded him with tolerant pity. Lewis was just finishing his studies at the University of California where he'd come under the influence of a radical instructor in social history. In a year he'd be launched on the world. It was to be hoped he'd have grown up a good deal by then, because the windmills he wanted to tilt against were likely to decapitate him with their swinging sails.

Especially as he never seemed to have sense enough to duck.

Morag sat quietly observing them all. She loved her grandchildren dearly, but she couldn't help wondering why, if Lewis had to be so idealistic, he also had to be so tactless. He must surely see that to irritate his father served no useful purpose: it didn't advance the cause of world brotherhood by one centimetre.

Gregor was certainly no idealist. Yet he had principles that had caused him to make sacrifices. It was no use harking back into the past and saying to Lewis, 'Your father gave up the prospect of being the acknowledged heir to the Craigallan Fortune in order to come out to San Francisco and work for the improvement of Spanish-American understanding.' Lewis's reply might well be: 'He hasn't done so badly out of it!'

She sighed to herself and was suddenly aware of Clare's dark eyes upon her. She glanced at her, saw her smile of understanding and the little moué of exasperation that compressed the wide mouth. She smiled back. Her heart warmed to the girl. At twenty-four, Clare was attractive in the strange style of the modern girl – not exactly beautiful, but so healthy and tanned and alive that she could turn the head of any man she wanted to.

Francesca worried about her, Morag knew. She had been described in the gossip columns as a girl-about-town. 'I don't think this is a good expression to have said about a daughter,' Francesca had confided to Morag, sounding suddenly less American and more Spanish than usual.

'Don't worry, my dear, she'll settle down when she finds the right man.'

'If she is always about-town, flitting here and there to every party, how will the right man ever find *her*?' mourned Francesca.

The workmen were taking hold of the old desk to move it into the big room on the left of the entrance hall. Gregor stood by, directing them. His son watched him, a smile of cynicism on his young, unformed features. Typical of Papa – he might talk about helping his neighbours but he was always the one to step back and give the orders.

Lewis took after his mother in looks. He

was more Spanish-looking than his sister, and he was glad of it now although he had suffered taunts at junior school; it made him feel closer to the workers whose cause he had espoused. In California at present, most of the manual workers were Mexicans. In times gone by California had imported Chinese, Japanese, Filipinos, jobless war veterans. At the moment the main influx came from Mexico where conditions were even worse then in the United States after the downward swoop of commodity prices and the Stock Market slump.

With the help of Jose and two workmen, the desk was manoeuvred into the house. Bess found a duster and cleaned away some of the grit it had acquired in the dry Californian air. She put a hand on Cornelius's shoulder. 'You sure you really want to use it? I'd think it would make you sad to remember.'

'Not a bit of it. Papa was always a believer in fighting back. That's what we're doing here, fighting back. Isn't it, Greg?'

'Right! Mind you, Mr Craig always belittled California. I remember when I asked him if he'd like to invest some of his money here, he told me he wasn't interested in growing lettuce.'

27

They laughed. They could almost hear old Rob's disgusted tones as Greg said the words.

'I suppose Grandfather thought growing oranges was a prissy sort of crop, compared with wheat?' Gina remarked.

'That was part of it. He was wedded to wheat... God, when I think of the hours we spent in the Chicago Board of Trade, sweating over the predicted crops and prices. He'd never have believed how low they're going now.'

'They'll recover,' Cornelius said. 'They always recover in the end. And even if they don't–'

'You can still make money on a bear market,' Gregor finished in chorus, and grinned.

'That only applies, of course, if you have money to invest in the first place. It's going to be a long time before I take a personal interest in futures.' Cornelius paused, considered what he had just said, and added hastily, 'I don't mean I'm not grateful to have this post at Regalo, Greg! Nor am I complaining about the salary!'

'I'd like to take this opportunity of saying,' Gregor began, with a little nod at Cornelius, 'while you're hanging on my every word...

We've just been remembering that Mr Craig didn't think too highly of California. He was an East Coast man – he loved New York and the power of money there. He could never have made his home in the West. But I think the Craigallan children can make a new start here.'

'Hear, hear!' cried Bess, applauding.

'The pioneers who reached California after terrible hardships thought they'd reached El Dorado–'

'Reached what?' Cornelius asked.

'El Dorado, you uneducated lump,' Gregor said. 'I'm trying to make a speech here, Neil. Would you kindly not interrupt?'

'Do you have to, *mi amado*?' Francesca inquired. 'It will soon be time to change for dinner–'

'Can I have a little respect here? Isn't this a welcoming party to the East Coast branch of the Craigallans? A man has a right to make a speech at a time like this.' Gregor was laughing, yet there was an undertone of seriousness in his voice. Watching him, Gina understood all at once that her Uncle Gregor was deeply moved. The settling of Cornelius and Bess here at Regalo was important to him. He really saw it as a new beginning.

'All I wanted to say,' he resumed, 'is that California really is a land of promise. I know the business world is all to hell and gone at the moment–'

'That is not a very elegant phrase for a speech, my husband,' Francesca observed. 'How can I restrain the children from using bad expressions if they hear their Papa say such things?'

'I'll rephrase that. To quote President Hoover, the business world is going through a period of readjustment at present. Is that better, *esposa mia*?' He paused for his wife's smile of agreement then went on, in mock solemnity: 'I believe California is going to come through this crisis better than most parts of the country. There are opportunities here we haven't even begun to tap. We've yet to build up our manufacturing industries. We have one of the best natural harbours in the world. The soil here is tremendously productive – we can grow almost anything we want to. I think this is the right place for Robert Craigallan's children and grandchildren to be making their home and I just want to say I know Cornelius and Bess will be very happy here.'

'We should drink to that, Gregorio,' declared Francesca.

'Well, it just so happens...' Gregor signalled, and Señora Entonches appeared bearing a tray with glasses while after her her youngest daughter carried between slim brown arms an ice bucket holding a magnum of Veuve Clicquot.

'You think of everything, Papa!' cried Clare, rescuing the heavy silver bucket from the little girl.

Lewis was quite annoyed to notice later that in the toasting and congratulations that followed, Jose Entonches and his wife not only took part but seemed genuinely to be enjoying it. How can you help these people, he cried inwardly. They don't even *want* to fight for their rights!

Gina was unaware of his inward arguments. She enjoyed the stay at Regalo but was equally pleased to return to the pleasures of San Francisco. The maid at Montemoreno handed a collection of telephone messages to her mistress soon after they entered, which Francesca sorted and handed around.

'For you, of course, Clare – and please don't spend all evening on the phone responding to them. Gregorio, there are six for you but you must promise to leave them until tomorrow if they are business calls.

Lewis – ah!' She parted with the slip carrying his message as if it were red hot. 'Lew, I wish you would not have that man ring you here!'

'Why on earth not, Mama? Harry Bridges isn't a criminal.'

'He is a union leader and a trouble-maker. You know I don't like him.'

'Now, now, Francesca, you know we agreed not to interfere in the friendships of our children. What are those you have left – are they all for you, darling?'

'Let me see... Yes, this one, and this – but this is for you, Gina. And this also. My word, you are in demand – and so soon after arriving. Here you are, the last two are for you.'

Gina sat down to read them. 'Mr Thomas Lessiter called and will call again.' 'Miss Alice Dignam called about the croquet party – please call her.'

And then astonishingly: 'Mr Wontner of MGM Studios called and asks you to confirm you will attend for screen test Tuesday ten a.m.'

Louella Parsons had not forgotten her promise.

## Chapter Two

Gina didn't trouble herself unduly about the summons. She sent a polite nine-word telegram to MGM: Thank you but regret unable attend screen test Tuesday. MGM for its part seemed untroubled by her refusal. She felt honour bound to let Miss Parsons know so she wrote her a little note, explaining that she had really meant it when she had said she didn't want to be in pictures but thanking her for her kind interest.

Gina found herself an agreeable job as a part-time secretary to the manager of the opera booking office. It was through her morning stint at the Opera House that she made a new friend.

'*Haben Sie zwei Billeten für mich?*' a deep voice inquired as she sat pecking out an urgent letter on the office typewriter.

'I beg your pardon?'

'*Billeten – für mich?*'

'I'm afraid you should be inquiring at the box office–'

'*Nein, danke, die Fraulein hat mir gesagt–*'

She rose from her place. He was a tall fellow, deep-chested, with unruly brown hair and a five o'clock shadow that was already beginning to show although it was only ten in the morning.

He stared at her helplessly. '*Sprechen Sie Deutsch?*'

'I'm afraid not. Don't you speak English?'

'*Englisch, nein.*' He shook his head with sad vehemence. '*Ich*' – he pointed to himself – '*singe in Oper.*'

'Run that by me one more time?'

He raised large, bony hands and waggled them in exasperation. Suddenly he took up a stance, opened his mouth, and began to sing. '*Toreado, en ga-a-arde, Toreador, Toreador!*' He broke off, gave her a questioning glance. '*Ich singe. Im Chor. Verstehen Sie?*'

Light dawned. 'I get it! You sing in the chorus!' A moment's thought gave her the rest. If he could sing in French, presumably he could speak it. 'Have you come for tickets for a friend?' she asked in French.

'Oh, thank God,' he said. 'I thought we would have to converse in mime. I should have two tickets for *La Bohème* tomorrow evening, but something seems to have gone wrong – have they been left with you?'

'Let me just look. What was the name?'

'Peter Brunnen.' He grinned. 'The fourth student from the right in the opening scene, baritone section.'

'You sing very well.'

'Thank you. I wish Maestro agreed with you enough to give me a solo line. Have you found the tickets?'

'Yes, indeed, they're here – I'm sorry, they should have been taken out to the box office for you.' She handed them over, and had enough interest to inquire: 'Friends? Relatives?'

'A Hollywood casting director and his wife. They're picking out singers for another musical.'

She couldn't prevent a little gurgle of amusement. 'How are you going to manage in Hollywood if you can't speak a word of English?'

'That remains to be seen. I'm hoping the film's director will be a German. Lubitsch, perhaps.'

'Good God!– You're not going into a film with Maurice Chevalier?'

'Why not, dear lady? The money will be very good and with it I can pay for lessons with Chaliapin.'

'And with Chaliapin, shall you speak Russian?'

'So long as he sticks to the dialogue of *Boris Godunov*. It's a pity there are no operas in English – I might have learned the language then.' His eye had come to rest on her left hand. 'You are a married lady?'

'My husband is dead.'

'Oh, I'm sorry. My wife is in Berlin... Might I, without offending you, invite you to have a drink with me some time, if you are free? I find it ... difficult to make friends outside the opera. And inside the opera there is so much competition, so much strain...' He paused. 'I'm sorry. That sounds like a plea for sympathy. I really only wished to invite you to a pleasant little *Weinstube* I've discovered on Market Street.'

'I should like that, M. Brunnen.'

'You would? Good! What am I to call you, *chère amie*?'

'I'm Gina Gramm.'

'Gramm. That is a German name?'

'Originally perhaps. My husband was an American.'

'What time do you finish work?'

'Midday.'

'I suppose you have many engagements in the afternoons?'

'Yes, I have plenty of things to do. But I should like to see your *Weinstube* some time.'

'Are you free today?'

'No, I'm sorry.'

'And on Saturday I have the matinée. Sunday?'

'No, there's a family gathering.'

'Ah, you have a family.' He looked momentarily sad. 'I come from a large family. It's nice, isn't it, when they gather for the midday meal on Sunday... Well, then, Monday. Are you free Monday?'

'Yes, I am.'

'*Enfin*! Shall I pick you up here at one o'clock?'

'That would be fine.'

'Till Monday, then.'

'Yes, till Monday.'

He tucked the tickets in his breast pocket, took her hand, bowed over it, and said in a very formal tone, '*Vielen Danken, gnädige Frau*,' before walking briskly out.

She laughed and shook her head. Opera singers! Already, in her short stint at the theatre, she had heard stories of their eccentricity and single-mindedness. This one certainly didn't lack initiative. She found she was looking forward to her date on Monday.

When she reached the office two days later, she found a note waiting for her on the office typewriter. It was in French. 'Great news – I've been offered a part in *The Desert Song* starring John Boles. Our date on Monday becomes a celebration – let me take you to lunch at El Prado.' She sat looking at the note feeling strangely regretful – she'd hardly met him and now she was never going to get to know him.

Just as she was putting on her jacket he put his head round the door. 'You got my note? Isn't it splendid?'

'Yes, indeed, I congratulate you.'

'I'm to be the fourth Arab bandit on the right this time. The Riff, they are called. The hero leads them in action but they spend most of their time singing. The plot seems absurd but they are spending a lot of money on it. *Colour!*'

She laughed. 'At least it's not Maurice Chevalier.'

'No, but unfortunately, the director is not Lubitsch either. Listen, I must go – it's *Aida* this afternoon, I have to put on my Egyptian tan. I'll tell you all about it on Monday.'

'I look forward to that.'

It was a source of inner amusement to her – a verification of what everyone else said – that he should take it for granted that she longed to hear all about his Hollywood offer. Although she guessed his age to be around thirty, there was something endearingly innocent about him.

Because they were going to El Prado, she dressed with care on Monday. Peter was in the corridor leaning against the wall as she came out of the office. 'Oh,' he said, impressed.

'Do you like it?'

'Very much,' he said, making an inch by inch study of the short sable jacket, the dark green silk dress, and the fine louis-heeled shoes. 'The only thing is... I find that until I get my salary cheque for December, I don't have enough money to take us to El Prado. I couldn't even borrow enough from any of the others.'

Shaking her head, she linked her arm through his. 'If only you had told me that first thing this morning... Is this too fine for a *Weinstube*?'

'To honour Rhine wine? Of course not!' He led her along the corridor and down the side staircase that brought them out at the back of the foyer. 'I thought you might be annoyed,' he confessed.

'At not being able to afford a high-class restaurant? Don't be silly. I come from a family that's just lost all its money.'

'Oh, that's sad! I didn't know.'

'How could you? Anyhow, let's talk about *The Desert Song*.'

As they walked along Grove Avenue he entertained her with an account of his interview with the casting director. 'He didn't like *La Bohème*. My agent translated for me. It seems he doesn't like stories with unhappy endings. *The Desert Song* has a happy ending. Americans are great optimists, I find.'

'Is that a criticism?'

'No, it's a fact. They believe in happy endings. Of course, they may be right.' He took firmer hold of her as they turned into Market Street and met the breeze blowing west from the Bay. 'Shall we take a taxi?'

'Is it far?'

'Not to me – four blocks. But I find the Americans in our company don't like to walk far.'

'Let's walk. It's a fine day. And it'll give us an even greater appetite for our lunch.'

The food was not really to her taste when it came – too heavy, the plate laden with sliced potatoes and puréed lentils. But the wine was excellent, a rich Jesuitengarten as good as the best Sauternes. She couldn't help knowing that an imported wine like this must be expensive, even if they were not drinking it at El Prado.

With great frankness, Peter was giving her the details of his salary for the film. 'Fifty dollars a week – it's very good compared with the opera and there's even overtime for the singers, although not for the actors, I believe. They've done all the action shots and the non-singing scenes. From now on they concentrate on recording the music.'

'I wonder how that's done?'

'Only the good lords knows. I'll write and tell you once I find out. And as soon as I can get the money together I'll send for my wife.'

'She's in Berlin, you said?'

'Yes, singing in a café quartet and taking lessons from Graumann. She has a better voice than me, but I have the luck.' He hesitated. 'Which is a pity.'

'It's a pity that you have luck?' She repeated, surprised.

'I have the luck, but she has the ambition.'

'Oh, now, surely you have ambition or you wouldn't have come to San Francisco–'

'I have a good voice. I want to use it well – but Magda wants to be an opera star.'

She let that go by in silence. 'Will she be pleased at coming to Hollywood?' she asked after a moment.

'It's better than singing Die Lorelei in a smoky café. And there must surely be good singing teachers in Hollywood – there are so many musicals being made now.'

'What's she like? Is she pretty?'

'I think so.' He produced a battered wallet and extracted snapshots. Gina beheld a sturdy, brown-haired girl in a well-cut skirt and blouse, looking straight into the camera with her chin defiantly set. 'That was taken in Stuttgart. We met there, both in the same company. Do you think she's pretty?'

'Very attractive,' lied Gina. In fact, she thought her a little overweight and rather pugnacious.

'Perhaps not for films,' Peter said with the dispassionate observation that comes from facing the facts of life in a stage career. 'And of course, like me, she doesn't speak English.' He paused. 'Gina, may I ask you a favour.'

She drew back, hesitated, then nodded. 'Don't ask anything difficult, though!'

'Could you give me some English lessons?' He flushed red. 'I have survived quite well so far, because there are German singers in the company and if they aren't close by, I can speak Italian and French. But I think it might be a big drawback on a film set, not to speak any English at all.'

'I'm no teacher, Peter...'

'I don't expect a miracle. But if you could teach me how to ask the way, and order a meal–' He broke off. 'Why on earth should you? You hardly know me, and I can't pay you until I get my salary–'

'I wouldn't be doing it for money, Peter.' She gave it a moment's thought. 'All right, how long have we got?'

'Two weeks.'

'And you're singing six times a week–'

'Not exactly – I don't appear in *Tosca*.'

'So we have fourteen afternoons and a couple of evenings. Tell me the phrases you think you're going to need.'

From his pocket he produced a crumpled sheet of paper. 'Where is the studio?' he read out. 'Where is the director?'

She met his eye as he looked up and they both began to laugh. He had been so sure she'd say yes to his request that he'd actually written out the words.

She took the paper from him but the words were written in German. 'Write them again in French.' He did so, and she noticed, as she'd done when he left a message on her typewriter, that he couldn't spell. She placed her finger on the first phrase and began.

Peter's apartment in North Beach, shared with three other male singers, wasn't a suitable place for study. So Gina, with her aunt's agreement, invited him to Montemoreno each day for a light lunch and four hours' work.

At first Francesca was dismayed by the whole thing. A penniless opera singer wasn't her idea of an eligible suitor for her niece. But when she understood that Gina regarded Peter purely as a friend she played her part well. Within a few days Peter Brunnen was an accepted part of the McGrath household: Francesca wheedled his laundry out of him to be done by their maid, Gregor lent him an overcoat when the supposedly mild San Franciscan winter turned suddenly cold, and even Clare – Clare, who really only liked people who could amuse her – helped coach him when Gina needed a break.

Francesca's kindness was all the more unforced because she realized Peter would soon have safely departed. But though he went, he didn't let the friendship die. He wrote, as he'd promised: mis-spelt French epistles about the madness of the film set, the touchiness of microphones, the shrill soprano of the leading lady Carlotta King, and comic accounts of his own struggles with the technical language of filming.

At the end of January, when he'd been gone for two months, Gina came home from the Opera House one day to the news that Peter had been trying to reach her by telephone. 'He asked you to call back, Mrs Gramm,' said the maid. 'Said it was important.'

The telephone number was written on the pad. Gina went up to her bedroom to make the call. She suspected some disaster, perhaps to do with the arrival of Peter's wife. But no, Peter seemed in good spirits when he answered.

'Thank you for returning the call. Gina, I wonder if you would like to come to Hollywood? For a little vacation?'

'Vacation?' Gina echoed. 'But … I haven't been working long enough to take a vacation, Peter.'

She didn't say that if she had, she certainly wouldn't choose Hollywood as a holiday centre.

'Aren't you curious to see the film stars, all the fine houses in Beverly Hills? I can get you into the studios to watch work on the set–'

45

'I don't think so, Peter, thank you.'

'Please come, Gina. I've reserved a room for you at the La Perla – nothing splendid, but it's quite nice, has a pool.'

She paused. 'What's this all about, really?'

'Come, and I'll tell you. Come, even if it's just for a few days – I need your help, Gina!'

She argued, but she knew she was going to agree. She could ask for a long weekend without causing any problems at the booking office. Moreover, she had just bought a small second-hand car and was quite glad of the opportunity to try it out on the drive to Hollywood.

Her aunt was dubious. 'Do you think this is proper, my dear?'

'No, perhaps not. Would you like to come as chaperone?'

'Heaven forbid! Besides, I have dinner guests on Saturday–'

'I'll go with you, Gina,' said her cousin Clare unexpectedly.

'You will not!' said Francesca.

'What's the matter, Mama? Do you think I'll run off with John Gilbert?' Clare laughed at the notion. 'Don't let's have a fuss about it, darling. Gina would probably welcome the company and I'm curious to see Hollywood. I promise to be good.'

Since, in fact, Francesca couldn't prevent Clare from going, she gave in with good grace. Gina wasn't entirely pleased with the prospect but when they at last checked in at La Perla she discovered her cousin had plans of her own.

'I shan't get in your way,' she said. 'I've a college friend who's on the film-editing side at Warner's – he's fixing up a few parties and things.'

'Clare, don't get carried away by–'

'Oh, relax, relax – you don't want to believe all you read about Hollywood in the papers! Joe is a respectably married man with a one-year-old daughter and a wife who does flower paintings.'

Thus reassured, Gina let Clare go her own way. Besides, it was only for a few days.

Peter called to take her to dinner that evening. 'We'll go to the Brown Derby. It's where everyone goes to be seen–'

'Do you want to be seen, then?'

'No, I thought you'd like to be there and spot the film stars showing themselves off. We'll go somewhere else if you prefer.'

She'd thought he was being pretentious at first but now saw that, innocent as ever, he'd merely wanted to please her. At his instruction she drove to the Brown Derby Restaurant where her car was whisked away from her by a parking captain and – because it was early – they obtained a table at once.

Peter ordered chicken a la king and a bottle of California wine with perfect confidence. His everyday English was heavily accented but passable. He asked about her activities but the real business of the weekend was yet to be mentioned, she felt sure.

It turned out he was waiting for the dessert before he broached it. 'Gina, I've been offered a part in another film.'

'How marvellous! Congratulations! Are you being given solos to sing, or anything?'

'It's not a musical, Gina. It's a comedy-drama called *Change Partners*, and I've got two scenes with about nine lines of dialogue in all.'

'Dialogue?' cried Gina loudly.

At the next table, heads turned.

'Yes, dialogue.'

'In English?'

'Of course in English! What do you imagine, that Hollywood is going to make films in German?'

'But, Peter, you can't speak English!'

'I can speak *some–*'

'But not enough to play a speaking role! And besides, what you *can* speak is parrot fashion.'

'Exactly!' He looked at her triumphantly. 'Gina, will you teach me these lines so I can say them properly?'

'Good heavens!'

'It wouldn't take long. There are only nine lines.'

'But you have a strong German accent–'

'Yes, that is partly why I got the part. I'm supposed to be a Viennese doctor–' He held up a hand. 'Now don't say that the Berlin accent is quite different from the Viennese – I've told my agent that and it doesn't matter. He says they'd give the part to a Frenchman or a Spaniard if he looked right. I've got the role because I'm tall and "authoritative".'

'But it's ridiculous–'

'No it isn't. Look.' He produced a few pages of typescript. 'This is the first scene. The heroine is suffering from recurrent lapses of memory and I believe I have to tell her it's due to a problem hidden deep in her psyche.'

She took it unresistingly, glancing at the lines, then put the paper by her plate. 'But Peter – do you *want* to take a speaking role in a non-musical film? What about the singing?'

'I can go back to that. The money for this is very good, you see, and ... I need the money.'

'To bring Magda over?'

He sighed and pushed away his plate of melting ice-cream cake. 'I sent Magda the money for her passage at the end of December but she used it to go to Italy.'

'Oh no!'

'The best singing teachers are in Italy,' he pointed out. He seemed to have no resentment over what had happened. 'Well, now she's in Milan, and she's taking lessons with Biardi, and hasn't even got a job in a café quartet – so I need this job, Gina, it's really very important to earn enough to send some to Magda. Otherwise she'll starve.'

Let her, thought Gina, thinking of those well-covered bones. Do her good. But she could see that Peter felt he must meet his responsibilities. All the same, she tried to resist. 'Shouldn't you think a bit about your own career? You might get a good part in a musical–'

'But I'd have to wait for that. This role in *Change Partners* follows straight away after we finish dubbing *The Desert Song*. I really want to take it. In fact...' he broke off and began to trace embarrassed patterns on the tablecloth.

'You've already signed on,' Gina supplied.

'Yes... Well, I had to – I told you, they had a Spaniard lined up to play it if I didn't take it.'

'And they signed you not knowing you can't speak English?'

He shrugged.

'You must have the best agent in the world!'

'Oh, he's good, all right – but he wouldn't have let me sign if I hadn't told him you'd teach me how to do it.'

'Peter!' But it was no use being outraged by him. Already she knew she was going to spend this so-called 'holiday' in coaching Peter to speak lines in English as if he knew what they were about.

She met the agent, Bert Kolin, the next day. 'Say, it's pretty big of you to rush to Peter's help like this, Mrs Gramm. I guess you know that without you, he wouldn't have got the part. And listen – it's just the first step. Mr Stahl likes the look of our boy Peter. He's planning a biggie for his next, *Back Street*, you know? From the bestseller by Fannie Hurst? He thinks there might be

51

a part for Peter in that.'

'But what about his singing?'

'He can always go back to that,' said Kolin with insouciance.

When Tuesday morning came, Peter had learned the lines so well that he sounded impressive. Kolin grinned. 'If they change anything during the shooting, we're sunk! But thanks a million, Mrs Gramm.' He hesitated. 'I wonder if you've any ambitions to settle in Hollywood? There are a lot of actors and actresses who need help in speaking dialogue.'

Gina withdrew from the suggestion. 'I've no training as a teacher–'

'You managed great with Peter. And didn't I hear you say you took lessons from Ellen Terry in London?'

'Well, yes, but...'

'That's a good enough qualification for anybody here! Think it over, Mrs Gramm. I could bring you a raft of clients. Better still, I could get you a job with one of the major companies as voice coach, dialogue coach. They're in despair at the standard of delivery they get from most of their actors now that sound is here to stay.'

'I don't think so, thank you, Mr Kolin.'

She went back to San Francisco, so exhausted that she was thankful to let Clare do the driving. Clare, for her part, was sparkling with delight. She'd had a wonderful time, partying around every evening and spending most of each day at somebody's pool. If she were asked what the difference was between this and San Francisco, she'd have had to say that she didn't feel her mother's anxious eyes hovering over her in Hollywood.

Gina wouldn't have given Bert Kolin's suggestion another thought but for a blow which fell ten days later. At the breakfast table, her Uncle Gregor was reading the financial pages of the *San Francisco Chronicle*. 'Gina,' he said from behind them, 'what was the name of the insurance company handling Cliff's policy?'

'Brokerage-Life,' she replied. 'Why?'

He rustled the newspaper. As he handed it across the table to her his handsome features were creased in concern. 'I'm sorry to give you bad news to start the day.'

She glanced down the columns. Her eyes soon lighted on the item he had been reading. 'Insurance Companies Fail,' she read. 'Five Offices File Suit.' The suit, she discovered, was for bankruptcy. The falling dividends on investments had made it more and more difficult to meet the claims on the companies' funds as major firms closed down or suffered loss. For some time now the insurance companies had been paying only a percentage on the annuities taken out with them.

Now the end had come. They had gone broke. There would be no more money.

Gina's income had been small, but it had been – so she thought – secure. With that, and the small salary she received for her work in the opera booking office, she had felt at least a partial independence. Now she saw that she would largely be living on Gregor's charity.

'It's not important,' Francesca cried when she understood the news. 'Tell her, Gregorio – she is always welcome here!'

'She knows that. She doesn't have to be told. Gina, don't let this upset you. By and by, if business picks up, the insurance firms may begin to pay something–'

'By and by? When this "recovery" comes that the President keeps foretelling?' Gina was trembling with reaction at the news. Until now she'd never realised how desperately she needed the reassurance of paying her own way.

She had never known actual want. But she

had seen it around her since the Crash. Moreover, she had seen how respect and consideration dwindled as income diminished. Even Greg had suffered, although he was by no means a pauper. The loss of his supposed inheritance had caused a difference in attitude towards him. Editors no longer courted him for his view on the economic situation; opponents on the matter of Hispano-American relations were not as polite as formerly.

The monthly cheque from Cliff's insurance policy had been immediately turned over to Greg against his protests. Gina had felt that she was thus paying for her very comfortable board and lodging and all the other benefits she received from being part of Greg's household. Her salary at the Opera House was pin money only; the job was intended for a lady who wished to occupy her time but didn't want to go in for 'good works'.

So far she had not needed to renew her wardrobe, which contained fashion clothes by Patou, Maggy Rouff and Irene Dana, unlikely to date for at least a year. True, she had invested in a car of her own, but she had wished to make fewer claims on Greg's cars – he himself used one and the other was needed for Francesca or Morag, since Montemoreno was some distance from the town centre. Now, in the first flush of feeling herself almost penniless, she regretted the purchase.

Unless she was going to decline into being Uncle Greg's poor relation, she would have to find herself a job. She consulted Morag on this point. Morag, who knew what it was like to be poor and dependent on a weekly wage, counselled caution.

'You don't know what it's like, Gina, having to report for work every morning and go through the daily grind–'

'But I've done that, to some extent, in the booking office–'

'Come now, darling, be honest. You've started work at nine-thirty and finished at one. When you wanted time off to visit Peter in Hollywood, there was no difficulty–'

'I know that, Grandma Morag. I know it's what most people would call a piece of cotton candy. But at least I know something about being in a job that pays a salary–'

'What are you proposing? That you try for a full-time job at the Opera House? I think you'll find, while economy measures are in force, that they won't want to take on any extra staff. You know, Gina … I hardly like to say this to you … but while you and other goodnatured ladies take up these part-time posts and accept peanuts for them, you're doing some poor clerk out of a full-time job.'

'Oh!' gasped Gina, colouring up.

'There, there, dear, don't take it so hard.' Morag patted her hand. 'You weren't to know that.'

Gina was so vulnerable after the blow from the insurance company that she felt quite stricken at Morag's words. The other woman, seeing tears glittering at the edge of the hazel eyes, turned quickly to less hurtful matters.

'Didn't you say Peter Brunnen's agent offered you a job?'

'Yes. Teaching voice production and diction.'

'What about that, then?'

'Grandma Morag, I'm not equipped for that–'

'Are you sure, dear? You had a year at a very good drama school – it was well-known for its grounding in the classics and for teaching how to project the voice–'

'But I never actually played Shakespeare or Sheridan–'

'But then you took singing lessons and

diction class in London, didn't you?'

'Oh yes, and Mr Kolin was very impressed about that because I studied with Ellen Terry–'

'There you are, then!'

'Grandma, I've no idea if I could teach!'

'It seems you managed very well with Peter.'

'Yes, but…'

'But what?'

'I liked Peter. I did it because he seemed to need help.'

'You could try it, at least, dear. If you didn't like it, what have you lost?'

Morag's attention was really not on Gina's problem. Morag was thinking about what to pack for her trip to Regalo, for she was off to San Joacquin Valley to visit with Cornelius and Bess. Bess's baby was due in about a month; Morag had been invited to stay until the big event, to help run the household during the last few weeks of Bess's pregnancy.

Gina thought it over. Indeed, if she went to Hollywood to set up as a dialogue teacher, what would she lose if she didn't succeed? She would be on salary so that, win or lose, she would be earning something. If she found she couldn't do it, she might find something else – not acting, because instinct told her she wouldn't like film-making. But there were so many ancillary jobs to do with films – there were the wardrobe departments and the make-up rooms and the props and the scene-making and the research on foreign or historical settings and the film-processing and the publicity and the sheer book-keeping...

Before she took the plunge, she rang her mother in New York. Ellie-Rose was delighted to hear her voice. 'Darling! This is a surprise. I thought with your new Spartan regime you had decided not to make long distance phone calls?'

'Mama, I need your opinion. Now that I've got no real income, I'm thinking of taking a job.'

'Good for you! What kind of job?'

When she heard it described, Ellie-Rose's enthusiasm noticeably waned. 'Oh ... Hollywood... Darling, do you think you...?'

'I don't know, Mama. I just don't know. Everybody says it's a terrible rat race but ... I wonder if that's just for the top rank of rats? A little mouse nibbling away at the job of helping people speak better...'

Ellie-Rose was thinking about something different. Gina was a very good-looking woman, likely to attract the attention of the predatory males of the film world. And she was a widow, still not quite back on an even keel after the shocks of the past year. This sudden friendship with Peter Brunnen was a symptom of her loneliness. Remembering her life in New York with Cliff Gramm, it was difficult to visualise Gina suddenly rushing to befriend a poor German singer.

'I wish there was something here for you, darling,' she said. 'But New York is full of desperate people these days, trying to make ends meet.'

'Never mind, Mama. I'll have to sort this out for myself.'

Her mother's opposition strengthened Gina's inclination to take up Bert Kolin's offer. She rang him next day, and was rapturously received. 'Say, Mrs Gramm, you couldn't have chosen a better time! I've got two clients – husband-and-wife team – Hungarian born, great comedians all their lives and now – whammo! They can't get a job for love nor money because they can't do anything but visual jokes. Say, listen, Mrs Gramm, how soon can you get here?'

He assured her he would negotiate a contract for her with MGM, would see that she received a salary of at least two hundred dollars a week to begin with, that an office would be made available for her at the studios in Culver City. 'You got a car? Yes? No problem, then. You'd better go into a motel for the time being but we can get you an apartment pretty soon.'

He took charge. Gina had to do nothing except present herself at the offices of MGM on a Monday ten days hence.

When she did so, she found she was being interviewed by the great Irving Thalberg himself – the Boy Wonder of Hollywood, the 'intellectual' of the film world. He was a slight young man, with a pallor that hinted at poor health, but exquisitely barbered and groomed.

'I'm grateful to Mr Kolin for bringing you to our attention, Mrs Gramm,' he said, rising from his desk to shake hands as she was shown in. 'We're in desperate need of help over getting voices that will record well.'

'You must understand, Mr Thalberg,' she said, 'I don't know anything about recording or the technical–'

'Who does?' he sighed. 'We're all still feeling our way. The sound engineers explain it to me, and I try to understand, but I no more understand why Warner Baxter recorded well in *Broadway Melody* than I do why John Gilbert's voice won't "take". But our chief problem is simpler – many of our great stars have never spoken a word of dialogue in their lives. For silent films, it was never necessary. They used their faces and their bodies. Now all at once they've got to reduce their physical action and use their lungs. They just can't do it.'

'And those that can,' put in Kolin, thinking of Hetta and Janik Cherna, 'are as understandable as Pekinese pug-dogs.'

Gina understood that the studio heads were so worried they were willing to try anything including Rosicrucian philosophy or Japanese wrestling, so long as it helped put understandable spoken dialogue on the sound track.

She had spent the intervening days in buying and re-studying some of the books on techniques she'd used at school. It didn't strike her then – though it did later – that they were all intent on teaching drama students how to speak like ladies and gentlemen, and East Coast ladies and gentlemen at that. This in fact was what the studios wanted: to turn their collection of truck-drivers, waitresses, shoe-salesmen and manicurists into scions of the East

Coast aristocracy.

The office supplied by the studio had all sorts of technical equipment installed. She was examining it gingerly when Peter Brunnen breezed in, a bouquet of carnations in his arms. 'For you, *chérie!*' he cried, embracing her so that the flowers were crushed between them.

Luck would have it that Louella Parsons, moving through the studio's premises as one honoured wherever she appeared, happened by in the corridor. 'Well, well!' she remarked, entering uninvited by the open door. 'What have we here. Why … it's Mrs Gramm, isn't it?'

'Miss Parsons. How nice to see you again,' Gina said politely.

'Aren't you the sneaky one, though! I thought you said you didn't want to be in pictures?'

'Nor shall I be, Miss Parsons. I've got a job at the studios, true – but I'm a voice coach.'

'A voice coach? Darling, isn't that just a leetle dull for someone as good-looking as you?' The little lady looked from one to the other, took in the bouquet of carnations, and smiled. 'Well, some of us get flowers and some of us get information. Nice to have seen you, dear. Good luck in the ... er ... job.'

Her view of the matter appeared in her column two days later. Generally she liked to deal with the big names, but if gossip items were scarce she would use whatever came to her notice.

'What new heart-throb at the MGM studios has arranged for his special friend to have a job as voice coach? We witnessed Peter Brunnen (he of the lovely Continental accent and sexy voice to match) welcome Mrs Gina Gramm with more than a bouquet when she was installed in her new office.' There followed a heart-rending piece about the loss of the Craigallan fortune, the plucky attitude of the beautiful Mrs Gramm in facing her sudden poverty, the wheedling done by love-lorn Peter Brunnen to have his *liebling* join him at Culver City Studios. 'You'll learn more of this romance from these columns, fellow film-fans, so watch out for my story on the course of true love.'

Miss Parsons was welcoming Gina to Hollywood.

## Chapter Three

In the San Joacquin Valley it was much warmer than on the coast. The breezes and the sea mists which kept the temperature of San Francisco at about the level of a fine October day in Boston never penetrated into this hinterland of orchards and farms.

Morag McGarth was enjoying her visit with Cornelius and his wife. Bess was blooming; her rather plain freckled face was already faintly tanned by the San Joacquin sun but pregnancy had also given her skin a fine glow of health.

'It's so lovely to have another woman to talk to, Grandma Morag–'

'But you have Mrs Entonches and the wives of the other workers, surely?'

'We-ell...' Bess sighed and shrugged. 'In the first place, my Spanish isn't all that good and they speak very little English. In the second place, they seem to be in awe of me.'

'In awe?' That made Morag laugh. No one could be more friendly and approachable than Bess Craigallan.

'It's a long tradition, you see. Land was owned in the old days by grandees who were way, way above the workers in station. You took your hat off when you spoke to them, and you certainly never hobnobbed with the *dona*. That view lingers on here in the San Joacquin.'

'That's nonsense!' But Morag found it was only too true. The women around the orchard smiled in friendly fashion when she approached, even stopped what they were doing to await her opening words. But they never seemed to have anything to say in return except, '*Si señora, gracias señora.*' The children, though delightful, were even worse. They hid behind their mothers' skirts, peeping out in awed interest. And they, darling though they were, seemed to speak no English at all.

There were in any case only four families permanently attached to the estate. Morag, with memories of the farm on which she had worked in New York State, found the system hard to understand.

It seemed that when the oranges were due to be picked, workers arrived by the hundreds. Where they came from, how they knew there was work for them, was not clear to Morag. And it seemed that once the oranges were picked and boxed ready for shipment to the main packing station or the juicery, the pickers disappeared.

The cultivation of oranges for the purpose of turning them into juice was one of Cornelius's main projects. 'Greg explained it to me before I came,' he confided to Morag. 'Orange juice is a big and growing market–'

'I wonder about that, Neil. Surely people prefer to eat the whole orange–'

'No, Greg's had a statistical study done and the figures show the there's an enormous potential market–'

'I really don't see where!'

'Well, it's like this, Grandma Morag. You might say it's largely thanks to Hollywood–'

'Hollywood!'

'Half the female population of America is trying to look like a film star – and they've got to lose weight to do it. There's even a comic song, Bess tells me: "My Wife is on a Diet!"'

'Yes, I've heard it on the radio–'

'Well, you see, orange juice or grapefruit seems to figure in almost every diet that Greg's researchers could get word of.'

Morag smiled in appreciation of her son's acuity. He had always been clever – quicker than most men to catch on to what was about to happen.

'And then you see,' Cornelius went on in the strange flat voice which was the result of his deafness, and which somehow could never reflect the genuine enthusiasm he felt, 'there's the change in the American lifestyle. A man used to get up in the morning and get ready for work – shave, brush his hair, get dressed – while his wife made griddle cakes or muffins to go with the bacon for breakfast. Now his wife has to go out to work too – or perhaps *instead*, in these hard times.'

'I see. So she doesn't have time to mix up a batch of batter for griddle cakes. But a man surely doesn't go out to work on a glass of orange juice, Neil?'

'No, there's cornflakes as well, or maybe bought sweet rolls... The point is, orange juice is being sold to the housewives as convenient and nutritious. So the sales are leaping upwards.'

'What you're saying, Neil, is that there's a lot of money involved.'

'Might be as much as a million dollars if we can get the right orange to produce rich, plentiful juice.'

'Good heavens!'

'It's a bit frightening sometimes,' Bess put

in, handing around little iced cakes as they sat on the shady veranda at tea. 'When we first came here, Neil and I thought we were just being given a do-nothing job out of the kindness of Greg's heart. But now we realise he's given Neil a really important project.'

'But you've handled important projects before, Neil–'

'Not involving fruit. I was a wheat expert, Grandma Morag. So I'm having to start from scratch here at Regalo–'

'Mr Entonches helps you, I suppose?'

There was the silvery chuckle of Bess's laughter followed by the strange croak that was Cornelius showing amusement. 'Poor Jose! He's scared to death of anything except handling the pickers and getting the oranges into the boxes. When we first arrived, he let us know he thought he was going to lose his job, because he couldn't understand any of Greg's questions about the productivity of the trees…'

'At least we've set his mind at rest about that,' Cornelius took it up. 'He understands now that I couldn't manage without him, and he feels he couldn't manage without me. I suppose he's right, too. If Greg had put in some young whizz kid with a degree from a horticultural college, Jose might have been out on his ear.'

Bess put aside the plate of cakes. 'I must really get it out of my head that I have to eat for two,' she sighed. 'My mother believes in that old saying, you know – she keeps sending me jars of chicken breasts and hickory smoked hams, as if we didn't have a market nearby in Fresno.'

The conversation turned to family matters and the business side was quite forgotten. But Morag, who had a lifelong interest in plants and flowers, looked with renewed delight at the acres of orange trees when she was driven out next day on a botanising expedition.

Her son Greg had insisted that she should take one of the family cars and with it a chauffeur, Erneste, a small dark man of intermediate age. Erneste couldn't understand why the señora should want to be taken up into the foothills north of the Kings River, but his orders were to convey the señora wherever she wished to go. He, personally, would rather have gone to Fresno, where at least there were stores and cafés.

Morag was interested in variations of the beautiful sand verbena which was now in bud at different levels in the hills. The flower grew in the same locale as the desert dandelion, yet one year the verbena would flourish and next the dandelion; no one knew why. This was to be the verbena year; when Bess's baby arrived, the flowers would be in bloom, a carpet of lavender colour, shading into the purple-red of the owlclover on the lower slopes.

She stood beside the comfortable sedan car, looking about her, shading her eyes from the bright, unclouded sun. California was a botanical wonderland. When the surgeon-botanists of Vancouver's expedition first explored the coastal hills of 1792, he sent back the first seeds and roots to Kew Gardens in England. Another expedition in 1816 had named the state flower, the Californian poppy, in honour of Dr. J.F. Eschscholtz, surgeon to their ships. Gradually the plants were observed and named, but there was still much to be done. It was Morag McGarth's hobby to gather information and send it, such as it was, to the universities who were cataloguing America's botanical heritage.

'I'm going to go up that path, Erneste,' she told the chauffeur. 'There's a little valley up there where I shall do some work.'

'Si, señora.'

'It's just after eleven o'clock now. At about noon, bring the picnic basket up and we'll have lunch.'

'Si, señora.'

'And, Erneste, don't fall asleep and leave me waiting for the coffee flask like yesterday!'

'Si, señora.' She was *la abuela*, the grandmama, and must be humoured therefore in everything, but why could she not sit in the parlour and knit like other grandmamas? He got into the sedan the moment she was out of sight and went quietly asleep with his chauffeur's cap tipped over his eyes.

Morag had a most enjoyable and profitable day. She had found two varieties of sand verbena which seemed to have a hairier stem and amplexical leaves, of which she had taken samples since they seemed relatively plentiful. She had also seen a miniature cactus which she was almost certain was, if not unknown, at least rare. She photographed it with the box camera her son had given her at Christmas. She'd had a pleasant rest in the sun after lunch and a good walk to wake herself up. Now she must get home to bathe and change, for at Regalo dinner was eaten early.

They were winding their way down the hill

road in shallow loops. Erneste's attention was on his driving but Morag was looking out at the scenery. Thus she saw, although Erneste did not, the little figure at the roadside.

'Erneste! Erneste, stop! Look, someone's been hurt!'

Erneste obeyed.

With a sound of impatience, Morag thrust open the passenger door. Erneste got out too, calling, 'Señora, please! Be careful! There are robbers in these hills–'

'Oh, rubbish, that's not a robber!' She gestured at the body. It seemed to be that of a young girl.

'Señora, it might be a trick–'

'Well, if it is, all they'll get is a few pressed flowers and the picnic basket. Oh, Erneste!' Now she had dropped to her knees beside the girl, and the reproach in her tone made the chauffeur frown. He was right to be suspicious – even if, on this occasion, the suspicion was misplaced.

The child stirred as Morag brushed away the tangled hair over her face. She opened her eyes. They were grey eyes, dazed now, and then frightened.

'What – what–'

'What happened? My dear, you seem to

have had a fall.' Morag helped her to sit up, and gently touched the girl's foot, which in its patched sneaker was swollen like a melon.

'Oh ... yes ... I remember ... Patsy ran away–'

'Patsy?'

'My dog... We were going to gather hedge-greens for supper–'

She made a sudden attempt to sit up on her own so as to scramble to her feet. The pain of her twisted foot made her gasp.

'Be still, now, child – you'll only make things worse,' Morag warned.

'But Mommy needs the greens for supper–'

'Never mind that. You've sprained your ankle, at least – you may have harmed the tendon, in fact. Erneste, help pick her up.'

'Señora?' cried the chauffeur, aghast.

'Oh, come along, she won't weigh much! Where do you live, my dear?'

'Up there.' She jerked her head so that the tangled light brown hair flew about. Morag looked in the direction she indicated. There was nothing to be seen.

'Are you sure, dear? I don't see a house.'

'Oh, no... Over the ridge – in the valley.'

Morag could distinguish a track leading

up among the rocks towards the crest of the slope that bordered the road. 'Is it far?'

''Bout quarter mile.'

'You'll have to carry her, Erneste–'

'I?' he protested. 'Señora, she is filthy dirty–'

'Nonsense, she's covered in dust from her fall.' But when she looked closer she could see that indeed the girl's skin had a film of dirt that was of longer duration than a few minutes. Soap and water were not a part of this child's daily life.

'Well, dirty or clean she's got to be carried home, and the car can't go up that track. Come along now, Erneste–'

'Señora, would it not be better to leave her here and let her family find her? If her dog has run home, surely the mother will send out–'

'Well, if you won't carry her, I must.' Morag made an effort to rise with the girl in her arms.

Next moment Erneste was carrying the girl and Morag was leading the way up the track. 'What's your name, dear?' she asked over her shoulder as they went.

'Melda. What's yours?'

'I'm Mrs McGarth, and this is Erneste. Now, Melda, does this track lead straight to your house?'

'Oh, ain't got no house, Miz McGarth. We got a wagon.'

'Wagon? What do you mean, a wagon?' She had a mental picture of a covered wagon of the old days, drawn by a team of mules or horses. Surely not! Or was the child perhaps delirious? There was no way of knowing how long she'd lain there unconscious from the pain of her foot. An hour or so in the sun, that might make anyone part with their wits.

'It's a big Ford, good for a few hundred miles yet, my Daddy says. Mommy and Daddy sleep in that and so does Chip – that's the youngest – and then of course we got a tarp for the rest of us now the dry's come.'

Morag could make nothing of it. The child spoke in a sing-song accent unfamiliar to her and with a faintness that betokened the pain she was in. Besides, now they were coming to a steeper part of the climb and Morag needed her breath for walking.

They crested the rise and began to descend. 'Señora,' Erneste panted, hurrying to catch up so that he almost trod on Morag's heels. 'Señora, pray take care! Her family are probably a gang of thieves – there

76

are many in the hills.'

'Oh, stop scaring yourself to death,' she replied crossly. She was beginning to feel physically weary. She'd been up since six, had spent an active day in the field, and wanted only to return the child safely to her mother so they could head for home and a bath.

They came round a bend in the track. She gave a cry. Erneste gasped: *'Que? Que?'* and tried to elbow past her.

They stood side by side, staring. In the shallow valley beneath them a transient-workers' camp was spread out.

It was the first Morag had ever seen. Down through the centre of the valley a stream threaded its way but later, when the summer gained strength, it would dry up into an arroyo. On either side of the stream the encampment spread, a huddle of tents, shacks and trucks. The tents were not of canvas but of old sacks or tarpaulins supported on tree branches and tethered with cord to stones. The huts were made of scraps of linoleum or old cardboard cartons, windowless, with an opening for a doorway but no door. Old fruit tins or coffee cans served as chimneys and from the chimneys came the scent of wood smoke as the inhabitants cooked their evening meal.

'*Diablo!*' grunted Erneste.

'But ... it's a *village*,' Morag exclaimed.

'Yes, and we had better leave the child here and get away from it as fast as we can, señora, for these people are like wild animals – it is well known!'

'Well, it's not well known to me,' she replied. 'And as for leaving Melda here to be found when someone happens along, that's ridiculous. Come on, now, Erneste – it's your Christian duty.'

Erneste looked as if he would have been happy to turn pagan just then, but had no choice except to follow *la patrona* where she went. At this moment, she chose to go down the rocky track to the village.

They were about a hundred yards away when the dogs noticed them and announced their arrival. They ran towards them, barking in excitement.

Then the village-dwellers were hurrying towards them. The dogs were called off or caught by their owners as they cavorted around them. 'Hey, lookee, Sam, we got visitors,' was the first remark. And then, 'Ain't that Melda Tompson you got there?'

'What you been doing to her?' demanded a tall, gaunt man in denim trousers and

78

patched shirt.

'We found her. Where does she live?' Morag asked, glancing about with authority. 'We ought to get her foot in a pan of cold water and send for the doctor.'

'The doctor?' snorted the man. 'Melda's folks can't afford no doctor! Come on, I'll show you.'

He led the way to a big old Ford truck which stood a little way up a slope in the shade of a cottonwood tree. From the truck to the tree was stretched a worn tarpaulin. Under this a few items of furniture were set out – a wooden table, a small bench, and a battered tin trunk with its lid thrown open to reveal pots and pans.

At the table, peeling potatoes, sat a thin woman in a print cotton dress. She turned her head at the commotion then leapt up when she saw Erneste's burden. 'It's my Melda! What happened?'

Once again Morag explained. 'I think the foot may be quite badly damaged–'

'Oh, I just knew something was wrong when Patsy came home on her own. Oh, poor child... Set her down there, if you would.' She led the way to a corner of the tarpaulin tent, close to where it touched the ground. Here she hastily spread a blanket so that Erneste could lay her down.

'Wouldn't she be better on her bed?' Morag asked, glancing about.

'Land sakes, this is her bed, missus. Now then...' She began to fumble at the laces of the sneaker.

'It'd save trouble to cut it off,' Morag prompted, thinking of the pain every movement must cause Melda.

'Cut it off?' The mother looked at her in consternation. 'What'd she wear if I cut if off? I'm not having no daughter of mine go barefoot!'

Someone had brought a shallow pan of water. Melda's shoe was eventually eased off so that the foot could be placed in the pan. Morag sat brushing the tangled hair off her face and whispering soothing words. 'It's all right, dear. It'll hurt less in a minute. When the doctor gets here he'll bind it up for you–'

When the child was more comfortable, Morag had time to look around. The villagers had gathered to watch the little drama. She saw a strange assortment of figures – tall rangy men from the plains of the Midwest, short dark Mexicans, one or two blacks, a couple with the unmistakable high-planed faces of the Magyar race, a few who looked like Filipinos.

All of them had one thing in common. They were poorly dressed. The men were in work clothes of varying degrees of patchwork, the women were in print frocks or work smocks. Some were barefoot. Few were very clean, and only the men looked as if they had had a square meal recently.

As for the children, they were heart-rending. Skinny, dirty, ragged, their noses running, their faces pinched... Morag had a sudden pang of memory. She recalled days in her youth when she had seen children like these – on the immigrant ship to New York.

Surely, in this rich country, there could be no child as poor and undernourished as those who had lived on weevilled oats and tainted water in the steerage of an immigrant ship? There were charities, public and private. Welfare facilities. Civic departments for social care, state authorities. Church societies for the succour of the needy.

How could this entire community have slipped through the network of benevolence and solicitude set up by the moneyed section of society?

For when she looked about, it was clear these people were destitute. They plainly had no money even for the basic necessities and as for medical treatment...

When she first had the girl carried up the track she'd expected to find a farming family – not rich, by any means, but with funds put by for emergencies such as calling a doctor. Then when she saw the shantytown she'd thought, 'There'll be a welfare physician who calls regularly.' But now she understood that they were totally on their own. No welfare department officials could ever have let these children become such little skeletons.

She went back to ask Melda how she felt. The eight year old was crying with pain. Morag remembered the little tin box of aspirin she carried in her jacket pocket when she went out on a day's botanising. Too much stooping in the sun could bring on a headache so she went forearmed. She produced the tin, opened it and counted the tablets: six left.

She said, masking her uncertainty with an air of assurance: 'Give her a half of one of these tablets now and the same again every three hours while she's awake.' She thought that was a reasonable dose for a child Melda's age, and it would help the little girl to sleep. While she slept, the healing process could start and Melda might be on the road to recovery.

All the same, a doctor ought to examine the foot to see if there was serious damage.

Melda's mother was thanking her profusely, setting about the business of cutting an aspirin tablet in half with a kitchen knife. As Morag turned away, her arm was grasped.

'Lady, are you a doctor?'

'Good heavens, no–' She shook her head at the questioner, a square-faced young woman in an advanced state of pregnancy.

'You got medicines, though? Listen, my Davey is sick – I dunno what to do for him – seems like I can't cure his sore throat and he don't want to eat–'

'I'm afraid I–'

'Look, just come and see him. I give him lemon juice with jest a *tech* of molasses but it don't ease him none. He just lies around a frettin', and with this–' she gestured at her swollen stomach – 'I ain't got the patience with him.'

While she spoke the woman was drawing Morag along with her. The pressure of the others in the crowd took Morag to a hut made of old tin advertising placards, strangely bright in the cool upland sunshine. *Princes Hair Tonic and Colorator,* proclaimed the hut's walls, and *Economy King Cream Separator, the Dairy Farmer's Friend* – ironic reminders of how to spend money the inhabitants no longer had.

The little boy was bedded down on a three-legged sofa. He was wrapped up well, playing with a toy gun whittled from a knot of wood. Morag knelt beside him to feel his forehead. He had a temperature but nothing remarkable so far as she could tell.

'Mammy, gimme a drink of water,' he whined.

'I dunno as I should give it to him. Y'know, I think the water here is dirty–'

'But if you boil it first–'

'Listen, every scrap o' wood to boil a kettle has to be carried up here. I can't go boilin' up water every time Davey wants a drink.'

'It seems to me you could boil up a kettleful and put it aside in pitcher – couldn't you? And it's probably good for him to have fluids.'

'You got any more of them pills you could give Davey?'

Morag tried to explain they were only common aspirin. But already she was being begged to come and cast a glance at another patient, an elderly man whose poisoned hand wasn't improving.

'We been putting on bran poultices,' his wife explained in a subdued tone when Morag had unwillingly inspected the inflamed hand. 'Y'see, he can't work while it's like that and we ain't got a morsel to eat so he's got to get cured real soon.'

'He ought to have it lanced,' Morag said, from the experience of seeing many an injury around the farms where she used to work. 'The skin's as tight as a drum–'

'Well, I kin take a darning needle to it if you think it's ready–'

'Oh, Mrs O'Malley, he should see a doctor–'

'Listen, lady, can I get you to say what you think of my sister? She's been sick and nauseous a week or more.'

So it went on. At length Morag took Erneste's arm and urged him to make a way for her to the edge of the shanty town. There she came to a halt. 'You have to understand, I'm not a doctor. But you do need medical attention to some of the things I've been shown. Now I'm going to leave now, and I want a couple of you to come with me back down to the car... I have to get back to my family, they'll be worried about me...'

Explaining as she went, she made her way with Erneste back to the road. In the car she picked up her holdall to find her purse. She handed over every cent it contained. 'Now I want you to buy Lysol or Cresol to disinfect with, and ask the druggist for painkillers and things to get down temperature – he'll know. Do you know of a good drugstore?'

'They's one in Del Rey,' offered the gaunt man who had challenged her when she first came into the village. 'The druggist ain't too uppity to serve us there.'

'Too uppity to serve you!' Morag was shocked. 'If you've got money, he's bound to serve you – that's his duty.'

'Problem is, ma'am, we generally don't have money. But I reckon if'n I show him a dollar bill as I get in the door, he'll be okay.'

'Señora,' urged Erneste, 'it's getting quite dark. Señora Craigallan will be worried.'

'You're right.' She nodded at the three men who had accompanied them to the car, closed the passenger door, waved farewell, and was driven home.

All the way home she was seething with indignation. When she arrived at Regalo, she was talking as she stepped out of the sedan.

'I've just spent a couple of hours in the most disgraceful place!' she exclaimed, raising her voice to drown out Bess's anxious queries about her lateness.

'Grandma Morag! Where have you been?' asked Neil.

'I've been in a scene from the history books, my boy! I never believed that in this day and age people could live like that! Do you know there are about a hundred people camped in a valley off the Pine Flat road, living in huts made of cardboard and getting their drinking water from a skimpy little stream? And starving – slowing starving to death, by the looks of them.'

'Grandma Morag, slow down – I can't make out what you're saying! You're so late home... Bess and I thought you must have had an accident. Are you all right?'

'I'm all right if you mean have I got my limbs intact. But I'll never be the same again after what I've seen. Now I want you, Bess, to telephone a doctor and send him right away to look at a man with an infected hand. And he should be ready to deal with what may be a dysentery outbreak – there are two or three children who're in a bad way.'

'Grandmama, Grandmama,' soothed Bess. 'Calm down! We held back dinner – aren't you hungry? It's nearly eight o'clock–'

'Oh, never mind that–'

'But I do mind, dear. Neil's had a hard day

87

and needs his food, and I'm ready to eat, myself.'

It dawned on Morag that Bess had had an anxious time. And that wasn't good for the baby.

As she sat down to the handsome meal that Bess's cook had kept waiting, she began instantly: 'Now, Neil, I'm going to be very slow and clear in what I say so you've no excuse for misunderstanding. I came across an encampment this evening on my way home, where people are living like animals. They've no running water, no sanitation, no medical care, and as far as I could gather no food and no money to buy it with. What I want to know is, how does it come about that the growers of this neighbourhood have allowed such a thing to happen?'

'Where was this, Morag?'

She described the spot. 'The nearest orchard, I think, is Turner Grove. Does the manager there know those people are dying on his doorstep?'

Neil let the maid take away his empty soup plate. 'That must be the place they call Scratchville, I think. But there are more than a hundred people in Scratchville, aren't there, Bess?'

'Some of them might be off picking the

lettuce, Neil. I think, Mrs Leiterman said she'd seen trucks and vans heading down-valley a few days ago.'

'Are you telling me that there are *more* than I saw living in that slum?'

'From what I've heard, there are about four hundred people as a rule. Or is that the camp at Velando Creek?'

Morag gave up any pretence at eating. 'There are other camps like that?'

'Of course, Morag. Scattered throughout the valley – and in Imperial Valley and down in Orange County and round Santa Barbara and up in the Greenhorns. Where do you think the pickers come from, when the crops have to be harvested?'

'You *know* people are living in camps and shanties?'

'Well, some of them live on the edge of the towns and come up into the valleys for the harvests. But there's a lot of movement – they follow the crops, you see. So they do tend to live in tents and vans. It's always been like that, I understand. It's like in the Wheat Belt – teams of tractor drivers or truckers hire on for the season–'

'Nobody in that village was hiring on anywhere! They all looked too weak to work. And as for the children–'

'I can see it's upset you, dear,' Bess said. 'Of course, there are unfortunates who can't get work–'

'I want you to call a doctor and send him out to that camp. There was a case of septicemia, and a child with a badly damaged foot and–'

'Morag, it's no use ringing a doctor and asking him to go to any of the transient camps. He'll just refuse to go.'

'Refuse! Neil, that's impossible! Those are sick people–'

'But the doctors around here refuse to treat them. That's the long and the short of it.'

Morag remembered the gaunt man's remark: he'll serve me if I show him a dollar bill as I go in the door. 'Is it because they have no money to pay the bill?' she demanded, her voice hard.

Neil looked distressed. 'They do get medical treatment, Morag. If anyone is taken ill while working on Regalo, or gets hurt, Jose tells me the doctor comes at once and we take care of the bill.'

'But if a child falls sick in one of those huts…? How does a sick child get a visit from a doctor?'

'I don't know, Morag. I've never been

asked that question before.'

'You must call the doctor who treats the workers at Regalo and send him out there–'

'But he'll ask who's going to pay.'

'Well, *we* are! For God's sake Neil, how can we sit here eating a three course dinner when there are people suffering from malnutrition a few miles away? It's our duty to pay for–'

'Listen, Morag, I understand that you're upset. But I've no funds to pay doctor's bills on that kind of scale–'

'Greg will pay. We only have to explain the situation to Greg and he'll foot the bill. I know my own son, Neil – he wouldn't let anyone suffer sickness or poor health when he could alleviate–'

Neil was shaking his head. 'I don't think you understand what you're proposing, Morag. I don't think Greg wants to get into a thing like that. It could run into a fantastic sum of money–'

'He can get public funds to help. There must be funds available–'

'I certainly wouldn't want to take a step like this without consulting Greg. After all, this orchard belongs to him, he has the final say over everything. It's not just the money, Morag – there are implications–'

'I'm going to ring him,' she said, jumping up from the table. 'I'm going to get him on the phone this minute and tell him–'

'Morag, please sit down and eat your food,' Bess implored. 'You've been out all day with nothing but a flask of coffee and a few tortillas. I don't want you collapsing with exhaustion–'

'I'm more likely to explode with indignation!' Morag flashed at her, and hurried to the hall where the telephone stood.

When Greg came to the phone at the other end, he was already quite alarmed. 'Is something wrong, Mother?' he asked. 'Rosita said you sounded close to tears.'

'Greg, I've been having a discussion with Neil about sending a doctor to see to some poor people in a camp-site on the Pine Flat road. Neil says he won't do it without your say-so.'

'Wait a minute, wait a minute – I don't understand. Send a doctor? Why has Neil got to send a doctor? It's not Neil's business–'

'It is his business! It's everybody's business! Those people have got to have help! Greg, it's a shame and a disgrace! There are children there who look as if they haven't seen milk in years, and old people with

92

injuries that are never going to heal unless–'

'But that's a problem for the public health authorities, Mother. I can't get into a thing like that.'

'Public health authorities! It looks to me there's never been a visit of any health authority to the place, otherwise it'd have been closed down months ago and they'd have been moved to proper accommodation.'

'Mother,' Greg said in a patient tone, 'there *is* no accommodation to move them to. Where are you going to put close on two hundred thousand migrant workers? Especially as half of them pack up and go home to Mexico when the harvests are over. The matter of a place to live is up to them. You say they're living in bad conditions – all they have to do is move on–'

'Move on to what? To another camp just like that? Greg, have you seen a place like that?'

'No, I can't say I have. But I've read about them in the papers – they make out all right.'

'You've got to do something! There are some very sick children there–'

'Mother, I can't just say I'll guarantee the medical expenses for an unknown number of–'

'Someone's got to do it. I can't believe you'll refuse to help when I tell you there's desperate need.'

'Now, dear, you're taking this too much to heart. If you'll let me have a day or two, I'll see if I can get one of the charities to send a nurse–'

'But that's not enough, Greg, not nearly enough! And they need help now, tonight–'

'Mother, be reasonable. And calm down. I'm surprised Neil and Bess let you get yourself in such a state. Let me get back to you tomorrow about this, after you've had a night's sleep and a chance to think it over.'

She persisted but in the end had to admit defeat. Her son was not going to leap to the aid of the sufferers in Scratchville. No one, it seemed, understood how bad things were.

When she went back to the dining-room Neil and Bess asked what Greg had said. She pressed her lips together and avoided giving a complete answer. She was astonished at her son's reaction. It must have been that she put the case badly – of course, yes, she'd been flustered, upset...

They ate dessert almost in silence. Bess and Cornelius kept up a conversation between them, perturbed by Morag's attitude. She, usually so gentle and imperturbable, was almost angry with them – and they hardly knew what they'd done to deserve her anger.

For her part, Morag was surprised by her own feelings. It was silly to be annoyed with Bess and Cornelius. It was sillier yet to be annoyed with Greg who, off in San Francisco, probably never even saw the pickers; he left all that to Jose Entonches.

But she was going to bring the problem forcibly to his attention. She had made up her mind. Tomorrow she was off to San Francisco to tell her son he must do something.

## Chapter Four

Her plan was frustrated at first for, when she stepped out of the big sedan next day about noon and hurried into Montemoreno, Greg wasn't home. Of course not, he'd be at the office of the Bureau.

No, he wasn't even there. He'd gone on a two day trip to San Diego, California's state capital.

'But he told me he'd be in touch today,

when I called last night–'

'So he will, Grandmama,' soothed Francesca. 'He'll ring Regalo from San Diego, and when Bess tells him you've come home he'll ring here.'

The call didn't come through until about nine that night. 'Mother, what are you doing back in San Francisco–?'

'I came to speak to you, of course!' she exclaimed, all her pent-up anxiety bursting forth in pettish annoyance. 'I've been trying to reach you for hours!'

'I'm sorry, dear, this has been a helluva day. I've been tied up until now, even had to have dinner with Gardener to talk him into... Well, you don't want to hear office politics. What was it you wanted to say to me?'

'Greg, you can't have forgotten! These people in the hobo camp–'

'Oh, that!' She could tell from his surprise that it had gone completely out of his head. 'I'm sorry, Mother, I haven't been able to give that a thought.'

'But it's urgent, Greg. Those children need proper care–'

'Yes, yes, I'll get to it, I promise. The moment I get back, I'll–'

'But that isn't until tomorrow–'

'I'm afraid so. Late evening, about ten–'

'And meanwhile Melda's foot might need putting in plaster, and the old man's hand isn't being lanced–'

'Mother, be reasonable! I don't even know what you're talking about. Are you sure you're all right? You haven't got a little fever or something–?'

'Greg, don't speak to me as if I were senile!' the unexpected anger in her voice made her son, at the far end of the telephone line, jerk in astonishment. His mother *never* lost her temper.

'All right, all right. I can tell it's important. Just let me get home and we'll talk it through.'

'Meanwhile have I your authority to send a doctor out there, with the understanding you'll pay?'

There was a pause.

'Greg?'

'I'd rather you wait till I think it over, Mother. You see–'

'Good God, boy, you have money enough – the new project for canned orange juice is going to bring you a million dollars, Neil says!'

'But there are political implications–'

'Political? What have politics got to do

with sick children?'

'Mother, politics comes into almost every-thing. Look what Lewis landed us in over that motion picture. No, no, I'm not rushing in where Democrats fear to tread!'

The attempted joke fell flat. Morag said in a cool tone, 'May I use my own money?'

She could hear him sigh. 'Of course you may. What a thing to say.'

'Very well.'

But she had very little of her own. Her beautiful ranch house in the Rockies had been sold to help pay off the mountain of debts that Rob left behind. Strictly speaking she could have kept the proceeds for the house was in her name, but honour had compelled her to add what she could to the Craigallan estate.

All she had was a few pieces of jewellery which Rob had given her. They were noth-ing elaborate; she had always insisted that diamonds and rubies weren't appropriate to her way of life. But she had a string of pearls, very pure and well matched. There were a couple of other things. She spent the next day going around the jewellers of San Francisco getting the best price she could for them.

Francesca was appalled, both at her parting with these few keepsakes of her darling Rob, and the fact that she should go and barter them in shops. 'It's so ... so unsuitable, Grandmama...'

'Nothing's unsuitable that'll put bread in the mouths of those children or buy medicine for them.'

She came home at evening with about two thousand dollars. She asked Francesca to recommend a doctor, one who went out to the poor and needy in San Francisco. Her daughter-in-law knew such things because she concerned herself with various charities connected with her church. She recommended Dr. Zagurra, who in his turn recommended a colleague in Bakersfield.

'I don' know eef he will be able to go eemediate, señora... You know, such a doctor has many, many patients who need heem.'

'But will you tell him it's quite urgent? And tell him – I will pay the bill.'

'I weel tell heem, señora. Two thousand dollar worth of doctoring – Mendoza understands well such theengs.'

For the first time in forty-eight hours Morag felt a little at rest with her conscience. She'd done what she could for the present, and when Greg came home she would persuade him to do more.

Unless the political difficulties made too great a barrier. What, exactly, were they? She didn't really recall the problem over the film. 'Greg said something about Lew causing him trouble over a film, Frannie,' she said as she settled down with her daughter-in-law after dinner.

'Oh, dear heaven, don't remind me. The trouble is still not over.'

'What was it – some student exercise in screen-writing?'

'Oh, no, if it had been only that, who would have cared. No, it was about Eisenstein.'

'Who?'

'You don't remember? The great Russian film director.'

It began to come back to Morag. In May 1930 Sergei Mikhailovich Eisenstein had arrived in the United States, nine months after being given leave of absence from his Soviet film studio. As far as she remembered, he'd left Russia because he wanted sound dubbed on his latest film but the Soviet studios weren't technically able to do it.

Jesse Lasky, one of the heads of Paramount Films, had been in Paris on business in the spring of 1930 and had been persuaded to invite the Russian to Hollywood. He arrived, greatly respected by those who'd seen his masterpieces of film-making but also greatly detested by those who were afraid of the Soviet Revolution. For a time there had been a honeymoon period with Hollywood. It seemed there were plans to make a film from a scenario by Eisenstein from Theodor Dreiser's great novel, *An American Tragedy*.

Then somehow it had all gone wrong. Hollywood no longer loved Eisenstein. The director, sent east to New York to finalise the financial details of the Dreiser film, was curtly told he was fired.

Radical students at Berkeley had been shocked at this unmannerly treatment of a great artist. They had set about finding a way whereby he could make films in the west before having to return to the restricted means of the Soviet Union.

And this was where Lewis McGarth came in. He had thrown himself heart and soul into the project. Some slight social contact with another radical, the bestselling American novelist, Upton Sinclair, put it into his mind to approach him for help.

Upton Sinclair had very little money himself – he seemed to give it away or let it trickle through his fingers – but his brother-in-law was a rich man. He also had rich friends.

Amongst them they had put together the sum of fifteen thousand dollars. Morag knew nothing about film finance, and in fact the actual amount no longer remained in her memory, but she remembered that when she heard of it she'd thought it rather a small amount of money to make a film.

Especially a film that was to be a historical drama of the politics of Mexico.

Greg himself had invested a little money in the film at first. His friends, likewise, had put some dollars into it – partly out of a wish to seem 'intellectual', partly out of curiosity to see what Eisenstein would bring out of that ill-fated country to the south.

But when Lewis went around with the hat again he began to get some dusty answers. His father said, 'You must think we're boneheads. The guy is just playing at film-making.'

'That's not so!'

'Listen, Lew, I made inquiries and I've found out that you can't make any kind of a film that's worth looking at for fifteen thousand dollars. All he wanted was spending money to amuse himself in Mexico.'

So illwill and resentment had cut the investors by half. Moreover, some political backwash had flurried around the family. Greg was accused of being involved with 'pinkos'. He was suspected of using his post in the administration to further the aims of discontented Mexican workers. The land-owners of the fruit-growing regions were watching him like hawks. If he dared do anything that, by spending money, im-proved the conditions of the pickers, they would cry 'Communist!' and life would be very difficult. He might even have to answer to Washington, might be dismissed, if his enemies could rig up a good enough case.

Morag had become aware, during her brief acquaintance with San Francisco life, that Greg wasn't completely beloved. He engaged himself on behalf of the Cali-fornios, the old families who had lost land or income by the take-over of the 'gringos'. He found lawyers for them, he investigated their claims, and sometimes he won back their estates.

He also mediated between Mexican employees and their employers in individual cases. This was done simply because they turned to him for help, as a well-known figure who spoke Spanish and understood the ways of the American court system.

But he had never taken part of any trade union claims nor did he want to. He steered clear of getting himself thought of as a 'champion of the Mexican worker'. He knew it would complicate his job beyond belief.

So when he reached home that evening and heard his mother's urgent appeal on behalf of the migrants of Scratchville, all he felt was an intense reluctance.

'I know, I know, Mother,' he agreed. 'From what you tell me, conditions are bad. But you have to understand that it's a state or federal matter – it needs government measures. No one man could possibly–'

'I'm not asking you to reform the whole of the Californian working arrangements, Greg. All I want you to do is help me improve the state of the camp–'

'Have you any idea of the money that would be needed?'

'But you know how to get money out of the state senate–'

'No I don't! And what's more, I'm not even going to try! If Harry Bridges can't get money from the senate for first aid posts on the docks for his longshoremen, do you really think I can get money for a gang of un-organised fruit pickers?'

'It's not so much for the pickers – it's their families, the children, the old folk–'

'I understand that. Mother, it's a lost cause.'

'I don't see how? Surely they have rights like everybody else–'

'No they don't,' said a new voice from the doorway.

Lewis had come home from Berkeley to spend the weekend revising for a forth-coming exam. He had been standing quietly listening to the argument.

His grandmother rose. She moved to-wards him and stared into his dark eyes. 'What do you mean, they don't have rights? Surely if we can get them to go to their senator–'

'Grandmama, those people have no votes. They can't influence the congress or the senate.'

'No vote?'

'They have no permanent address so they aren't on the electoral register.'

Morag drew in her breath and sat down on the nearest chair. She saw in her mind's eye the crowd who had surrounded her and suddenly realised that they were non-persons – ghosts, wraiths, human only in that they were hands and backs to work in the fields and orchards. Otherwise they had no importance.

'I'll tell you another thing,' Lew went on. 'Half of them are Mexican, and they're illegal immigrants – wet-backs who slipped across the Rio Grande without permission. If you cause a fuss and draw attention to them – if they seem to be causing trouble – they'll be deported.'

'No, no! If they can be employed, they must have a right to–'

'Nothing of the kind, Grandmama. You just don't understand. The orchard owners employ them when they need them and dismiss them when the crop's in. They're expected to move on to the next job and, if there isn't a crop to be picked, they're supposed to disappear. The Mexicans go home. The others starve quietly until they can start on the next crop.'

'Mother, don't take everything Lew is saying at its face value,' Greg intervened. He was weary after two days' strenuous argument in San Diego on behalf of the Spanish-speaking part of the San Franciscan population. The last thing he wanted was more argument.

'But is it true they have no vote? Is it true they've nowhere to go when the crop is picked?'

'There are welfare provisions. Thousands of them move into the cities for the winter and are looked after–'

'Oh yeah?' Lew interrupted, his voice brittle with anger. 'You only have to read the reports of the debates in the city council to know how they hate having to commit money to welfare for the migrants. It's cut down and cut down – and *you* do nothing to prevent it, Dad!'

'What the hell am I supposed to do?' Greg exploded, at the end of his patience. 'I've a job on my hands as it is – I have a commitment to–'

'You could stand for the council. You know you'd get in – dammit, Dad, you have plenty of support and you'd get more–'

'I don't want to be a councillor! I'm not a politician–'

'Are you saying you don't play politics? What were you doing in San Diego, then?'

'That's exactly what I mean. I had a specific problem to discuss and I discussed it. I can't waste my energies campaigning on behalf of people I don't know–'

'All right, I get it. You'll spend weeks and

months getting back ten acres of land for some little Californio widow who spends all her time in a black mantilla in church, but you don't do anything for the kind of people Grandmama saw – the people who really need it.'

'The little Californio widow needs it. It's just as hard, starving in a black mantilla. Besides, *she* would never ask for welfare–'

'She would if she'd swallow her pride–'

'But why should she? Why, when with a little patience and perseverance, we can get back her income and let her live out her life in dignity?'

'I'll tell you why!' Lew shouted. 'Because it's a waste of energy and intelligence that could be used for better purposes!'

There was a rustle of silk in the hallway. Francesca came in wearing a long ruffled dressing-gown and slippers. She'd gone up to bed once she'd seen her husband safely home, feeling that Grandmama would rather talk to him alone.

'What is all this noise?' she asked in her soft voice. There was reproof in it, and although she didn't turn her eyes on her son, the reproof was for him. She felt he should know better than to have a rowdy argument at eleven o'clock at night when

Greg had already had a hard day.

'I'm sorry, Frannie – did we wake you?'

'I was not asleep, Greg. Lew, I didn't expect you home?'

'I've some reading to do–'

'Then should you not be in your room, doing that, rather than shouting at your father?'

'I'm sorry, Mama, but he got my goat–'

Francesca sighed. 'Why is it that whenever you come home these days, there is nothing but dissension? I understand you feel strongly about your politics, but must we suffer for that?'

'Mama!' Lew exclaimed. 'Haven't we always heard how you fought for what you thought was right in the Philippines? Do you want me to do less than you?'

'I fought for my own people–'

'And that's what I'm doing!' declared Lewis, his dark Spanish eyes flashing with outrage. 'Half the people that Grandmama has just become aware of are *our* people – Mexicans who have no one else to–'

'Lew, do stop romanticising things,' Greg said in a very weary tone. 'This family has nothing in common with Mexican-Indians who come into the country illegally–'

'How can you be so heartless?' Lew

shouted. 'Don't you *care* that they're manipulated and exploited and deprived of human dignity?'

'Lewis, I don't think that the amount of concern can be measured by the noise we make–'

'Mama, Spanish good manners can be a way of turning your back on what you can't face–'

'Now stop that, boy!' Greg said suddenly. He didn't raise his voice but the anger in it made them all turn to look at him. 'I don't mind your cockeyed political theories but don't you start being snide to your mother or I'll–'

'Greg,' Morag said, reaching out a hand. 'Don't. Don't speak to him like that. It's my fault. I shouldn't have brought this problem into the house–'

'It was here already, Grandmama. Dad's known for years that the Spanish-speaking population is being swindled and down-graded by the gringos but it would be too unpleasant to come out in the open and say so!'

'I think, my son,' Francesca remarked, 'you had better go to bed.'

'It's no use trying to treat me as if I were a two-year-old, Mama–'

'You behave like a two-year-old! Flailing fists and silly babble–'

'Oh, Francesca,' Morag reproached. 'The boy talks sense, even if he expresses it too harshly.'

'So you think, Grandmama. You have not had to bear with him for three years or so. Ever since he went to university we have had lectures about how to alter the world. If it were so easy, why has it not been done?' Francesca swung back to her son. 'It is late. We have had enough. Let us all go to bed.'

'But Grandmama was asking Dad to help the migrants–'

'That is enough, Lew.'

'No it damn well is not, Mama! You can't shut me up just because you want peace and quiet–'

'Lew, I told you,' Greg said. He stepped close to his son and took his arm in a steely grip. 'Will you behave yourself, or do I have to throw you out bodily?'

'You and who else?' demanded Lewis.

'Lewis! Lewis!' At the threat of actual physical violence, Francesca flew to their side and grasped her husband's wrist. 'Don't be angry with him, Gregorio. He didn't really mean to speak to me like that–'

'All right, let him apologise.'

'For what? For saying I won't be gagged? It'll be a cold day in hell first!'

'All right, then, out! Outside until you learn some manners–'

Greg was pushing his son towards the hall when a soft, slithering sound made him pause and turn his head. What he saw made him let go Lewis so quickly that Lewis actually staggered.

'Mother!' Greg cried.

Morag had gone down to the floor in a dead faint.


## Chapter Five

At Gregor's knock, Francesca came to the door of Morag's room and opened it just a crack.

'I rang Dr Weker,' he reported, 'but he's at friends. They gave me the number to contact him. Should I–'

'Oh, no, I don't think so, dearest. She's recovered, says she feels tired, thinks she has a little cold coming. She just wants me to help her into bed.'

'I blame myself,' he said. 'I should never

have let that row develop in front of her like that. Her health has never been good–'

'Now, don't worry, my husband. She's been doing too much these last few days. First that encounter with the migrant camp, and then she's been all round San Francisco selling her jewellery–'

'Doing what?' He was appalled.

'I'll explain it all to you some other time. For now, dearest, let me get her to bed and to sleep.'

Morag heard the whispered colloquy though she couldn't make out the words. 'Tell Greg not to worry about me,' she said when at last she lay down between the cool sheets. 'He's always worried about me, ever since he was a boy... I've been rather silly, haven't I ... at my age? I'll be right as rain in the morning.'

But she was not. She woke after a restless night, feeling that she was suffocating. She rang the bell at her bedside and Francesca came running, forestalling the maid.

'What is it, Grandmama? What's wrong?'

'My throat's closing up, Francesca! I feel ... I can't breathe ... I don't know what's ... Frannie, I think I'm really ill...'

Francesca hurried to the telephone. Greg had got up too, and was about to go to his mother when Francesca caught him by his dressing-gown sleeve. 'No, *mi querido*, don't – it is something serious. Don't go in asking questions and making her talk. I think she should be kept very quiet.'

The doctor arrived within twenty minutes. He had been the family physician ever since they moved out to the West Coast, had taken a look at Morag from time to time when Gregor thought she looked tired or over-strained. He went into the bedroom, was there for some time, came out looking extremely grave.

'No doubt about it, I'm afraid. She'll have to go to an isolation unit.'

'What!' Greg made to pass him, but Dr Weker barred his way.

'Now don't be a fool, McGarth, diphtheria's very infectious–'

'Diphtheria!'

'I'll make arrangements for an isolation ambulance to come at once. Then I want your household to line up – all of you – because I need to take throat swabs. And you'll all have to stay indoors and not be in contact with anyone–'

'Weker, look here–'

'Don't give me any argument, McGarth. I'm sorry, but diphtheria is a notifiable disease and you *must* abide by the rules. Where's the phone?'

Francesca, pale and frightened, led the way to the instrument. She sank down on a hall chair while he made the necessary arrangements. Greg stood with his arm protectively around her. When Weker had put back the receiver he said: 'Any other family members at home?'

'Lewis is home for the weekend–'

'Send for him. And please ring for the servants.'

Seeing the necessity of it, Gregor did so. The maid came, and went back to the kitchen to summon the cook and the kitchen boy. Lewis had slept through everything so far, but came downstairs looking heavy-eyed and bewildered when his father pulled him out of bed.

'Now, listen carefully,' Weker said, frowning from under bushy eyebrows. 'Mrs McGarth has to go into hospital because she has diphtheria. Everyone in the household must have tests done to see if the infection has spread. Tell me what Mrs McGarth has been doing in the past few days – say, over the past week?'

'She's been staying on my place in the San Joacquin Valley. Good God!' added Gregor, in horror. 'Bess is pregnant—'

'I'll have to ring the health authorities there.'

'Ha!' Lewis said with a bitter laugh. 'She so much wanted to get the health authorities moving in Fresno – now she's succeeded!'

'The health authorities? What on earth d'you mean?'

They told him the story of the Scratchville camp. He looked scared. 'Oh, lord, those places are breeding grounds of infection! Well, at least from what you tell me it's only three days since she was there, so in between she's probably not spread the disease—'

'Perhaps not even to Bess and Cornelius,' Gregor said. 'She seems to have gone to bed early that day because she was upset, and left first thing next morning.'

'Let's hope so. I don't think it would be good for a pregnant woman to get diphtheria.'

The ambulance came rushing up the drive, scattering gravel. Out leapt two white-coated figures carrying white boxes. Two others came from the back with a folded stretcher. Dr Weker went upstairs with them to supervise the removal of the patient.

When Gregor tried to accompany him, the doctor pushed him back unceremoniously. 'Don't be a fool, man! I know you're anxious about her, but there's no point laying yourself open to infection. Think of your wife!'

Gregor turned back, irresolute. Francesca put out a hand towards him. He went with her into the drawing-room, where the attendants with the white-enamelled boxes were bringing out equipment. They donned gauze masks.

In ten minutes the test swabs had been taken and put in their glass stoppered bottles. Having said only ten words or less, the two men climbed back into the front of the ambulance.

Greg looked out of the window as the doors were shut on his mother in the back. 'No,' he groaned, 'no...'

But in a moment it was gone.

It was still only six-thirty in the morning. By nine, checks had been made on the household at Regalo. No one there felt ill, but swabs were taken as a precaution. A team of health workers had been sent to Scratchville. That evening the newspapers reported an outbreak of diphtheria which had already, unknown to the authorities, caused four deaths and resulted in eighteen other cases. The camp was in quarantine. 'Oh, great,' muttered Lewis, 'they'll probably put it behind barbed wire!'

Dr Weker reappeared about six in the evening. He was looking serious, his ruddy face pale and his eyebrows more ferocious than ever. 'Now, McGarth, this isn't good but I don't want you to be too worried. Francesca ... I'm afraid your test has shown up positive.'

Gregor made a strangled sound and put his arms round his wife. She huddled against him, trembling with dismay. Lewis, until then trying to be stoical, put his hands up to his face to hide his sudden and unexpected tears.

'It's all right, don't be upset, it's just in its early stages so we can give antitoxin straight away and ten to one it'll be a minor infection.'

'What is it – an injection? Can you do it now?'

'Sure, sure – I've come to do it for every-one, but...'

'But what?'

'Francesca will have to go into the iso-lation unit–'

'No! I won't allow–'

'You've no say, McGarth. It's the law of the state. She's got to go to a special unit – and it's best, because she can get expert nursing and supervision.'

Francesca looked up at her husband. 'It is best, as he says, Gregorio. I would not wish to stay here, endangering you.'

'No, that's nonsense–'

'It's the way it's got to be, I'm afraid. Can we go to your bedroom, Mrs McGarth, so I can do the injection? And then perhaps you'd like to put a few things together to take with you–'

'You're not taking her now?'

'The ambulance will be here in a minute. Afterwards I'd like to inject the rest of you.'

Gregor understood that he was caught, powerless, in a system that was inexorably rolling over them. He watched as Francesca led the way from the room. When Weker came downstairs again Greg asked: 'And my mother? I rang at noon – they said she was "receiving treatment" – what the hell does that mean?'

'They're trying to get her temperature down and keeping her breathing more or less normal. Her throat and neck are very inflamed. And you know, McGarth... Her lungs can't cope with this kind of strain.'

There was a tiny silence. 'What are you telling me, Weker?' Gregor said.

The doctor was making his way down the hall towards the servants' quarters. 'I think you have to face the fact that she may not recover.'

'Weker!'

The doctor paused before he laid his hand on the green baize door. 'I'm sorry, my dear fellow. I think you're strong enough to have the truth.'

It had never occurred to Lewis McGarth that he would ever feel sorry for his strong, confident father. But in that moment, when the agony of protective love was so strong on the older man's face, his heart went out to him. He went to him, put an arm about his shoulders.

But he could think of nothing to say.

If Morag had known she was grieving her son, it would have worried her. But she was beyond the reach of happenings in the everyday world. She was in the midst of a happy dream.

In this dream, she was in the alpine garden of her ranch house in Colorado. She was kneeling by a narrow terrace of soil where she was planting a fine, rare Soldanella. The plant, strangely, was in flower and stranger yet a soft fragrance surrounded its purple blooms. She leaned down to bury her face in the clump of coin-shaped leaves but a hand placed on her shoulder restrained her.

'Now then, sweetheart, don't put your nose in the flowers – I want to talk to you.'

She looked up. It was her own dear Rob, as she had last seen him – tall, still upright, the short thick beard that hid his facial scars streaked with one bar of white.

'What are you doing here?' she asked him in her dream. 'I thought you'd ... gone away?'

'Gone away? What gave you that notion? I've been here, Morag, waiting for you.'

She began to get up. His hand under her elbow helped her to her feet. 'I'm getting old,' she sighed, 'old and stiff.'

'Not you, my dear, not you.' He linked her arm through his. 'Now shall we go and look at the rest of the garden? Your pink Douglasia are in bloom?'

'They are? In February? That's early, Rob?'

'Well, count your blessings, my love. Come along.'

They picked their way up the steps he had had carved for her in the rock of the mountain garden. And so in her dream they walked together to look at the flowers, and the dream became the reality from which she never awoke.

If it had not been that Francesca was ill and demanded almost all Gregor's attention, he couldn't have coped with the grief of losing his mother. They had always been very close, closer than most parents and children because from his boyhood he had worried about her. It was in his nature to be protective towards his womenfolk: he would have done anything to shield Morag from harm. What he found hard to forgive himself was that he had not been with her at the end. The quarantine laws had made it impossible.

Francesca's illness took a beneficent course. The maid, Rosita, also had to be taken into isolation but she too made a good recovery. But no one else succumbed to the infection.

While Francesca was convalescing, Gregor took his mother's body east to New York, to be buried alongside his father. Rob's legal wife, learning of the plan through a duty letter from Ellie-Rose, sent a cable: Forbid Burial Next My Husband.

It gave Gregor some satisfaction to send the reply that she had no rights in the matter. He had bought and paid for the plot in which his father was buried and had bought also the plot alongside so that Morag could lie beside the man she had faithfully loved for almost sixty years.

Simple though it was, all the family came to the funeral, except Bess Craigallan: the baby was due almost any moment.

Ellie-Rose had asked them to her apartment in Queens after the funeral. They gathered there, a sombre group, rather scary to young Bobby, Ellie-Rose's thirteen-year-old. Her husband John was subdued: a second generation Italian and from a Catholic background, he had thought the funeral, according to the rites of the Scottish Presbyterian church, too brief and businesslike.

'I've something for you, Ellie-Rose,' Gregor said, taking a small package from his jacket pocket. 'Mother made a will – she'd nothing much to leave except her personal jewellery and trinkets, and the day before she was taken ill she went all round San Francisco selling those. But I bought them back because, you see, she left you this locket. It's got a little picture of Mr Craig that goes inside.'

'Oh, Greg...'

'Why did she sell her things, Uncle Greg?' Bobby inquired with innocent curiosity.

'Because she was trying to raise money to help some very poor people, kid,' Lewis explained. 'She'd seen them on her visit to Uncle Neil. Incidentally, Neil, what are you doing about them?'

Cornelius had turned away and so had not been aware his nephew was addressing him. Gregor answered for him. 'What can he do? It's a vast problem, far beyond the resources of any one grower–'

'D'you know what happened to the people at Scratchville?'

'I heard the health authorities had quarantined the place–'

'Yes, that's what they did – slapped an isolation order on it, carted off the worst cases to a field hospital, kept the rest under guard until they'd been declared free of infection and then – *moved them on*!'

Gregor stared at his son. Cornelius, turning his head, had caught most of the information Lewis was conveying.

He nodded. 'The place was buzzing with deputy sheriffs and temporary officials, Greg. They gave them three days' grace but after that time they had to be on their trucks and cars and headed out. Then they burnt the place, I hear.'

'Burnt it?'

'Threw kerosene over it and put a torch to it. They said it was to make sure the infection was burned out but...'

'But it was to make sure they wouldn't come back,' Lewis finished for him. 'Dad, now your own family's been involved in it – now you've seen how their lives are interlocked with ours – you have to do something!'

'I don't see what.' It was a sigh of unwillingness. 'It would take legislation – and though I have a few friends in the Senate, I don't think I could lobby them successfully on–'

'You could try!'

'You don't understand the difficulties, Lew. To you, everything is black or white, good or evil. My business in the San Joacquin Valley is meshed in with other growers, who would resist to the bitter end any attempt to change the pickers' conditions–'

'Did they really burn their houses?' Bobby put in, with something like tears in his voice. 'That's a terrible thing to do!'

Bobby's big brother Curt decided it was time to lighten the atmosphere. He went round with the Chianti his stepfather had provided, thus turning the conversation. He had questions to ask his sister Gina, about her Hollywood life. Hollywood interested him. There seemed to be money there, and perhaps opportunities for the likes of Curt.

Curt had brains but didn't like to use them. His greatest talent lay in the field of sports: he played tennis to championship level but the Depression had put an end to his ambitions in that sphere. His job as athletics coach at a boys' prep school in Maine bored him to death. Moreover he sensed the job was none too safe. Attendance at the school was falling off because parents couldn't afford the fees. Staff was being 'let go'; he had a feeling he might be next.

'Is there any kind of opening for a guy like me?' he asked Gina. 'I don't mean in the studios – but, for instance, what do folk do with their spare time in Hollywood?'

'They don't have much spare time, oddly enough,' his sister told him. 'You'd be surprised. When you're working on a film you're on the set soon after five in the morning and then you stay there all day until shooting ends – that depends on how temperamental the director is, but generally they pack up around six. After that, most of the people just go home and fall into bed.'

'But they can't *all* work at that pace. And there are gaps between films. I mean, you read about parties and country clubs–'

'Well, yes, I suppose that's true. Beverly Hills is full of party-givers, and they swim and play tennis…'

'They play tennis, do they? I mean, they play it a lot?'

'Oh, devotedly! Second only to swimsuits, tennis frocks are the favourite off-duty wear of the starlets.'

'You don't say! Think there's an opening for a tennis coach?'

His cousin Lewis listened to him with indignation. 'That's right, move out there and help them to fritter their time. Conspicuous waste, that's what it's about – everybody has to have a pool and a tennis court and if they can afford it, a ranch up in the hills where they go riding–'

'There's nothing wrong with that, Lew. If they have money, why shouldn't they spend–'

'I tell you it's all wrong – and even when they're working, they're churning out rubbish. A dream factory, that's what it is –

if religion is the opium of the masses, movies are the drugstore sleeping pills!'

Gregor listened to it all, only half his attention on it. His mind and his heart were with Francesca, the far side of the continent, making her recovery from diphtheria in the care of a nursing home. He wanted to get back, to see her installed in the comfortable house in Pacific Heights.

As yet, Gregor couldn't see beyond that. Everything had happened too fast, had cut too deep. He looked at his daughter Clare, unusually quiet and sad in her black dress. He listened to his son making his declarations about the rights of the people. He glanced at Ellie-Rose and her husband, busying themselves with the small tasks of hospitality.

Were they achieving anything, any of them? With Rob Craigallan gone the mainspring of the family seemed to have wound down. And with Morag gone, the safe warmth of affection seemed diluted. What would hold them together now?

The telephone rang in the hall. Ellie-Rose was occupied so Gina went to answer it. She came back, her sombre face suddenly radiant. 'Neil!' She went up to him, touched him on the arm to make him look at her. 'A message for you! Bess's baby was born an hour ago – you have a son!'

Cornelius broke into a smile. He looked at the others, speechless in his delight. 'Is she ... is everything all right?'

'Yes, fine, the doctor said to tell you you have a fine boy. Bess sends her love, the message says she'll ring when they let her use the telephone later this evening and will you have someone standing by so she can talk to you.'

There was something poignant in the moment. And suddenly Gregor knew what held them together. They needed each other. Cornelius, parted from Bess, couldn't hear her speak on the telephone – he needed someone to be there to relay to him what his wife was saying.

Gregor took his half-brother's hand in his and shook it warmly. 'Congratulations, Neil. Here's to the young Craigallan.'

They held up their glasses, smiling and nodding at Cornelius. 'To the young Craigallan...'

There was something hopeful in it. Cornelius's son was the future. Gregor felt the grief and depression lifting from his heart.

But if only ... if only Morag could have been here to know that Bess's baby was

here, to rejoice that the Craigallan name –
the name of her beloved Rob – would be
carried on.

## Chapter Six

Gina Gramm wasn't really very pleased to
find her young cousin Clare on the
threshold when she opened the door of her
Hollywood apartment.

'Clare! What are you doing here?'

'Visiting you, cousin, if you'll have me.'

Gina stood back to usher her in. Clare
walked with a purposeful step into her
living-room, to throw herself into a big
armchair. 'Gina, please let me stay with you
for a week or two. Everything's so gloomy
back home.'

Gina had shut the door and followed more
slowly. She'd guessed something was wrong.
People didn't make the long drive from San
Francisco to Hollywood for nothing.

'Tell me first of all, how's your mother?'

'Oh, picking up, picking up. But Dad
tiptoes around her as if she were Dresden
china, and he's so...'

'What?'

'I don't know the word... Downcast? Grief-stricken? He can't seem to come to terms with the fact that Grandmama was an old lady and likely to die in the natural course of events.'

'You have to admit that her death wasn't the calm quiet passing-away that he probably expected.' Gina herself had been deeply affected by Morag's death. The quiet friend of her childhood, the presence that had filled her Washington home while Mama was off in London during the war...

'I think he's still blaming himself for what happened. He'd have liked to keep her wrapped in tissue paper if he could. And it makes life so ... difficult. *I'm* not the type to be kept in tissue paper, Gina!'

'No,' Gina agreed. Clare was the type to like activity and conviviality. She had a lot in common with Gina's brother Curt – a swallow dipping and flying over the surface of things, glorying in physical prowess and freedom.

'Can I stay? I promise not to be a nuisance. You know I've friends and acquaintances here. I won't get in your hair.'

There was nothing to do but accept her as a guest. Family, after all – one couldn't say

131

no. But Gina found that her work as a voice coach kept her very busy. She didn't really want to have to entertain her cousin and though Clare might say she could occupy herself, even in Hollywood parties and picnics didn't go on for ever.

It would really be better if Clare had a job of some kind. She had insisted on going to university, chiefly because most of her friends were doing so. There she had taken what Gina regarded as a non-subject called History of Art. She did in fact have a degree. But from all that Gina could gather, her cousin had spent her university days in a round of entertainment. Perhaps, in fact, the determination to get to college had been simply to get away from her mother's watchful eye.

Gina knew that Francesca had hoped her daughter would marry soon after leaving college. Many girls did. But though Clare was clearly popular with men, she showed no inclination to 'settle down'. In the eyes of Francesca, brought up in a strict Spanish home in the Philippines and still influenced by her early environment, her daughter was heading towards long-term spinsterhood. What, three years past her twenty-first birthday and still unwed?

What Francesca didn't know – or chose to ignore – was that though Clare was unmarried, she was almost certainly not an old maid. There had been relationships. How deep they had gone, Gina had no means of knowing. Her uncle Gregor wasn't the type to complain about family problems but she'd seen enough to know that he worried about Clare and the succession of men friends who seemed to come and go in her life.

Here in Hollywood there were certainly plenty of men. But there were also plenty of girls – girls younger than Clare, and more openly attractive, in fact working hard at being attractive. In a way, it might do Clare good to be in competition with some of these eighteen- and nineteen-year-olds with their carefully-tended bodies, their platinum hair, their provocative clothes.

Ever since Jean Harlow burst upon the world in Howard Hughes' spectacular war film *Hell's Angels*, Hollywood had been full of sexy, curvy, thinly-clad blondes. Compared with them, Clare's tall slender athleticism and her nut-brown hair were almost negligible.

The thought comforted Gina. She needn't feel too much responsibility for Clare in any case, for she certainly didn't stand in the role of guardian or mother-figure to her. There was only seven years' difference in their ages: no one could expect Gina to run herd on her younger cousin.

Before she set about getting dinner for two, she rang Gregor in San Francisco to report Clare's arrival. 'She's asked to stay with me for a couple of weeks. I've said okay. Is that all right with you, Uncle Greg?'

She heard him sigh. 'I blame myself, Gina. I know I try to keep the house too quiet. But I want Francesca to make a complete recovery, and it's too bad to have Clare driving up to the door at two a.m., waking us all up...' He let his words die away, aware perhaps that they held too much complaint. 'Is it all right with *you*, having Clare to stay? When she left she gave the impression she had a standing invitation from you.'

'Well, it's not exactly an ideal situation What I thought was, Uncle Greg – suppose I got Clare some kind of a job?'

'A job? Clare?' The thought clearly amused him. 'She never sticks at anything. She's done little bitty things – helped put together one or two exhibitions, worked with Professor Gibbons on the research for a book about Impressionists. But nothing ever lasts long.'

'It doesn't have to last long. I don't think she's planning to take up permanent residence in Hollywood. But I might be able to get someone to take her on – just to get her out from under my feet part of the time.'

'I leave it to you,' Gregor said. 'But somehow or other Clare has always gone her own way, Gina. I just thank you for taking her in when her own home has become unattractive.' He hesitated. 'By the way, I don't want you to be under any financial strain–'

'Oh, she won't eat enough to make me feel the cost of entertaining her–'

They argued a little over money arrangements then Gina called Clare to the phone to add a word before hanging up. 'It's funny,' Clare remarked when they sat down to the meal. 'When I'm away from home I always feel closer to Dad than when I'm there. Do you know' She coloured. 'I think it's because I don't feel in competition with Mama!'

'Very Freudian,' said Gina with amused irony. But there could be truth in it. Perhaps being away from home, not being required to live up to the standard of her mother, might be best for Clare.

Her cousin spent the rest of the evening ringing round among her friends in Hollywood and Los Angeles. She soon had a programme of activities that seemed to take in the next few weeks. But the day inevitably came when nothing was written into her pocket diary, when she had shopped for everything she thought she needed in fashion stores and seen all the movies at the local theatres, so that the next couple of days seemed to stretch ahead, empty and without promise.

Gina had already prepared for this moment. By now she had her own circle of friends in the film world, mostly men and women on the technical side. 'What would you say to doing a little work for one of the studios, Clare?' she inquired as they sat at breakfast on the sunny balcony of her apartment.

'Work?' The idea didn't seem to fill her with enthusiasm.

'Something in your line. Global Films is planning a big Biblical epic – in fact shooting starts on the outdoor scenes quite soon. But they're still working on the research for the sets – what kind of goblets did they drink out of, for instance, and what was the design on the soldiers' armour –

that sort of thing.'

'Good lord, Gina, I don't know anything about Old Testament life–'

'It's New Testament. I think the film's called *The Woman of Magdala*. I know a bit about it because I've been hired out by MGM to train some of the bit players in how to speak their lines – somehow the director doesn't think it seems right, having a Roman centurion sound like a Brooklyn taxi driver. They're ferreting about in the art department, trying to find out about Roman houses and everyday living.'

'But why, if it's about Mary Magdalene? She surely didn't spend much time in Roman houses?'

'Oh, they've concocted a story about a Roman general who loves her and there's a lot about his career and Roman politics and so forth. You know what Hollywood scripts are like... Anyhow, there's a job there if you want it – they need to know about Roman art and so forth – I could introduce you to the assistant art director?'

'Oh, I don't think so, thanks, Gina.'

But after a day or two of kicking her heels, waiting for the weekend when the working population of Hollywood would be free to play with her, Clare changed her mind. It was either that, or move on somewhere else – and she didn't feel she could park herself on friends for more than a few days at a time. Nor did she want to go back to San Francisco as yet.

The assistant art director came for drinks that evening at Gina's invitation. He was a youngish man, thin and harassed looking. What he wanted above everything else was to have people working for him who knew what they were doing but would not show off to his boss, the art director, thus undermining his own position.

'I really must explain, Mr Wohlberg–'

'Dick – call me Dick – we're all on first name terms in my department.'

'Well, then, Dick,' Clare resumed, 'I must tell you I've never specialised in Roman art.'

'But you have a degree.'

'Oh yes. But my speciality was really French art.'

'All the same, you know how to find your way round a library, and to correspond with experts on sources abroad.'

'Oh yes, of course.'

'Our problem at the moment is that we have to get a set of interiors for a ... er ... ahem a house of ill repute in Rome. It's a damn funny thing,' he said with some resentment, 'you can find out what the inside of a noble villa looked like but almost nobody wrote about the sporting houses!'

Clare laughed. 'What you want is the stuff from Pompeii.'

'There you are! You come up with it at once. It took me three weeks to discover there were brothels among the ruins there! Now look, when can you start?'

'Oh, I don't know that I–'

'Come on, Gina's told me you're looking for something to do. I could get you taken on for the length of the shooting – that would be until January. What d'you say?'

Clare promised to be at his office next day on the lot, to see whether she thought she'd fit in. Salary and conditions could be settled then. She was still playing it very cool but Gina could tell she was rather pleased at the thought of being part of the film community.

Gina too was pleased. But she would have been less so had she foreseen the affair that was to spring up between her well-brought-up cousin and the notorious Vartan Dackis.

Dackis was the producer of the film, *Woman of Magdala*. He dropped in on the art department to complain that he needed some idea of the size of the rooms so that he could talk about camera angles with the cameramen. Clare, as 'expert' on the subject of the house of pleasure in Rome, had to explain the drawings and diagrams to him.

'How long have you been with the art department?' he inquired as he watched her slim hand with its unpainted nails pointing out the details of the sketches.

'Two weeks, Mr Dackis.'

'Two weeks, huh? And already you're making more sense than anybody else I've discussed it with. Listen, why don't you join me for lunch in the commissary at one? I could explain what I need – it seems clear we have to have these "colourful" wall paintings but I don't want them to distract the eye from the actors – see what I mean?'

Clare agreed she did. She also saw what he meant about meeting him for lunch in the commissary. This was a way of letting the rest of the company know he was taking an interest in her. His technique was well-known – he marked out a girl as quarry and then never let anything prevent him from capturing her.

You had to admit he had his attractions. Apart from the fact that he was a Hollywood producer, powerful and influential, he was goodlooking. He had come to America in his teens; Vartan Dackis was an Americanised version of his Greek name. He was compactly built, rather swarthy, with thick springing black hair and black eyes that matched with the 'Latin Lover' image so popular with movie-goers. But instead of entering the lists as an actor, Dackis had worked his way up from clapper boy to director to producer.

Clare couldn't help being flattered that he was interested in her, though she wondered why. She heard the explanation in something he said over lunch. She was shown to Mr Dackis' table as soon as she appeared in the commissary, a large airy room on the fourth floor of the technical building on the Global lot. He rose to greet her and to introduce her to the three other people already gathered there.

'I want you to meet Miss McGarth,' he said, taking her by the hand and almost presenting her. 'She's new in the art department. Any queries about the night life of Romans, I want you should go straight to her.'

The others made welcoming noises. There were two men and a woman, the latter instantly recognisable from the photograph that accompanied her column in the *Los*

*Angeles Examiner* – Louella Parsons. 'Mc-Garth?' she repeated. 'Now wait a minute – that beautiful Mrs Gramm is related to the McGarths.' She looked expectantly at Clare.

'Mrs Gramm is my cousin.'

Louella put up a hand to pat her feathered hat coquettishly. 'Well, well, Dack... This is the first time you won't have to groom one of your protégés for stardom. Miss McGarth actually knows which knife to use, I imagine.'

Clare looked at her in surprise. The words were spoken in a vague, inquiring tone which took the sting out of them, but the malice was there all the same.

To her amazement, Dackis rose to the bait. 'Miss McGarth is a real lady, Lollie,' he said, flushing a little under his olive skin. 'Don't speak like that about her.'

'And as to stardom,' Clare put in, 'I'm on the technical side.'

'But you hope to move into acting,' Miss Parsons supposed aloud. 'Although, really, one wonders what kind of a role Dack has in mind for you'

Clare decided to ignore the barb. 'If you'll excuse me, I'll just go and fetch my lunch–'

The commissary was supposed to be a

place of total democracy. Everyone was directed by arrows to queue with a tray at the service counter. But in fact the tables used by the directors and producers were served by waitresses. One now hurried forward to fill Clare's glass with iced water, to wait with poised pencil for Clare's order of tuna fish sandwich and black coffee.

'You're not on a grapefruit diet, then, dear?' Miss Parsons inquired. 'No, perhaps not – you've no flesh to lose, really. What kind of film have you in mind for her, Dack? A Western? She'd look good in pants and checked shirt.'

To her own surprise Clare took exception to that. 'Miss Parsons,' she said, 'I've told you I have no acting ambitions but if you insist on supposing I have, please don't talk about me as if I'm a laboratory specimen.'

The other woman smiled and nodded. 'Got spirit too, Say, Dack... This is a new departure for you. Do keep me informed of the progress of the romance.'

With this she rose, nodded her thanks for the salad and coffee which she'd scarcely touched, and trotted away to another table.

'Old witch,' growled Dackis. 'Don't pay any heed to her, honey. She likes to needle folk so they blurt out things she'll print.'

'She took a big interest in my cousin Gina when she first came to Hollywood,' Clare said, 'but if I remember rightly her curiosity wanes when the great romance fails to blossom.'

This was her way of telling Mr Dackis that there would be no 'great romance' between them. She was undeniably intrigued that he should single her out, and she had some idea now why – she was so totally different from the other girls who begged for his attention. But that was as far as it was going to go.

In this she was an optimist. Vartan Dackis had no intention of being turned down by any girl he beckoned to. He was deaf to ladylike hints. As they rose from the table to go back to their various employments he said to Clare, without troubling to lower his voice much, 'Pick you up around six? It would suit me best if we went straight from the studio but if you want to go home to change–'

'Excuse me, Mr Dackis–'

'Dack, call me Dack. That's the name I let my friends use.'

'Very well, then, Dack. I'm sorry, I can't meet you at six. I have an engagement.'

'Oh, is that so? Well, okay, I guess I've a

meeting with Joe Seldman that I ought not to cancel. When can you get away? Nine o'clock? Ten?'

'But I don't want to get away,' she said, almost laughing. 'I don't think you understand. I'm spending the evening with some friends. I shan't have space to do anything else tonight.'

He stood studying her. She was almost as tall as he, so that he stared directly into her eyes. The steady black gaze was almost mesmeric. 'What's the play, lady?' he said with a little jerk of irritation. 'Not fancy enough the way I invited you? Okay then, let's put in a few hearts and flowers. I'd like for you and me to make it together because you're a real thoroughbred, I can see that. So come on now, what time will you be through with these friends of yours?'

'About midnight, I imagine. And then, Mr Dackis, I shall be going to bed – alone.'

His answer was a frown of disbelief and then a smile. 'Oh, you the kind that didn't let a boy kiss her on a first date? Well, let's play it that way. What about tomorrow night? If you want to be romanced, I'll take you somewhere nice – how 'bout Victor Hugo's? We can have a champagne supper first.'

She loved the bluntness of that 'first'. When she laughed, he thought he'd won his point. 'Is that it, then? Pick you up to go to Victor Hugo's tomorrow? Wear something pretty.'

'I'm sorry,' she said. 'I have plans for tomorrow evening.'

'Dack!' someone called from the door of the commissary. 'Dack, your office is paging you on the outside Tannoy–'

'Just a minute, dammit!' he roared in reply, turning his head. He looked again at Clare. 'Come on now, Clare, let's get this settled. I don't have all day to play games. What evening are we going to get together?'

'Do you know what the word "never" means, Mr Dackis?' she inquired.

He stood, irresolute. 'Dack!' shouted the voice from the entrance. He moved away then stepped back. 'Listen, lady,' he said in a baffled voice, 'I haven't got the hang of you yet, but it won't be long, it won't be long...'

When he had gone Clare was aware of many eyes upon her in the big long lunch-room. She felt herself colouring up. It was almost as if she had put herself on public exhibition. She hurried away, heading for the comparative quiet of her corner of the

146

art department.

Hollywood was full of predatory males, ready to promise a screen test, a walk-on, a place in the chorus line. What made the situation between Clare and Vartan Dackis unusual was that he had nothing she wanted. She didn't want to be a star, she didn't want to see her name in lights or on the credit list as a writer.

'Hey!' he said, stopping her as she crossed the main thoroughfare on the lot with a design board under her arm. 'I want you in my office at four this afternoon.'

She stopped, let the board lean against her leg on the ground. 'Oh, really?' she said. 'What about?'

'We never had that conversation about the interior of the bawdy house.'

'I see. Very well. Do you want me to bring my sketches and research notes?'

'Oh sure, bring them.'

'Very well, Mr Dackis.'

When she got back to the art department she was thoughtful. In the end she decided she had a bad headache, asked for the afternoon off, and left the sketches and notes with the producer's secretary as she made her way out of the studios at about two-thirty. She had put a note with them in the big envelope explaining that she didn't feel well enough to stay on the job today but she hoped everything would be clear to him from her folio.

His reaction was amused annoyance. He rang her at home that evening. 'How's your headache?'

'It's much better, thank you.'

'I couldn't make much of the notes you sent. I'll need to see you tomorrow – you'd better stay on after work.'

'I'd rather not do that, Mr Dackis, I–'

'Listen, I've got to settle this problem about the sets before we put money into painting them.'

'I understand that, Mr Dackis. Very well, I'll ask Mr Wohlberg to stay on tomorrow evening too – he has some thoughts about the colours to be used in the interiors.'

There was a pause. 'If Wohlberg is the expert, perhaps we don't need you in the art department, Miss McGarth?'

She knew he thought that would pull her up short. In these hard times, jobs were hard to come by. Most girls would go on their knees to beg not to be fired. She shook her head to herself. 'That's up to you, Mr Dackis,' she said in a very cool tone.

I don't need the job, she was telling him.

You can't blackmail me, just as you can't bulldoze me.

He was a hateful man. And yet he was fascinating. He would use any weapon to get what he wanted. His lack of scruples was like something out of the Middle Ages, in the style of an Italian duke trampling over enemies – or, no, he was like a Norman baron, accustomed to getting what he wanted by force of arms.

The pursuit had been going on for a little over two weeks when Gina began to get worried. Hollywood gossip had let her know that her cousin was the latest target for the interest of the predatory Vartan Dackis. It was a source of cruel amusement that he was getting nowhere.

'Listen, *Liebling*,' Peter Brunnen said to her. 'You have heard what they are saying? Well, I want to warn you. Dackis is a man who will never admit defeat. If Clare really is not interested in him, it would be better if she left Hollywood.'

'That's absurd, Peter. We can't let him chase her out of town!'

'But it rankles.' He paused. 'That is the word – rankles? Or do I mean wrinkles?'

'You mean rankles, but I can't take it seriously. Good heavens, there are thousands of girls in Hollywood. Why doesn't he amuse himself with one of *them*?'

'Who can understand the mind of a man like that? Success is everything to him. He can't bear to fail. And if Clare won't give in to him, he has failed.'

Gina valued Peter's opinion. He was now fairly launched on a Hollywood career, happy to get good roles in secondary feature films, conscientious in learning his craft as a film actor. Kolin would groan to Gina: 'I can't get the guy to chuck his weight around. He's got the chance to be a big star – but he won't fight hard enough. Mr Nice Guy, that's him.'

'Perhaps, he's lucky, Bert. The ambitious ones are the unhappy ones.'

'It's on account of that bitch of a wife of his,' Kolin mourned. 'He wants the safe, easy money, so he can send it home to her and she can go on training to be a great singer. But I'll tell you this. She gets another six months out of him – and then if she doesn't land a role in grand opera she can pay for her own ritzy tutor!'

'You couldn't stop him sending her money–'

'Oh, couldn't I? I can get him to sign a contract that ties up every penny he earns unless I give the say-so. I don't want to do it to him, Gina, but she's a millstone round his neck – he should be living it up a little, buying a nice house, making a show of his success so I can lever up the prices of his next film. You talk to him, Gina. He'll listen to you.'

But all her efforts ended the same way. 'Magda is my wife, I must support her.'

'But I thought you were planning to bring her out to Hollywood.'

'She prefers to come when she has had some good roles in Europe – then she can break into the Hollywood musical as a lead singer.'

What it meant was that Magda wasn't prepared to come and be just Peter Brunnen's wife. Although Gina had never met her she began to feel a real dislike for her. But Peter would never hear a word against her. A quiet, tolerant observer of most other people, about Magda he was blind: 'She has a superb voice, she has it in her to be a great artist' – and that was an end of it.

Peter's anxiety about Clare made Gina more watchful. When a package came by special delivery one Saturday morning, she stood by while Clare opened it. Inside was a jeweller's velvet box, containing a very showy pair of diamond earrings. A card lay among the satin pleats of the interior.

Clare smiled and handed it to her cousin. 'Wear these this evening for me,' it said. It was unsigned.

'And what does that mean, may I ask?' Gina said, hearing herself sound tart and disapproving.

'It seems to mean he's going to be at the Zeitlingers tonight.'

Both women were going to the party. Herman Zeitlinger was a director who had just brought in a very expensive movie exactly on schedule after a very long stint on location. Before he settled down to cut and edit, he was throwing a gigantic jamboree to help him unwind. He and his wife were famous for their parties – they invited hundreds and threw open their estate, a rather grandiose house in Beverly Hills with a parklike garden. Rona Zeitlinger was fond of saying that she wanted her gatherings to be 'like family' but the family that gathered were always very well-dressed, very success-ful, or very beautiful.

'Those earrings are just the kind of thing that would look good at the Zeitlingers,' Gina laughed. 'But you'll send them back, won't you?'

'I'll do better yet. This evening I'll hand them back to Dackis in person.'

'Oh, Clare–!'

'What's the matter?'

'Don't do that. Don't make him look a fool in public. He's quite a dangerous man.'

'How can he be dangerous to *me*? He's just a pushy Greek with too big an idea of himself–'

'Well, if that's so, why does it make you sparkle with pleasure to have him dangling after you?'

'Don't be silly, Gina! I haven't the least interest in him!'

'All right. Prove it by quietly returning his gift.'

Clare shrugged and laughed. 'All right, if it alarms you so much. Lend me a pen.' On the back of the card she wrote: *Sorry, these wouldn't match my dress for this evening.* She then closed the box, put it in the stiff envelope and re-addressed it to Dackis's home. Gina rang for a special delivery boy and the package was handed over to him.

Gina was still worried. Those diamonds had cost a pretty penny. A man who sent a gift like that was not to be easily put off.

At the party he was nowhere to be seen. 'In a huff,' Clare whispered to her cousin,

153

'because I didn't take the bribe.'

'Clare, if you think you have the power to affect his plans like that, don't you think you ought to be very careful what you do and say to him?'

'Oh, nonsense. If he wants a scrap, I'll give him one.'

Mrs Zeitlinger surged up to greet them. She was unsure who they were but they were good-looking – in fact the elder girl was a positive beauty – and that was always an asset.

'Come along dears, you know the Pounders, do you? And there's Frank Johnson – oh, and Cecil – yoo-hoo, Cecil...'

Waiters brought trays of drinks. Gina and Clare parted company to join people they knew. From time to time Gina caught a glimpse of Clare's brilliant blue satin gown but after a while she ceased to keep track of her.

She was dancing with a former pupil when a little commotion drew her attention. Vartan Dackis had arrived, with a small party. Hanging on his arm was a little slender redhead and hanging from the redhead's ears were the earrings Clare had sent back. They would have looked ostentatious on anyone but on this tiny girl they looked like

154

chandeliers on a robin redbreast. Gina glanced about for Clare. She discovered her standing by the drinks bar, staring in vexation. It was one thing to send back the gift, quite another to find he'd bestowed it at once on someone else. Good Lord, thought Gina, she's just interested enough to want to hang on to him if she thinks she's losing him.

Dackis accepted a drink from a passing waiter then escorted his pretty little friend onto the dance-floor. The rumba was the dance of the moment: the redhead danced well. By and by it so happened that the couple passed the spot where Clare was standing in conversation with a tall blond Western actor.

'Hi there, Clare,' Dackis said. 'That the dress you meant? It could do with a diamond or two to help it along, if you ask me.'

Clare broke off her chat, turned her head slowly to take in Dackis companion. 'They're helping where they're needed,' she remarked.

Gina couldn't quite hear what was being said. She worked her way round the group between herself and Clare. She was just in time to hear Dackis say, 'Laurette, I want you to meet Clare McGarth. You know what she specialises in? She knows all the dirty bits about Roman orgies.'

Laurette giggled. 'Really?' she asked. 'I mean ... no kidding ... you into that kind of thing?'

'No, that's Mr Dackis' idea of a joke,' said Clare. She smiled. 'If you've known Mr Dackis long you'll be aware of his keen sense of humour.'

At this point Gina intervened. 'Clare, David Guyles is wanting to meet you.' She took her cousin by the arm but Dackis barred her way.

'Listen, I'm in the middle of a conversation here–'

'I'm sorry,' Gina said, allowing a note of surprise to show. 'I didn't realise it was anything important.'

Dackis hesitated. 'Well, I guess it wasn't. Why should I waste my time on a high-hat broad, anyway?' For the first time his gaze really focused on Gina. 'You a friend of hers?'

'I'm her cousin, Gina Gramm.'

'Oh yeah, I heard of you. You teach folk how to talk and everything.' He stared at her. 'A gal with your looks could do better than that!'

'Thank you, Mr Dackis, you're very kind, but I'm happy with my work.'

'You're a family that's got no ambition,' he complained. There was a perceptible lessening of hostility in his manner. 'But you sure got class... Listen, you here with friends? Because if not, I'd kinda like for you to join my party. Laurette here, and her agent Sam, and Monty Littler – we're short on womenfolk.'

'There's no reason why we should not join forces.'

Clare tried to signal her disagreement but Gina refused to take any notice. Later, when they had gone to a bedroom to freshen up, Clare muttered: 'I can't think why you did that – we don't have to kowtow to him.'

'There's no reason why we can't be decently polite to him, Clare. And if you want my opinion, you should either make up your mind to get a job elsewhere so that you need never run across him, or else you should take up with him and be done with it.'

'Take up with him?' Clare echoed, with so much force that another guest, powdering her face, turned to stare. Clare lowered her voice. 'You know very well that I can't stand the man!'

'Perhaps. But you're enjoying the role of the one girl he can't lassoo.'

'That's not true! I've done everything I can to discourage him!'

'Everything except have a civilised conversation? Let's see what we can achieve with that, Clare.'

Clare was annoyed and couldn't help showing it. 'He has as much civilisation as a rhinoceros,' she said, as they returned to the party, 'but have it your way.'

Dackis had had the waiters put two big round tables together so that his friends and the two girls with their escorts could sit together. By and by there was a big convivial group making so much noise that oddly enough it was possible to have a private conversation.

Gina took the initiative. 'I intervened on purpose earlier on,' she said, 'because I thought you were about to have a stand-up fight with my cousin.'

'I might try that,' he said with a grin. 'I've tried everything else.'

'Mr Dackis, why don't you just let it go?'

'I *never* let go. Not when I want something, that is.'

'But why should you want Clare so strongly? Is it simply because she's the first one to say no?'

'Women are always saying no,' he told her. 'They never mean it.'

'When a woman says no, you take it for granted she means yes?'

'Sure.'

'And if she says yes, you take it for granted she means no?'

He stared, and then surprisingly his face creased up and he began to laugh. It changed him. Gina felt she had seen those features in some old painting or bas relief – 'Satyr Laughing', a dark, mischievous face giving in to the mirth of mortals.

'You're a sharp lady,' he said when he recovered. 'But you know? – you're all right.'

'Does that mean you see my point?'

'What's your point, exactly?'

'That you ought to give Clare credit for using the English language with correctness. When she says no, she means no.'

'She tell you that?'

'We just had that conversation, in the powder room.'

'I kind of hate to believe she means it. I'll look a fool if she gets away.'

'Not if you turn her into a friend. There is such a thing as friendship, you know.'

'Not between men and women, Mrs

Gramm. That's naive.'

She shook her head. 'I speak from experience.' She considered a moment, her wide
mouth turning down in a little grimace of
distaste. 'Perhaps it's not easy to believe in
friendship in a place like Hollywood. Values
get so distorted here.'

'You don't like Hollywood? Best place in
the world! I been here since I got off the
boat and I tell you, there's more chance to
make your mark here than anywhere else in
Christendom.'

'You never worked anywhere else in
America but here?'

'Well, worked my passage across on the
cargo boat – but that was a Greek trader.
When I landed my wages gave me enough to
take the train from New Orleans to Hollywood, but I reckoned I'd need a stash to
keep me going if I couldn't get a job straight
away. So I bummed across – hobo stew, box-
car beds... God, it was rough. Took me six
weeks and I ended up stinking like a skunk
because I never stayed in a hotel so I never
took a bath.'

Gina listened with unfeigned interest.
Although Dackis was often spoken of in
Hollywood chit-chat, she'd never heard
anything about his early days. 'You came

from Greece,' she murmured. 'Could you speak English?'

'Oh, say, you think I was stupid enough to come here to work and not speak the language? On the Corinth Canal, lots of sailors spoke English – not classy, not like you, but good enough. And at first, when I was a gofer, I didn't have to say much – I just had to say yes-sir and no-sir and fetch and carry. God, I was happy in that job... When I got down off the market truck that brought me into L.A. I got the dollar bills out of my shoes and I went to a cheap hotel and I had a bath and then I checked out and went to the shops and I bought me a new suit and new shoes and changed into them in the men's room in the station. I put my old clothes – the ones I came from Greece in – I dumped them in a trash can. And then I hitched a ride to Hollywood and I just didn't stop bothering the gatekeepers at the studios until I got that first job.'

She nodded in appreciation. 'You understand what I really mean when I say that's quite an epic.'

'From the Greek *epos* meaning a tale or a song...' He paused, then murmured something in Greek, a memory of times past.

'Do you ever go back?'

'Na-ah!' It was a snort of derision. 'What's to go back for? Nothing ever happens in Corinth. My mother, God bless her, all she'd want is for me to marry some good Greek girl she'd pick out for me. She'd have the matchmaker in the house before I arrived! And my family have done enough marrying for all of us – my kid brother, he's got a good wife and four kids, and my sisters, they done all right, I saw they got good dowries. I wanted Mama to buy a little hotel for her old age, but she didn't want to do that, afraid of the book-keeping, you know, so I bought her into the shipping business, just a little import-and-export with a manager she can trust.'

'Perhaps you ought to marry, Mr Dackis. You sound like a good family man.'

'All us Greeks are family men. That Greek tragedy the eggheads go on about – that's all family feuds, you know.' He was pleased with this show of erudition. 'And, say, call me Dack. That's what my friends call me. And I'll call you Gina, right?'

The conversation was broken up by the demands of the others. The party was now entering its early-morning stages, when the wilder guests would put on their exhibition – nude swimming in the pool, or an over-erotic tango, or some other proof that they were free spirits. After the dance floor became the stage for a can-can by three starlets, Gina decided it was time to leave. With Hollywood she had come to terms, but not with the excesses that seemed to follow on too much scotch and bourbon.

Dackis was unwilling to see her go. 'Say, the party's really just starting! Don't quit now!'

'It's not my kind of thing, thank you, Dack. Nice to have had our talk.'

'Yeah,' he said, glaring in annoyance as she took the arm of her escort and moved off.

Both girls slept late next day, Sunday. As they were slowly coming back to life with cups of black coffee and the Sunday edition of the *Los Angeles Express*, the doorbell rang. A florist's delivery boy stood at the door, hidden behind a huge basket of magnolia.

'Good gracious!' Gina's impulse was to call to her cousin, It's for you! but first she tipped the boy then examined the card.

It was the same kind of card that had accompanied the earrings yesterday. The message read: An epic always contains a garland for the victor.

'What does *that* mean?' Clare wondered aloud when she read it.

'It was something that occurred in the talk we had.'

'You mean ... these are for you?' Clare drew back. 'He's sending *you* flowers?'

'I don't know. The card isn't addressed to either of us.'

'I certainly didn't talk to him about his Biblical epic! In fact, I hardly exchanged two words with him.'

'Well, that was what you wanted, wasn't it, Clare?'

'It seems you knew what *you* wanted!'

'Don't be absurd–'

'Don't let those Latin good looks mislead you, cousin. Underneath it all, he's the bastard he appears to be.'

'Listen, Clare, he's nothing to me. I was only being polite, trying to defuse the bad situation between you two.'

'Polite? Well, you seem to have called out something new in him. Flowers instead of showy jewellery, little private jokes instead of public commands – you must have that special touch.'

'He's really quite interesting when you get to know him–'

'Oh, really? Let me say the same thing you've been saying to me. He's a dangerous man – and small-minded, too. Don't you see he's doing this to get back at me – to let me know he's transferred his interest to–'

'That's nonsense. And even if it were true, since you were so positive last night about not liking him, what does it matter?'

'It matters that I hate to see you taking it seriously,' Clare said with a flash of anger. She looked hard at her cousin. 'You are, aren't you?'

'What is there to be serious about? A basket of flowers after a party–'

'Vartan Dackis doesn't waste his money on flowers for nothing, Gina. Don't fool yourself he's the gentlemanly type who's just being courtly. Those flowers mean he's trying to open up a relationship with you.'

Gina began to collect together the coffee pot and the cups. She took them into the kitchen and began to wash them. Clare came after her. 'Gina, you do understand what I'm saying, don't you?'

'Of course.'

'Are you going to encourage him?'

'I'm not going to do anything except thank him for the flowers.'

'But that's what he wants. When you call, he'll take it on from there.'

'We'll see.'

'You really do find him attractive! Are you

165

out of your mind? He'll tread you under like all the others.'

'He and I talked about friendship last night. Perhaps that's what he needs – a friend.'

'A friend!'

'They're rare in Hollywood, Gina.'

'I give up,' Clare said. She stalked out of the kitchen and presently could be heard barging about in the bathroom and her bedroom. She reappeared dressed in a tennis dress and jacket as Gina was collecting up the scattered newspaper sections in the living-room.

'I've a date with Herb,' she said. 'Shan't be back till late. Have a good day.'

'Same to you.'

Clare collected handbag and gloves, made for the door, then paused. 'If you're going to thank Dack for the flowers,' she said, 'don't do it today. Don't appear too eager.'

'Very well,' Gina said, smothering a smile at being given advice by her younger cousin.

But she didn't need to put through a call to Dack. About one o'clock, when she was thinking of going out for lunch, the phone rang. It was Dack himself. 'Did you get the flowers?' he demanded.

'Yes, soon after we got up.'

'Is Clare there?'

'No, she's gone out.'

'What did she say about the flowers. She was miffed, eh?'

'Somewhat.'

'Somewhat! Gee, lady, you use some funny words! Somewhat! I bet she was hopping mad!' A pause. 'I meant her to be, Gina.'

'I guessed that.'

'You sore at me?'

She hesitated. 'I'm a little disappointed. I thought we'd established last night that the thing about Clare is over.'

'Yeah, well, it is now. I had to pay her back, Gina. That's my style, you see. Us Greeks, and our feuds.'

'Being a Greek is no excuse, Dack.'

'Oh, you going to give me a lecture? For if you are, I won't invite you to my party.'

'What party?'

'My poolside party. I've got a pitcher of dry martinis on ice and a heap of salads and things, and I already invited a bunch of folk to help demolish 'em. Like to come? It's a nice day for a swim.'

She was about to say no, yet when she thought of the afternoon ahead, it didn't seem inviting. Lunch alone in some Hollywood restaurant, a session of work on recordings of a difficult pupil... 'All right, Dack,' she said. And to the devil with Clare's warnings.

'I'll send my car for you. Be ready in half an hour.'

She spent that half hour trying on and taking off the casual clothes she'd bought since coming to the film city. Sunday brunch was a favourite gathering for which sportswear was the fashion. She settled at last on a bright yellow sundress of thin poplin with ribbon shoulder straps, and slender-strapped gold sandals. In her bright holdall she took swimsuit and suncream.

The group of people at Dack's house were a motley collection, mostly from Global studios but some from others. They were cameramen and lighting experts, script-writers and sound engineers. They had wives and sweethearts with them, even a few children. Gina felt that Clare would have been surprised at the scene. She also felt that she had been paid some kind of special compliment in being invited today.

From two until eight there was splashing and laughing and over-eating and dancing. Then the mothers of the children began saying that they ought to get the kids home to bed, and little by little the party broke up. Gina said, 'Will you lend me your car and driver, or will you ring for a taxi for me, Dack?'

'Don't rush away. Listen, I got a nice dinner planned for us–'

'You don't mean you *intended* to have me stay on?'

'Sure I did. We never had a chance to talk properly in the midst of all that din. I thought we could crack a bottle of Greek wine, eat some mezze, catch up on what we don't know about each other. I mean, honey – I talked a lot about me last night, I never heard much about you.'

'There isn't a lot to say about me.'

'Come on.' He put an arm about her and walked her indoors from his big front porch, where they had been waving off his brunch guests. 'You're Mrs Gramm – is there a Mr Gramm?'

'He died in the early part of last year.'

'A widow... It's hard being a widow. My poor old mother, she was left a widow at twenty, with four kids. You got kids?'

'No.'

'Are you pleased or sorry about that? I kind of like kids myself. It was nice today, having them around.'

In the over-ornate dining-room a table was laid for two. There were even – oh, cliché of Hollywood romantic films – candles waiting to be lit.

'Can I be shown a mirror so I can make myself presentable for all this?' Gina said with a little chuckle. 'My hair's a mess after an afternoon in and out of the water.'

'Sure, Alfred will show you.' He rang the bell; his manservant appeared to usher Gina to a bedroom on the first floor, hung with expensive pink silk and gilt mirrors. Gina put the beach-bag with her damp swimsuit in the washbasin of the adjoining bathroom, and towelled her hair dry. She washed her face and was sitting in front of the dressing-table in the bedroom, about to apply fresh make-up, when the half-open door of the room was pushed wide.

Dack was there. He leaned against the jamb, watching her. 'Do I bother you?'

'Not a bit. You've seen women on the set putting on their lipstick, I imagine.'

'None of them looked as good without it as you do, Gina.'

'Don't tell lies, Dack. You employ some of the most beautiful women in the world.'

'Maybe. But I never met one like you before.'

He came into the room, stood behind her, and studied her reflection in the big gilt mirror. He ran a hand over her chestnut hair, smoothing it to her ears. Then he ran his fingers under her chin. Cupping her face, he tilted it up towards him. He leaned over, and kissed her.

If she wanted to prevent anything more, now was the time to draw back. But there was so much animal passion in the touch of his mouth that she had no will of her own. She strained her face up to his, kissing him with a sudden urge of physical desire that seemed to come from nowhere.

When he began to slip the thin straps of her sundress from her shoulders, she arched her back in pleasure, like a cat feeling the warmth of the fire. When he carried her to the bed, her arms were about his neck, already drawing him as close to her breasts as she could. Where was she now, the girl who had mourned her lack of physical joy in the marriage with poor Cliff Gramm? What was so different now, between herself and this man she scarcely knew?

And when at last they made love, she had a momentary vision of the laughing faun of her memory – pagan, fierce, yet with magic within his power.

## Chapter Seven

Peter shook the folded newspaper under Gina's nose. 'Is it true, what it says here? You have taken this impossible man as your lover?'

'What impossible man?'

'Vartan Dackis, who else?'

'I read the newspaper this morning, I don't recall it saying anything about lovers.'

'Oh, you have taught me English so good,' declared Peter, 'that I can understand what is said and what is unsaid. These sentences say that you and Dackis are having an affair.'

'Read that into it if you must. I'm not obliged to respond to the gossip in the newspapers, said or unsaid.'

'But to the anxiety of a friend you must respond! Gina, this man is so ... so unsuitable! Uncultured, unprincipled–'

'Have you actually met Vartan Dackis?'

Peter hesitated a little. 'No, not actually met. But everyone knows what he is.'

'From things "unsaid" in newspapers?'

She shrugged, and picked up the script on her desk. They were in her office, a suite of some splendour into which she had recently been moved. She couldn't help sensing that it was done because she was now someone of 'importance' in the Hollywood hierarchy; the mistress of Vartan Dackis the producer. MGM didn't want to offend Dackis by seeming ungenerous to his 'friend', hence the huge wide room with its deep carpet and picture window, and the little secretary in the outer office to do the chores she had done herself until a week ago.

Peter had come for a lesson on pronunciation of some difficult lines in a new film. 'Come along, Peter, let's get to work.'

'Oh, work, work... That can wait. What is important is to rescue you from this stupid mistake! What can you *see* in him, Gina? Everyone knows he thinks only of himself. And he makes such bad films!'

'His films make money, Peter.'

'But artistic values are more important than money–'

'Oh, indeed? What kind of artistic value do you place on the films you make?'

The flash of irritation surprised him. He gave a look of reproach. 'I have to take what work I can get, Gina–'

'That's *your* excuse. Dack's would be just as good, I daresay, if he even bothered to invent one.'

'Mine is not an invention! You know how things are— But in any case it's not me we are discussing, it is this man Dackis–'

'No it isn't.' She came to him across the wide office and put her two hands on his arm. She looked up into his long angular face. 'Don't let's quarrel, Peter. I don't interfere in your private life, you don't interfere in–'

'Me? I have no private life. You know I don't – what is this American phrase – play around. I'm too busy – work, dialogue lessons, music, exercise to stay in shape.'

'I wasn't talking about any girl friends you might have in Hollywood. I was referring to your wife.'

'My wife? But she is in Milan,' he said, taken aback.

'Do I lecture you about how wrong it is for her to pour away your money on lessons with the highest-paid teacher in opera? Do I tell you she's unsuitable?'

There was a very strange silence while Peter slowly folded his long form into one of the leather-covered armchairs. He was half-frowning. 'Did Bert tell you to say that?' he asked.

'No. But I know he thinks the same.'

'I had no idea you thought like this of Magda.'

'I have really no thoughts of Magda, Peter darling. But if you want to take up a reproving attitude about Dack, I can do the same about Magda.'

'It's not the same thing. Magda and I are married. It is duty that makes it important to look after her. You have no duty to Dackis. To the contrary – you ought to have enough discrimination to keep away from such a man. Gina, you must have heard of all the other women.'

'I know there have been women.'

'Do you know that Melita Mills … ah … the English word has gone – *Selbstmord*? What is that in English?'

Although she had picked up some German from Peter, the word for suicide had never yet figured in their conversation. But she could translate it from its parts – self-murder.

'I know Melita Mills took an overdose. From all I hear, she was a very unstable person.'

'She left a note saying Dackis had driven her to it. That is what I am told.'

'But that's just the kind of thing an unstable woman would do. It proves nothing.'

'Then what about the little girl – they say it was four years ago – she brought a court case.'

'Yes, a paternity suit. She settled out of court.'

'Only because he paid her off.'

'Peter, all this is just Hollywood tattle. And it's in the past. I don't talk to Dack about his Hollywood past.'

'What do you talk to him about, that is what I would like to know! You have nothing in common with such a man.'

How could she tell him that Dack called to something purely physical in her make-up, something she had never known was there until he summoned it up? Peter – dear, good, kind Peter, who never kissed anything but her cheek or her fingertips – how could he be expected to believe that an almost obsessive passion bound her to Dack?

She wasn't a child, nor was she the type to surrender herself to a silly infatuation. She knew that this desperate need for Dack's body would pass – how long it would endure she couldn't tell but it was so intense that, like a fierce fire with little fuel, it must burn out soon.

Meanwhile she had no intention of giving up her relationship. It was important to her, and to Dack. From what she knew of his sexual career, he was likely to lose interest in her in a month or two. So be it. But so long as it lasted, no one was going to talk her out of it.

'Are we going to do any work on this script, or not? The studio pays me to give you lessons, you know.'

'I'm not in the mood for it,' Peter said, surprisingly. He was the least temperamental of actors. It was a measure of how upset he was. 'Gina, everyone is talking about you. It's got worse since Clare moved out. They say Dack threw her over for you, and you had a jealous row.'

'There was no jealous row. My brother Curt turned up in Hollywood with nowhere to live so it made sense for Clare to rent an apartment and have Curt to stay.'

'Your family are so respectable! What must they think, your Uncle Gregor and Aunt Francesca? Their well-brought-up daughter Clare living with her cousin?'

'They know it's perfectly innocent–'

'That's not what people are saying!'

'How often do I have to tell you? Hollywood likes to think the worst of everybody.'

177

'But you don't deny that you and Clare aren't friends any more?'

'I'm friends with Clare.'

'She is not friends with you. She was very … how do you say *schädlich*?'

'I don't know and I don't want to. Clare will get over her vexation.' Gina sighed. 'Peter, this script…?'

'We will begin on it tomorrow. It's not so difficult – we just have to decide which lines I have to speak with an accent and which have got to be very clear English.'

'I notice you're an exiled Russian prince this time. It's very romantic.'

'Please don't make fun. I'm trying very hard not to let them put me in a film where I have to play a Hungarian hussar, but I'm losing the battle. When they found out I learnt to fence for operas like *Les Huguenots*, they began planning a duel scene so I think I am trapped.'

She went with him to the door of the outer office. 'Think more kindly of Dack's films, then,' she said as he bent over her hand in farewell.'

'Of his films, yes. Of the man, no.'

She watched him stride away along the corridor. As she turned back, her phone was ringing. Her secretary, newly hired by the film company, looked up. 'It's Mr Dackis again. He rang while you were in tuition.'

'Put him through.' She took the call in the inner room.

'Sweetheart, is that you? Nancy said you'd told her to hold all calls.'

'That's right, I had a pupil. I'm free now – what did you want?'

He had plans to propose for the evening. She agreed to them, her mind still partly on the argument with Peter.

'Gina? Honey? You don't seem very keen.'

'I'm sorry, Dack. I was miles away. Yes, of course, dinner with the Grubers – that suits me fine.'

'What were you thinking about, then? Someone more important than me?' He was joking, but he was still anxious to know the answer.'

'Oh, it's just some disagreement I had with Peter Brunner. Nothing serious.'

'What did he say to upset you?'

'He didn't upset me. We had a disagreement, that's all. About a script.' It was only a little white lie. She could hardly tell him that Peter had been begging her to break off the affair.

'He's got his nerve, arguing with you! He's supposed to be taking lessons, isn't he? Not telling you your business. You got many pupils who give you a hard time?'

'No, certainly not, and Peter didn't give me a hard time. He's too good a friend to quarrel with me.'

'Yeah, I guess so...'

Bert Kolin dropped in next day. 'What you been saying to friend Peter? He chewed me out about criticising his wife with you.'

'Oh dear! We had a kind of squabble yesterday. It wasn't about Magda, really – it was about something else. But I snapped back at him about Magda. I'm sorry, Bert. Was he cross?'

'Ah, not him. You know Peter. He's one sweet guy. But I think you might have done him a favour. I been trying to talk him into setting a limit for the kind of money Magda gets. He's less strong against it.' Bert nodded so vigorously that ash from his cigar fell down the front of his straining waist-coat. 'By and by I might get him to put his foot down with that dame.'

'Oh yes, and Ben Lyon might marry Mickey Mouse!'

Bert eased himself in the roomy armchair. 'I might take a drink if you offered one.'

'I'd offer, but I have a pupil coming in ten minutes.'

'I can drink a small scotch in ten minutes, Gina.'

Thus pressured, Gina brought out the decanter from the cupboard hidden among the fake books on the shelves. She'd had no say in the decoration of the rooms but the drinks cupboard rather amused her. As she handed him his glass she said, 'How is Peter doing?'

'He's doing good. He's got a film coming up – real heart-warmer, about a captain of hussars who's wrongly drummed out–'

'He mentioned that. He doesn't want to do it, Bert.'

'He didn't want to do *The Prince of Nowhere* but he saw sense by and by. Listen, Gina, you know how this town works. Until you're one of the biggies, you have to take what you're offered. Peter isn't one of the biggies so if he wants to keep working he's got to accept silly scripts. What's it matter? Folk don't go to the movies to see Shakespeare.'

'I hear that Thalberg has ambitions to do Shakespeare.'

'He'll never get the backing.' Bert sipped. 'You're looking great these days, sweetheart. Always were a great looking gal, but you seem to have something special about you.'

181

He pursed his fleshy lips. 'Could it be love?'

Gina sighed inwardly. His heavy tactfulness only served to call attention to what he intended to say. 'What if it were love, Bert?'

'I s'pose that means Vartan Dackis. Is it right, what I hear?'

'I don't know what you hear.'

'Baby, don't get involved with Dackis. I know he's got sex appeal and power and money – but he's also got a mean streak as wide as Hollywood Boulevard.'

'So people keep saying.'

'It's true, believe me. So at the moment you haven't come up against it – I s'pose you're in what might be called the honeymoon period.' He grinned. 'Joke. But listen, if you ever came up against him, you'd learn the truth of what I'm saying. He plays rough.'

'I'm not going to quarrel with Dack, if that's what's worrying you, Bert.'

'No, I reckon not. Not many people quarrel with Dack. But he might quarrel with *you* and if he does, watch out. Honest, Gina, I could bring you half a dozen acquaintances who've got the wounds to show from tangling with him.'

She couldn't help but be impressed by his earnestness. So she did him the justice of taking him seriously. 'He was rough with Clare – I'll give you that. But that was all due to a misunderstanding. He didn't realise what kind of a girl she is, and when she fought him off he got angry. I don't think he'd ever be like that to me.'

'I sure hope not.' He put his glass on the desk and struggled out of the armchair, complaining, 'You have to have young, fit students – old guys like me would use up a lot of energy sitting down and getting up!'

'You're not old, Bert. But you're very kind.'

'Yeah, sure, Mr Soft-shell, that's me. I just don't want you go get hurt, girlie.'

'I'll be all right, Bert.'

She was sure this was so, because although she recognised the truth of what Bert had been saying, she couldn't imagine Dack having any reason to be angry with her. She had told him everything about herself, so that he knew he was the only man in her life – the only man, indeed, who had ever made her feel a complete woman. She wouldn't irritate him with ambitions to be a star, as doubtless many women had done. She was prepared to accept the situation between them on the terms he offered and to let the affair run to its inevitable close without rancour on her part.

But she was surprised to learn that that was not enough.

After a weekend together, Dack said to her: 'Tomorrow I'm busy all day, and I've an evening meeting with Sam Goldwyn at his house on Laurel Way. It won't be too late ending but you understand I'll be pretty bushed by then – we'll be talking money.'

'Of course. It's all right. I hope the conference with Mr Goldwyn goes the way you want it to.'

'Tuesday, I've booked seats for us at the Barn Theatre – they've got a musical in from Chicago and the broad in that seems to have talent. I thought we'd take a look–'

'Oh, I'm sorry, Dack, I can't. I have a previous engagement.'

'You have a *what*?' It was a snort of surprised amusement. 'You mean you've got a date?'

'Oh, I wouldn't put it quite like that.' She laughed. 'I'm going to a sneak preview.'

'Who's got a film coming on? *The Front Page* isn't coming on yet – I hear they have trouble with the Hays Office.'

'It's Peter's film – *Storm of Gold*.'

'Peter Brunnen? Oh, say, you can give that a miss – it's nothing important–'

'It's important to Peter,' she said. 'I promised him I'd go.'

'You can get out of it easy.'

'But I don't want to.'

'You don't want to?'

'No, I want to see Peter's film. Don't forget, I helped him learn the dialogue. I want to hear how it sounds.'

'Oh, professional interest, is that it? I can arrange for you to get a look at the film some other time – Sam Goldwyn'll have it, he gets all the new films to show at home–'

Gina was shaking her head. 'You don't understand. I promised Peter I'd go to the preview and I want to keep my promise. It's not as if my opinion on the musical at the Barn is of any importance–'

'That's not the point, Gina! I want you there.'

'Well, I'm sorry, but we can go some other night.'

Dack frowned. 'I've got things planned for other nights.'

'So have I.'

'In future, you ought to check with me before you put dates in your diary.'

'Oh, now, listen, Dack...' She was about to say she couldn't plan her life around him, but then she saw that there was a thundercloud on his brow. Perhaps now was not the time to tell him that she valued her independence. She said, 'It would be better not to get our lines crossed, I suppose.'

As she drove from Dack's house to her office in the MGM studios she thought over that conversation. It was a little worrying. He had a possessive streak that made him difficult at times.

The preview on Tuesday was at a picture house on the circuit owned by MGM. Although it was supposed to be a 'sneak', avid movie-goers knew which theatres were used on which nights by the companies to gauge the reception of a brand new film. On the day in question the sign would go up on the marquee: Preview Tonite! Pre-release Showing! And then the name of the film with its stars, or the names of the stars and then the film title – whichever was deemed more important.

On Tuesday night the marquee lights spelt out: *Storm of Gold*, Peter Brunnen, Tilda Martin. Gina calculated that it meant Peter wasn't yet more important than the film but had first billing before his co-star.

'Not bad, eh?' Bert Kolin was pink with pleasure. 'Not bad for his third movie. If it takes with this audience, that part in *The*

*Emperor's Hussar* is his.'

Gina took his arm to walk down the aisle to the area which had been roped off for the important people. The rest of the audience was already in place, their heads turned away from the screen, watching to see who would arrive. Peter had to escort his co-star. When they came in, Gina was delighted to hear a spatter of applause. But it was probably for Tilda Martin. She was an established favourite.

When the lights went down the opening music was full of swooning violins and trilling flutes. It was the kind of film Gina would never have bothered to go to if Peter hadn't been acting in it, but she was able to say to Bert with perfect truth that she'd enjoyed it.

'Yes, it went down well,' he said, watching the audience applaud as the closing shot faded out. Ushers were moving down the aisles, handing out cards so that members of the public could enter their verdict on the film. Bert, an old hand at previews, watched how they accepted the cards: they were taking them eagerly, which meant they had something good to say. When they'd been bored or irritated there was always a growling reluctance to take the cards.

For her part, Gina had something else to look at. Sitting two rows back and to her left was Vartan Dackis, glowering at her.

'Dack!' she said aloud, though he was too far off to hear her.

'What say, honey?'

'There's Dack!'

'Where? Oh, gee – if I'd known he wanted to look at the preview I could of sent him tickets. Gee, what's he doing here?'

I think he's checking on me, Gina could have said. Aloud she said: 'He knew I'd be here – I expect he's come to take me out to supper.'

'Ask him to come to the party, Gina. It won't be much, 'cos Tilda's got to be on set at five in the morning, but we thought we'd have a coupla drinks.'

'Yes, of course.' Now the crowd was moving out along the aisles. Gina moved with them until she came level with the row in which Dack had been sitting. 'Dack,' she said, determined to see the bright side of it. 'How nice of you to come! Did you enjoy it?'

'Na-ah! I hate these small-scale second feature things.'

'Did you miss out on the musical?'

'Stopped by before I came on here. Don't

188

think I'll bother with the girl. She's got good pipes but she can't project worth a damn.'

Now they were side by side, moving towards the entrance. 'There's to be a little celebration, Dack. Want to come along?'

'No, it isn't my film—'

'Please come. Bert would love to have you come.'

'The director'll think I'm being nosy.'

'No he won't. I'm sure he'll be pleased.' He'll think you're looking at him with a view to hiring him. So will Tilda. Even Peter might think so – but Bert will put him wise.

Without much persuasion Dack joined the group who were heading for a nightclub called The Web. Prohibition was still in force but it was always possible to get liquor if you knew where to go, and The Web had a reputation for selling decent imported wine as well as hard spirits. It was well understood by the Hollywood police force that to raid The Web would be the height of bad manners and result in a sudden diminution of funds available for police charities.

The purpose of the party was to wait for the first editions of the Los Angeles newspapers. The film critics always had tickets for the previews; they used them frequently but sometimes, if they felt the film was beneath their notice, they ignored them. However, Bert had spied Alberti of the *Examiner* and O'Hearn of the *Tribune*. Reports would have been phoned through, to be set in the reserved spot on the arts page. The papers would hit the streets soon after one a.m.

Gina sat with Bert and the director. They were at one corner of a long table. Somehow Dack was at the other end with Peter and Tilda. The conversation was all about the film, mostly complimentary – more complimentary than was entirely deserved but Gina understood the need for over-emphasis. Nothing in Hollywood was ever just 'good': it had to be 'great' or 'stupendous'.

By and by Tilda said goodbye. She had to get a couple of hours' sleep before facing next day's make-up call. Her agent would ring her at four-thirty. Time went by, people table-hopping to say they'd heard the film was great and to offer congratulations. Food was brought, the expensive, banal food of the Hollywood nightclub – chicken à la king, cherries jubilee. No one ate much; until the papers came, nerves were too highly-strung for eating.

At last the pageboy arrived staggering

under a load of newsprint. Hands seized copies, the pages were discarded until the review columns were reached. 'He says it's "gripping". Gee, I thought he'd say it was better than "gripping"...'

'O'Hearn calls it "touching". "A touching performance by Tilda Martin..." Oh, say Peter–! O'Hearn went for you in a big way! "A simplicity of style that exactly suits the talking picture..."'

'"That rich, easy voice..." Yeah, Alberti would go for that. He's an Italian opera buff.'

They took the reviews to pieces, trying to assess the box office appeal of the film from these first reactions. Gina could hear Peter laughing with relieved delight.

'Congratulations!' she called to him, the length of the table.

'For what? For being called "simple"?' he joked back.

'Can't you speak the goddam language?' Dack said in a loud voice.

'Peter was just being modest,' Gina said, sensing the hidden anger in him. 'He–'

'Modest, huh. What kind of jerk is he? He just got two good reviews from two good critics – why can't he just be glad about it and shut up?'

Someone muttered that Mr Dackis had had too much to drink. The words somehow surfaced among the soothing murmurs from everyone else. 'Drunk, am I?' Dack snarled. 'Drunk or sober, I can still make better films than that mug of mush we just saw!'

He got up, upsetting both his own drink and that of his neighbour. Gina, with a glance of anguish at Bert, hurried after him as he stormed his way among the tables and into the vestibule. There she caught up with him. 'Dack!'

'Let go of me!' he growled as she took his arm. 'Go back to your friends–'

'Come on, now, Dack, don't be like this. I only wanted to be at the preview and say good things about the film. We can leave now, if you want to.'

'Oh, stay, stay and talk gush to your sexy-voiced hero–'

'Come on, let's go home, Dack. I could do with a good club sandwich and a cup of coffee after that skimpy supper. Shall I rustle us up something to eat?'

'Well … I could do with a bite… Sure you want to leave?'

'Of course I do.'

'We-ell… Yeah… Okay … I'll get a cab.'

The events of the evening were forgotten in the domestic chores of getting a sandwich and making coffee in her little kitchen. Dack hovered around her, trying by his manner to excuse himself for his behaviour. But he would never say aloud that he was sorry; this she knew instinctively.

She hoped it was all washed away in the passionate love-making that followed. If Dack was more domineering, less considerate than on previous occasions, she understood; he was insisting on his mastery in face of what he thought was a threat from a rival.

But though she understood she was distressed. How could you handle a man who was so jealous that even common friendship drove him to rage?

She determined to be very careful about her relationship with Peter – to avoid him except in the professional environment. She couldn't avoid him altogether for she was still tutoring him for his part as the exiled Russian Prince and might be called upon to work with him on the hussar role.

Then she discovered that Peter had been assigned to another voice coach. 'I don't know why,' he said when he rang to tell her. 'It's a man, a Broadway director – Wickstead, do you know him?'

'Oh yes, he's got a big reputation—'

'Well, he talks rubbish. He tries to direct me as an actor. I say to him, I can act, and if I'm wrong my director will put me right. All I need from you is how to pronounce and phrase the words – but he doesn't listen. I'm going to ask to come back to you, Gina. You and I get along fine.'

His request was agreed to. When he came for his resumed lessons he was quite indignant. 'No one could explain why the change was made in the first place.'

But Gina got the explanation next day. 'Is that right, you're teaching that guy Brunnen again?' Dack demanded.

'Why yes, I am.'

'Did you ask to have him back?'

'No. Peter asked. He didn't get on with Wicksted—'

'Hah! He didn't want to lose tabs on you, you mean! If he thinks he can counter my moves, he's got another think—'

'Dack! Do you mean you arranged to have him moved to another teacher?'

'Sure I did. I dropped a word in the right ear and it was done next day. And I'll do that again tomorrow, only this time with bells on.'

'But that's absurd, Dack—'

'Listen, I don't want you seeing that guy.'

'What on earth for? There's *nothing* between Peter and me.'

'Not from your side, mebbe. But I saw the way he looked at you. He's hooked on you—'

'Nothing of the kind! He's got a wife in Europe that he's devoted to—'

'Yeah, a long way off, in Milan, right? You think he doesn't want consolation—'

'How do you know Magda's in Milan?'

'I had inquiries made, that's how.'

'You – you've been checking up?'

'Sure thing! I like to know the opposition.'

'But there isn't any opposition, Dack,' she said, desperately. 'Peter and I are friends, that's all.'

'There's no such thing as friendship between a guy and a girl. I told you that. And I intend to see there isn't even friendship—'

'But you can't choose my friends for me! I can't have that, Dack! I won't let you—'

'Oh, you won't, huh? You'll do as I damn well say, lady, or you're going to regret it.'

She was too angry to weigh her words. 'What will you do?' she asked. 'Hire someone to have me beaten up? Force me to take an overdose like Melita Mills?'

'Say, you snide little party-princess! Where do you come off accusing me of–'

'You don't deny you've used rough stuff in the past, do you? Not to mention going backstage and whispering with your flunkies. What's so stupid is that you're wasting your time! If you could just behave like a civilised human being you'd understand that Peter and I mean nothing to each other–'

'If he means so damn little, why are you in such a lather about not giving him lessons?'

'It's the principle of the thing–'

'Principle! Oh, yeah, principle! That's what those egghead writers from the east always go on about when we tell them their screenplays need editing. Principle? My principle is to have nobody hanging about in my backyard–'

'You don't own me, Dack! And you've no right to interfere in Peter's life–'

'I'll do more than interfere. If he's so important to you, I could easily get him out of the way–'

'What are you saying? You'd hire some goons to–'

'Oh, nothing physical. In this dorp, you can get rid of an actor easy. There's always somebody just longing to step into his shoes.'

'I think that's enough,' Gina said. She picked up her bag and gloves. 'I think we'd better say nothing more or we'll both be sorry.'

'Here, what are you doing? We've got a date at–'

'Not today, Dack. I'm going home. Perhaps when we've both had time to cool off, we'll be in touch again.'

'You stay where you are!' He seized her by the wrists, so harshly that she dropped her handbag. It fell to the floor, scattering its contents over their feet, but neither of them noticed.

'What are you going to do?' she demanded, staring into the black, menacing eyes. 'Hit me?'

'Gina–'

'That's what everybody said you'd do. I had warning enough.'

'Gina, I...' The fury went out of him. He released his hold.

She turned and walked out of his house. Her car stood in the drive with its keys in the dashboard. She got in and drove off, stricken by what had just occurred.

She thought he would ring, or send a gift in token of apology. But nothing happened. Next day went by, and the next. She was hanging on to her determination by her fingernails; her physical need of him was torment.

Bert Kolin dropped into her office on the morning of the third day. He looked very worried.

'A hell of a thing has happened,' he said.

'What?'

'Peter lost that role in *The Emperor's Hussar*.'

She sat back in her chair, staring at him over her handsome desk. 'Oh, Bert ... I thought it was all signed and sealed?'

'So did I. But they've decided to use Antonio Salvo instead.'

'But ... he's much older.'

'Yeah, and they've got to teach him to fence for the part. Stupid, isn't it?'

'It's incredible!'

'Gina... They're saying Dackis bitched it up for Peter.'

She drew in a deep breath.

'You think it's true?' Bert persisted.

'It might be.'

'I could see he was jealous as hell the night of the preview. Trouble is, Peter won't take it seriously. He won't believe it.'

'Even if he believes it, what could he do?'

'Stop seeing you.'

'Is that the answer, Bert? To knuckle under?'

Bert began to wander along the bookshelves, poking at the leather-bound spines of the ornamental books. 'I don't want you should take this wrong, Gina,' he said, 'but if you're really in love with Dackis you should play for the big stakes. Throw up your job, let him provide you with an income, and get a gold ring on your finger. That's not going to be easy, but it'll be a lot better than running an affair with him while you hold a job where you see other men.'

'I don't want to marry Dack, Bert! It's not that kind of relationship.'

'You don't want to marry him? Most women try for that.'

'We wouldn't stay married for a year. It would be madness.'

'You mean you think there'll be a break-up?'

'Of course. He's not the kind who can stay with one woman. He gets bored easily.'

He turned to stare at her over his shoulder. 'You say that as if you don't even like him much.'

'Liking and loving are two different things.'

'You saying you love him?'

'I...' She fell silent for a moment. 'Let's not discuss it. What's to be done, Bert? Can you get back *The Emperor's Hussar* for Peter?'

He shook his head. 'That's dished. What's worrying me is if it happens again. Too long a gap between pictures, and Peter could be on the breadline.'

'He could go back to opera.'

'Would it be that easy? Besides, there's Magda – he always worries about Magda.'

'Let Magda worry about herself.'

'Try to sort this out with Dackis, Gina. Keep him off Peter's back.'

'The only way to do that is for Peter and me to break off our friendship.'

'Okay, then do it that way.'

'Will Peter go along with that?'

'Does he have to know? Just keep out of his way.'

Gina got up from her desk and moved to stare out of the window, at the busy scene below where the film studio's main road went by.

After a moment she said, 'I'll do my best, Bert.'

'Thank you.' He came up behind her, kissed her on the top of her head. 'You're a doll, Gina.'

The trouble was that Peter wouldn't be avoided. He was now busy filming *Prince in Exile* so he came for no more speech lessons, but he turned up at odd moments at her office, stopped her in the commissary, called at her apartment. Once he said in a reproachful tone, 'Have I offended you, Gina? Why are you so unfriendly these days?'

I'm trying to save your Hollywood career, she could have replied. But she held her tongue. 'I'm busy,' she said. 'I've a lot of work with this Biblical film now they're shooting the interior scenes. It doesn't matter if soldiers in the battle scenes shout in American accents but they want the Roman senators to sound more "classy".'

He was only partially satisfied. She tried, after he had gone, to think of some way of quarrelling with him so that they would not see each other again – but Peter was so difficult to quarrel with.

And all the time she could feel the unrelenting pressure of Dack's possessiveness upon her. He even hired a private detective to keep surveillance on her. At first she couldn't believe it, but when for the third time she'd seen the same tall untidy man in the Panama suit in the same beat-up Buick, she challenged him.

'Are you following me?'

'Me? No, lady, of course not.'

But he was there next day, in a Ford this time. She walked up and leaned on the edge of the car window. 'Mr Dackis is paying you?'

He gave a little gasp of apprehension. 'I never told you that, miss.'

'So it's true. Well, all right, you have to earn your money, I suppose. But it's just so … degrading.'

Degrading. That was the word. To be so inexorably tied by mere physical need to a man who behaved like this…

When they were together, all they did was bicker. To Gina it was so distasteful that she could never understand why he didn't just stay away, but he seemed to like it that way – arguing, getting aggressive and abusive, and then washing it all away in a tide of passion when they went to bed together.

Until next time they met, when the arguing began again.

At the end of August Dack began talking about a vacation, a trip to New York that would for him combine business with pleasure. She tried to imagine herself introducing Dack to her mother and stepfather and knew it was impossible.

Yet she found she didn't dare tell him she couldn't go. It came as a shock to her to realise she was actually afraid.

Her cousin Lewis arrived on a visit. At first she was worried in case he was thinking of trying for a job in Hollywood now that his university career was over, but it was nothing like that. On the contrary, Lewis knew what he was going to do: he was going to help campaign for the Democratic candidate in the presidential election. But first there was a worry of his own to deal with.

'You know that film of Uppie's?'

'What? No, I don't think I–'

'The one Eisenstein is making in Mexico.'

'Oh, that.' Uppie was Lewis's name for Upton Sinclair, it seemed. 'What about it?'

'Uppie is terribly worried. Eisenstein keeps cabling for more money, but we never find out what happens to it. And I think he's running us into debt down there.'

She noticed that Lewis had identified so strongly with the author and his family that his problems had become Lewis's.

'Perhaps in the end there'll be a marvellous film.'

'Oh, the man's a genius, no mistake about it. But the thing is, Gina, Uppie and his wife really need someone to go and sort of ... catch hold of things, water everything down a little. First of all, they need someone to explain to the Mexicans that Eisenstein doesn't have unlimited funds.'

'Then why don't they get someone...' she stared at Lewis. 'You speak Spanish. Are you saying that you've got the job of going south to deal with Eisenstein?'

'Yes, and it's been suggested I should ask you to go with me.'

'Me?'

'Yes, you. Hollywood has some money invested in this, and you remember Jesse Lasky first invited him to the States–'

'I heard something about that, I think.'

'Mr Lasky would like someone from the Hollywood studios to go and rescue him from his own mistakes but he doesn't want Paramount to become visibly involved. When he heard I had a cousin working for MGM, he suggested I should ask you to go with me. MGM are willing to release you on unlimited leave.'

'Mexico!'

'I know it's a long way from anywhere, Gina. And a hell of a lot to ask when you have your own career to think of–'

'No, no!' Mexico! Out of reach of Dack,

out of reach of his private detectives... And a reason to go, a suggestion from Mr Lasky of Paramount that could be regarded as equal to a command. A chance to step out of the trap she was in, to get away from Dack without rousing jealousy of another man, to free Peter of the unending and unfounded suspicions that were wrecking his career... A chance to be herself again, her real self, not a puppet belonging to Vartan Dackis.

'What do you think, Gina? Would you do this for me?'

'I'll go,' she said.

## Chapter Eight

Gina's first sight of Mexico was almost enough to make her change her mind. 'Oh, God,' she exclaimed.

Lewis, who was driving her car, spared her a glance. 'Don't judge Mexico by Tijuana, Gina. This is just a tourist trap.'

The trouble was, it was a trap designed for the very worst kind of tourist. Southern Californians in need of a drink could evade

Prohibition by simply crossing the border and soaking up tequila in Tijuana. The shop windows were full of Mexican dolls, girl dolls in the exaggerated ruffled skirts of the café dancer, matador dolls in *traje de luz* outfits that glittered like fractured glass.

There were other windows, decked with live girls. Gina stared at them in amazement as they drove past, wondering what they could be – until it dawned on her they were brothels.

'Lew!' she gasped.

He kept his eyes on the road, but went slowly red. 'I tell you, the rest of Mexico isn't like this!'

'It better not be, or Eisenstein will find he's making a pornographic film!'

Eisenstein had been in the 'waist' of Mexico, at the port of Salina Cruz, filming bawdy sailors, and beautiful maidens with great starched ruffles over their heads. Then he had moved west to look at the Zapotec ruins in the province of Oaxaca, where Nature had obligingly provided him with a real earthquake. His plan was now to visit Yucatan, about another four hundred miles away, so it was the devout intention of Lewis and Gina to catch him in Oaxaca City.

The roads were bad, and as they climbed

the twisting mountain roads the altitude made Gina dizzy and breathless. But the sights of this new and alien country glimpsed through the grimy car windows stirred Gina's imagination, banished all thoughts of Hollywood, and almost made her forget the man she had left without a word.

After days of dusty driving they stopped in Mexico City to rest and recuperate. After a welcome bath and dinner in the Hotel El Presidente, Lewis set about telephoning Sergei Mikhailovich Eisenstein. The Mexican telephone system was never good, but the earthquake in Oaxaca Province provided the perfect excuse for failure, and Lewis spent over an hour before he got through.

'Ah, McGarth, it is you! How charming of you to telephone me. Mr Sinclair cabled me that you were coming. How nice.'

Eisenstein had an impish sense of humour. He had decided to take up the position that Lewis McGarth had been sent as interpreter and the young woman, Mrs Gramm, as a mere visitor. Nothing would have induced him to admit to Lewis that they had come from backers sorely tried by his uncommercial outlook.

Lewis found the director urging him to stay in Mexico City, to seize the opportunity of witnessing the dances in Guadalupe Square on Assumption Day: 'I hear they are really fascinating, my dear friend, you should not miss them.'

'But Mr Eisenstein, I've come on purpose to join your crew–'

'But first you must see Mexico City, no? It is foolish to be in this beautiful country and not take every chance to look at the folk festivals. Stay a week in Mexico City.'

'No, thank you, I believe you'll have moved on from Oaxaca within the week–?'

'Oh,' Eisenstein said, a little dashed. He'd hoped to be safely off in the Yucatan Peninsula when the snooper from California turned up in Oaxaca.

'We'll be with you late tomorrow, Mr Eisenstein. In time for dinner, I hope.'

'That will be delightful,' Eisenstein said heartily, and hung up to say in disgust to his friend Alexandrov, 'A spy from the money-grubbers of America, alas. And his woman.'

'They're coming, then?'

'Yes, but we can keep them occupied with sightseeing while we get on with the real work.'

'We had better do something to make

them feel welcome, Sergei. They might report badly about us and the money would be completely cut off.'

'Tcha!' sighed the director. 'Money ... what a nuisance it is. I never realised until I left the Soviets that money really is an evil.'

'But these people who are coming are not necessarily evil. I believe the young man was helpful in putting us in touch with Upton Sinclair in the first place.'

'Better if he had not! What an old woman *he* turned out to be!'

'Oh, Sergei, be reasonable. He persuaded his friends to invest money in this film. It's only natural he should worry–'

'He knows nothing about film-making. Why doesn't he leave it to those who do? And this young man, McGarth – he is not a film expert. He has just left university, I believe.'

'Where he studied economics, Sergei. Maybe he understands money?'

'Oh,' said Eisenstein with deep gloom.

Gina and Lewis arrived in Oaxaca earlier than they expected. They found an un-believably beautiful city, nestling in a lush green valley and glowing beige-pink against the blue sky about the Madre del Sur mountains. The hotel, the Dos Rosas, looked clean and comfortable. The receptionist told them in fluent English that Señor Eisenstein was out on location, expected back for dinner at eight.

Having unpacked and had a drink, they decided to go in search of the film crew. The cameras were set up in an alley giving access to an ancient square where the remains of temples built before Columbus had been used as the foundation for a lovely little Catholic church.

The light was fading. Eisenstein was shooting a wedding celebration in the square, with a mob of laughing, dancing people surrounding the young bride and groom. The Kleig lights glared down from gantries above the old trees. Music thrummed from a mariachi board.

Gina stood staring with some amazement. A scene like this would have cost a small fortune in Hollywood. 'My word, he's spending money here,' she said to Lewis.

'Oh yes – but don't forget, everything is much cheaper in Mexico.'

It would need to be, she thought. The scene went through, the crowd surged about in happy enthusiasm, the director shouted 'Cut!' and the big lights were turned off.

As a large group sauntered towards the

lane in which Gina and Lewis were standing, Lewis engaged some of them in conversation and discovered that they were being paid fifty cents Mexican per day and had been working for five days. 'Can't quarrel about the rate of pay,' Lewis said to Gina when he had translated.

'How many people do you think were dancing in that scene, Lew?' Gina inquired.

'Oh... About two hundred?'

'Two hundred times fifty cents is a hundred dollars. That's five hundred. Don't you see, Lew? No wonder he's exceeded his budget a dozen times!'

The crew were busy packing up. It seemed best to go back to Dos Rosas to await them there. As they strolled back, Gina said: 'The whole idea was impractical, Lew. Now I've seen the kind of thing he's shooting, I see that he could never do it on the kind of money Sinclair was supplying.'

'But I don't really understand what he was shooting there. I saw the script he prepared for Uppie – it had nothing about a wedding fiesta in a city square.'

The script Eisenstein had given to Upton Sinclair consisted of a prologue, an epilogue, and six separate stories intended to show the recent history of Mexico as it affected the common people. Although not be any means a documentary, it had been intended to use what was available in the locations, not go into any elaborate production.

But when Gina read the shooting script that night after they had had dinner with the film crew, she knew the outlook of the director had changed. Enchanted by the fierce beauty of Mexico, he'd been unable to resist showing it to the filmgoer.

'But, dear lady,' he replied when Gina remarked on the expansiveness of the treatment, 'it would be a crime to come to Mexico and stay indoors shooting two people or three – outside on the playas and markets is where life is really lived.'

She looked at him with helpless reproach. He was a year or two older than herself, not much taller, with a great square head covered with thick, bushy dark hair. His face was full of liveliness – charm had been his weapon all his life. He set himself now to charm this lovely lady from Hollywood who, unfortunately, seemed to know something about film-making.

That first evening set the tone of their subsequent relationship. Gina urged economic sense: Eisenstein parried with artistic enthusiasm. Both were right – the difficulty was that they weren't talking about the same film. Sergei Mikhailovich was in the middle of a love affair with Mexico which he was determined to translate to film, and damn the expense!

Because he had worked only in films made for the Soviet government, he'd never had to worry about money. If he needed a hundred extras, he demanded a hundred extras and the Department of Culture sent them.

Gina argued with him about his methods. Lewis begged him to consider the dilemma in which he was placing the kind-hearted old man in California, whose friends were now refusing to send another penny to the film-maker. Eisenstein muttered that an old man who worried so much about money could scarcely be called a true socialist.

The film-making in Oaxaca ended four days later. The company packed itself up and got ready to depart for Yucatan, where the scenes for the prologue would be shot.

'I can't go to Yucatan,' Lewis groaned. 'I've got to get back to San Francisco! I promised to help work for the Democratic campaign, I can't waste any more time here!'

The Democratic convention had nominated Franklin Delano Roosevelt, Governor of New York, as their candidate. Exactly what the Democratic policy was, no one was quite sure – but it had to be better than the Republicans', who had let the country slip further and further into the Depression. America was more than halfway through 1931 and yet the promised 'upturn' hadn't come. Men were standing in line in the great manufacturing cities for a bowl of soup and a slice of bread. Something had to be done and though no one knew exactly what, Roosevelt seemed to be the man to do it.

Compared with all this, the few thousand dollars being lost by Upton Sinclair and his friends seemed unimportant. 'Look here, Gina,' Lewis said, 'you really know more about films than I do. You stick with Eisenstein, try to make him pull his horns in. I'll have a good long talk with Uppie when I get back and try to explain the situation.'

'You will?' Gina said with some amusement in her hazel eyes. 'Exactly how?'

'I'll manage,' Lewis said, with the confidence born of desperation. Thus speaking, he boarded the train at Oaxaca station and was borne away on the start of his long journey back to San Francisco.

Yucatan was just as wonderful to Gina as Oaxaca. Merida, the city Eisenstein used as base camp, was white and clean and full of windmills pumping well water. After the long two-day drive, back-breaking and bumpy, the Hotel Montejo looked like paradise though it was small and old-fashioned by American standards.

Eisenstein and his assistant director Alexandrov had asked to be passengers in Gina's car: they wanted to look for locations for future shooting as they travelled. Their cameraman, Tisse, and his camera boy together with trunks, cases of exposed film, and other bulky luggage went by train. Eisenstein clutched to his chest a briefcase containing the screenplay. Exactly why he bothered, Gina couldn't understand; she'd already realised that he worked in a very free style, almost improvising as the location demanded.

What had annoyed her almost as much was the fact that, having asked to go by car so as to spot good scenery, Eisenstein went to sleep as soon as they were moving.

'You must forgive him,' said Gigori Alexandrov. 'It is always the same. While we are filming, he is demonic – never sleeping,

215

always active even when we are not actually on the set. He stays up almost all night, planning shooting angles, sketching moves for actor or camera– But then, when there is a lull, he becomes strangely lazy. This sleep of his, it is like a lethargy...'

'That's quite all right, Mr Alexandrov,' Gina said formally. She'd agreed to act as chauffeur as a means of breaking down the barrier between them. It wasn't in Eisenstein's nature to be rude to a lady. But since he regarded her as a spy and a hindrance, he'd done everything he could to evade her.

He hadn't bothered to hide his satisfaction when Lewis said he had to get back to San Francisco. The female cousin would remain ... well, he could handle the female cousin. The heat, the exhaustion, the boredom of continual re-takes... And if those didn't floor her, he would turn her head with his quick, bright charm, dazzle her with his intellect...

Gina didn't begin to understand him. She sensed that he really was a genius, but something irresponsible and egotistic marred him. And yet, wasn't that often true of men of genius? The great painters of the past, the great poets – how many of them had been upstanding characters? So, just as he used sweetness and winsomeness as weapons, she used feminine wiles. So far the match had been more or less a draw.

In Merida he was a blaze of energy. There were takes to be done for insertion in the part of the film called 'Fiesta', the section about the amorous picador. In fact, anywhere that Eisenstein espied an attractive locale, he set up his cameras.

He was shooting a monstrous footage – Gina had tried to find out how much was already in the can but Eisenstein managed to evade a direct answer. 'Oh, but one always shoots too much,' he said, waving a slender brown hand. 'That is part of the art. It is the cutting and editing that produces the real effect.'

'In Hollywood, producers and directors try to bring in the films as close to the required length as possible–'

'But in Hollywood they can control their sets and locations–'

'They also,' Gina went on firmly, 'spend a limited amount of time on shooting. It's called a shooting schedule. About two months, usually–'

'Agh! Two months! How can one translate the soul of Mexico onto celluloid in two months!'

After great difficulty, Gina put through a long distance call from Merida to California, and reached Upton Sinclair. 'As far as I can gather, Mr Sinclair, he can't foretell when he might finish shooting. I really don't know what to say to you.'

'My dear Mrs Gramm, I don't know what to say to *you*! I've looked at the rushes of the footage he's already sent for processing here. I don't understand any of it. It does bear *some* resemblance to the outline he showed me in the first place—'

'Oh, I shouldn't rely on that,' she said hastily. 'He grasps at inspiration—'

'Inspiration,' she heard the author groan over the hiss and crackle of the long-distance line.

'The problem is, if you try to get strict with him now, he just won't listen. I have to tell you... I think he's really in love with Mexico.'

'Well, my dear, I know it's a beautiful country—'

'To him it's more than that. It's a chance to make film poetry – a chance I think he knows will never come again, certainly after he goes back to the Soviets.'

'If it were just my own money,' Sinclair said in a despairing tone. 'I wouldn't mind so much if it were just my own money. But my friends have invested...'

As a result of this phone conversation Upton Sinclair sent his brother-in-law to supervise the finances of the film company, but this only worsened the situation. Hunter Kimbrough was an anxious, well-meaning man, but he irritated Eisenstein almost past bearing. If Gina was a spy, at least she was a good-looking spy. Hunter Kimbrough was middle-aged, conservative, and took an instant dislike to Eisenstein's beloved Mexico.

A state of tension arose: the air was like thunder around the production team. Each evening when Eisenstein and his colleagues returned, worn out, from a day's shooting, Kimbrough wanted to cross-question them about what they had spent, how many peasants they had paid to take part, how much footage had been shot, what the cost of transport had been.

'Lay off a little, Mr Kimbrough,' Gina begged. 'You're driving him to something foolish.'

The foolishness turned out to be the vast project to film the section called 'Maguey', which took place in an arid hot region, the Llanos de Apam. Here huge estates stretched as far as the eye could see, and among the tall Maguey cactus the peasants still toiled, extracting juice from the plants to make *pulque*, a popular Mexican drink.

This story had a larger cast than any of the others. Local inhabitants were talked into playing the parts. There were ten chief roles, several supporting roles, and a cast of peons and horse-riding characters called *charros*. As might have been foreseen, discipline among this mob was almost impossible.

Gina wrote a long calm report to Upton Sinclair with a copy to Mr Lasky at Paramount. She counselled tact and caution. For his part, Kimbrough counselled quite the opposite. The result was that Sinclair actually sent a cable to Joseph Stalin, begging him to recall his film genius. The Russian dictator replied that he had no interest in a renegade like Eisenstein.

The bitterness and anger this caused was predictable. Eisenstein went back to Merida to film more exterior shots for 'Fiesta'. He went to Chapala to film white pelicans and Indios paddling dug-out canoes. He had the roof torn off an old Tehuantepec mansion so as to film dancers from above. He organised a bullfight to keep the interest of an actor who had a job offer in Spain.

It was as if he knew the whole project was heading straight to hell, but intended to go there in style. Even Alexandrov, who was like a brother to him, could do nothing with him. In desperation Gina took an airline flight from Mexico City to Los Angeles, and from there drove in a hire car to Upton Sinclair's house.

The white-haired old author greeted her with genuine pleasure. So far they had never met, but he had kind feelings about any friend or relative of Lewis McGarth to begin with, and after Gina's heroic efforts over the film, he spoke to her as if she were an angel.

'I don't know what we're going to do, Mrs Gramm,' he groaned. 'Bills keep coming in, I keep sending bank drafts... Do you know that the insurance on the film and equipment is running us into thousands?'

'I'm sorry, Mr Sinclair. I do understand and sympathise, I do indeed. But Mr Eisenstein is being driven beyond his tolerance by the continual complaints and interference–'

'But what choice do we have? We *must* curb him somehow! He keeps going off on some new project – do you know he's at Xochimilco now, filming the Flower Festival? There wasn't a word about the Flower Festival in the original screenplay!'

Mrs Sinclair, known as Mary-Craig, moved restlessly. 'I don't think it's right,' she said. 'My husband shouldn't have to act as manager and general factotum to a foreign film director. It's making you quite ill, isn't it, darling!'

'That's not the point, dear. It's our responsibility to the people who trusted us with their money–'

'I see that, Upton. I'm not arguing against that. But after all, you have your own work to do. Mr Eisenstein doesn't seem to consider that you are a creative artist too!'

After Gina had gone to her hotel she thought about that. Was Upton Sinclair a 'creative artist' in the same sense as Eisenstein? He was a bestselling author, famous for his Lanny Budd character. One great novel of protest about the Chicago stockyards would probably live – *The Jungle*. But was he as innovative, as strangely-new, as Eisenstein?

That was really not the point. What mattered was that the strange film called *Que Viva Mexico* should be continued until, at last, Eisenstein had shot enough material and could settle down to the cutting and editing that would produce the final work of art.

Next day she went again to the Sinclair home outside Los Angeles, in time for a luncheon invitation. Others connected with the project were there, including Lewis. The American election was just past – Roosevelt was in with a huge majority but could not launch the great recovery plans until he was inaugurated in the new year. At first the conversation was about Roosevelt, the hopes he had engendered, the feeling of optimism and new beginnings he brought with him.

But by and by the conversation turned to Eisenstein and Mexico. Lewis, inevitably partisan on the side of the Sinclairs, offered to go to Mexico again to remonstrate with him.

'No, my dear boy, you have your own life to live. I've come to a decision with regard to the film. I put through a call to Hunter Kimbrough last night after Mrs Gramm left and we had a long, long talk. Mary-Craig and I discussed it all early this morning. Friends, I think we ought to put a stop to the whole thing before we lose any more money.'

'Oh, no!' gasped Gina.

But the sound was lost in the general murmur of approval from the other five guests gathered around the Sinclairs' table. Heads nodded, glances of understanding were exchanged. What they were thinking was: All film directors are megalomaniac, and this one's a Russian to boot.

When she could get a word in Gina tried to champion Eisenstein's cause. 'You don't understand his methods – nor do I, I freely admit, but if you had seen Sergei at work you'd know that something tremendously valuable is being evolved.'

'Yes, quite, dear Mrs Gramm. But will it be a saleable film?'

She couldn't maintain that it would. She did her best, but they listened with that tolerant look that means the decision has already been reached. They approved of her in many ways, but she was, alas, female: likely to be run away with her emotions – and every one knew that Eisenstein was a very attractive man.

After lunch Lewis put that very point to her. 'I notice you referred to Eisenstein as Sergei. Is there ... well, you know ... anything between the two of you?'

She smiled ruefully. 'On his side, nothing. He's too obsessed with Mexico to want any emotional entanglements. On my side, there's a sort of unwilling admiration and friendship.'

Her cousin looked unconvinced. 'You got very rattled when Uppie said he was cancelling the project.'

'So would you be, if you understood what it meant!' But she caught back the rest of her words. What was the use? The decision had been taken.

Upton Sinclair asked her to return to Mexico as messenger. He gave her a bulky letter which she was to present to Hunter Kimbrough personally.

She would gladly have refused, but she was still being paid a salary by MGM for 'carrying out special research on location.' She must earn her money. So she accepted the manilla envelope, put it in her handbag, and went to her hotel to pack and phone for a plane reservation.

She was snapping shut the locks of her suitcase when her bedside phone rang. 'Gina?' said a slurred voice.

'Who is this?'

'You coming to Hollywood, or shall I come to you in L.A.?'

'Dack!'

'Yeah, baby, it's Dack! Thought you could

get rid of me by walking out, did you? No woman ever walked out on Vartan Dackis!'

He was drunk, very drunk, and very angry. She shivered as she heard the vengeful tone of his voice. And she groaned at the publicity machine, which ground on over private lives no matter how much it might harm them, and which had disclosed her whereabouts.

'Dack, I've no time to talk to you now. I'm leaving for the airport–'

'Yeah, get you! The girl adventurer! Pan-American's prize passenger! What you trying to prove, Gina? – that you're more important than me?'

It surprised her to be asked that, because in the past couple of months, since becoming so immersed in the Eisenstein film, she'd almost forgotten Dack. At first she had had moments of physical longing that had made her weak, but little by little he'd vanished from her heart and pulse and nerves.

'I'm sorry, Dack, I have to go now–'

'Don't you put the phone down on me, babe!'

But despite the fury in his voice, she did so. She was in such a rush to catch her plane that she had no time to worry over Dack's resentment, nor the fact of his being thoroughly drunk at four o'clock in the afternoon.

In the dusty airport building in Mexico City there was the same delay and inefficiency as on her outward flight. But in the streets there was bustle and enthusiasm. In the courtyards of some of the lesser hotels, a cactus had been decorated for a Christmas tree. As they took the turning that led to Gina's hotel the road was blocked by a procession led by children carrying a platform with little statues of Mary, Joseph, and an angel.

'It's the *posadas*,' the taximan explained in good English. 'From now until Christmas Day they'll be going from house to house, "seeking lodgings", and at one or two each night they get gifts from the *pinata*.'

The group, each member bearing a candle, threaded its way past. There was laughter and delight on every face. How awful, Gina thought, to be coming with bad news into a scene so full of happiness...

It was late. Inquiry at the reception desk gave her the information that Mr Kimbrough had retired at ten with instructions to wake him at five so as to be ready to go grimly out with Señor Eisenstein's camera crew. No sense in waking him to give him the letter and, as she herself was very tired, it would be easy to be still asleep when they set out next day.

But the time had to come in the end. When the cars drew in at the hotel court-yard next evening she was on the porch to greet them.

'Oh, Mrs Gramm, so you are back,' said Sergei Mikhailovich. His tone implied that he wished she'd stayed in California. 'How is our friend and benefactor?'

'Worried, Mr Eisenstein.'

He sighed and shrugged. He looked ex-hausted. The slight figure in its white shirt, stained with sweat where the braces for his drill trousers criss-crossed, was drooping and listless. She could tell at a glance that filming hadn't gone well today.

'What did Upton tell you, Mrs Gramm?' Hunter Kimbrough asked, shouldering his way past Tisse who was carefully bringing in his camera.

'Can we talk, Mr Kimbrough?'

'Sure, sure... Just let me get a bath and a change of clothes. How about if I meet you in the bar for a drink in half an hour?'

Eisenstein looked at Gina, to see whether he too was invited. When she dropped her glance, he went into the hotel without another word.

Gina was waiting with a scotch and soda for Kimbrough when he appeared. He downed it quickly. 'God, what a day! We trudged miles among the cactus around Pachuca looking for the ideal location to have a horse-chase. I mean, Mrs Gramm, you can ride horses from anywhere to any-where – what difference does it make which stretch of cactus-country you choose?'

Sighing, she opened her handbag and took out the letter. 'Mr Sinclair asked me to give you this. Another copy is coming by mail.'

'Oh? Legal documents?'

She said nothing, simply waited while he tore open the envelope and began to read the contents. After a few seconds he looked up. 'I think I need another drink!'

She summoned the dark-skinned waiter, who came with refills as if by intuition. 'Closing it down?' Kimbrough said. 'Eisen-stein's going to hit the roof.'

'I tried to argue against it–'

'You did? I can't think why! It should have been closed down after that man had spent three months in Mexico! Do you realise that he left Hollywood almost exactly a year ago? That he's spent almost twelve months on

229

this film and it's nowhere near finished?'

'I realise that, Mr Kimbrough, and I'm not excusing him, but I just wonder if anyone understands his purposes–'

'I understand them, by the lord Harry I do! He's stringing it out as long as he can so as to avoid going back to Russia, where he probably got slung out because he's a charlatan! No, I'm glad Upton and Mary-Craig have come to their senses at last. But,' and he sank lower in the big cow-hide armchair, 'I'm not looking forward to telling him.'

Tell him he did, by going to Eisenstein's room before dinner. As far as Gina could guess, there was a hell of a row. Kimbrough at last came downstairs to eat dinner with Gina, but none of the Russians came, nor did Agostin Aragon, the young student who had acted as guide and interpreter to Eisenstein at his own expense.

The next day showed the result of the conference the four had held in Eisenstein's room. First, they insisted the film must be finished according to plan; Upton Sinclair and his fellow-backers had promised support to make an entire film.

When Kimbrough stoutly maintained that there was not enough money, that they would be left stranded in Mexico without a peso if they tried to carry on, Eisenstein gave him a scornful stare. Really, for a communist, he was very aristocratic.

'So, with the money, you can blackmail me. Very well. I accept that we are much over our budget and must curtail our work. But I insist we must finish the episode that we are working on now. It would be madness to cut us off in the middle of filming the story – and the most dramatic scenes are yet to be shot, the scenes of the murder of the peons.'

'No, it's out of the question.'

'But if you close us down now, what good does it do? You have material for the prologue, the epilogue, and almost complete footage for "Fiesta" and "Sandunga". Unless we shoot the rest of the "Maguey", all the work we have done on that is wasted. Surely it is better to finish that episode, at least?'

The battle went on all day. Kimbrough put through long distance calls to Los Angeles.

The final result was that Sinclair and his fellow-backers decided to let Eisenstein finish the shooting of 'Maguey'. The Russian director was delighted: it almost seemed to compensate for the loss of the rest of the film-making. Yet the tension among the group took its toll. Eisenstein was ill, with a recurrent high temperature and dizziness. Kimbrough dismissed it as 'temperament' though it was clear Eisenstein was often very unwell.

Yet he worked like a demon. Meanwhile the backers tried to negotiate some means of having the film speedily made ready for the screen. There was some dismay when the news came that they'd signed a contract with Amtorg, the Russian Trade Agency in New York. All film was to be shipped untouched by Amtorg to Moscow, whither Eisenstein would go to cut and edit.

'So,' Eisenstein said with bitterness to Gina, 'I am to be shipped home too – like the film, as if I were the property of someone else.'

'But surely you want to go home?' Gina urged, although she'd sensed for a long time that he did not.

The director shrugged. 'What choice do I have?'

He tried to give himself a choice, however. When Eisenstein went to New York in March of 1932, Gina went with him to see her commitment through to the end. She was startled to be told by her stepfather John Martin that Eisenstein had gained access to the cans of film and had begun work on them in a cutting room belonging to a private film company.

'Say, is that right that your Russian pal is negotiating with Movietone News to sell some of the travelogue bits of his film?' John inquired.

'Not as far as I know! I don't think he's entitled to do that – his contract stipulates that all the footage belongs to the company who put up the money.'

'Well, maybe I got it wrong. But I hear he showed some fifteen minutes of film to a newsreel company.'

'He's not allowed to *do* that,' Gina cried. 'Oh, why must he resort to these backdoor methods? He knows as well as I do that legally he's not allowed to touch that film until it's delivered to the studio in Moscow!'

Her stepfather shrugged. 'The word is, he's trying to raise enough cash to get back to Mexico and film the rest of his epic.'

'Oh, lord… I'd better get in touch with Mr Sinclair.'

Afterwards she wished she had not. The strict letter of the law was with Upton and his friends, but the film belonged, in its truest sense, to Sergei Eisenstein. When the lawyers descended on him and threatened him with a court case if he insisted on 'tampering' with his own work, he was almost ill with anger.

'What do they know about it?' he cried to Gina. 'They are fools, all of them! Grigori, tell her – tell her how we sweated and suffered to make that film! It belongs to *us*.'

'Not in American law, Sergei Mikhailovich,' the assistant director sighed. 'Mrs Gramm was right to put a stop to what you were doing before you actually sold anything to anyone else. I believe that, under this country's law, that would have been regarded as fraud.'

'Fraud? I? How dare you, Grigori!'

Gina's heart ached for him; he looked so fine-drawn that a puff of cigarette smoke would have knocked him over.

They were at dinner in the dining-room of the Biltmore, using funds Gina had managed to acquire for him by arranging some paid interviews. Her own expenses were still being paid by MGM although they expected her back in Hollywood the moment Hollywood's small investment in the film was safely protected by its delivery in Moscow. Moscow! The very word brought shudders in film companies' boardrooms. It was being kept very dark indeed that one or two of the studios had invested small sums in the project. Of course, had the film been a roaring success, Hollywood would have been only too delighted to announce that they had backed the Russian genius.

As the conversation at their table grew less angry, Gina and the two men leaned together to speak in lower tones. All at once a presence became noticeable at Gina's back. She turned.

It was Vartan Dackis.

'Nice to see you, Gina. Going to introduce me to your highbrow boyfriend?'

'Dack – what are you doing in New York?'

'Oh, conferring with the bankers over my costly epic. Roosevelt has put the fear of God in them. Well, so this is the boy wonder, is it? Hello there, Mr Eisenstein.'

'Good evening,' Eisenstein said in surprise. Although there was little actually offensive in Dack's words, his tone was a sneer.

'Hear you've eventually finished your masterpiece. I'll say this for you – it may not be the greatest film ever made, but it'll sure be the longest.'

Eisenstein glanced at Gina. 'Your friend is interested in my film, Mrs Gramm?'

'This is Vartan Dackis, a producer for

Global Films. You know Mr Eisenstein, Dack. And this is Grigori Alexandrov–'

'Yeah, yeah, his assistant. Took two of them to shoot about seven hours' worth of film – if he'd brought any more of his commie pals, they might have made a film twelve hours long.'

'Dack, what on earth is the matter with you?' Gina cried.

'Nothing at all. Just thought I'd show an interest in this new friend of yours. So long for now, Gina.' With that he turned smartly on his heel and marched away.

'He cannot be a friend of yours!' Eisenstein said. 'He is a barbarian!'

'It's too difficult to explain.' Gina went back to talking of the film.

They discussed it for a long time. The anguish he felt over losing control of the film here in the United States, the necessity to go back to Moscow where other, and perhaps more stringent, restraints would be laid on him... He looked near despair.

When at last they broke up to go upstairs, Alexandrov went up first, to the room he shared with Eisenstein. Gina signed the bill for the meal and then went up in the lift with the director.

At his door they paused. He seemed so sad

that she stood on tiptoe to give him a goodnight kiss. As she touched him, some roaring thing was launched upon them, she was thrown sideways, and a pair of strong hands seized her by the throat.

The scream she began was cut off in her windpipe. A flood of red rose in front of her eyes. Through it she saw Dack, face clenched in bitter fury. She heard, through a roaring in her ears, shouts and cries. Then she lost consciousness.

When she recovered she was in her own room. An elderly maid or housekeeper was bending over her with a glass of water. Behind her were other figures. When she struggled to sit up, restraining hands were placed on her shoulders. She tried to turn her head to see who it was. It hurt her neck so much that she gave a gasp of pain.

'How are you feeling, Mrs Gramm?'

'I'm … all right.' It was a hoarse whisper. 'What … happened?'

'Don't you worry about it, dear. He's gone,' said the maid.

'What? Who – was it Dack?'

'We've got him locked up in the manager's office,' said a heavy voice. When she turned her head with care, she saw a bulky man wearing a fedora hat even though he was indoors. 'The house detective, ma'am. Don't you bother your head about your assailant – we'll get him out of the hotel in a minute or two.'

'But what … what…?'

Eisenstein replied to the unspoken question. 'I think he was trying to kill you, Gina.'

'Oh no.'

'Look, Mrs Gramm, I hate to ask this when you're still in shock and all, but do you want to bring charges against him? If you do, I'll call the cops.'

'No! No, please don't.'

Even hazy as she was with pain and reaction, she could see the relief on his face. 'Well, I admit I'm better pleased if we just keep this quiet. Don't do the hotel no good, a thing like this – people like to feel safe in a classy place like this. Okay then, we give him the bum's rush as soon as he calms down.'

'Is he – is he drunk?'

'Who's to say? He's had a few, but I'd say he's a bit touched. Ranting and raving about … well, never mind what he said, he's nuts.' He moved towards the door. 'I'll put him in a taxi to go to his own hotel, right?'

'A moment, sir,' Eisenstein put in. 'If nothing is done to restrain him, he might do this again!'

'I hope not! I wouldn't like another fight in our hotel corridors–'

'I was thinking of Mrs Gramm's safety, not your hotel's reputation.'

'Oh. Well, yes, there is that. I s'pose ... look, I'll have a pageboy sit outside your door tonight. How's that, lady? You feel happy with that?'

Gina shivered. She had really thought she was dying as Dack's fingers squeezed the life out of her. 'I ... I can go to my mother's apartment, if you'll call me a cab.'

Half an hour later Gina was with Ellie-Rose and John in their apartment in Queens. John was angry when he heard the story. 'You should have brought in the police,' he said. 'The man's a menace.'

'He's ... unbalanced, perhaps,' she agreed. 'I hadn't realised how bitter he would feel...'

'Thing is,' John went on, pointing his cigarette at her, 'he goes free and goes back to Hollywood. What happens when you get back to your job there?'

'I don't know,' she said. 'I'm too tired to think about it now.'

Ellie-Rose helped her to bed in the little spare room. 'Darling,' she said. 'I know you're not fit to think about it at the

239

moment. But I just want to put the thought into your head. Wouldn't it be better to stay away from Hollywood?'

Next day Gina's throat was a dark purple on the outside, and a fiery rasping furnace inside. She stayed indoors, drinking soothing fluids provided by her mother. The phone rang, with inquiries from Eisenstein and other acquaintances in New York.

But the most alarming call was from Dack. 'How did you get this number?' she asked in panic when she heard his voice.

'I looked it up in the phone book, what else?' he said. 'I had a dossier on you, don't forget, Gina.'

'If you've rung to apologise, don't bother. I don't want to hear it.'

'Don't speak to me like that, honey. You know I didn't mean it.' There were tears in his voice. 'I was a little high – I took a pill or two, to see me through the interviews with the money-men. Gina, I'm coming to see you–'

'Don't you dare!'

'But I got to see you! I got to explain–'

'If you come here, I'll call the police!'

'You can't treat me this way, baby. I need you. I got to see you and persuade you–'

'No, I don't want to see you. I don't want

to, ever again. It's over, Dack, don't you understand that?'

The self-abasement vanished. Fury surged through the tones that replied. 'Nothing's over unless I say so. You belong to me and never forget it.'

She slammed the phone down. She was trembling with anger and then, over-whelming the anger, fear.

She knew her mother was right. She couldn't go to Hollywood, she couldn't stay in New York – she couldn't be anywhere Dack could reach her. She must get away, as far away as Mexico. Another country, an-other community, where Dack could have no influence.

She thought about it during the next few hours and by evening had come to a decision.

She had enjoyed her time as an actress in London. She would go to London again.

## Chapter Nine

Lewis McGarth was sorry but not surprised at the fiasco resulting from the Eisenstein film. Since his sympathies were entirely with Upton Sinclair and his friends, he had none of Gina's regrets over the outcome. Besides, he had so much else to think about now that Franklin D Roosevelt was in power.

The New Deal rose in America like a golden sunrise. Some thought it was the only hope for the country. But there were others who saw in it the beginning of communism. They were very angry and, worse, they were very frightened.

They retired behind such bastions as they had. And there were still plenty of Republican strongholds. The State of California had a Republican Governor, and when the state elections began to loom, campaigning began with a fervour that hadn't been known for years.

Lewis's work in the Economic Research Force gave him even more insight into the injustices of his home state. He knew there was great wealth there – but it was in the hands of a few. 'We've got to change things, Dad,' he insisted to Gregor McGarth. 'I want you to switch parties this time – I want you to vote the Democrat ticket.'

Gregor shook his auburn head. 'No, I've never been a party man and I'm not going to start now. Besides, who the devil could you get to stand for Governor in the Democrat camp that has a midget's chance?'

'I'm working on it,' Lewis said.

Gregor smiled. He'd come to terms now with the fact that his son was an incorrigible idealist, was never going to make any kind of a businessman. 'You'll have to find a film star to stand, if you're going to attract any support!'

'Well, not exactly that.' He hesitated. Perhaps it was too early to say anything. Yet he wanted to know what his father, a very shrewd man, would say to the idea. 'We're trying to persuade Uppie to stand.'

'Sinclair?' It was an explosion of astonishment. 'That idiot?'

'Dad, he's not an–'

'He is too an idiot. Anyone could have told him he wasn't going to get a film from that irresponsible Russian! Nobody'll vote for him, even if you could get him to stand as a

243

Democrat – and he won't, he's too much in love with that idiotic Socialist Party he belongs to. Socialist – yes – no idea how to handle money!'

'Dearest,' Francesca said, laying her hand on her husband's arm. 'Don't go on blaming Mr Sinclair for the loss of that investment. You didn't have too much money in the scheme.'

'No, thank God for that!'

'Oh, for Pete's sake, Dad! There are other things in life besides getting a good return on investments! There are people in California actually *starving*! And they'll go on starving under a Republican administration – that's why we've got to change things.'

Gregor looked around his comfortable living-room. He had no real desire to change things much. He would never be as rich as his father Robert Craigallan, but he was doing well enough. He had a position in society, a wife he adored, children who, though something of a disappointment, were off on their own and in control of their lives.

Although he and Lewis disagreed over politics, there was a bond between them, of friendship and tolerance. Morag's death and Francesca's illness had brought home to

Gregor that some of the things Lewis worried about were important: sickness and malnutrition had to be dealt with. The only point on which they disagreed was the means.

Lewis said no more for the moment. When at last the famous author Upton Sinclair was persuaded to join the Democratic Party and allow himself to be nominated as candidate for the Governorship of the State of California, he threw himself into the work of campaigning. He was very fond of the old man but, more than that, he had faith in him.

Sinclair's 'platform' became known as 'EPIC' – 'End Poverty In California'. It had something of the elements of 'a chicken in every pot', used by former campaigners. The message was, this is a land of plenty, so let's share it out more equally.

The question immediately asked was: How? For this, Upton Sinclair had an answer in several parts. One of them was that if he was elected he would put through a Bill in the State Senate whereby a substantial tax would be levied on that booming money-earner, the Hollywood film industry.

'That stupid old pinko!' howled the big

producers. 'How can he say the film industry has money? Doesn't he know there's a Depression?' It would have been more convincing if the parties and automobiles of Hollywood had figured less in the gossip columns. When this was pointed out to them, they ordered their stars to be less conspicuous – but old habits die hard.

Sinclair, wily enough in his own way, would use a recent photograph of some ermine-clad actress to point up his speeches. 'All I'm asking,' he'd say with an engaging smile, 'is that they should sell a mink or two.'

Sam Goldwyn, asked his opinion, went on record with a deathless remark which conveyed his real opinion of the world of letters. 'Sinclair's only a writer,' he said, 'what does he know about anything?'

The campaign rocketed on, amidst threats and actual physical attacks against the Democrats. The newspapers were almost solidly against Upton Sinclair. The whole Hollywood publicity machine was at work against him too. And yet … and yet … his meetings were always packed, he drew the crowds and called forth the cheers.

Mary-Craig Sinclair began to be really worried. Anonymous letters arrived at their

Beverly Hills home threatening that if Upton Sinclair actually succeeded in being elected, he would never live to take office. 'You don't want to pay any heed to those, dear,' her husband said with blithe confidence, 'you always get cranks at a time like this.'

Quietly, Mary-Craig had a word with the young men who were working for her husband's election. 'Try to protect him,' she said. 'Don't let him walk in among the hostile crowd – he thinks sensible argument and goodwill can win over everyone, but … but…'

Lewis patted her hand. 'We'll look after him, Mrs Sinclair, don't you worry.'

But it was less easy than he supposed. The meetings were broken up by cudgel-wielding thugs, but even more alarming, shots were sometimes fired on the outskirts of the crowd as they came out of the halls.

There was one man Lewis began to notice in particular. He'd show up at an indoor meeting, sitting near the front. He would listen with his arms folded, impassive, but his burning black eyes would be fixed all the while on Sinclair. Only once so far had he ever taken action: he stood up to ask a question at a meeting in the Los Angeles prizefight stadium.

'You're out to ruin the film industry, right?'

'My friend,' Upton Sinclair replied, 'an eight per cent levy won't ruin anything as rich as the film industry.'

'You're gonna take money from us – yet you gave money to that highbrow Russkie to throw money away in Mexico.'

'We learn by our mistakes, sir. I now see it's more sensible to take money from films than to give it.' Laughter.

The dark-eyed man glared about at the audience. 'You can laugh,' he snarled, 'but I'm not gonna let this bunch get away with it.'

Shouts of 'Sit down!' and 'Rubbish!' broke out. The next questioner spoke up, and Lewis lost track of the dark-eyed man. But his intensity, his repressed fury, worried him. Nor were matters helped when, a few days later, a letter arrived enclosing a bullet. 'I got another one like this for you,' the letter said.

What could it mean? 'Oh, it's a distressed mind at work,' Sinclair said, waving a bony hand dismissively.

'But it seems almost as if he's got some personal grudge...'

'He thinks he has, no doubt.'

'Do you think it's that guy who asked about the Eisenstein film the other night?'

'Why should it be he?'

'I don't know. He's been at your meetings so often, glaring at you as if he holds you responsible for something … something personal, almost.'

'It can't be, my boy. I don't know the man. And there's no way of knowing whether he sent this rubbish or not.'

Lewis turned it over, with other anonymous threats, to the police. But he knew very well the police weren't going to do anything about it. Even if they'd taken it seriously, they weren't likely to be able to protect the Democratic candidate from a determined madman with a gun.

One of the biggest meetings before the poll was at noon in the Los Angeles Opera House. The place was packed. Lewis McGarth, with the other young male campaign staff, were patrolling the aisles for troublemakers, for they had promised the Opera House management that no damage would be done.

In a seat about five rows back in the stalls, Lewis espied the dark, stocky man who had asked about the Mexican film at a previous meeting. For some reason it worried him that the man had chosen a seat near the aisle this time – as if to leap up and get away quickly? When the platform party filed on stage, Lewis took up a position in the aisle a little way behind the man.

The meeting ran its usual course. Upton Sinclair explained his policy, claimed he had party backing for what he hoped to achieve, called upon his supporters to vote for him, and then asked for questions.

'Yeah, I got a question,' said a middle-aged woman, rising to her feet in the dress circle. 'It says in the *Los Angeles Times* where you're encouraging a load of bums to come to California because they're gonna get hand-outs! We don't want to support no more bums – we're hard put to it to support ourselves. What you got to say to that, Mr Sinclair?'

The white-haired old man hitched his jacket lapels. 'Well now,' he said, thinking it over in his bright, alert mind. 'You know the owner of the *L.A. Times* is Harry Chandler?'

'Yeah,' murmured the audience. 'So what?' called a voice.

'I'll tell you so what, my friend. Harry Chandler came to California on a freight train with only five cents in his pocket, twenty-five years ago.'

The audience stirred and chuckled.

'So you see, even if you come out here as a hobo, it doesn't mean you won't work and make a success.' The old man threw out his arms. 'Move over, Harry Chandler! Give the other bums a chance!'

There was a roar of laughter. The audience, prepared at first to be critical, was totally won over.

It was as if this laughing conquest was just too much for the man in front of Lewis. He leapt to his feet. 'You can't laugh at what you've done to me!' He shouted. He was struggling to get something out of his pocket. Lewis glimpsed the dull glint of steel, the curve of a gun-butt. He jumped, grabbing the man by his shoulders and heaving him sideways into the aisle. 'Help! He's got a gun!'

Immediately the nearest ushers rushed to his aid. They smothered the man in a heap of young, vigorous bodies. Between them they heaved him up, thrashing and wrestling. Spittle flew from his lips as he was frog-marched up the aisle to the policemen boiling into the Opera House from the foyer.

The incident was played down in the newspapers. An unbalanced opponent of the Democratic candidate had been taken into custody, charged with disturbing the peace, and released into the care of a sanatorium specialising in the treatment of alcoholics. The man's name meant nothing to Lewis.

But, later, when he heard more details, understanding came to him. The public relations manager of Global Films had hastened to the police station almost as soon as the gunman was charged. Great efforts were made to hush up the whole affair. 'It won't be good for Hollywood if this makes a big splash,' the authorities were warned.

And since Los Angeles never wanted to harm Hollywood, the gunman was allowed to plead diminished responsibility under an assumed name.

'What's his real name, then?' Lewis asked the young lawyer who had ferreted out this information.

'He's a guy called Vartan Dackis – produced that Biblical epic that was such a flop last year.'

'Dackis?' Lewis said, startled.

'Yeah, you know him?'

For a moment Lewis almost blurted it out. But good sense checked his tongue. 'I heard

252

of him,' he said.

Dackis! So that was why he had seemed to hate Upton Sinclair – because he held him responsible for Gina leaving Hollywood. His life seemed to have gone completely to pieces after Gina broke with him.

Lewis had heard something about the attack by Dackis in New York before his cousin sailed for Europe. The man had physically attacked her in her hotel.

'Is he safe in that sanatorium?' Lewis demanded.

'I hear they've got him under sedation. I talked to the PR man. He says Dackis is all washed up in Hollywood – nutty as a squirrel's cage. By the time they've dried him out in the clinic, he'll be more or less sane again, but they're pensioning him off, sending him home to drink himself quietly to death in Greece.'

'Thank God for that,' Lewis said. 'We don't want any more attacks on our man.'

Though there were other threats, in the end the threats were wasted. Upton Sinclair failed in his bid for the Governorship of California. The Republican candidate was returned with a handsome majority.

It was only what Gregor McGarth had expected. Cloudy idealists like Upton

Sinclair were never going to be taken really seriously by the electorate. Nevertheless, there were things that needed to be done in California, things that the Republican legislature were never going to bother with.

Although his son might have been surprised to know it, Gregor had plans to ameliorate the conditions of the Californian fruit-pickers. His mother's words haunted Gregor – 'I can't believe you'll refuse to help!' After her death, he reproached himself: if he had done more for the migrant workers, they might not have been living in a disease-ridden camp for his mother to stumble upon.

Gregor had been brought up to believe that self-reliance was the ideal way of life. But his mother had always had compassion for those who couldn't cope – an endless patience with the shortcomings of others and pity for the feckless poor. How much the more so for the hardworking yet poverty-stricken migrants on whom the fruit-growers depended for their harvest?

He had waited until after the election to see if, by any chance, the electorate of the state might choose a Governor with a reform policy. Now that it was clear there was no help to be expected from the state government, Gregor set his own plans in motion. He had allotted the income from his new juice-canning project – as yet not large – to the idea.

He had held long and frequent consultations with Cornelius and Bess. Three years' experience with the transitories had shown them what was needed most.

There were to be cabins in an open block around a central courtyard. There was to be room to park their rickety trucks and cars at the back of each cabin, because if the family was large, the children would need to sleep in the vehicle.

'I'm against that,' Cornelius said in his croaky voice. 'I think we should build a nursery room for the children, with little pallets in a row so they get a decent night's sleep.'

'Ah, no,' Francesca said, with a shake of her dark head. She had taken a keen interest in the planning. 'The families will be mostly Mexican and you know, with them, the family is very important. If you start telling them their children must sleep elsewhere each night, they will feel threatened.'

'Oh, you,' Bess said, giving her husband a loving push with her fist. 'You think because in your lab you can put things here and here, you can do the same with people. Well, you can't. And how would you like it if little Cory were taken off to sleep in a separate building fifty yards away?'

'Cory has a room to himself. He doesn't have to share it with his parents and four brothers and sisters…' But Cornelius knew he had lost the point. He sat back now to watch the discussion on the lips of the others.

A site was chosen on the edge of the Regalo estate. Experience had taught Cornelius that the migrants wouldn't like to be too close to the *casa de patron* and in any case, it would save building a long access road for the vans.

An architect was hired, plans were drawn. 'This is going to cost a buck or two, Mr McGarth,' the architect muttered as he sketched out what Gregor asked for.

'I know that. I'm prepared to pay. But bear in mind – I'm not building the Ritz!'

'I wonder if you realise what you *are* building?'

'What, in your opinion?'

'Trouble, sir, trouble!'

Of course Gregor expected trouble, and it soon was forthcoming. The other growers were enraged. 'What's the idea, putting up cabins for those tramps?' they cried. 'After they went on strike last year in Imperial Valley? They don't deserve special housing, they deserve prison!'

'Come on, Buffy, you know they only went on strike because the growers drove the wages down to thirteen cents an hour, and they knew they couldn't live on that.'

'We sure won't get 'em for thirteen cents an hour this year after that shemozzle – but I'm not paying a cent above fifteen. And I won't get 'em for that if you start mollycoddling 'em! You'll give 'em big ideas about what they should expect.'

'Well, I think they should expect to live in accommodation that doesn't take a day to erect and a day to take down, and is liable to collapse in a storm,' Gregor said in a peaceable tone.

'Okay, okay, so you give 'em a couple of shacks – but for God's sake, why do they need a shower block? Couple of faucets at the end of the track – that's what they're used to and that's what they should get. And what's this about a central courtyard where they can have a kind of barbecue? D'you want them to get the idea it's all a picnic?'

'Don't get in a fret about it. You know the migrants always like to congregate outdoors for an hour or two over their evening meal. I'm only giving them a few benches to sit on.'

'You'll be building 'em tennis courts next! No good ever comes of mollycoddling workers!'

'Look, it's hardly mollycoddling to provide a simple cabin so they can get a good night's sleep and stay out of the rain if we have a wet night. All I'm doing is supplying four walls and a roof–'

'But I hear you're only going to charge five cents a day!'

Gregor could have replied that five cents a day to a man earning a dollar seventy-five for a twelve hour stint was three per cent of his income. He could imagine the uproar it would cause among the orchard owners if taxes were increased by three per cent. Instead he said, 'I tried to choose a figure I thought they could afford.'

The truth was, he'd thought of providing the accommodation free, but he knew it would start a furious row. The rental he had decided on was purely for show: he intended to plough it back into the upkeep of his accommodation block.

'Goddammit, McGarth, it's that soft-hearted son of yours that put you up to this!

You should have more sense!'

'If you want to know,' Gregor said, 'my mother suggested before she died that I should do something for the migrants. This is by way of being a memorial to her.'

That was enough to make his colleagues in the Fruitgrowers' Association offices look a little abashed. 'Why couldn't you have just endowed a hospital ward, Greg?' said Tom Lindless, who was a good friend.

'Because Mother wanted me to prevent disease, not help cure it. Come on, fellows – if you give the fieldworkers somewhere half decent to sleep and eat, it's bound to increase efficiency–'

'The way to increase efficiency,' said Arnold Buffy in a savage tone, 'is to tell 'em you'll fire 'em if they're sassy!'

Despite the mutterings and arguings, Gregor pushed on with his idea. He wanted the accommodation ready for the next orange harvest on Regalo.

But little setbacks occurred. A load of building material went astray. A station wagon carrying construction workers to the job one morning was run off the road by a heavy truck that didn't stop – luckily no one was seriously hurt. A man laying the drainage either slipped or was pushed so that he nearly suffocated in a minor cave-in.

'Do you think someone is trying to tell me something?' Gregor asked with grim amusement of his friend Tom.

'If so, are you getting the message?' Tom snapped back, in a manner unlike his usual slow-spoken self. 'I'd think it's clear by now that your present ideas aren't popular.'

'I can't think why they're getting in such a state about it. Nobody asks them to follow my example, but surely I'm free to do what I want on my own land?'

'Whatever else you are, Greg, you're not naive. You must have known they'd get edgy.'

'Once the scheme is finished and in action they'll see it's harmless. In fact, they may even take it up themselves. I don't think they've noticed, Tom, that the big business combines are beginning to buy land in California. How will the estate owners hold their pickers if factories start to spring up offering much better conditions and good wages?'

They were in the Growers' Club, a sedate businessmen's club in Sacramento, handy for strolling along to the Capitol for a lobbying session. Others were sitting around at this hour of the evening, having a pre-

260

dinner drink, waiting perhaps for some politician to join them for a sage discussion of policy. The fruitgrowers of California had immense influence, which they used with guile and force.

Tom nodded over his highball at a group in a far corner. Well-tailored, well-barbered, glowing with that veneer which comes from having a good valet, they were typical of the men who ran the Growers' Association.

'Do you really think you can influence this bunch to look that far ahead?' he muttered. 'They've either owned their land for a hundred years or they're in partnership with a big food-producing chain that's almost unassailable. They're not going to change their habits just because you get a case of the conscience-stricken.'

'All right, let them run their business the way they want to, so long as they do the same by me. I'm not trying to change the world, you know, Tom. All I want to do is try something that my mother would have wanted to see – a little lessening of the hardships the transients have always had to endure. If you look at statistics–'

'Oh, statistics!'

'Don't sneer at them. They have their uses. Lew has statistics to show–'

'If we're going to run our businesses by any facts Lew supplies we'll be *giving* our money away to the poor and needy. I'm surprised at–'

'Listen, Lew can show that almost every epidemic of flu or scarlet fever or whatever begins in the area of a transient camp. He can show–'

'Oh, great. If you quote that kind of thing to anyone else, you'll only make them hard on the transients. They've been run out of California before now, and it could easily happen again.'

'Not so easily now. Okay, when it was Japanese or Mexicans – you could get up a scare and then accuse them of being illegal aliens. But a lot of our migrant workers are from Oklahoma and Texas and Kansas now. You can't run them out so easily.'

'I suppose that's true.' Tom thought about it. 'I don't know whether that makes it better or worse.'

'In any case, I wouldn't give these facts to anyone except you, Tom. I know you won't spread 'em around. I just want you to understand that when I try to give the pickers a bit of comfort and hygiene, it's not entirely because I've gone starry-eyed. I don't forget that my mother died of a disease she contracted in a shanty town, and that my wife was very sick from the same infection. It just seems like sense to do something about it.'

Tom was unconvinced. In his view, public health was a matter for the health authorities.

The camp was still not quite completed when Cornelius, in consultation with Jose Entonches, his foreman, sent out word that he would need orange-pickers in three weeks' time. In the last week of May, Gregor took Francesca to Regalo to inspect the place.

They stayed in the big house with Cornelius and Bess. Francesca amused herself most of the afternoon by playing with young Cory, so that when she proposed to go down to the cabin area, Gregor forbade it. 'You haven't had your rest. Leave it a while, *querida*. After dinner, perhaps.'

'But it will be dark then, Gregorio.'

'Good gracious, don't you know we have every amenity, including electric lights?'

After dinner, Gregor allowed himself to be sidetracked by the estate foreman, who had a long tale of woe about personal disagreements with one of the permanent workers of the estate. It was so long and complex that it couldn't really be discussed with Señor Craigallan, who didn't understand enough Spanish for the nuances. 'Take your shawl, darling!' Gregor called after his wife as she was about to get into the car with Cornelius. 'It's chilly this evening.'

She draped her shawl about her shoulders, and gave him a wave. On the drive to the cabin site only Cornelius spoke. It was difficult to have a conversation with him when he was driving because he had to keep his face turned to the road. He explained to her that about four families of pickers had already arrived and moved in, seeming delighted with the accommodation although the laundry block still lacked its doors and windows, and the hot water system for the shower block seemed to be defective.

'Oh, but it's charming!' Francesca said as she saw the little settlement spring to life. Cornelius had touched a switch for lights in the 'main square'.

Indeed, the architect had done his best to avoid any appearance of institutionalism. Although the cabins were built from board planks they had been whitewashed, and the corrugated tin roofs had been painted red. Invited into the first cabin to see how the residents had settled in, Francesca saw a businesslike kitchen screened off from the main room by fretwork bricks. The rest of the cabin was a plain square, with two beds that folded down from the wall. It was spartan, but the migrants were accustomed to sleeping on the ground under canvas – to them it was palatial.

The people in the cabin happened to be Mexican. Francesca had a long talk in Spanish with the mother. The children, ranging in age from an undersized teenage boy to a child of three, stood around in respectful silence.

'Come and look at the laundry facilities,' Cornelius invited.

'*Si, si, el lavadero – e maravilloso, señora!*' – and Señora Pantano bustled ahead of them in an almost proprietary manner.

The laundry room was a great rectangular hall with channelled concrete floor, sinks, taps and drying racks. No effort had been made to decorate it. It was purely functional, lit by four high-powered light bulbs hanging under plain white shades.

All of a sudden, those bulbs went out.

'Damn!' said Cornelius. 'It must be the fuse gone. Stand still, Frannie – I'll get the torch from the car–'

But as he spoke, a strange sound drowned

his words. A thudding of footsteps on the dusty track outside – the footsteps of many people, running in silence from the entrance gate.

'Neil!' called Francesca. But of course he could not hear her, nor know that she was speaking since he couldn't see her face in the dark.

In the sudden darkness, she moved towards the spot where they had been standing. Her foot caught in a drainage channel. She went headlong.

Señora Pantano, buffeted by this falling figure, screamed in terror. Her husband, hearing her from outside, came running. Cornelius collided with him in the doorway. As they swayed and struggled, all the other lights in the settlement went out.

Women in the occupied cabins cried out in alarm. Children dashed outside to see what was happening. Unexpectedly, a crowd seemed to gather in the little central square.

The darkness was suddenly filled with menace.

The four families who had moved into the Regalo cabins numbered about twenty-eight persons. Most of them had scurried outside at the cries of alarm from the laundry block. Now they found themselves colliding with others – but the others seemed bulkier, clad in leather jackets and heavy boots, wielding sticks or clubs.

The light from the stars, inadequate though it was, showed these others to be strangers – tall, thick-set, well-fed. Now a flickering light was added to the stars – torches were being lit. The sharp smell of burning naphtha crept among the buildings from the wad of rags tied to sticks.

Cornelius had managed to free himself of Miguel Pantano's grasping arms. He hurtled outside. In the fluttering light of a dozen torches he saw a band of armed men with pick handles.

He couldn't hear the shout of 'Let's do it, boys!' But he saw a group of intruders lurch across the central square towards the first line of cabins. He called: 'Stop! What are you doing?' but the challenge was lost in a wave of whoops and war cries.

The Mexicans were crying out in fear. 'Vigilantes, vigilantes!' How often had they been harried from their camps by them? The women began to run indoors to snatch up what they could before taking to flight. The men tried to grab the intruders, to delay them.

Cornelius could make them out now in the light of their own torches. There were about two dozen. Every second man held a torch and a stick. Others had iron bars or truncheons. A few seemed to be armed with guns – bulky, wide-barrelled weapons.

Cornelius ran among them. 'No, no – what are you doing? You can't–'

'Get going, shithead! Pack up and move out!' snarled the man he grabbed. He got a blow on the shoulder that sent him down to one knee.

Some of the migrant men had formed a line to stand fast and fight. Children were crouching in the cabins, wailing in terror. The scene was hellish – scurrying figures in a yellow-red smoky light, shouts and screams, the sound of blows, tall shadows whose arms lunged up and down in furious attack.

But the camp's inhabitants were proving unexpectedly stubborn. They had been given a fine home, for once. They couldn't, wouldn't allow themselves to be driven out.

'Smoke 'em out, boys, smoke 'em out!' shouted the leader. There was a sharp report from one of the short-barrelled guns. Something surged through the flickering darkness to break the window of the bath-house and roll, smoking on the floor.

The smoke-bomb exploded without much sound, scattering grey-yellow fumes. They curved upwards in the still air, enclosed by the bath-house walls. 'Don't shoot indoors, Sam, it won't do no good there!' roared the vigilante leader.

There were three or four reports as other teargas bombs ripped through the alleys of the settlement. Two landed in the square, the others sent acrid fumes floating in the breeze. Tears started into the eyes of the migrants trying to fight off the vigilantes. The intruders, forewarned, donned masks.

Now they were terrifying – like monsters, their faces alien and remorseless, great round eyes staring after their prey in the torchlight. The small children ran to their mothers, grasping their skirts. The mothers, too frightened to know what to do, scooped them up and ran into the nearest corner to cower in horror.

'Aw, it's gonna take hours to empty it first! Put a torch to it now!'

A cheer rang out at the command. The men with the torches ran to obey. Straw, paper, anything that would burn was caught up, set alight from the torches, and tossed into the cabins.

'No, stop – this is insane!' shouted Cornelius, staggering up to tackle a torchbearer aiming at a cabin window. 'There are *people* in there–'

Too late. The torch went glittering into the shack. The man, unbalanced under Cornelius's attack, fell sideways. One of his companions ran to drag him up. They backed off, confronting Cornelius.

'Go on, pack up and git!' they shouted at him. 'Clear out, you white trash! Get into your truck and vamoose!'

Cornelius could hear nothing. All he could see in the uncertain light of the flames was a face like an armadillo's, with eye-pieces reflecting back the fire.

'Get out of here, you thugs!' he ordered. 'I'm going to call the sheriff–'

He started towards them, angrier than they were. He was going to pull the gas-masks off, find out who they were.

One of them had no weapon – he'd lost his cudgel and thrown his torch into the cabin. The other had the teargas gun.

'Stop!' he warned. 'Hold it, punk! I'm warning you–'

Cornelius wasn't even aware they were speaking to him. 'Who sent you here, you madmen?' he demanded, reaching out to

270

grab the canvas chinstrap.

The man with the gun saw a figure taller than himself. There was anger and determination in it. In a minute it would reach him, hold him for arrest.

He pulled the trigger. The teargas shell rushed out, taking Cornelius full in the chest.

From the doorway of the laundry Francesca saw him go down. She screamed and ran towards him. 'Neil! Neil! Oh, *Redentor sagrado*...!'

But no calling upon the Saviour could help Cornelius Craigallan. He lay on his back staring with blank eyes up at the sky above the red light of the burning cabins. His life-blood had rushed out of him through the huge hole torn by the teargas grenade.

'*Dios, Dios!*' wept Francesca. She fell to her knees at his side. She dragged her white shawl embroidered with roses from her shoulders. With it she tried to staunch the blood still pumped by his failing heart.

The man who had fired the gun was appalled at what he'd done. He dragged off his gasmask to see more clearly. Horror made him angry at the woman weeping at his feet. 'Bloody Mex!' he roared. With the butt of the gun he knocked Francesca aside.

He kicked at her. 'Bloody bums! Get up, run for it, get out of here, you!'

Francesca, pushing herself up, dazed and sick from the blow to her head, threw out her hands to him. 'Help me!' she begged. 'He's dying!'

'Git! Come on, *tamale*, move–'

'No, Chuck – don't let her go – she *seen* you–'

'Aw, quit shivering – who's gonna listen to a Mexie–'

'No, Chuck – we can't risk it–' He picked up a length of board from the burning cabin. He began to pound at Francesca.

'Hey, Joe – that's a woman–'

'You crazy or something? She can put us in jail!' Frenzied, he slammed the smoking board down again and again. Chuck stood uncertainly by, watching, the gasmask dangling from a finger.

'I ain't never killed no woman,' he muttered.

'You killed her man, though. And now it's okay – she'll never testify.' Joe straightened. 'What's it matter, she's only a wetback.'

He turned his head to listen. The noisy old engines of the migrants' trucks were starting up. 'They're going,' he said. 'Let's herd 'em off.'

Chuck hesitated beside the two bodies. Then with a shrug he followed his colleague to the track leading to the entrance gate. One or two terrified figures were still running towards the ancient vehicles which were beginning to trundle out on to the spur road.

Suddenly full of roisterous good humour, the vigilantes pulled off their face-masks, helped throw the last escapers on board. They chucked some scattered belongings in after them. They stood in a cheering band to see them off. They screamed and catcalled as the last of the trucks rocked up on to the metalled road.

Then, in the distance, another sound could be heard – the steady hum of a good car engine. 'Somebody's comin' from the house–!'

'They seen the flames–'

As quickly and silently as they had assembled, the attack group faded into the orange trees of the Regalo estate.

They had been there only a little over ten minutes. They left burning cabins, a wrecked bath-house and laundry, and three bodies. One was a thirteen year-old-boy who had been trapped in a burning building. The others were Cornelius Craigallan and Francesca McGarth.

## Chapter Ten

The sheriff of San Joacquin County was paunchy, bulky, sweating, and abjectly apologetic. 'What can I tell you, Mr McGarth? Seems like they were just a bunch of drunks on a toot that got out of hand.'

'A bunch of drunks? With teargas?'

'Yeah... Well ... when my men got on the scene they didn't smell no teargas.'

'It was strong in the air when I got there. And if you analyse those scraps of metal, I think you'll find they're part of a teargas grenade.'

'They're at our laboratories in Sacramento now.' Alvert moved from one foot to the other, heavy and uneasy. 'Even if that's what they are, Mr McGarth, guys coming out of the army bring things like that for souvenirs. Mebbe even steal 'em for fun, when they're training with the National Guard.'

Gregor invited the man to sit down. No use to make an enemy of him, although he wasn't going to rouse himself to help track down Francesca's murderers. 'Have you traced any of the migrants?'

'Naw! 'F you ask me, they're to hell and gone in Mexico by now.' I would be, if it were me, Alvert added inwardly. What gasoline gypsy wants to be rounded up as witness in a thing like this? Kept hanging about in Fresno until the case comes on – if it ever does – with not a cent coming in while the fruit and vegetable harvests are being picked out in the countryside, and you're losing your chance of a job for the whole season.

'My foreman tells me one of the families had a truck with Oklahoma registration plates,' Gregor said. 'The Siggetts. They wouldn't head for Mexico.'

'Mebbe not.' But they're over the state boundary by now, thought Alvert. They all took off like a covey of partridge, and you ain't gonna find them anywhere near Regalo Orange Orchard, so give up the idea. 'I've put out a call-in on them, but we didn't get a hold of that idea until yesterday morning and I reckon they'd a covered a thousand miles in them thirty-six hours.

'You got to figure, Mr McGarth,' Alvert said as kindly as he could, 'them folks don't want to be looked at by a peace officer. You know what they're like – they don't exactly steal, but things go missing off of washlines when they're around, chickens stray away from the coop and don't come back, a sack of flour disappears from Mitchin's Stores. So they don't aim to be noticed at any time, and they sure don't want to be picked up and questioned too close.'

Listen, you're a smart guy, he was saying to Gregor, though not in so many words. You had a college education and all that. You must know we're not going to get any witnesses to come forward.

Gregor understood that all too well. Alvert had been elected by the population of San Joacquin County with the help and agreement of the estate owners. No one would ever reach any office in the San Joacquin Valley who didn't go along with the views of the men in power.

He was sure that the vigilantes who broke up the migrants' settlement on Saturday night had been hired to do it. They had been given instructions to end any foolish schemes by Gregor McGarth, told to take torches and staves, and had been armed with teargas to flush out any stubborn men who might make a stand against them.

Then it had all got out of hand. Gregor

understood that. With dark anger he acknowledged that the planners of the attack had never meant anyone to die. Least of all any relative of Gregor McGarth, not his brother, and certainly not his wife, his wife…

When he reached the burning cabin site on Saturday, his first thought was: bastards! This is their way of making *sure* I get the message!

He'd been angry then, but it had been an anger of the mind – they don't agree with my ideas, they play dirty to stop me, what fools they are.

Then alarm had leapt upon him. Where was Cornelius? Where was Francesca? He ran among the dancing flames of the cabins, feeling the heat beating through his evening jacket. 'Frannie! Frannie! Where are you?'

Cornelius's Ford had been parked about a hundred yards away from the cabin site. It was empty. So were the alleys and the central square. No one was fighting the fire. Where was everybody? Had they all run off – to hide? Did that mean, not just one fire-raiser with a can of gasoline but – oh, God!

'Frannie! Frannie!' He was terrified now. If Francesca and Cornelius had stumbled on a gang of men sent to scare out the migrants…!

Jose Entonches found the bodies, in the alley between the first and second row of cabins. 'No, sir,' he said, barring the way as Gregor ran up, 'don't look–'

But nothing would have stopped Gregor. He fell to his knees beside the two bloodied heaps, seeing them flicker in and out of vision in the light of the fires.

In a way, that was why he hated the murderers so much – because he couldn't even remember Francesca as she had been in all her dark beauty. Now she was a bundle of bloodied clothing, a mash of flesh and bones and brains. Even when he tried to summon up the formal portrait hanging over the fireplace in the drawing-room of the house in San Francisco, the features slipped and melted, became blurred with red – unrecognisable, unreal.

My darling. My pure beauty. My one love, my soul and my reason for being. Reduced to this ugly huddle in the hellish firelight.

Jose Entonches had driven like a madman to the house to telephone for the police and a doctor. A doctor! As if anything could be done for the two bundles of gory flesh in the dusty ground between the cabins…

Later Gregor realised that the deputy in Fresno had been laconic about trouble at Regalo. Only when Jose kept sobbing: '*Asesinato* – murder, murder!' did he begin to pay heed. It was easy to guess that he'd been given a hint of 'a bit of fun' at Regalo, something he needn't take too seriously. But a death... Even if it had been only the Mexican boy, whose charred remains were found at daylight in a corner of one of the cabins... There had to be a post mortem and a burying, at the expense of the county, even for a no-account Mex. But Jesus! – the killing of Mrs McGarth and Cornelius Craigallan, and nothing 'accidental' about it either! He'd dived to the phone to call Alvert in Sacramento.

Alvert was genuinely appalled. Apart from pity for McGarth and Craigallan's widow, he had feelings of foreboding. There would be all kinds of trouble. McGarth would expect him to go to extreme lengths to track down the perpetrators. And there was just no way he could do it.

Not all the drifters and travellers who came through California were honest men looking for work. There were thieves and troublemakers among them. Alvert could imagine such men being easily recruited to come and roust the greasers into leaving their fine new camp. There might have been a stiffening of local rowdies, to show them the place and lead the attack. But it was ten to one that most of the men involved in the incident had boarded a train and were now long gone, quick to put distance between themselves and trouble.

Even if they were local, even if they'd stayed put ... Alvert wasn't eager to track them down. Nobody was actually saying that the men had been hired to make the assault on the cabins, but if they had, people with money were behind it. Alvert made it his policy not to offend people with money.

And if you were to say: Well, they've just been responsible for three deaths, Alvert would answer that you could bet on it they'd never meant that to happen. They weren't really *guilty*.

'You can depend on me to do all I can, Mr McGarth,' he told Gregor. 'And I'm having my boys go over the area of the fire with a fine tooth comb – if there's anything by way of evidence, we'll pick it up.' He held out his hand in leave-taking. He knew, as McGarth shook it, that the other man didn't believe a word he'd said. Well, hell, you couldn't blame the guy for feeling sore. It was a dam'awful thing – and, if you came right down to it, probably wouldn't have happened if Mrs McGarth hadn't been such a Mex-looking lady. Alvert understood the thinking of the people amongst whom he lived: he was fairly sure Francesca had been killed because in her loose dark dress and Spanish shawl she looked like the wife of a migrant worker. No vigilante would ever have harmed a *white* woman.

Bess came downstairs when she heard the police car drive off. 'What did Sheriff Alvert have to say?' she asked.

'What did you expect? He sees no prospect of finding the men who did this.'

'No.'

She sat down on the dark oak settle, dry-eyed, self-contained. Apart from one awful spasm of tearing, wrestling violence, when she had wanted to rush the pallet on which Cornelius's body was brought in, she had been very quiet. When Señora Entonches took her in her arms, encouraging her to weep, she'd said, 'No, it would upset little Cory.'

This was her excuse, and her reason for continuing to exist. Cory needed her.

Little Cory couldn't imagine where Daddy had got to. He didn't come to breakfast

Saturday morning, but that sometimes happened if there was work calling him away at the far side of the orchards. But he didn't come home to lunch either, nor even to play with Cory at bathtime.

When he inquired where Cornelius was, Mommy said, 'He's gone on a trip, Cory.'

'To Fresno?' That was where Daddy often went.

'Farther than that, Cory.'

Cory looked at his mother with attention. She was pale, and wearing a plain black dress quite unlike the pretty floral prints she usually wore. Clearly she was upset because Daddy was away. 'Home soon,' Cory said with an emphatic nod, to comfort her.

She made no reply. It was strange – she didn't seem to want to talk to him. Stranger yet was the eldest daughter of the Entonches family, hired as part-nursemaid, part-playmate. She kept hugging him, and bursting into tears for no reason at all, even when he hadn't pushed her or pulled her long black hair.

Señora Entonches – Tia Carmen – was busy in Cory's room next day, helping Mommy pack all his belongings in a big tin trunk. 'We going on the train?' he asked hopefully.

'Yes, dear, we're going to San Francisco.'

That was nice. Cory liked the big cool house in San Francisco. The garden wasn't as big as Regalo, but there was a pool and a fountain. And the cook would give him sugar cookies. And there was a cat, Alonso, who made a beautiful noise in his throat when you stroked him.

Yet Montemoreno wasn't as enjoyable as he expected. Everyone there seemed strangely quiet. And Aunt Frannie wasn't there. That was strange. She'd been staying with them at Regalo, and he'd thought she must have gone home to San Francisco when he didn't see her there.

He lingered in the doorway of a room where she often sat with her embroidery. It was cool and shaded. Her embroidery hoop lay on the drum table where she had left it, waiting for some new piece of work to be inserted. The box with her needles and beautiful coloured threads stood nearby, closed. A big standing frame, holding a tapestry banner for St Martin's Church, loomed in the shadows in its dust-cover, like some big square ghost.

Uncle Greg spoke quietly from behind. 'What are you doing here, Cory?'

The toddler stared up at him. 'Where's

Aunt Frannie?'

His uncle seemed to take a long time to reply. 'She's gone away, Cory.'

'With Daddy? To a far place?'

'Yes, boy.'

There was no reason for it, but desolation swept over the child. He ran to his uncle, threw his arms round his legs, and hid his face against the dark cloth of the trousers. 'No, no!' he wept. 'I want Aunt Frannie! I want Daddy! Where are they?'

He felt himself being picked up, cradled in his uncle's arms, his face against his shoulder. 'Shh now, shh! It's all right, Cory. Don't cry, there's a good boy. I'll take you to Mommy, but first you must stop crying.'

When the passionate storm had subsided, Cory stared into his uncle's face, so close to his own now he was held in those strong, secure arms. For the first time he seemed to see that Uncle Greg was like Daddy in some strange way – something about the tilt of the head, the shade of the hair, the turn of the lips. In other ways, quite different, of course – Uncle Greg could speak like Mommy in a voice that went up and down, not like Daddy who sometimes sounded like a creaking wagon wheel or the monotonous throb of an old engine. But oh, it would be so good to hear that voice again...

The house in San Francisco filled up with other people in dark clothes. It dawned on Cory that they were all people he saw at party times like Christmas or Thanksgiving, only now they were different, not laughing, not bringing presents and teasing him by holding them out of reach. They spoke to him kindly, too kindly. They kept telling him not to bother Mommy, until he began to be afraid she too had gone away like Daddy. Only Uncle Greg understood at once and took him to find her, sitting quietly in the garden under a shade tree, staring before her almost as if absent-minded.

'Spend some time with him, Bess,' Greg said to her in a low tone. 'He's getting scared.'

So all day she kept him with her, which was good, but next day everyone went out of the house in long black cars, and when Cory ran down to the driveway gates to stare at them leaving the grounds he saw a little crowd of strangers there watching too. And there were men with cameras who called to him, 'Hey, kid! Kid, look this way! Smile, huh? Wave! Hey, kid, you're Cory Craig-allan, right?'

But Aunt Frannie's maid had hustled him

away, and the gardener acting as gatekeeper had turned his back on the strangers and their strange pointing, flashing boxes.

After the funeral the family gathered at Montemoreno to discuss what to do next. 'Bess has told me she wouldn't want to stay on at Regalo after what's happened,' Greg said, 'so I've asked her to live here.' He didn't say aloud, to run the household now that Francesca is dead. But they all understood that.

'I'd only be in the way at Regalo,' Bess said. 'It was Neil who ran the place.'

'Jose has got a bad case of the jitters,' Greg went on. 'I offered him the manager's job but he's scared to stay there in charge after what's happened.'

'I don't blame him,' Lew muttered. 'There's a lot of anti-Mex feeling now that jobs are so hard to find.'

'What are you going to do about Regalo, then?' Ellie-Rose asked. She was trying to take an interest. The murder of her brother had hit her hard. All through her girlhood she'd felt protectively bound to Cornelius and the affection for her brother had never wavered. Now that he was gone, part of her life seemed ended.

Ellie-Rose had sought comfort in doing all

she could for Bess. Yet Bess was handling her grief very well. She was too quiet, perhaps, but she was functioning, and once she had actually to take over the reins of Francesca's household she would find enough occupation to tide her over. Bess's parents had come to San Francisco for the funeral, looking old and shaken. Times were hard with them, after the Wall Street Crash. Ellie-Rose had a secret conviction they were relieved at not being asked to take in their widowed daughter, the fine old family home in Chicago being long gone to reduce living expenses. Ellie-Rose had been prepared to offer Bess a home in New York if there had been any need. Now everything seemed taken care of – Bess accepted her new role as housekeeper without demur. She did it for Cory's sake, no doubt. There was no strong bond between Bess and Greg but they got along well enough.

Gina had flown over from London to be at the funeral. As Ellie-Rose looked at her beautiful daughter, she sensed that life was not treating her particularly well. But who was finding the living easy these days? Ellie-Rose's journalist husband kept his finger on the economic pulse, and told her that in London too there were lines of unemployed men pleading for work, respectable men reduced to playing mouth-organs in the gutters for pennies.

'Are you making a living, Gina?' she asked in a moment when the general discussion was interrupted by the appearance of the maid with drinks and snacks. 'You seem thinner.'

'Oh, it's fashionable to be thin,' Gina said with lightness.

'That doesn't answer my question, Gina.'

'I get by, Mama – what d'you expect? The casting director at Pinewood Studios has an arrangement with me to help him find actors with good American accents when they need them for roles in British movies. And I give lessons to British actors who need to speak like Bostonians or Chicago gangsters. It's not big business but something always comes along.'

'Couldn't you come home now, Gina? That awful man Dackis has been sent back to Greece or wherever he came from – you wouldn't be under threat any more.'

Gina blew out a breath. 'I didn't much care for Hollywood, Mama. London's more my sort of place – and I've a chance of going to Paris in the fall.'

'Paris!'

'Yes, wouldn't that be something? They're making a film about the Paris underworld, with a couple of episodes where the crooks are supposed to go to see colleagues in New York so I'm going to supervise the French-American accents.'

'I'll come and visit you in Paris,' Ellie-Rose promised with a smile, 'as soon as I save up the fare. How did you get this chance?'

'Oh … well … I've a friend in the film industry there.' Gina said no more, but Ellie-Rose got the firm impression that the friend was a man. Well, why not? Only she did rather wish Gina would meet someone suitable and settle down into a proper marriage. Even marriage with a Frenchman would be better than nothing…

Ellie-Rose's elder son was at the gathering too. She eyed him from across the room. He was as handsome as ever, and untouched by time or hardship as far as she could see. His tanned features glowed with health. He was clad in quietly formal clothes yet you could tell he was hard and muscular, more accustomed to action than to sedentary pastimes.

On his wrist he wore a very expensive gold watch. On first sight of it Ellie-Rose had exclaimed, 'My word, coaching tennis must pay better than I thought if you can afford that kind of thing!'

Curt laughed. 'Good lord, I didn't pay for it! It was a present.'

She was about to say, 'Who on earth gives you presents like that?' when good sense made her close her lips on the words. For she was suddenly sure that he had been given the watch by a woman – a rich woman, she guessed.

Later she found the chance for a moment alone with Greg's daughter Clare. Clare shared an apartment with her cousin Curt in Hollywood. It was one of those casual arrangements that had become a fixture somehow. It suited them – they went their own way and never bothered each other, yet had the pleasure of a better standard of living by sharing expenses.

Ellie-Rose asked, 'Do you and Curt have friends in common, Clare?'

'Not many.'

'He said that expensive watch was a present. I wondered if you knew…?'

The girl shook her head. 'That's the kind of question you don't ask, Aunt Ellie.'

That could only mean that Ellie-Rose had guessed correctly. The more she thought about it, the more she knew she was right.

Curt could never afford his expensive tailoring and handmade shoes on the kind of salary he earned at the Redwood Country Club.

She was oldfashioned enough to be shocked. Her niece Clare seemed to think nothing of it, but to Ellie-Rose it was shameful. And when she thought of Curt's father, it seemed even worse. The upright Senator Gracebridge, now regarded as something of a national hero because of his death in Flanders at the hands of a German sniper...!

After dinner that evening she went to the study of her half-brother. He was clearing up some paperwork to do with his post as director of the Bureau of Hispano-American Relations. She said: 'Greg, what do you intend to do about Regalo?'

If he was surprised that she should take an interest, he made no mention of that. He shrugged. 'I'll have to put in a manager,' he said.

'I was wondering if...'

'What?'

'Could you give the job to Curt?'

He was so taken aback that for once he showed his emotions completely. He stared at Ellie-Rose. 'Curt?'

'Yes, he... Well, after all, Greg, he's thirty-four years old and nowhere in the world. Coaching tennis! He ought to be doing something with his life.'

'That's up to him, Ellie-Rose.' Privately Greg thought Curt a charming waster. He'd been bright enough at school, but somehow he had never lived up to his father's expectations. That was simply because, as a child, he'd been puny. His father had wanted a fine, rough-and-tumble son but instead had had a scrawny little thing held back by some slight heart defect. By the time Curt's physique changed for the better through his prowess as a swimmer, it was too late.

Greg had watched with some sympathy as Curt emerged into manhood. He'd seen him strive to excel, had been pleased when – rather too late for success – Curt had reached the lower rungs of the Wimbledon Tennis Championship.

But, like many young men, Curt had suffered deeply from the Wall Street disaster. The girl he'd hoped to marry and of whom he'd genuinely been fond had grown tired of waiting for him to find a job with a decent income. Then the prep school had folded.

As far as Greg could see, Curt's philosophy was: What does it matter? He took nothing seriously. Amiable as a friendly dog, careless as a swallow, Curt drifted through life. His looks seemed to improve as he grew older. He was tall, tanned, goodnatured.

Ellie-Rose said: 'Greg, I'll be honest with you. I'm really worried about Curt. He seems to me to be living far above any income he could make at his job.'

'What are you suggesting?' Greg asked, frowning. 'That he's into something underhanded?' Awful rumours reached San Francisco about the way people lived in Los Angeles and Hollywood. Drinking beyond bounds, drug-taking, parties at which young girls were handed around like tasty dishes... Yet none of that seemed to be a likely field for Curt. He was too easygoing for wickedness.

'I don't know if you'd call it underhanded. I just feel ... well ... he's ... he's perhaps moving in circles you and I wouldn't approve of.'

Greg didn't say, I don't feel it's my business to approve or disapprove of Curt. He was fond of Ellie-Rose, although not with the same fierce, protective love he felt for his own immediate family. 'I can't offer Curt the job at Regalo,' he said, going back to first base. 'It's not the kind of thing you hand out just because it's a member of the family–'

'You gave the job to Neil!'

'But Neil knew what he was doing, Ellie-Rose. He had years of experience in agriculture. He got to grips with citri-culture from first principles – and in a way that was why I offered him the job, because he could do what Jose could not. Now I've got this expensive project launched, for the production of juice oranges. I can't let Curt walk in on that and start giving orders – he wouldn't know what was a good juice orange and what was a fruit-bowl product.'

'He could learn, Greg. He was bright at school. He just didn't bother too much academically once he found he could get all the applause by being an athlete.'

'Listen, my dear, I quite see you want to do something for Curt, but I can't take on a thirty-four year old ignoramus. I can get a keen young fellow right out of university who knows everything and wants to use it.'

'Please, Greg! Curt really needs this break.'

'But he's never even looked at me as if he wants to talk jobs–'

'No, because as long as he can live an easy life in Hollywood he won't bother.'

'I don't get it, Ellie-Rose. What is it you say he's up to?'

A fiery red spread over her fine clear skin. 'I think he's letting women keep him,' she said in a stifled voice.

'Are you saying ... he's a gigolo?'

'Don't use that word!' She started up from her chair, turned about the room putting her hands through her short silvery hair. 'Greg, I can't let myself even think that about my own son!'

To tell the truth, Greg found it almost amusing. How typical of Curt to find lonely rich ladies whom he could befriend, to his own advantage. Of course, being a tennis coach afforded ideal opportunities of meeting women with lots of money and time on their hands. And surprisingly enough, Hollywood was full of them; wives of producers and directors, who seldom saw their husbands and, when they did, found them tired and irritable.

Greg was pretty sure no actual money changed hands. It wasn't on any sordid level. Curt wouldn't enjoy life if it was lived like that. But charge accounts at the exclusive stores, restaurant bills signed-for on the understanding that they would eventually be paid by someone else, a foreign sports car on perpetual loan from a generous friend...

'Look, be reasonable, Ellie-Rose,' he murmured, going to her and putting a friendly arm around her shoulders. 'Now you've told me this, do you really think Curt would accept the job if I offered it?'

They both thought of Regalo – miles from anywhere, comfortable enough but equipped only for country life. It was the kind of place a family man would enjoy, but a footloose bachelor accustomed to parties and elegant women would go mad there. And that was leaving aside the fact that Curt had no scientific training, knew nothing about growing food products.

'But he can't expect to go on forever just ... just...'

Living off his immoral earnings, was what Greg knew she was thinking. He gave her a hug. 'I can tell it shocks you, my dear, but in Hollywood everything's different.' He thought of Clare, and felt a shiver of apprehension. His own daughter ... what did she get up to in that whirl of self-indulgence? She had a job that seemed to please her, and friends of whom she spoke with affection. He had always taken it for granted she lived a totally normal life. But she shared her apartment with Curt; was it possible to touch pitch and not be defiled? But then he thought, Oh, come … defiled … nobody could be defiled from contact with Curt.

He gave his attention to comforting Ellie-Rose. 'Why don't you talk to Curt?' he said. 'You're his mother, after all.'

'But … you see, Greg … I was away all through the war. I sort of lost touch with him, and Gina too.'

'All the more reason why you should be able to talk to him. You're not a possessive, interfering mother. You should be able to say that you're worried.'

'I can't, Greg. I can't ask him if he's living off women!'

'No, of course not. But it's quite reasonable to ask if he has any plans for the future. After all, even a tennis coach must have plans, ambitions… Ask him what he intends to do, whether he expects to keep the same job for ever.'

'I'll try.' She shuddered away from the thought even as she agreed. She knew she wasn't going to broach the subject with Curt. She was afraid that, in his lazy, goodnatured way, he'd say, 'Why, no, Mama, I've no plans – as long as my looks hold out I can't see why I should bother.'

Greg's reason for not giving Curt the job was genuine enough, but there was another. He wanted his son Lewis to take it on. Lewis had no training in agriculture but he had a degree in economics which ought, by all the laws of logic, to fit him for handling the business side. To help him with the citriculture, Greg planned, as he had told Ellie-Rose, to hire an eager young graduate.

But when he put the idea to Lew, he got an unexpected reaction. Lew stared at him, then said in a tone of anger and disappointment, 'You're my own father, but you don't know me at all!'

'Don't know you? What does that mean?'

'Did you really expect me to take on the management of Regalo? Help you to exploit those itinerant workers who work for a pittance? Help you to perpetuate the serf system that shores up Californian agriculture?'

Greg felt the accustomed tide of love and exasperation. Why did every conversation with Lew turn into a political argument? 'I don't exploit the itinerants,' he said. 'I hire them and when the job is done, they move on. It's by their own choice–'

'Choice! What choice do they have but to accept fourteen cents an hour? What choice do they have except to spend the money in the orchard-owner's food store?'

'Now, Lew, you know I don't run a company store – any worker on my land is free to go into town and buy–'

'Only they're too tired to make the trip, and they can't afford the gasoline, so they buy from a truck that comes out from Fresno charging fancy prices–'

'Listen, you know I take no share in any of that–'

'I know you tell yourself so. But if you wanted to, you could insist the prices on that grocery van were brought down to–'

'The man's entitled to a profit for taking the trouble to go out to the orchards–'

'He's not entitled to screw them into the ground for a bag of sugar and a bar of soap! Do you know how much the driver takes as his own personal cut?'

'I've told you, I play no part in any of that–'

'And salve your conscience that way – oh, I understand! You think because you built a decent living block with sanitation and a square for them to run their socials, that absolves you from guilt. But you really give them nothing–'

Greg got up from his desk. The abruptness

of the movement made Lew pause.

'Lewis,' his father said in a tone of quiet anger, 'I've given more to these people than you have.'

'Given? What have you given?'

'A mother, a wife, a brother. Have you given as much?'

For once, his son was silenced in an argument. He frowned, looked down.

'You can say that I gave them unwillingly. Damn right! I wouldn't have sacrificed a hair of your mother's head for any man or woman on this earth. But I wanted to do something for the migrants because your grandmother begged me to. I didn't do it out of idealism, and you may say that negates the act. All right, think what you like. But I tried to do *something*, and I paid for it. What makes it worse is that it was paid for by the lives of others. If I'd been shot to death by a teargas gun or battered by a thug, that would have been more logical – I was the one interfering with the natural order of things. But no, it cost the life of your grandmother from disease, it cost the life of your mother and your uncle by attack. So don't say I've given nothing.'

Lew had never heard his father speak so much about his personal feelings. It embarrassed him. Somehow he felt it was all right for him to pour out his emotions about injustice and morality, but not for Gregor McGarth to speak of loss.

'You don't want the job at Regalo. All right,' his father went on. 'But don't give me any lectures about it, Lew. Although I don't agree with your ideas, I respect your sincerity. Do me the justice of respecting mine. I want to run the orchard successfully because it's to my advantage – but I want to be fair to my employees. I work within the system, I don't try to change it too much. And one day, son, you'll find that my way works while you're still making speeches about equality and freedom.'

'You're wrong, Dad! The system is going to collapse in a horrible mess one day–'

Greg gave a snort of disbelief. 'I've been hearing that ever since I was a boy, but things still go staggering on as before–'

'Staggering. That's the word. After what happened in the Stock Exchange, do you really believe things can go back just as they were? And if that weren't enough, look at those madmen in Europe – Mussolini, Hitler–'

'Oh, they're posturing idiots! Nobody takes them seriously.'

'Maybe that's where we're wrong, Dad. Maybe we ought to take them seriously and stand up to them before they get too big for their boots.'

'You mean, shoot guns at them? Lew, we had all that twenty years ago. We don't want it again. You'll see, the dictators will show themselves to be incompetent and absurd, and we'll settle down to normal again.'

'You mean, the "system" will go on working to your advantage as usual.'

'Why do you knock it? You've got to come to terms with it some day, Lew. I'm not a rich man, but I'm not poor either. Everything I own will come to you one day. You ought to know how to handle it when it does.'

Lew shook his head in violent rejection. 'No! No, don't leave me your money, Dad! I don't want it!'

'Don't talk like a fool—'

'I mean it! If you leave it to me, I'll give it away. I don't want to be a capitalist—'

'For God's sake! What's in a name? I don't think of myself as a capitalist – I just own some property, that's all—'

'Yes, and you think it gives you the right to control other people's lives. I never want to get caught in that trap. I'm serious, Dad. If

302

you're thinking of me as controller of the McGarth fortune, forget it.'

Greg looked at his son as if seeing him for the first time. 'You're saying that you're disinheriting yourself.'

'I don't believe in inherited wealth. It's against my principles.'

A silence developed, which grew till it actually seemed to have weight and pressure. Then Greg drew a quiet breath. 'Very well,' he said. 'If that's what you want. I tell you now: if you refuse to take over the land I've bought, I shall leave it to your cousin Cornelius.'

Lew shrugged. 'That would be better, really. He carries the real name, doesn't he? The Craigallan name. That's what you've always wanted – to see that old brigand's name perpetuated, to see the family of Robert Craigallan back among the movers and shakers. Leave everything to Cory, then, and put it back where it should be, under the Craigallan name.'

'That's not the reason, Lew–'

'I don't care what your reason is. All I know is I don't want to be trapped in an inheritance I wouldn't know how to handle.' He paused with his hand on the doorknob. 'Don't be disappointed about it. You'll see –

it's best this way. I'd only have disappointed you, and your ghost would have come back to haunt me as I made a mess of handling your money.'

When he had gone, Greg went with dragging footsteps back to his desk chair. He sank into it, strangely exhausted. He felt a vast loneliness. Francesca, to whom he would have turned with this disappointment, was gone. She, with her gentle voice and gentle touch, would have soothed it all away – but she wasn't there. Only shadows and silence remained in her stead. Shadows and silence. It seemed that everyone he loved had left him. Death had taken his mother and his wife. His half-brother too, for whom he had had respect and affection.

His children, who should now be closer to him than anyone else in the world, seemed separated by some unbridgeable gap – Lew whose mind he couldn't fathom, Clare who pursued her own life in a town he distrusted.

'Francesca,' he whispered, 'Francesca...'

But there was no reply. She would never reply to him again. There was no voice to speak to him, no heart to beat for him alone. There was nothing in the world of any use or value.

Nothing, except to find her murderers and make them pay. It seemed a cruel and a harsh ambition, but it was all he had left.

## *Chapter Eleven*

Peter Brunnen came to the funeral in San Francisco, a fact duly noted by the newspapers. 'Filmstar Brunnen told me in his heartthrob voice, "The McGarth family were very kind to me when I was learning English for my first Hollywood role. Though I knew Cornelius Craigallan only slightly, Mrs McGarth was a true friend." When questioned if he would be re-united with Mrs Gina Gramm, who has flown from London for the funeral and with whom at one time his name was romantically linked, Brunnen smiled. "Mrs Gramm has been abroad for over a year. Of course I shall be seeing her." Brunnen's wreath, seen at the ceremony, was of dark red carnations...'

At the graveside he stayed in the background, only shaking hands and expressing sympathy as did so many others. But he took Gina aside for a moment to murmur,

'Let's meet, Gina. I'm staying over until tomorrow at the Fairmont.'

'I don't think I can get away this evening, Peter. I owe it to the family to stay with them.'

'Sure, I understand that. I shan't be going back until tomorrow evening – could we have a meal?'

'Are you flying back? I could meet you at the airport for a drink.'

He nodded, not wishing to press her. She looked wan and sad in her black suit and hat. The two deaths had hit her hard. He knew she had always thought a lot of her Aunt Francesca, whom she'd described to him once, rather enviously, as the only married woman she knew who was still totally in love with her husband.

When she explained to her Uncle Greg that she was seeing Peter off on the evening flight, he touched her hand. 'Tell him I appreciated his being here. Frannie always took an interest in him – said he was wasting his voice in Hollywood.'

'I'll be back for dinner. But if I'm a little late, tell Aunt Bess not to wait for me.'

Already it was an accepted fact that Bess was the lady of the house. She knew, as she went out to the waiting taxi, that the thought saddened him. Already, Francesca was being replaced.

Peter was in the bar of the airport building. Prohibition having been repealed two years ago, he was sampling one of the local wines. He summoned the waiter to pour a glass for her as she took the chair across from him. 'This is called a Sauternes,' he remarked, 'though why, I don't understand, since it's quite a passable dry wine whereas real Sauternes is sweet.' He watched as she unbuttoned her jacket and eased it back from her shoulders. 'Well, how are you, Gina Gramm?'

'I'm all right. How is Peter Brunnen?'

He shrugged. Although it seemed absurd to say so, his shrug really was Continental – one of the things that made him popular as a second-rank star. She studied him, thinking that although he was successful enough, he didn't look particularly happy. His long frame was clad in a very good suit, his hair was expertly barbered to control its thick unruliness, his nails had been attended to by a professional manicurist. Yet there was a wistful air about him.

'I saw your latest film that got to London,' she said. 'I thought you were very good.'

'Which was that – *Captain Carlo*?'

'Oh, no, it wasn't Spanish – it was about Poland under the Czar.'

'Ah, *Rendezvous in Cracow*. Yes, that wasn't bad, as a matter of fact. But don't go to see *Captain Carlo*. It's terrible.'

'Peter!'

'Really, it's nothing but *kitsch*. If you ask me, I look about as Spanish as liverwurst, but nobody listens when I try to object.' He sighed. 'But never mind that. What kind of thing are you doing in London, Gina? Are you happy there?'

She explained about the ancillary work that gave her a living but avoided any financial details. She could see him taking in the fact that her black suit was not very well-fitting, having been borrowed for the funeral trip. The blouse she wore with it was a good one, pure silk with hand embroidery on the little round collar, but it dated from the time she'd been a pampered rich girl. Her bag and shoes were far from new though of excellent quality.

Peter had learned many things in Hollywood, and one of them was to assess who had money and who had not. It was clear to him that Gina was only getting by in London.

'Why don't you come back to Hollywood?'

he suggested. 'The Mad Greek got packed off to his homeland, so you'd be quite safe.'

She sipped her wine. 'No, Peter, although it was because of Dack that I dashed away, I don't feel any urge to come back.'

'No?' His deepset eyes examined her. There had been a little tinge of longing in the smile with which she softened her refusal. 'There's something that calls you back to London, then. And the name of this call is…?'

'He's in Paris, actually. He's called Michel.'

Peter made a face. 'Oh, a Frenchman! I won't argue against competition like that! Is he nice, this Michel?'

'I think so.'

'Is it serious?'

'Who can say?' She pushed her wine-glass about on the tablecloth, making little ripples on its damask surface. 'He's married,' she burst out. 'That's the difficulty.'

'Ah.' He reached out and covered the hand fiddling with the wine-glass with his own; large, warm, and comforting. 'Is it a real difficulty? He loves his wife? Or what?'

'Oh, he… They get along all right… You know what the French are like, Peter. They compartmentalise… The problem is, Michel's a Catholic of a tepid sort but his wife is devout. So there can be no divorce.'

'And where does that leave you? Does she know about you? Are they still together as man and wife?'

'Oh, of *course*! Oh, don't get the wrong idea, Peter. Michel and I don't see each other all that often. Not at present, that is... Although I'm hoping to move to Paris later in the year.'

'Is that wise, Gina?'

She made no reply to that. The waiter appeared with two little bowls of peanuts and salted crackers. 'You're a fine one to talk about being wise,' she said to Peter with a laugh, to turn the subject. 'You're the one who kept sending half his income to a wife the other side of the world! I went to Covent Garden, Peter, to hear her sing. She was Michaela in *Carmen*.'

'You did? In the spring, you mean? What did you think? I heard her sing the role in Milan last year – I went especially for her debut.'

'She seemed pretty good to me.' If the truth were told, Gina had gone to the Opera House determined to dislike Magda Ledermann but had been beguiled by the voice. It was pure, clear, strong, and true. She had to admit that when Peter declared his wife had a real talent, he'd been correct.

Gina had sent a little bouquet of flowers and a note wishing her well in her first London appearance, explaining that she was a friend of Peter's from California. She'd received a very cold reply: 'Your name is familiar to me from hearing my husband mention it. I thank you for your good wishes, M Ledermann.'

All right, thought Gina, if she doesn't want to be friends, it's okay by me. Later, through a journalist friend who collected gossip items for the evening papers, she learned that Magda had a reputation for being friends only with important people. Gina, of course, was a nobody, especially these days and especially in London.

She decided not to waste any more money on expensive seats at the Opera House just to hear a voice which, though beautiful, came from a singer who seemed to have no heart at all.

'In Milan she got good reviews but the audience didn't take to her,' Peter was explaining. 'Italian opera-lovers are very choosing.' He paused. 'Choosing?'

'I think you mean choosy. Why didn't they choose Magda, then?'

'She says it was due to intrigue among the

lead singers. That's why she jumped at the chance to come to Covent Garden – she says she'll never get to the top in Italy because there's prejudice against non-Italian singers.'

'Well, Covent Garden isn't bad, is it?'

'No, very good. I tried to persuade her to come straight to New York from Milan – there was a chance of an audition with the Met.' He fell silent.

'Well, go on – why didn't she come?' Gina urged, guessing that he wanted to discuss it with someone.

'I don't know what to make of it, Gina. She said … she said she didn't want to leave Europe, because she'd had a hint that the Fatherland would call her to a role in German culture.' He raised his eyebrows in disbelief.

Gina smothered a smile. The Fatherland! Really, what grandiose words these people used. 'Well, that sounds good, Peter. I expect she'd like to make a name for herself back home – Local Girl Makes Good. It's a natural ambition.'

'In Hitler's Germany?' he gave her a glance that was almost a glare. 'You were off in Mexico at the time, struggling to help that silly Russian. But didn't you read in the newspapers, how the Nazis had butchered each other? The Night of the Long Knife, the papers called it. I can't understand what Magda is thinking of, wanting to go back to Germany and sing for that bunch of assassins.'

'But she probably doesn't take any interest in politics, Peter–'

'If a German ambassador takes her out to dinner and tells her she should await a summons from Hitler, that's politics. Or close enough.'

'Oh, come on! I imagine an ambassador is like all the rest. If he's trying to impress a pretty woman, he'll make promises he has no intention of keeping.'

'You haven't been listening! It's true, a man will promise what he thinks a woman wants. What appals me is that he should feel Magda would be tempted by a "promise" like that.'

Gina might have said, But you've always known Magda was ambitious. She might have added, And rather selfish. But he didn't want to be told that. She said: 'Singing's her business, not international politics. She probably hasn't a clue who or what the Nazis are, or what they want–'

'She knows. She wrote me an angry letter

313

when I was rude to the emissary they sent–'

'They sent an emissary to *you*?' The moment she'd said it, she was sorry for the unintended slight in it.

But Peter, the least vain of men, gave a shrug and an angry laugh. 'You may well be astounded. I was too. But it seems he went the rounds of the German contingent in Hollywood, telling them they owed it to their Fatherland to show disgust at the Jewish plot.'

'What Jewish plot?'

'Hollywood, it seems, is part of an evil plan by the Jews to sap the moral will of the civilised world. Through Hollywood films they spread their decadent culture.'

'Oh, they can't really believe that!'

'It's possible they do. But in any case, what they want is for a large number of German actors and technicians to go home to Germany, there to make speeches about how happy they are to return to a decent moral climate and serve the Fatherland. And what's so bad, Gina, is that some of them actually believed what that silly man said.'

'But not you.'

'Oh, no, I told him to–' He broke off. With a glance of mischief he said, 'Well, though I taught you some German, you didn't learn the words I spoke to him!'

'And Magda was upset about that?'

'She told me I was being wilfully blind to the great opportunities in UFA films, just waiting for me if I would go home. When I wrote back saying I preferred to take up the opportunities Bert Kolin found for me, she got even angrier. She wrote that I ought to be ashamed to be under obligation to a Jew.'

'Oh.'

'Yes, oh! It grieves me to think my own wife should have picked up any notions from the propaganda of Doktor Goebbels. My one hope is that the offer – the command – whatever you choose to call it – will come to nothing and she'll eventually come to America. But from her point of view, you see, it makes better sense if she returns to Berlin and I take up the offer of a contract with UFA.'

'Maybe it *would* be better, Peter? You think so poorly of the films you're making here – perhaps you'd get better roles in Germany?'

He sighed. 'It would be nice to get something sensible to do. Particularly now that Magda is financially independent. But I'm certainly not going to talk contracts with the German Ministry of Propaganda.

It would be like talking business with an orang-utan – they're totally unpredictable.'

'Why don't you see if Bert can get you some work in England? Or in France – you speak good French.'

'Bert is trying for a part for me in a Jessie Matthews film – do you know her?'

'Oh yes, we've met. I did some dubbing for the French version of *Evergreen*. I think she's shooting a film called *It's Love Again* at the moment.'

'Yes, but the one after – I think it's to be called *Head Over Heels* – there's some talk of having a lesser Hollywood star as her partner, to try to open up the market for the film in the States.'

'And that's you? You'll be going back to singing!'

'If it comes off. I don't know. Bert's working on it. I do feel...'

'What, Peter?'

'That I ought to get to London if I can while Magda is still there. If not, I have a feeling... You know, we see each other so seldom. In the five years since we have left Berlin, she to go to Italy for voice lessons and I to the San Francisco Opera chorus, we've met twice. Once in Brussels when she was singing a minor lead in *Orfeo*, and once in Milan when she first sang Michaela in *Carmen*.'

And both times, thought Gina, you went to her, she didn't go to you. 'It certainly isn't a good recipe for a successful marriage, darling.'

'I want it to be a successful marriage. We had so much in common when we were students but then, when I began to get singing roles and she didn't...'

A voice over the public address system called Peter's flight. He rose, left a note on the table for the wine, and held out his hand to Gina. 'I didn't mean to bore you with all that. I wanted to talk about *you*. Letters don't really convey much. But now I know about Michel I understand why you don't write often. And I hope it works out for you, Gina.'

As she made her way home Gina thought over that conversation. Even if Peter made it to London, she didn't think it would do much for his shaky marriage. She had a feeling Magda had considered him for years mainly as a meal-ticket, and now that her own career was taking off and she no longer needed him, he was a nuisance. Particularly if he wasn't going to comply with the rules invented by the new German government.

From Peter's side it was less simple. He still had affection for his wife, or at least a strong sense of duty. Gina knew, from the newspaper cuttings occasionally sent to her in London by her mother, that Peter Brunnen was regarded as an eligible bachelor in Hollywood. He was often mentioned as squiring this starlet or that movie queen. She had no doubt he had his little affairs, like all the others.

But he still took his marriage seriously. The ties he and Magda had formed during their student days still bound him, if not her. That wouldn't be so bad if Magda still cared for him, but Gina was almost certain Magda felt she had 'outgrown' Peter. His money had been necessary to her when they first parted, he with a job and she with none. But now that she was having some small success, and was being promised great things by the Third Reich – what need did she have of Peter Brunnen, minor star of B feature films?

I'm so lucky, Gina thought. No matter if there are all kinds of drawbacks between me and Michel, he really cares for me. And he's *there*, in Paris, where I'll be joining him soon.

When she thought of the long parting Peter had endured, and the loss suffered by her Uncle Greg and her Aunt Bess, she was filled with a sense of amazement for the good fortune she had had in life. True, she and her young husband Cliff had missed the high peaks of passion, but they had been genuinely in love. In her wild affair with Vartan Dackis there had been elemental sensuality which had sprung from genuine sexual attraction.

She had been granted one of life's greatest favours; she had given and received love. What if times were hard, what if her income was precarious and her future uncertain – she had been blessed, and she was grateful in the moment of insight granted to her as the taxi took her home through San Francisco's vertiginous streets to Montemoreno.

Dinner was just about to be served. She couldn't help noticing that her cousin Clare was unusually quiet during the meal. When it was over, Bess went up to put Cory to bed, accompanied by Ellie-Rose who had taken it upon herself to stay close to the new young widow. Ellie-Rose knew what grief was; she too had suffered great loss.

Curt went out on some engagement of his own. Gina was about to follow Clare to the drawing-room when to her surprise her Uncle Greg detained her with a glance.

They went to his study. 'Gina, you're more my daughter's age than anyone else–'

'Oh!' She guessed she was going to be asked to deal with some problem. 'Listen, Clare and I aren't close, Uncle Greg.'

'But she went to you when she left home to make a career–'

'Yes, that's true, but she moved out quite soon.'

He looked perplexed. 'Didn't you get on? I thought you had a lot in common.'

Yes, we had, we had a man in common, thought Gina. Although a long time had gone by, she wasn't sure Clare had forgiven her over Vartan Dackis.

'I've been away a good while, Uncle Greg. We've been completely out of touch.'

'That's too bad. I thought you might be able to find out what's troubling her.'

Gina shook her head.

'It's so odd... D'you know, Gina, she asked me for the job of managing Regalo.'

'What?'

'Yes – when I told her Lew had turned it down she said, "Give it to *me*." I thought she was joking, but she wasn't.'

'Does she know anything about growing oranges?'

'Not a thing. She's always regarded it as a

bit of a joke – Daddy's hobby, Daddy's way of getting himself in among the landed gentry of the county. I couldn't get anything out of her – I mean, when I asked her why she should want to bury herself at the back of beyond with the Entonches family, she just said she was tired of Hollywood.'

Gina laughed. 'Well, that figures. Hollywood is the kind of place you can have more than enough of. Especially if you're not on top of the heap.'

'It may be that. But why should she want to hide herself away on a fruit farm in the San Joacquin Valley? Why not somewhere more glamorous? She wouldn't explain. I was wondering...' He looked at Gina with hope... 'I was wondering if you'd have a word with her?'

'If there is some special reason, she wouldn't tell *me*.' She hesitated. 'I take it you told her she couldn't be manager of the orchard?'

'Of course. It would be an affront to Jose, to put a woman in over him – and a woman who knows nothing about the business, at that. There are no women in the fruit-growing estates – it's a man's world. Besides, she's not serious about it. What I mean is, she's not really thinking of making a career in orchard management – she's just running away from something. I thought you might find out what.'

'I'm sorry, Uncle Greg.'

'Well, never mind,' he said with regret. 'Perhaps one day she'll tell me.' He sighed. 'I want so much to help her, Gina. I just don't know how. It's the same with Lew. There's a gulf, somehow...'

Gina turned the talk to her departure, which was next day, and got away quickly. She was quite determined not to antagonise Clare by interfering in her affairs. However, Clare tapped at her room door about half an hour later, as Gina was packing.

'Gina? Are you busy?'

'Not especially. Do you want something?'

'Daddy took you aside to have a private talk, didn't he?'

'He ... we had a chat, yes.'

'About me?'

Gina searched in the drawer of the tallboy for an elusive pair of silk stockings. 'Why should we talk about you?'

'Because I got him worried earlier on today – and it was the last thing I meant to do. What did he say to you, Gina?'

'You just described it as a "private talk", Clare.'

'All right, I'll tell you what he said. He said I'd asked for the job at Regalo and could you find out why I wanted to leave Hollywood.'

Gina smiled. 'Yes, he said exactly that.'

'Poor Daddy,' Clare said with absent-minded fondness. 'He wants so desperately to be helpful and comforting, but he's really the last person who can do anything.'

Gina turned from her suitcase with a suppressed sigh. 'It's a man, I suppose.'

'Yes.'

'What's the trouble? Doesn't he love you?'

'I think he does.'

'What then?' She thought of Michel. 'Is he married?'

'No.'

'Someone in some kind of trouble – hooked on booze? Drugs?'

'No.'

'Well, for heaven's sake, Clare, if you want to confide in me, *confide*! I can't be the least bit of help if I don't know what kind of man he is.'

'He's wonderful!' Clare said, her dark eyes shining like pools reflecting starlight. 'He's clever and nice and well-educated and ambitious and handsome...'

'Well! If he's such a paragon and you love

him and he loves you, where's the problem?'

'He's Chinese.'

Gina met Clare's glance. She felt for the edge of the bed and sat down on it slowly. 'Chinese?'

'He's American-Chinese. Fourth generation – his people came from Canton as coolies for the railroad. He's the eldest son – has two sisters older than he and a brother younger, but he's the pride and joy of his parents.'

'Go on. What does he do – how did you meet him?'

'On the set at Paramount. He's one of the top cameramen, Gina – stars actually ask for him by name.'

'Which is what, by the way?'

'Kay Yung. In Chinese, it's Yung Kay – the family name is Yung. Oh, Gina, if you could only meet him! He's so quick and bright – so perceptive.'

Gina listened to a song of praise about Kay Yung. Allowing for the natural exaggeration of a girl very much in love, he sounded an attractive man. He had worked his way through university, taking a science degree, and then gone on to photography through hobbyist interest which turned into a career. The roll-call of films on which he had worked was a list of notable artistic successes. And, though Clare didn't say so, he made a lot of money.

'But of course the racial prejudice thing is just making it all impossible for us,' Clare said, tears whispering in her voice. 'Everybody agrees Kay is marvellous at his job, but the minute he's seen around with a "white" girl, attitudes change. And of course it's hopeless even mentioning marriage.'

'Yes,' Gina agreed with anxiety. 'I should think your father would be very much against it.'

'*My* father!' Clare cried. 'It's *his* family that would cause the most fuss. They idolise him. They expect him to marry a Chinese girl of good family and perpetuate the clan name. They're terribly oldfashioned people.'

Gina knew nothing about China or the Chinese – except that the country had been invaded a few years ago by Japan and was having a hard time from the Japanese Imperial Army. The Great Wall of China, symbol in itself of China's endurance, had been occupied by Japanese troops. There had been some talk of air raids by the Japanese Air Force on the northern cities. Whether it was true, or only sensational journalism, there was no way of knowing.

The Chinese of San Francisco were a large community – self-sufficient, known chiefly for their industriousness, their restaurants, the strange decor of their own quarter known, inevitably, as Chinatown. If Gina had been honest, the idea that her cousin was in love with a member of that community was very odd. The Chinese were waiters, clothes-pressers, shopkeepers. It somehow seemed incredible that Gina could even have got to know one well enough to fall in love.

'It sounds as if you've chosen a tough row to hoe, Clare,' she remarked with sympathy. 'Was that why you asked for the job at Regalo – just to get away from the situation?'

'It all seems so hopeless! Kay loves me, I know he does. But you see, he's so damned honourable. He keeps pointing out what an awful life it would be for me, married to a "yellowman". He knows what prejudice is – he's had to combat it to get where he is in Hollywood. And mixed marriages cause so many sneers and insults...'

'How ... er ... how far has it gone? I mean, are you and he...?'

'Lovers? Good lord no! Kay keeps saying that if we got involved and it came out, they'd crucify us both – me, particularly. And you know, Gina … the only way to do it would be sneaking about under cover of darkness. And we're neither of us the type for that.' Clare leaned against the back of the chintz-covered bedroom armchair and began to cry with one hand shielding her eyes. 'It's such a mess,' she sobbed. 'The best thing seemed, just to walk away from it.'

Gina knew from experience how strangely difficult it was to avoid people in Hollywood. The film community was a small one, after all, and if you could stay away from parties there was still the working situation, where you were in the same building or the same lot or conferring with the same set of technicians. To Clare, Regalo must have beckoned like sanctuary to a medieval sinner.

'If you are not going to marry him, why don't you make a complete break?' she suggested.

'That's what I was trying to do–'

'No, I mean, go a long way away. Why don't you come with me to London?'

'London!'

'Yes, why not?'

'But … but … what would I do in London?'

'Why should you do anything – for a while, at least? You could live on your allowance from your father. It's easier there, living on a low budget. They don't expect you to show off so much, have a new car every year, wear a mink the minute the weather turns chilly. You might find a job of some sort after a bit, if you really felt you had to. And you could share my flat.'

'But … wouldn't I be in your way?' Clare said, sitting up and mopping her eyes with a little scrap of fine cambric.

'Well, I hope to be in Paris within a few weeks. I'd be in Paris a couple of months, perhaps into January.'

'I don't know what to say.'

'If you're serious about ending this thing with Kay, the best way is to make a clean break. I mean – be honest, Clare – Kay could have gone to see you at Regalo or you could have taken a train from Fresno to Hollywood any time you wanted to.'

'Yeah… And anyway it was silly to imagine Daddy would hand over his precious orchard to a nincompoop like me. It was clutching at straws to suggest it.'

Privately Gina thought it had been a way of signalling her desperation. Perhaps, if Uncle Greg had been more persistent, Clare would have at last confided in him. But it was better this way. If she could persuade Clare to go back with her to London, it would spare Uncle Greg the distress of knowing that his beloved daughter had made a fool of herself over a totally unsuitable lover.

When the idea was put to him, Gregor McGarth felt a pang of loss. Clare was going across the Atlantic. That seemed so far away. True, they had seldom seen her since she moved to Hollywood, yet she was at least within a day's drive. But now she was going far out of his reach.

He tried to look on the bright side. At least she would no longer be sharing an apartment with Curt. Hitherto he'd thought of him as some sort of kindly big brother to Clare; now that he knew where his income came from, he seemed less dependable.

As to the reasons for Clare's restlessness, Gina confided only enough to seem reasonable. 'It's an unhappy love affair. Uncle Greg. Nothing awful has happened but I think it's wise for Clare to get away.'

'I'm glad she's going with you, Gina. You see, you were wrong when you said you were completely out of touch.'

So it seemed now. They hadn't even

mentioned Dack. That was a forgotten incident, part of the foolishness of the past for both of them.

Gina's London flat was in the artists' quarter, above an oil and paint shop in the King's Road, Chelsea. It wasn't much of a place by the standards Clare had been accustomed to in Hollywood – a narrow steep staircase led up from the door at the side of the shop, giving access to a small landing from which three doors opened off. The large room, over the shop's customer area, was the living-room. Gina had furnished it with pieces picked up for shillings in the secondhand shops of nearby Fulham. Yet it was comfortable and welcoming.

'My,' said Clare when she was shown in, 'this is nice! You've an eye for colour, Gina.'

'Marvellous what a little tin of enamel paint will do. Look this will be your bedroom. It's got suitcases and junk in it at the moment but we'll clear it out and go shopping for a bed tomorrow. And this is my room, next to it.' She threw open the door to show the quiet white-painted room with its sprigged muslin curtain and bedspread. 'And here's the bathroom – a bit primitive by your standards, but everything works.'

Clare fell in love with the bathroom. It had

a bath with legs and a mahogany surround, an ancient copper gas geyser for hot water, and a washbasin and toilet of china bearing a design of phoenixes in flight. 'Oh, it's darling!' she cried. 'I must sketch it for use in a period film—' She broke off. That part of her life was gone. She had thrown away an interesting job in the studio's art department to come to London.

Putting her toilet things in the bathroom cabinet, she found a man's razor and hairbrushes. She had too much tact to ask to whom they belonged.

Later that evening she put through a long-distance call to San Francisco to tell her father they had safely arrived and that she loved the tiny flat.

Greg heard her excited voice with a sense of deep relief. That was more like the Clare he liked to remember – the eager little girl running to him to show him an autumn leaf, pulling at his hand to go into an ice-cream parlour. The listless desperation of her manner when she asked him to let her live at Regalo had scared him. But now, thanks to Gina, she was restored to him as something like the daughter he loved, who was looking forward to a new beginning.

He too had a new start to make. He had to

accustom himself to waking in the morning without Francesca beside him, and to breakfasting alone in the pretty room that always reminded him of her. Bess was too tactful to appear downstairs. She busied herself with Cory instead. But at the end of the first week of his widowhood Gregor saw her passing the door of the breakfast room and called: 'Have you had breakfast, Bess?'

'I'll have it later, after you're gone.'

He rose and went to her, napkin in hand. 'Come on in, Bess. I understand what you've been doing, but we can't go on like this. You're mistress of the house now – we ought to eat together to plan the day.'

Bess saw the pain behind his eyes as he said the words. For a moment she was going to refuse. Then she understood that this was part of his determination to face the world without Francesca.

For her, in a way, it was easier. She was in new surroundings. Nothing here spoke to her of Cornelius – except Cornelius's little boy, who had settled in at Montemoreno as if he had always belonged there. For his sake she wanted everything to go smoothly. And she owed it to Greg to fit in with his wishes in every way.

She came into the breakfast room. Greg

ushered her to a chair across the table. He handed her a little silver handbell. 'Ring for Rosita,' he said.

She shook the bell. The maid appeared as if she had been waiting outside in the passage – as indeed she had, since she heard the master summon the new mistress into the room.

'Bring another place setting, please, Rosita,' Bess said, 'and fresh coffee.'

'Si, señora. And toast and *mermelada*, as usual?'

'Yes, please.'

Rosita went to the kitchen. 'At last it is settled,' she told the cook and Erneste, the chauffeur-gardener. 'The señora will be taking breakfast with the señor.'

'About time,' grumbled the cook. 'So much fuss, making separate preparations.' The domestic staff took a keen interest in all that concerned the señor. They had dearly loved Francesca and for her sake wanted all to go well for Gregor.

He found it quite endurable to have Bess across the table from him instead of Francesca. Partly it was because she was so totally different – almost plain whereas Francesca had been so beautiful; brisk and businesslike where his wife had been diffident. And with enough intelligence to know they had difficulties ahead of them if they were to share a home.

Greg went to his office at the usual hour. He had a busy morning, and then in the afternoon he had to chair a meeting of businessmen from the counties neighbouring San Francisco: San Mateo, Santa Clara, Alameda, and San Joacquin. There were problems with the maps of old real-estate holdings in all four counties.

Some of the old Spanish families, in indignation, were threatening a joint law suit against the proposed building of a series of dams which would alter the watercourse of the Calaveros River. The project was a civic undertaking but the backing of the businessmen had brought it ahead in the Capitol in Sacramento because it was clearly to the advantage of the farmers and orchard owners. Their haste had meant that the ownership claims of the old families might well get set aside by special legislation, so as to hurry the beginning of the work.

'We all understand, of course, that the Garcia and Rodriguez families have claims,' Dick Galdeston said after they had been in session for about an hour. 'When the bill goes through the Senate, there will be provision for compensation–'

'The old families are quite aware of that. Mr Mendoza? Would you like to explain the situation?'

Mendoza, lawyer for the claimants, made a longish speech about the losses his clients would incur if the bill was pushed through the Senate. 'The disagreement about the validity of the maps makes a great difference to the amount of money they can claim. Their view is that the land is undoubtedly theirs–'

'Look here, Mendoza, the spread under Walnut Valley was sold by the Garcias to that Japanese melon-grower, and *he* is selling to the highways authority–'

'The land was never sold to Mitsubuko. It was on a long lease. The papers are in my office, where you can inspect–'

'It you want to make a fight of it, Mendoza, it's simply a matter of who you believe. Mitsubuko has documents which say he bought the land.'

'For eighteen thousand dollars? My dear Mr Ballard, you can't really believe that.'

'Sure I believe it,' Ballard said with a grim laugh. 'Those damn Japs made the best bargains in the whole of California – they bought when land couldn't be worked because of the war and labour troubles and God knows what else, and they got it for peanuts. What else d'you expect from Nippos?'

'Gentlemen, let's not go off on side issues,' Greg said. 'The validity of Mitsubuko's sale of his farm is something we can check on. The main problem is to hold back the passage of the bill in the Senate until this can be straightened out all around–'

'The hell it is!' cried Stanton Latham, throwing a cigar stub towards a loaded ashtray. 'I want that bill through the Senate as soon as possible. I need that water coming over my land within the next five years if I'm to expand into cotton–'

'Fat chance you have of getting pickers for cotton,' Galdeston interrupted. 'They won't pick fruit for less than twenty cents an hour – you can't make a profit on cotton at that price.'

'Oh, it'll come down,' Latham said, 'it's bound to.' He glanced at Greg. 'That is, if soft-hearted landowners don't give them ideas above their station.'

'Now, Stan, McGarth was only trying an experiment,' soothed Galdeston. 'And now he's seen what a mistake it was, he's not going to do it again.'

'That right, McGarth?' asked a voice. 'You going to shovel away the ashes and forget it? It sure was a mistake!'

Greg hesitated. 'I shan't be rebuilding in the foreseeable future, if that's what you mean.'

'Good man! It's only a fool who doesn't learn by experience.'

'But I'm going to find out who was responsible and see that they hang,' Greg ended, as if the other man had not spoken.

'I don't see how you'll do that,' Galdeston said in a tone of polite regret. 'As I heard it, the sheriff's getting nowhere.'

'That's what I hear too. The appeal for witnesses to come back has done no good. So how's he going to find out the guys that did it, with no descriptions to go on?' someone asked.

'I know the sheriff has come to a dead end. But that doesn't end it as far as I'm concerned. I intend to find the men and have them tried for murder.'

'You do? How are you going to do that?'

'I've contacted a firm of private detectives. They're working on it now—'

'Aw, private detectives! What can they do that the cops can't do? You're throwing your money away,' Galdeston said.

'Oh, I can be of some help to them,' Greg said. 'I have contacts throughout the state. I've been able to give them introductions that may prove useful.'

'Among your Spanish friends, you mean?' Joe Barrald suggested, with a hint of scorn.

'Among those, yes.'

Dick Galdeston sat up straight, to look with attention at his well-polished cowboy boots. He affected Western dress, to draw attention to his whipcord muscles and tanned face. 'Listen, McGarth, we're sorry as hell at what happened to your wife and half-brother, but don't lose your sense of proportion. It was clearly a drunken spree that got out of hand. The guys responsible probably don't even remember what they did.'

'I remember,' Gregor said. 'And I think the men who paid them remember.'

'Paid them?'

'What the hell d'you mean by that?' There was a sudden rush of questions.

'It was too much of a co-incidence that they struck my place just when the new cabins were filling up with workers. It was meant by someone as a lesson to me. I intend to find out who paid the fire-raisers.

I'll do it through my own contacts if the police won't do it.'

'I never heard such rubbish!'

'What d'you think you're pulling here, McGarth?'

'Is he out of his head, or what?'

Over the noise, Dick Galdeston raised his voice. 'Are you saying you'll use your position to pursue a personal vendetta?'

'I shall use whatever means I can. The police would welcome my help, I feel sure.'

'Say, you ought to be careful what you do, McGarth,' Galveston advised. 'You're a government appointee. If you start misusing your office, you could be quite easily be removed.'

The other landowners looked at Galveston nervously. He rose to his feet, a tall, handsome figure in slim tan trousers and matching shirt with piped edging to the pockets and cuffs. He picked up his wide-brimmed hat from under his chair, dusted it mechanically against his leg.

'I guess as far as I'm concerned the business of the afternoon is over,' he said. 'When we re-convene, I hope we talk a lot more sense than we have today, both as regard the land rights and everything else.'

'Hear, hear,' murmured the others, and

rose to follow him.

All except Rafael Mendoza, the lawyer. He stood by the table putting documents into a Morocco leather attache case. 'Mr McGarth,' he said, 'I don't know why I should feel it, but I think you made an enemy today.'

'That may be so,' Gregor agreed.

'I should be very careful. Mr Galdeston is a very wealthy man, very powerful. He has many, many friends in Sacramento.'

Greg shrugged. 'I know that.'

'He will watch you now, like a hawk.'

'What interests me is that he should be so upset over my plan to use private detectives.'

Mendoza shook his silver head. 'No doubt he simply wishes to have the affair forgotten. "Let sleeping dogs lie".'

'Too bad if his wishes have to be disregarded, then.'

'For you, it may be too bad. He could harm you, Mr McGarth.'

'I don't think so,' Greg said.

But before the month was ended, he was proved wrong. He was summoned to Washington for a conference, which in fact turned into a speech of instruction by the director of the department. For reasons of economy, the government had decided to close down its office of Hispano-American Relations in California.

## *Chapter Twelve*

If rich fruit-growers had really plotted to strip Gregor McGarth of his job so as to prevent him from investigating the murder of his wife and half-brother, they had made a big mistake.

Gregor didn't like to claim idealism for himself, but he had taken the post with the Bureau of Hispano-American Relations out of a wish to help solve the racial antagonisms of the region. It had taken up all his working day and much of his spare time.

Now the federal government had told him he was no longer wanted. Very well, he was free now to follow his own wishes.

And his main wish, his burning desire, was to find and bring to justice the men who had killed his wife.

He had no doubt in his own mind that Dick Galdeston was responsible for the so-called economy cut that had put him out of office. That in itself was significant: it seemed to mean that Galdeston had a reason for not wishing the truth to come to light.

To pursue a search for grounds to indict a man like Galdeston was a risky business. It would have to be done with subtlety and concealment. That meant having people work for him at several removes, and it meant the expense of large sums of money – for Gregor knew that if Galdeston was involved, it would take long months and hard work to uncover his tracks.

Gregor would have been prepared to spend every cent he had to pay for the inquiry. But now he had been set free by some misguided intriguer to earn the money to pay his investigators. One of the things Gregor did best was to make money.

He had always had a natural aptitude for business. The first time his father, Robert Craigallan, had taken him to the Chicago wheat exchange he had been like a young stallion scenting a herd of mares. He had worked with his father, had learnt from him, made a fortune with him, most of which had gone down the drain with the rest of the Craigallan money in the crash of Twenty-nine.

That had not worried him unduly, if he were to think only of himself. Since settling in San Francisco he had bought some land – the orchard estate in the San Joacquin Valley, some coastal lots – which brought him income additional to the salary from the government. Now that salary was gone and in its place he had a 'pension', commensurate with the length of his service but so meagre that it would have meant a great change in living style if it had been his only resource. But with the money coming in from the estate, he was still comfortably off.

That wasn't enough, now. And the dismissal from his post had set him free to make the money he needed. He had not the slightest doubt he could do it.

His first step was to contact the West Coast office of Vinnison and Charle, who had been stockbrokers to the Craigallan family since Robert Craigallan first had ten dollars with which to play the market. He had two days of talks with a young star of the West Coast department, Al Stolovsky. He began to read the financial journals with greater interest than hitherto.

By the time a month had gone by, he had enough feel for the market to start making his moves.

The Depression was still casting its chilly gloom over the world's industries. But Franklin Roosevelt was determined that the United States should lead the way out into the sunshine. It was profitable to invest in government bonds. Then, looking around, Gregor saw that the motor car was becoming more and more a necessity. When he went to Los Angeles on business, he noted that the public transport system was almost non-existent. You had to own a car in that great, sprawling city to be able to go about your business.

It was clear to Gregor that Los Angeles wasn't the only American city built on those lines. So automobiles were going to be a rising market for some time to come. And so was the fuel they consumed.

From the fall of that year into the late summer of the next, Gregor busied himself chiefly with the making of money. He sensed that property in California was going to be a good investment and put more money into it. He had experts from an oil company make geological tests on some land he owned on the coast, and the signs were hopeful – there could be petroleum under his acres of beach sand.

It began to get too big to handle from his

home. He opened an office. He needed people he could trust to man it, so his thoughts turned to his son.

Lewis was working for the New Deal administration in Bakersfield, running a survey on spending patterns of mobile construction crews. The area was having many new roads and water channels built, but the sudden influx of hard-drinking, hard-living engineers with money to spend had upset the locals.

Gregor drove to Bakersfield one weekend to see his son. He put up at a pleasant motel on Highway 99, noting with amusement that the manageress brightened considerably at his arrival and patted her blonde hair into place.

'Is there anything I can do for you?' she inquired with a smile as she handed him the key.

'No, thanks, I'll be going out to dinner by and by – can I get a good steak in the restaurant?'

'Sure can. And you can get drinks by the pool if you just signal to the boy.'

'Thank you. I'm expecting someone, by the way–'

'Oh?' she said, disappointed.

'When he arrives, will you tell him I'm

waiting for him in the restaurant? He'll be along about seven.'

'I certainly will,' she said, brightening. 'Have a nice evening, now.'

'Thank you.' As he went to unlock his cabin Gregor thought about her. She was an attractive woman, perhaps in her late thirties, her blonde hair certainly not natural but well cared for and her perfume not obtrusive.

Perhaps… Yes, perhaps… It had been a long time since he had thought about a woman. Over a year since his wife died…

Lewis turned up rather late. He looked dishevelled and tired. 'Sorry, Dad, something came up at the last moment. Have you ordered yet?'

'No, I thought we'd have a drink first. What'll you have?'

'Scotch on the rocks.'

The cocktail waitress took the order. Gregor studied his son. Lew was working too hard. He looked worn and thin. He hadn't bothered to change before coming on from his office in Bakersfield. His shirt was crumpled, his suit needed pressing. Only the bright dark eyes – so like his mother's – had the same energy still.

They sipped their drinks. Lewis sighed

and relaxed. 'It's been a hell of a day,' he said. 'I would have got in touch and cancelled this meeting, but you were on the road somewhere.'

'I'm glad you didn't. I wanted to talk to you about something important, Lew.'

'Yeah, I can guess. Come into your new business with you and help you make money. Well, you ought to know, Dad, it's a waste of time to say it.'

'It won't be a waste when you hear the rest. Lew, I'm not back in harness making money just for the love of it. I have a reason–'

'Oh yes, I know – you feel you have to provide for Bess and young Cory – as if Regalo itself weren't enough for the kid.'

'It's not that. Listen to me, Lew. Don't jump to conclusions all the time. I need money at my command–'

'I can't see why you need *more*. You can't live in more than one house, eat more than one dinner–'

'Don't give me basic Marxist twaddle. Of course I can't live in more than one house. But I can *use* money, I can make it work–'

'So as to earn more money. I know, it's the classic stock exchange crap–'

'I need it to pay people to work for me.

I've got a plan that's been in operation for nearly a year–'

'Why does it always seem to give so much pleasure to have other people at your beck and call?' Lewis wondered. 'I've seen it so often–'

'Oh, for God's sake, stop *patronising* me for a poor benighted capitalist!' shouted Gregor.

At neighbouring tables, diners turned their heads to stare.

'Listen, Lew,' Gregor said more quietly, 'I need the money to help me track down the men who killed your mother.'

If he had intended to silence Lewis he couldn't have chosen a better way. The younger man stared at him with his mouth half open and his black eyes like pools of dark amazement.

'Now will you listen to the rest of what I have to say?' his father went on. 'I've got some leads on who hired those thugs. I'm trying to track down witnesses who can identify them. The whole thing costs a fortune to run, and it's a kind of thing I need to give my attention to. I need someone to keep an eye on the San Francisco office from time to time while I'm away. I need someone I can trust, for information comes through it that has to do with the investigation.'

'My God...!' said Lewis with something like a groan.

'Do you understand? I'm not just piling up money for the sake of it – though it's good to have it again, I don't deny that. I won't pretend that I don't enjoy being someone to reckon with in the financial arena. But that's not the main point. I needed cash to pay a small army of private investigators and I went back to the stock exchange to make it.'

'But I thought the police had closed down the inquiry? That there was nowhere to go with it?'

'Oh, Lew! You know better than that, surely. The police didn't bother too much. They maybe had a shrewd idea of what they might uncover and didn't want to know. They're only too happy to leave it in the filing cabinet. But there *are* leads – not very clear as yet, but that's coming along.'

For a moment his son stared down at the table. Then he took a sip of his whisky before saying, 'I understand your feelings. But will it really do any good to have six or seven men arrested? They were probably put up to it by somebody else – we all sensed that. What good is it to punish them?'

'I'm not aiming at the cat's-paws. I want the people who paid them. In the long run I'll get them. But I need help, Lew. I need someone to stand at my back. I want that someone to be you.'

The waitress hovered with the menus. 'Would you care to order now, gentlemen? And can I get you another drink?'

They ordered steaks and salad. It seemed to Gregor that his son was glad of the excuse not to answer his request. When the girl had gone with a saucy sway of hips, Gregor put out a hand and caught Lewis's sleeve. 'Answer me. Will you come into this with me?'

'Oh, Dad! If only you'd confided in me from the start!'

'What do you mean?'

'I thought… When I saw you going into the stock market, manipulating shares… I thought you were just burying yourself in the pleasure of making money for the sake of something to do. I'd no idea you had a use for the money. I wish I'd…'

'What's all this about, Lew? You're not going to say no to me?'

'I have to, Dad.'

'What on God's earth for? You can't be doing anything more important than helping me track down those murderers!' To his own surprise, his voice was thick with rage. He withdrew his hand from Lewis's arm, leaned back. 'Is that it, then? You think trotting around collecting statistics for the New Deal is more important than justice for your mother?'

'Justice... I suppose that's what it is. But there's revenge in it too, isn't there?'

'Yes, revenge! Why the hell not? Don't you want to see them suffer, the bastards that cut her life off?' He shook his head, perplexed and hurt. 'She never harmed anyone in her life, you know, except when she had to fight to survive in Manila. But she knew what it is to want revenge. Her parents were killed by guerrillas, she didn't just run away afterwards – she stayed and fought. That's what I want us to do, Lewis. I want to fight back. And who else should help me, if not you?'

'I can't. I'm going away.'

'Where to? Look, if it's some silly job for Roosevelt, put it aside for now. The Depression is still going to be around in six months' time, you'll still have plenty waiting for you when we crack this thing.'

'No, I'm not going to do something for Roosevelt. I'm going to Spain.'

Gregor frowned and was silent. The waitress came with two huge oval platters bearing steaks an inch think. She set them down, offered mustard, french dressing for the salad, refilled their glasses of iced water, and went away with a smile of encouragement.

'May I ask what the devil you're going to Spain for?' Gregor inquired as soon as she was out of earshot.

'You must have seen the newspaper reports, Dad. The Republican Government is losing the fight against Franco's armies. I'm going to help them.'

'Help them? What, by collecting statistics?'

'I'm going to fight. I'm joining the International Brigade.'

Gregor pushed his plate of food away untouched. 'You're going to carry a gun?'

'Yes.'

'For the Republican Government of Spain?'

'Yes.'

'You think it's more important to fight for them than for justice for your own mother?'

Lewis coloured up under his pale skin, turning away so that he didn't need to meet the accusation in his father's eyes. 'I don't know about that. The whole thing is new to me. I haven't had a chance to weigh them one against the other.'

'But now that you do?' Greg returned eagerly. 'Now that you know? You'll stay and help me – I know you will.'

'I can't, Dad. I can't back out now.'

'Good God, of course you can! It's not as if you're conscripted. You're a volunteer, right? You can change your mind.'

'I can't, Dad,' Lew said, in agonised tones. 'A bunch of us are going together. I can't chicken out at the last minute like this. They'd think I was scared.'

'What does it matter what they think? You'd know you had a good reason to change your mind – the best reason in the world–'

'No, it isn't,' Lew broke in. 'It's a personal vendetta, when you come right down to it. All right, I'm not saying you're wrong to want to bring them to book – but there's something bigger at stake in Spain, Dad. It's the fate of a whole country.'

'Lew, I'm not indifferent to what happens to Spain. For God's sake, your mother was Spanish, we have relations over there still. And let me tell you, they'll be on the opposite side from you if you land in their country to take up arms for the Republicans! What's it got to do with us? There are half a dozen countries in turmoil–'

'But this one we can maybe save, Dad! In this one, the fate of democracy is being decided–'

'Oh, for Christ's sake! Spain's had a dozen governments since the war. If this one fails, another will take over–'

'But it'll be a Fascist government. And don't you understand – Germany's just waiting to see whether it really pays to take up arms. She's watched Mussolini invade Ethiopia and get away with it, but after all, they think the Ethiopians are just a bunch of savages. If Franco can take over a developed nation–'

'Lew, I don't want to argue politics. I'm asking you, for the sake of your family – for family honour, if you like – to stay here in California and help me run down those killers.'

They sat looking at each other. Then after a pause Lewis McGarth got up stiffly and held out his hand. 'I'm sorry, Dad, I signed papers this afternoon that give me passage on a ship leaving New York in two days' time for Spain. I can't change my mind, I have to go. Wish me luck.'

A frightening mixture of emotions seized Gregor McGarth. Anger, resentment, grief, anxiety, affection, and at last a tinge of pride.

For, however wrongheaded the boy might be, he had the courage of his convictions. He was going to fight for the right, as he saw it. Good lord, how can you be such a fool, Gregor cried within himself to his son. He understood that Lewis saw himself as Ivanhoe on a white horse, fighting the wicked black knight. But war isn't like that, he wanted to tell him, not at all like that!

Gregor had seen war, in the Philippines when he rescued his brother from captivity and brought home Francesca as his bride. He had seen it again in Mexico as he tried to steer the negotiations for peace between his own country and the revolutionary government. Both times he had seen Spaniards – men of Spanish descent – in combat.

The Spanish can be very cruel, he wanted to warn his son. Don't think it will be easy. You'll be lying out in the sun, with your tongue sticking to the roof of your mouth from thirst, and your clothes smelling of your own sweat and dirt. You'll be running and jinking to avoid rifle fire, you'll be leaping and falling into ditches to take cover from shells.

And if you're hit – oh, God, if you're hit – there'll be no maiden with her hair in a golden fillet to tend you. There'll be flies pestering the wound, and some untrained first-aid corpsman to slap a dressing on it, if you're lucky, and then back into the lines unless you're so bad they have to truck you to a hospital.

He wanted to groan, don't go! Don't expose yourself to horrors you've never even imagined. Even if you come through un-scathed physically, you'll have nightmares, you'll shiver sometimes in the sunlight from some sound, some smell conjuring up what you've experienced.

It all exploded in a growl of loving irritation. 'Sit down, you fool! What did we order all this food for if you're going to march out before we've even tasted it?'

Lewis faltered. 'We-ll… There seems no point in staying if all we're going to do is argue…'

'We're not going to argue. Sit down, eat your dinner. You look as if you need it. And if all I read about conditions in Spain is right, you may not get another meal like this for a long time.'

His son stared at him. A foolish grin began to form about his mouth. He subsided into his chair. 'I never could fathom how your mind worked,' he confessed, and picked up his knife and fork.

The rest of the meal was taken up with a description by Lewis of his travel plans. He and two other young men were setting off from Bakersfield next morning, to reach New York by the evening of Friday, when the *Aurelia* was due to sail for Cherbourg with a party of American volunteers. After that the organisation was vague; there would be an agent in Cherbourg to send them on, it wasn't thought politic to reveal his name or the route they would take.

Neither man ate very much of the excellent steak. They ordered coffee and brandy. They sat over it for a while. 'I really have to go, Dad,' Lewis said. 'I've got things to clear up at the office tonight so it can be handed over to my assistant.'

They went out to the car park. Lewis's shabby Buick was close to the drive-out. Gregor walked to it with him, stood helplessly by while his son got in. 'So long, then,' he said.

Lewis pressed the starter. The car coughed

and groaned, but wouldn't start. 'Oh, God!' cried Lewis. 'It would act up tonight, of all nights. I've *got* to get back to Bakersfield!'

He got out, put up the bonnet, fiddled with connections. 'I don't know. It may be the spark plugs…'

Gregor gave a shaky sigh. 'All right,' he said, 'take mine.'

'What?'

'Take my car.'

'But how will you get back to San Francisco?'

'I'll hire one, for God's sake!'

'But then – your Caddie will be in Bakersfield–'

'I'll have someone drive it back to me, of course. Lewis, if you can't organise a hiccup like this, how're you going to organise a war?'

'I'm not going to organise it, Dad. I'm just going to help fight it.'

Gregor took him by the shoulder and pulled him close. He put his arms around him and hugged him with the protective love that always welled up in him when his children were in trouble. 'Look after yourself, Lew,' he muttered. 'Try for the love of Mike to grow up a bit while you're away!'

Lewis returned the embrace. For a moment

his Spanish heritage took over, he held his father close murmuring, *'Padre, padre, espero poder escribirle – eso non es adios eterno–'*

'But it *is* goodbye, *hijo mio*.'

'But I'll be back soon. The war won't last long.'

'No it won't last long.' But you'll be on the losing side, some inner wisdom told Gregor. Thank God his mother didn't live to see this moment…

When the handsome black Cadillac had driven off, Gregor stood for a long time watching the other traffic passing the entry to the motel's parking lot. The highway was busy, the night-time trucks and buses went surging by in a blare of sound and light. He saw an old Ford van, laden with household goods, stuttering along the slow lane. It reminded him of the migrant workers among whom, dispersed and lost, were the families who might recognise the murderers of Francesca and Cornelius if only he could find them.

He went to his cabin. It was air-conditioned by a unit fixed into the lower half of one of the windows. He lay down on his bed, listening to the hum of its motor, listening to the sounds of the other residents settling down for the night.

But he knew he wouldn't sleep yet. He got up, and some time after midnight, went out to pace about in the landscaped grounds, over the manicured lawns, along the side of the blue-tiled swimming pool which glimmered in the reflected neon light of the motel sign.

A voice called softly. 'Mr McGarth?'

He swung about. It was the manageress. 'Mr McGarth? Is anything wrong?'

'No, thank you. I'm just not ready to sleep.'

'You suffer from insomnia?' she asked in a throaty, sympathetic voice. 'Oh, I do too. And I always find the best thing for it is a good nightcap – a good shot of bourbon with no ice. I've got some in my cabin, Mr McGarth. How about sharing a nightcap with me?'

He hesitated.

'I just got off duty,' she said. 'The night manager comes on at midnight. The owners don't think it right to have a woman on duty at night, you know?' She came up and put her arm through his. 'My name's Alda, Alda Jusset – that's French, originally, my people came from Marseilles. You're of Irish descent? I like the Irish, they're so poetic.'

'Scottish, my parents were Scottish.' He fell into step with her. Why not, he was thinking. I'm not going to get any sleep so why not?

She was kind and helpful, more eager than he for their love-making. She held him in her arms and murmured, 'I know, something's gone wrong, but never mind, honey, everything passes in the end.' She kept him with her until the first faint rays of light began to show at the sides of the window-drapes. 'I have to get some sleep now,' she said with a sigh. 'I've got work to do, after all. Will I see you when I get back on duty?'

'No, I have to get back to San Francisco.'

'So, it's goodbye, then. Goodbye, sweetheart. I hope everything turns out all right, whatever it is.'

'Thank you, Alda.'

They didn't say, If ever you're in San Francisco, look me up. Or, Perhaps you'll be by this way again. They both knew this was a once-only event.

She was already snuggling down to sleep as he dressed. He hesitated a long while about whether to leave some money on the night-table but decided that would be crass. After some thought he put his gold cigarette lighter there, and scribbled a note: 'Just a memento.' She could keep it or sell it, it didn't matter.

He ordered breakfast, then while he waited for it telephoned for a hire car, arranging for the Buick to be towed away and repaired. It would be stored in the big garage at Montemoreno until Lewis came back. He wouldn't let himself think, If he comes back.

He drove away early, feeling sad and dissatisfied and empty. There was some self-disgust in his state of mind. How could he have gone to bed with someone so casually – a woman he didn't even know beyond the name and the few words they had murmured to each other in the darkness?

Francesca, Francesca, he said over and over to himself as he drove home to Montemoreno. It was like a litany said in penance. But it didn't exonerate him from his self-reproach.

## Chapter Thirteen

The band was playing 'Harbour Lights'. The vocalist was singing with his face close to the stand microphone: 'Then those same harbour lights, Will bring your love to me-e.' The svelte figures of girls in bias-cut evening gowns moved dreamily in the arms of men in dinner jackets.

Clare McGarth was the energetic type. She was foxtrotting as if she enjoyed it. Her partner, with plans for what remained of the night, was trying to save his strength.

He was more than a little tight. The champagne in the Causerie Club was expensive but he had the money to pay for the three bottles consumed by himself and his guests. His name was Ronald Talhurst, youngest son of a wealthy noble family. His family didn't approve of his 'goings-on' in London, particularly his association with an American girl of no parentage worth mentioning.

American girls weren't much in favour in London at present. One of them – and not very young or sexy, either – had captured the heir to the British throne. For several agonising months the British had been the subject of tittering gossip all around the world, and more especially in America, where it hurt most.

Now the agony was over, the former Edward the Eighth was now the Duke of Windsor, Wallis Simpson was the Duchess of Windsor, and a very suitable young man married to a very suitable young woman and with two pretty little daughters had succeeded to the throne. The coronation had taken place, London had been *en fête*, and yet ... and yet...

It had been a worrying year. The French had been working hard on their Maginot Line, as if they really expected the Germans to attack. The town of Guernica had been destroyed by Franco's airmen. There had been a two-week bus strike in London, raising hobgoblins of fear about Communism and the breakdown of society. Japanese troops in China had taken, with apparent ease, Peking, Tientsin and all the provinces adjoining. Benito Mussolini had visited Berlin and been given a show-off reception by the Nazis who really seemed to have endless regiments of handsome blond young men to parade before him with banners.

Worst of all, as far as the McGarth family were concerned, the Spanish government had been forced to retreat to Barcelona, so that it was clear the end was in sight. The last letter received from Lewis McGarth had been from some shell-battered little village in the north, speaking reassuringly of reinforcements expected every moment and the hope of some relief from the still-fierce September sun of Spain. Since then, nothing, although it was almost December.

Gina Gramm sat at a table on the edge of the dance floor watching her cousin swaying in the arms of the thin, elegant Englishman. At her side, Peter Brunnen was wrinkling his nose at the poor quality champagne in his glass. 'Why can't they have some good German hock?' he muttered. 'Cheaper and better than this fizzy rubbish.'

'We'll go soon, Peter. I promised Clare I'd rescue her from Ronnie and she's just given me the sign.'

Peter made a face. 'You women!' he said. 'We think we're laying such clever traps and all the time you have your escape route worked out!'

'Oh, well if that lad thought he was going to get Clare drunk on nightclub champagne, he has another think coming, as they say here.'

The song's reprise having ended, the band swung to a close with a long rattle on the snare drum. It was time for the players to have a break for a smoke and a beer. One o'clock in the morning, and the customers were beginning to think about wending their way home – or wherever else they had in mind.

Clare arrived at the table looking fresh and untired. Her dress of strawberry satin set off the remains of her summer tan. She must go to Elizabeth Arden to have it removed, for the winter season was well under way and it wasn't considered good taste to look tanned after November – not unless you were in Monte Carlo or Cannes, and even there the French girls liked to gleam ivory-white in their long dark gowns.

Clare's partner sank down on a chair. He looked much less chipper than Clare. 'We'll have another little drinkie, shall we?' he suggested. 'Just to keep the party going.'

'I'm afraid we can't, Ronnie,' Gina replied with the faintest of winks at Clare. 'I promised I'd get Clare home by one-thirty – she has a golf date for ten tomorrow – today, I mean – at Sunningdale.'

'Oh, good Lord, plenty of time for that—'

'But I need my sleep if I'm to play well, Ronnie dear. So I really must go.'

'Righty-o, then, I'll just have the car brought round—'

'It's kind of you, Ronnie, but we've ordered a taxi,' Gina said. 'So it's goodnight for now. Thanks for a lovely evening.'

'But look here—'

'Night-night, Ronnie,' Clare said, stooping to plant a little kiss on the top of his smooth head. 'Give me a ring some time and we'll do it again. You foxtrot awfully nicely.'

Peter shepherded them out. In the foyer the doorman whistled up a taxi from the rank at the corner. They were getting in before Ronnie Talhurst could gather his wits about him and his energy to come after them with a protest.

Clare had given the address of her flat. The two girls had moved out of the King's Road to a handsomer and larger place in Belgravia. Clare's father had raised her allowance by a very large degree once his income began to flourish, so that she was spared the necessity of finding a job of any kind. When she moved out of Chelsea and invited her cousin to go with her Gina had no compunction in accepting. A good address was an asset in making a success in London.

They invited Peter in for coffee and a sandwich. He was complaining about the scantiness of the food in the nightclub. 'Not enough to feed a sparrow,' he said, 'and I suppose they charge the earth for it?'

'I think they do, but most people don't go for the food.'

'I wonder what they do go for?' he mused. 'The band was quite good but the wine was terrible.'

'Oh, you and your thing about wine! Most people don't care so long as it makes them feel pleasantly pie-eyed.'

'Pie-eyed? My God, what have pies got to do with being drunk? I shall never understand the American language!'

'Here,' said Gina, giving him the bread on a board with the knife, 'cut yourself two thick slices. What will you have in it? Ham? Cheese?'

'I suppose you have no *Liverwürst*? No? Well, I must make do with ham.' He built himself a huge sandwich.

Gina watched in fascination. 'I don't know what happens to all the food you eat, Peter. You never get any fatter.'

'Thank God. I'm told part of my fascination is the lean and hungry look.'

'Nonsense, it's the voice,' Clare remarked, setting out cups and saucers for the coffee. 'That rich, soft voice. It's like dark sherry – makes women movie-goers feel weak at the knees.'

They talked about the film Peter was making at Denham. The project with Jesse Matthews had fallen through, but Bert Kolin had negotiated a part for him in a new film with that interesting director Alfred Hitchcock. It was to follow *The Lady Vanishes*, which had recently been a big box office success both in Britain and America.

Meanwhile Peter was filming *Present Company*, a comedy-drama about an accident-prone teacher of languages. It allowed him more chance to act than anything he'd done in Hollywood, which made him enthusiastic.

'Did Magda like it?' Gina asked, referring to a visit he had arranged for his wife to the set.

He shrugged and was silent. Then he turned to Clare. 'Clare, may I ask you something?'

'Me? Yes, of course. What?'

She was surprised. Although she and Peter had become quite good friends, it was well understood that he was more attached to Gina.

'Are you in any way involved with that young man who was with you tonight?'

'Ronnie? Good heavens, no!'

'Or anyone else?'

'What's this about, Peter? Are you making a study of my love-life?'

'Yes, I am,' he said, replying seriously to the quip. 'I'm doing it on behalf of a friend of mine.'

'Really? You amaze me. Who can be so interested in my affairs?'

'Kay Yung,' Peter said.

At Clare's gasp of hurt surprise, Gina looked up. She'd thought her cousin had managed to forget Kay in the months in London.

'What about Kay?' Clare asked, putting out a hand to steady herself against the kitchen table.

'Have you heard from him?'

'No. We agreed there was no point in keeping in touch.'

'I believe he still thinks the same. But I think he's wrong, Clare. He's been going through a hard time.'

Clare flashed a look at Peter from her dark eyes which seemed to ask, And do you think

I haven't? But she bent her head and made no reply.

'You saw about those Japanese planes sinking the USS Panay?'

'Well … yes, I read it in the newspapers. Why?'

'It stirred up an awful lot of anti-Japanese feeling in America. The State Department managed to smooth it down on the diplomatic front but ordinary people were very upset.'

'What has that to do with Kay?' Clare asked, frowning.

'My dear girl, don't you understand, those angry patriots, they don't know a Chinese from a Japanese! They've been going round beating up anyone with a yellow complexion and slanted eyes. Kay was chased by a gang of boys in a car on the freeway–'

'Oh, no! He didn't have a crash?'

'He did, Clare – he turned over. Luckily he got off with cuts and bruises, but he had to be rescued from the young men – his assailants, is that right? – by the highway patrol.'

'That's terrible! That's awful! Were they put in prison? I hope they were! I hope they locked them up and threw away the key.'

'Clare, that's not the point. That isn't what

371

I wanted to tell you. Kay was told by the police that if he wanted to avoid prosecution – no, persecution – he ought to wear a badge.'

'A badge?'

'They're on sale all over the West Coast. "I am a Patriotic American" Or "I am Chinese American"–'

'Good God!' Gina exclaimed. 'That's like what we hear about the Nazis – making the Jews wear the Star of David...'

'It certainly isn't what you and I would enjoy,' Peter said with a grim nod, 'and Kay got very angry. So he went and volunteered for the army.'

'What?'

'He said he'd do better than buy a badge, he'd wear a uniform. So he went into the army base at Glendale and signed on.' Peter paused. 'Signed up? Signed on?'

Gina shook her head at him. This was no time for the finer points of the English language. 'Where is he now?'

'In training camp. He called me just before I left Hollywood.'

'How ... how does he sound?' Clare asked, her voice trembling with a mixture of emotions that she could scarcely control.

'Not particularly happy. His family are

urging him to get out of the army – I believe there is some method of revoking the decision within a certain time, and perhaps there is a fee to be paid. But he won't do that. He's suddenly become a very angry and stubborn man.'

Clare looked stunned. 'Kay? Defying his family? No wonder he's unhappy.'

'It's not that. He told me he'd hoped to be sent to China after basic training – there's a small contingent of American troops guarding the embassies and consulates. But they're planning to send him to an army information unit. He's going to make documentary films for the army.'

'Well, that makes good sense, if you ask me,' said Gina. 'Didn't you tell me, Clare, that he was one of the best cameramen in Hollywood?'

Clare said nothing. Peter took it up. 'He was indeed – I wasn't important enough to have him on any of my films but I heard what others spoke of him, and of course I met him from time to time. I … ah … I was aware that you had been friendly with him, Clare. Someone gossiped to me about it. Forgive me for telling you that. But it made me feel that … you might want to know what happened.'

'I still can't believe it. Kay – in the *army*!'

'When I told him I was coming to London and might be seeing you, I asked if I should tell you this. He said no. And then he said… "Write and let me know if she's married some other guy by now".'

'As if I could suddenly marry someone else! He must have *known* I wouldn't!'

'It is more hard to be sure of what other people are feeling than you seem to think, dear Clare,' Peter said. His smile had a tinge of ruefulness. 'But, when I learn that you are not interested in other young men, I think you might like to have the address of Kay Yung at his training camp. Also his telephone number, *ja*?'

'Oh, Peter! What an angel you are!'

'Here they are,' he said. He took an address book from his inside jacket pocket. He then looked at his watch. 'I should like to remind you also that though it is nearly two in the morning in London, in California it is the afternoon – which might make a very suitable time to telephone to a young man at an army training camp.'

'Oh yes! Oh, what a good idea! Oh, Peter!' She rushed upon him, kissed him fervently, hugged him hard, and ran out of the kitchen, across the hall, and into her bedroom.

Peter brushed his unruly hair down after the encounter. 'Well, it is always pleasant to play cupid.'

'An unlikely form for cupid to take. But thank you, Peter.'

'I am pleased to do it. There are enough unhappy people in the world, no?'

'I agree.' Gina got up, refilled their coffee cups. 'More to eat? Some cake?'

'Cake?' He looked hopeful. But when she produced the thick rich English pound cake from a tin, he shook his head. 'No one makes cakes like those I used to get in the Unter den Linden cafés...'

'You couldn't afford cake in those days, Peter.'

'Oh sometimes ... yes ... when I had made some money singing Bach in a church festival...' He sighed and shook his head. 'I wonder if they still have church festivals these days? Or is it all arm-salutes and flag-waving?'

'Peter, what happened with Magda? You avoided speaking of her when I asked earlier.'

He drank his coffee.

'Don't you want to talk about it?'

'What good does it do? Her mind is made up.'

'To do what?'

'To go back. She has been offered the role of Senta – *Senta*! – in *Der Fliegende Hollander* at the Berlin Oper in February.'

'I don't know opera, Peter. Is it a very good offer?'

'You don't know *The Flying Dutchman*? Senta is the heroine. It is a very big role. A great honour – I don't know how she will handle it – her voice is not a Wagnerian voice. Not yet, at any rate.'

'Surely the director of the opera wouldn't offer her the part–'

'The director of the Berlin Oper does as he is told!' Peter said with sudden disgusted anger. 'The Nazi bosses tell him what to put on and who to hire, and he does it. I am ashamed – *ashamed* – to see what is happening. And Wagner – all the time it is Wagner. The music may be magnificent – although for me it is too grandiose, too self-important – but this sudden admiration of Wagner is because Adolf Hitler thinks his music typifies the great German soul. And so Magda is going home to sing for him.'

'Is that it? That diplomatic thing really came off in the end?'

'It seems so. I suppose the opera director tried not to go along with it but in the end whoever pulls the strings has made the puppet dance. So now Magda goes. She leaves in two days time. She has to rehearse the role – she has never sung it, never expected to, if she were to tell the truth.'

Gina listened with distress but with perfect acceptance. She'd always expected Magda Ledermann to get to the top of the opera world and this unexpected glorification of German singers in German opera was just the opportunity she needed.

'Did you try to persuade her not to go?'

'Of course! I tried to tell her that in the first place these idiots now in power must fall in some *coup d'etat* one day. It is inevitable. Also I said that artistically it was a mistake, that the rest of the world had no respect for musicians who elbowed out Jewish performers and took their place. That to sing Wagner for Adolf Hitler would do her no good in her future career.'

'And what did she say?'

'She told me I ought to be reported as an unpatriotic German.' He laughed. 'And she said I should withdraw from the Hitchcock film, because his last – *The Lady Vanishes* – was very anti-Nazi.'

'Oh, Peter.'

He got up and began to collect up the

used coffee cups. He put them in the sink and ran water on them.

'Don't bother with those. The daily will do them in the morning, Peter.'

'It is pleasant to do it. It reminds me of when we were poor music students, Magda and I. She would make pretty little meals from scraps of expensive meat and noodles, and I would wash up the dishes afterwards, still feeling hungry but never liking to tell her I would rather have had a big piece of bread and cheese...' He put the cups and saucers one by one on the enamelled draining board. 'What happened to us, Gina? I thought we loved each other enough to survive separation, but it wasn't so. We just drifted apart.'

She wanted to say, It's not your fault. You did your best. She went up to him, put her hand on his arm. 'Don't grieve about it. These things happen.'

'I haven't told you the worst.'

'What's that?'

'She wants a divorce.'

She stared up at him.

'I'm an embarrassment to her. She's going to be an important singer. Von Ribbentrop has recommended her personally to Hitler. She doesn't want to have it said she has a husband who makes second-rate films for foreign film companies.'

'Is that what she said?'

He picked up the cloth and began to wipe the cups with unnecessary vigour. 'No, she just said we had been separated so long she felt I was a stranger.'

'Whose fault is that?' Gina cried. 'You asked her often enough to come to Hollywood. You even sent her the money–'

'What does it matter whose fault it is? I came to London on purpose to repair our marriage. I thought once we spent time together, slept together as man and wife... But even that was no use. She didn't want to. She ... she's had lovers, and I don't blame her for that. I have had my own consolations, God knows. But she made it so clear that I came second-best to the others.'

Gina was angry on his behalf. Why couldn't he be angry too? But she knew the answer. It was because he was the kind of man who formed strong attachments and couldn't easily break them. Magda had been his first love and so far was his only real love. Without her his life would seem to have had little purpose – for it was because of Magda he had given up his own ambitions as a singer and become a film actor.

'Perhaps it's best,' she suggested, as gently as she could. 'Perhaps it's best to have it ended, and make a new start.'

If Peter had any reply to that, it was prevented by the eruption of Clare into the kitchen. 'He's fine! He was so pleased to hear from me! He... he hardly knew how to speak to me. Oh, Peter, thank you for telling me!'

Gina smiled at her fervour of delight. 'You got through all right, then?'

'Oh yes, it was just as if he were in the next room. He was surprised at first ... I ... I maybe sounded a bit strange. I was in floods of tears. Anyhow, I'm flying home tomorrow. Where's the directory, Gina? I must telephone Pan-American and see if I can get on the Clipper. I promised Kay I'd... Oh, I'm so happy, Gina!'

Her thrilled excitement was infectious. Gina hugged her in congratulation, Peter shook hands and kissed her. They helped her find the number for Pan-American's office. When she went back to telephone, Peter said he thought it was time to go home and leave them to sort themselves out.

She went to the door with him. 'It's awfully late. Have you a studio call for tomorrow?'

'No, they're doing something technical with special effects, a long scene in which I don't appear.'

'Thank you, Peter, for what you did for Clare. She's all of a sudden a different person.'

'And you, Gina? You too are a different person. Where is the confidently happy woman I spoke to at San Francisco airport?'

She shook her head, looking away.

'What happened? Did the wife cause trouble?'

'Yes. But not in the way you mean, Peter.' She sighed. 'I met her, you see. When I went to Paris for that limited teaching contract. And once I'd met her...'

'I see. She was too nice for you to want to hurt her.'

'It was simpler even than that. I just ... couldn't understand why Michel would want anyone else. We didn't quarrel or anything, I just found I was avoiding him. So that was the end of it – what does that sad poet say? "Not with a bang but a whimper."'

'I'm sorry. Or at least – perhaps I'm glad. It seemed a waste for you to be in love with a man who couldn't give you anything worth having.'

'Oh, it was worth having, Peter. He was really fond of me. But it seemed better to end it all while we were still friends, rather than… Oh well, it's a small thing, compared with you and Magda. I hope she changes her mind, dear – about the divorce.'

'I don't think she will.'

They kissed a friendly goodnight. She closed the door behind him. On the bedroom extension she could hear Clare exclaiming: 'Not until day after tomorrow? But that's awful!'

The day after tomorrow – and then Clare would be re-united with the man she loved. Happy for her, and yet with something like envy, Gina went to fetch Clare's suitcase from the roomy cupboard off the hall.

The next day and a half were a rush of packing, telephoning, letter-writing. Gina neglected her own little office in Wardour Street to help clear up Clare's affairs. 'The lease of this place is paid up until next June so please feel free to stay on here, Gina. And there's quite a big balance in my bank account in Piccadilly – I've made arrangements so that you can draw cheques on it until the money runs out.'

'Oh, but I can't–'

'I'm sure Daddy would want it that way.

And these clothes I'm leaving – I don't mean to be patronising, but if you can make any use of them, please do, Gina. Or sell them – they're couture clothes, you ought to get something for them. And if Ronny Talhurst rings, tell him I've gone home. That'll shake him! – he thought he'd manoeuvred me almost into bed with him.'

'Instead of which, you're rushing off to the arms of another man.' Gina paused. 'What's going to happen, Clare? Between you and Kay?'

'We're going to get married.'

'He's asked you?'

'No, but we talked about his family. He says he's gone against their wishes once, he feels he might get into the habit. And I know he wants to be married, to have children. Children are very important to the Chinese.'

'And to you?'

Clare's face was lit up as if from within by a soft, slow warmth. 'Oh yes,' she said in a low voice, 'I'd love to have Kay's children.'

When she had gone, the big flat seemed strangely empty. Gina became aware that she was alone, far from home in a strange city where rumours of war became more frequent with each passing week. Winston Churchill made a great outcry about what

383

he called the 'appeasement' of the Italian dictator Mussolini by the British Prime Minister, Neville Chamberlain. In Spain, General Franco drove on to Vinaroz, which he took after a bloody struggle. Germany under its new foreign minister, Magda's friend von Ribbentrop, made extravagant claims over parts of Czechoslovakia but backed down when the other European powers stood firm.

'That is the way to treat Adolf Hitler,' Peter declared to Gina. 'If they only have the sense to go on saying no to him, the population at home will get tired of doing without decent food and clothes and will throw him out!'

Clare telephoned every now and then. She was extremely happy. She and Kay were to be married in June, when he had finished training and been assigned to his film-making unit. 'The army have given us a really marvellous honeymoon!' she told Gina. 'What do you think, they've posted Kay to Hawaii!'

'Oh, what marvellous luck! Hawaii! That's an absolute dream island, I hear!'

'Kay's awfully pleased. Of course it's beautiful scenery – what he calls photogenic. We sail in three weeks.'

'What about the wedding, Clare?'

'It's going to be at City Hall,' Clare said, with what Gina heard as a faint shadow of regret.

'Your mother would have wanted a church wedding, Clare.'

'But that would have meant a long argument with the priests about the religion of the children. And Kay's parents wouldn't have liked it.'

'Are they going to be there?'

'Of course. Eldest son gets married – the parents have to be there!'

'And Uncle Greg?'

'Him too.'

'How did he take it when you told him about Kay, Clare?'

'Well, it wasn't the most enjoyable moment of his life,' Clare said, 'but he survived.'

She remembered it as she spoke. Her Aunt Bess had given a little celebratory dinner for Clare's unexpected return home, as yet unexplained. After the welcome-home cake had been cut and a piece put by for young Cory, Claire had asked to speak to her father alone.

He took her to his study. 'Well?' he said. 'I knew there was something behind this sudden dash back to California.'

'I'm getting married, Daddy.'

His face changed. Something that was half a frown, half a smile, went across it. 'To some handsome European? This Ronnie Talhurst you've mentioned in your letters?'

'No, to a man called Kay Yung. I left California last year because it all seemed so hopeless, what with prejudice and Kay's parents being likely to oppose the marriage…'

'Kay Yung?' Gregor said, suddenly hearing the name.

'I've known him a long time, Daddy. This isn't a sudden decision. I'd like to bring him to meet you tomorrow.'

'Are you telling me,' Gregor said, 'that you've fallen for a Chinaman?'

Clare was surprised at her own anger. 'He's a sergeant in the United States army,' she said in a very sharp tone, 'and is fourth generation American, which makes him more American than me, because I'm only third generation.'

She'd expected an argument from her father. And true enough, he looked very surprised, very dubious. She hurried on: 'We could have had an affair but we didn't want that. We want to settle down. I've wasted enough of my life, Daddy, rushing around after silly things. Now I realise what's really important. I want to get married and have children.'

To her amazement her father laughed with genuine delight, throwing an arm about her shoulders. 'Well, daughter,' he said, 'they ought to be lively little imps, my grandchildren – Scottish-Spanish-Chinese inheritance! They ought to be worth watching!'

So now there was to be a civil ceremony in San Francisco, and then Clare and Kay were to sail to Hawaii, where they would have two weeks' honeymoon before Kay had to report for duty with the U.S. Army Information Cinematographic Unit.

There were two more pieces of family news during that twelvemonth. Lewis McGarth surfaced in the Basque region of France, having been smuggled out by an underground rescue team run by anti-Franco peasants. He was safe and, apart from the after-effects of a leg wound and extreme exhaustion, well enough. Since the doctors ordered him to stay in Biarritz to recuperate, Gina volunteered to go visiting him. She found him changed: thinner, darker, and less idealistic. He was bitter about the course of the war in Spain. 'The United Nations isn't going to do a damn thing to save the legal Spanish government,' he said. 'They're going to let Franco build up for his big offensive in Catalonia and when he's got the whole thing mopped up and under control, they're going to recognise a Fascist government.'

'You can't know that for certain, Lew. When they get around to it–'

'Get around to it! By the time they stop kow-towing to Hitler and Mussolini, Spain will be under Franco's lock and key.'

'You did all you could, Lew... Put it behind you now.'

'As easy as that?' He frowned at her, dark brows coming together in a dark face thin and gaunt from months of poor food and lack of sleep.

'You have to stop fighting some time. Put it behind you, go home to see your father. He doesn't say much about it but he must be lonely, Lew – his two kids have been away from home for years and now Clare is off in the Pacific, for at least two years.'

'I can't go home.' He shook his head in slow but complete rejection. 'Back there, it's all so ... unreal. What do they know about real life? I wouldn't fit in, Gina. No, I'm going to stay in Europe. That's where the balloon's going to go up one day.'

'Oh, nonsense! I do wish people would stop warmongering! Everything calmed down beautifully after that visit the British Prime Minister made to Munich.'

'Gina, if you believe what that old fool said about "peace in our time", you believe in the Tooth Fairy.'

Nothing she could say would change Lewis's mind. He wouldn't even agree to come to London – back to civilisation, as she phrased it – when the doctors declared him fit. He said he liked the Pyrenees, he intended to stay there. She had an awful premonition he intended to get involved with the anti-Franco mountaineers. But she didn't pass on that premonition to his anxious father.

The other event in the family was the death of Luisa Craigallan in Naples at the age of eighty-three.

Once more Gina volunteered to go. She made the long journey by ferry and train to Naples, arriving very weary on the actual day of the funeral. The official from the American Consulate was the only other mourner. He escorted Gina back to the apartment where her grandmother had lived her last days – a grandiose, mouldering set of rooms in a once-fine villa out along the road to Sorrento.

If she had left anything of value, it had been taken – by thieves or local officials ('The same thing,' muttered John Panton of the consulate. 'Bunch of Crooks!') Her income lately had come from investments made on her behalf by Gregor, but anonymously. She, still hating him, had willed them to her idol, Mussolini. When Gina rang her uncle to tell him, he laughed. 'True to form right to the end,' he remarked. 'Your grandmother never forgave old Rob for fathering me. If there really is a hereafter and they meet there, I bet she's turning her back on him this very minute.'

As to the shares willed to the 'strong man' whom Luisa had so much admired, Gregor wrote them off as a bad debt.

When Gina got back to London she found a little flux of work awaiting for her. Several days went by while she made telephone calls, arranged appointments. Then she bethought herself of her friends and rang them up. She found to her consternation that Peter Brunnen had gone.

An acquaintance explained that the film with Hitchcock had fallen through. Hitchcock was in Hollywood now, planning to film Daphne du Maurier's *Rebecca* in which there was emphatically no part for Peter Brunnen.

Gina took another look through the mail that had collected during her absence but could find nothing from Peter. She waited a few days; nothing came. At length, worried for reasons that had no logical basis, she put through a long distance call to Bert Kolin in Hollywood.

'Gina? Gina Gramm! Say, imagine hearing from you, kiddo! How's tricks in London?'

'Not bad, Bert, not bad. I just got back from Italy and I'm trying to catch up–'

'Italy? Been on holiday? I always wanted to see Rome, you know–'

'Bert, the reason I'm calling is, I wondered if you could give me Peter's address.'

There was a sudden little pause at the other end.

'Bert?'

'I … er … I don't have an address for Peter right now, Gina.'

'What do you mean? Has he changed agents?'

'Changed? Naw, Peter wouldn't do that to me.'

'Then where is he?'

'To tell the truth, honey, I don't know.'

She found it too extraordinary for words. An actor's agent must know where he is. Above and beyond that, Bert was Peter's friend. 'You mean he's back in Hollywood and he hasn't contacted you? Is he disappointed about Hitchcock?'

'Peter isn't in Hollywood, Gina.'

His voice was so flat and unemotional she knew he was very upset. 'What is it, Bert? What's happened?'

'Peter went to Berlin in January.'

'What?'

'I don't know where he is. He didn't discuss it much with me. He left London somewhere around the 28th January and I had a letter dated 8th February saying he was okay and would be in touch. Since then, nothing.'

'But that's over a month ago, Bert!'

'Yeah, well, you know, the mail's been a bit haywire with all these crises that keep coming up. I rang the hotel Peter wrote from in Berlin – that was last week. They said he'd checked out. So maybe he's on his way home.'

'But then the film contract must have fallen through?'

'What film contract?'

'Didn't he go to make a film for UFA?'

'He went,' Bert said with sudden savagery, 'to look for that bitch of a wife of his!'

The story he could tell was scanty. Peter had agreed to Magda's wish to have a divorce and expected to hear from her German lawyer by and by. She had sung Senta in *The Flying Dutchman*, had had several other roles and been well received by the Berlin opera audience. Then, quite suddenly, her name no longer figured in the programmes. More odd still, she didn't contact Peter about a divorce nor did she reply to his letters.

Bert didn't know what steps Peter had taken at first. He thought Peter's parents had been asked to check her address with the Opera House office. It seemed nothing had come of that. Having waited for news for about four months, Peter had decided to go himself in January, the more especially as the films he'd been working on were finished and the Hitchcock film had been cancelled.

'Oh, well...' Gina said. 'I suppose he has a perfect right to go to Berlin to talk to his own wife. But I wish he had let me know.'

'Me too – I wish he'd get in touch.' Bert

coughed. 'Say, Gina … you don't think anything could have happened to him?'

'Like what?'

'I dunno. Germany's a funny place.'

It certainly was, these days, for people of
Bert's religion. But Peter was what Hitler
called an Aryan.

'He might have had an accident, I
suppose?' Gina said. 'Did you contact his
parents?'

'I don't get any answers. I wonder if they
moved?'

'But then the letters would come back.'

'D'you think so? The mail's all to hell and
gone these days, and I haven't tried to
telephone because I don't know who to
call.'

'What about the American Embassy?'

'But Peter's a German national, Gina.'

She'd forgotten that. She'd come to regard
him as an American despite his German
accent and his occasional pretence of
despising things American. 'I suppose,' she
said in a tone of doubt, 'I could make
inquiries at the German Embassy in
London…'

'Would you? Would you, Gina? I'd be
damn grateful! I just want to hear from him,
is all.'

'I'll do it tomorrow, Bert.'

But it wasn't so easy. The officials at the Embassy were not inclined to be co-operative. They wished to know why she should interest herself in Peter Brunnen, who had gone home to Germany as a good German should in time of crisis. 'Does he owe you money? Have you any claim on him?'

'None at all,' Gina said, offended. 'It's simply a matter of friendship. I haven't heard from him in three months, and I wondered how to get in touch, that's all.'

'We have no knowledge of the whereabouts of Herr Brunnen.'

'But could you enquire? Could you find out if he's in a hospital for instance?'

'You believe him to be taken ill?'

'No, it's just a possibility. Or he may have had an accident.'

'We have more important things to do, *gnädige Frau*, than inquire after friends of American ladies. I'm sorry, but if Herr Brunnen went home, as was very proper, he is probably too busy now to keep up friendships abroad.' Improper friendships, was implied by his tone, as he eyed her stylish slim-waisted dress of floral silk and the carefully applied cosmetics on her fine features. Such things were very un-German: German women wore print frocks and no make-up.

Gina tried every method she could think of. She got friends in the film business to put out feelers as to whether Peter had gone to work for UFA. She got friends in Fleet Street to ask foreign correspondents for news. Nothing emerged. Nor could she learn why Magda Ledermann had ceased to appear at the Berlin Oper.

At the beginning of August, her anxiety had reached such a pitch that she was sure something bad had happened. She gave her assistant instructions what to do with the various pieces of business expected, found other voice teachers for the pupils she still had in hand, and with the money left in Clare McGarth's London account prepared to go to Germany.

'You're absolutely out of your mind!' her friends warned. 'English visitors are very unpopular in Germany at the moment.'

'But I'm an American, so that's no problem.'

'Gina, everybody's in a state of jitters. There may be war at any moment.'

'Nonsense,' said Gina.

She arrived in Berlin on the 24th August.

Eight days later, Germany invaded Poland. Two days after that, Britain and France declared war on Germany.

## Chapter Fourteen

For Gregor McGarth, the long search for the killers of Francesca and Cornelius had begun to show success.

During 1938, the director of the detective agency came to him with a lead. 'One of my agents has been contacted by a migrant worker. He won't give a name, and he says he won't speak to anyone but you, Mr McGarth.'

Gregor had questions at once. 'Who is he? Have you found out? What reason does he give for wanting to speak to me?'

'He's going by the name of Davison but who knows whether that's his right name? And so as to his demand to speak to you directly ... I don't know what's behind it. I told him we'd pay him for information no matter who he spoke to.'

'I'll see him.'

'Say, I'd be a bit careful, Mr McGarth. He

wants to meet out of town – and you know there are people who'd like to put a stop to your inquiries. It could be a set-up.'

That was quite possible. There had already been two remarkable 'accidents' in Gregor's life. A car had almost mown him down on the corner of Vallejo and Polk one quiet Sunday morning when he went out for a walk to clear his head after a sleepless night. And when inspecting a motor launch he was thinking of buying at the China Basin, a packing case had suddenly toppled from a neighbouring boat and almost driven him through the deck.

'Does he seem a suspicious character to you?' he asked O'Dowd.

'No, I can't say he does. And he's as nervous as a kitten himself.'

'Then I'll meet him. You can have one of your men come with me.'

'Oh, no, he wants to speak to you alone. But I can have a man tail you – this guy is edgy but I don't think he knows surveillance methods.'

The meeting was arranged among the huts and trenches of the construction site left over from the building of the new Golden Gate Bridge, on the Marin County side. It was just after sundown on a hot August evening. Heat mist was forming over the land, the air was heavy and damp. Gregor shivered as he got out of his car on the coastal boulevard and walked to the point under the stanchions that had been arranged as the meeting place. Through the fog, across the bay, the lights of San Francisco twinkled intermittently like distant stars. The foghorn on Treasure Island sounded regularly, like a lost sea monster.

'Mr McGarth?' The touch on his arm took Gregor by surprise. He'd been looking towards the water.

'Yes, Who are you?'

'Never mind that. Listen, Mr McGarth, I owe you a good turn and I want to repay it.'

'Me?' Gregor peered at the man in the dimness. 'But I don't know you.'

'No, but I met your mother once, Mr McGarth. Mrs Morag McGarth.'

'But … that was years ago!'

'I ain't had so many good turns that I forget them over a few years. Your Ma came to our camp in the San Joacquin, Mr McGarth, and she brought my Melda home when she broke her ankle.'

'Melda? I don't remember the name.'

'No, reckon your Ma didn't think to tell you. But she came with her driver, him carrying Melda, and she went around in our camp and she gave out every cent she had in her purse right then and there. And a few days later we got doctors and nurses, though it was too late for some of us with the sickness. We all knew who'd done that for us, Mr McGarth, and seems to me most of us would have done what we could for the lady in return, only we heard she died right soon.'

'Yes, she did.'

'You know, Mr McGarth, we didn't have no money to send a wreath. But we mourned for her all the same. Us gasoline gypsies don't find many friends.'

Gregor didn't know what to say. The fervour of the man's manner alarmed him; he sounded almost unbalanced. 'I was told you had information for me?' he said.

'I hear you're trying to find the men who set fire to the cabins at Regalo.'

'Yes,' Gregor hesitated. 'Were you there?'

'Naw, we was east in Mariposa County at the time. But word gets passed along, you see, and we heard you'd hired detectives.' He gave a little laugh, short and bitter. 'Some of 'em tried to work among us, mingle, you know – see what they could pick up. But you can tell a spotter a mile away –

they got too much flesh on their bones and they don't mind coming in with half-empty baskets. So folks stay away from the likes of them. You can't be sure what they're keekin' on. Some of 'em's after us union men.'

'All I'm interested in is information about the men who murdered my wife and brother.'

'Yeah, well, I can't help you there, Mr Mc-Garth. But I got information.' He paused. 'Is there a reward? I ain't doin' this for the money, but Melda's growed up with some sickness that needs a doctor and I ain't got the money to pay one.'

'There's a reward,' Gregor said. 'If the information is helpful, I'll pay your daughter's medical bills.'

The man caught his breath. 'Say,' he murmured, 'you *must* be rich!'

'What's the information?'

'A friend of mine was in a bar in Portland, Oregon, beginning of this year. There was this guy there, cryin'-drunk. He's left his woman in Fresno and she wouldn't come north to be with him. In fact, she was suin' for divorce, had found another man. I hear he was real cut up about it. When my friend asked him why he couldn't go back to Fresno for her, this drunk said it wasn't safe, he had to stay out of California because of what he'd done.'

'Go on,' Gregor urged, as the man stopped to drag his donkey jacket closer about him, against the encroaching fog.

'Cut a long story short, this drunk guy said he'd helped roast a coupla folk in a camp site in the San Joacquin. My friend pricked up his ears and paid for a few more drinks – he was flush with the dinero, won a pot in a poker game. Seems this guy had been hired to teach some misguided orchard-owner a lesson, burn out his new cabins and scare off his workers, only it went wrong and folk died.'

'What's this man's name? What's his address in Portland?'

'My friend didn't get no address. You can't ask for an address in a bar-room. But the man's name is Fisler, Walt Fisler, and he works for the Coastal Bar Construction Company – or at least he did in February. Sorry it took so long to get the information to you, but my friend didn't understand the story was important and we ain't seen each other until recently.'

'Thank you.' Gregor took out his pocket-book, extracted a hundred dollar bill, and held it out. The man looked at it, but backed away.

'I can't change no hundred dollar bill,' he said. 'I show that in a store, the owner'll call the cops, he'll think I stole it.'

Gregor could have kicked himself for his stupidity. 'Just a moment.' He felt in his pockets, took out all the loose bills and change. It amounted to twenty-one dollars and forty cents. In his pocket book he found four tens. 'Can you change a ten without trouble?'

'Oh, sure, sometimes a family can earn ten dollars in a day, the cashier'll pay us with a big bill.'

'Here, then, take it. And I'll send you the rest – in small bills.'

'Send it? I ain't go no address where the mailman calls, Mr McGarth.'

'Can you go into a post office, ask for mail that's been sent there?'

The other hesitated. 'I reckon,' he said.

'Tell me the name of a post office – somewhere where you'll be in three days' time.'

'I'll be picking melons in Napa, if I get took on.'

'I'll send it to Napa then. What name?'

'Lewis, Abel Lewis.' He put out a hand as Gregor produced a notebook with a gold pencil in its spine. 'Don't write nothing down, Mr McGarth. You got powerful enemies.'

'Yes,' Gregor agreed. A thought struck him. 'Do you know who they are?'

Lewis turned away. 'I know who they are down where I'm living, Mr McGarth. But I don't know who they are up in your world.'

'Wait!' Gregor caught at his jacket. 'I meant it, about paying for your daughter's medical treatment. Have you got a doctor?'

'I suppose ... we can find one.'

'Look, here's the name and telephone number of my family doctor.'

'We got to be on our way to Napa, Mr McGarth.'

'I'll arrange something. You could leave her a few days, could you? In a hospital for a check-up?'

'Yeah ... reckon... He's a real good doctor?'

'The best.'

'Cos Melda's real sick. She's been bad about a year.' Lewis squared his shoulders. 'All right, Mr McGarth, I'll call your doctor first thing in the morning. And I thank you kindly. So long, now. And tell the guy in the black car with its headlights off that I never meant to do you any harm.'

Gregor mailed the money as soon as he

reached home. He rang Weker to warn him there would be a call from Abel Lewis. He reported everything he had learned to O'Dowd, who sent a man at once to Portland. Fisler had moved on, but patient inquiries revealed that he had come south to Fresno in hopes of convincing his wife their marriage could survive.

Found at last, he was persuaded to make a deposition. He, of course, had taken no part in the wickedness of the others. He'd been hired to 'throw a scare' into some Oakies and Mexes. He'd been appalled when the prank turned into a felony. He didn't know any of the men with whom he'd worked that night, except by first names and nicknames. He hadn't seen them since, didn't know where they lived.

As to pay, he'd been paid, and paid well, by an unknown paymaster, a small fat man in a dark suit and with his hat pulled down over his forehead.

But one piece of information he was able to give. The equipment for the raid had been supplied by the little fat man, the pick handles and the gas guns. The gas guns and their grenades had been brand new, supplied in their cartons. And tacked to one of the cartons had been the name of the shop: Parton Guns and Tackle, Goading, Idaho.

The proprietor of Parton Guns and Tackle had nothing to hide. He had sold the guns and teargas grenades quite legally. They were to be used, he remembered, to clear out a colony of bats that had taken up residence in a cave wanted for storage.

He looked up his records. The payment had been by cheque. The cheque was from Lake Lucid Boating Hire, Forest Glen, Trinity County, California. The signature was that of the manager, Michael Mott.

Michael Mott, interviewed, was surprised and, according to the report of the O'Dowd agent, alarmed. But he agreed after some prevarication that he had indeed bought the gas grenades, to get rid of bats in the Pikonat Cave, where he stored some of his boats in winter. 'No law against it, is there?' he inquired.

Further inquiries disclosed that there were no bats in Pikonat Cave, nor had there been. If there have been bats in any enclosed space, they leave a covering of droppings. Pressed, Mott said he'd cleaned up the cave. Nothing that could be advanced to him about the impossibility of such a feat would alter his explanation.

It was further discovered that the Lake Lucid Boat Hire Company was owned by Richard Galdeston, of Sacramento, California.

Dick Galdeston was coldly amused when Gregor McGarth called on him. 'I heard your detectives were pestering my man in Forest Glen,' he said. 'What do you think you're doing?'

'I'm uncovering proof that you hired and armed the men who killed my wife.'

Galdeston shook his head. 'No you're not. You're wasting your money and being a nuisance. Why don't you just give it up, McGarth?'

'You admit that your manager in Forest Glen bought those grenade guns?'

'Yes, of course.'

'I have proof that they were used at my orchard – at first to intimidate the workers and then to kill my brother.'

'You can't prove they were the same grenade guns.'

'I have a signed statement that shows the boxes from which the guns were handed out to the criminals came from Parton Guns and Tackle. The owner will testify that they were the guns paid for by Mott.'

'Will he? And so what? The boxes could

have been stolen from Mott's office.'

'He never reported any such theft.'

'Well, maybe they were replaced without his noticing they had been borrowed.'

'Are you saying you knew nothing about the use of those guns at Regalo?'

'Certainly. And you can't prove anything different.'

'We'll see about that,' Gregor said. 'Perhaps I've gone as far as I can go, but the District Attorney will do better.'

The District Attorney was almost curt with him. 'What have you got?' he demanded. 'You've got nothing. Some gas grenade guns were purchased, paid for by a firm which Galdeston owns. You can't prove he knew anything about it. You can't prove he had anything to do with it.'

'Those thugs were hired by someone who wanted to prevent any improvement in the working conditions of the pickers. It was undoubtedly a landowner – you go along with that, do you?'

'Let's say I do. But you can't prove Galdeston was the landowner.'

'*You* can prove it. You can interview everyone in the Galdeston organisation until you get the chain of command–'

'Mr McGarth, we already interviewed

everybody we thought could help us, at the time of the crime. We got nowhere then, and we'll get nowhere now.'

Gregor studied the lawyer in his smooth grey pick-and-pick tailoring. 'Are you saying you won't go after Galveston?'

'That's what I'm saying. You've spent two years and a lot of money on it, and what have you got? A cheque signed by a man who's employed by Dick Galdeston. That's all there is – you can bet there's nothing else in writing anywhere. And it isn't enough. The legal system can't function with evidence like that, Mr McGarth.'

Gregor took his leave, amazed and angered at the lack of co-operation. He had been certain that Galdeston would be brought to book by further investigation on the part of the authorities.

But if the law couldn't make Galdeston pay for what he had done, Gregor could. He would exact retribution himself. Not by carrying out sentence of death – oh no, that would be murder, it would lead in its turn to retribution on the part of the law, and Gregor had no intention of ending his days in Alcatraz.

But there were other ways of making Galdeston suffer. He was a rich man, a proud man. It might be worse for him to be ruined financially than to face a court case.

It took much thought and planning to set his revenge in motion. But though it was difficult, it was less dangerous than the work of tracking down the guilty man. Galdeston knew the District Attorney had turned down Gregor's plea for action. He thought himself safe.

He was, on the contrary, very vulnerable.

Anyone who makes his income from the growing of perishable foods is at risk. There's only a certain leeway between perfection and putrefaction. Gregor arranged matters so that Galdeston couldn't get his peach crop picked.

After Abel Lewis's daughter received the medical treatment she so urgently needed, Gregor kept in touch with him. Little by little the man began to thaw out to him, and it became clear that he was involved in the organisation of yet another new trade union for the migrant workers. This one was called the Harvesters Union, with all the troubles of its predecessors: lack of funds, intimidation from employers, harassment by 'vigilantes', lack of stability among the workforce, fear of pricing themselves out of jobs.

The Harvesters Union received a mysterious large donation to its funds. When it called on its members to refuse to work for Galveston Orchards unless they got twenty cents an hour, they responded. Galveston's peaches ripened on the bough. Toughs arrived with staves to force the pickers to accept sixteen cents an hour. They resisted. Busloads of innocent Mexicans arrived to go into the peach orchards. The strikers picketed them, persuaded them to wait until the wage went up to twenty cents.

The strikers were called upon to disperse. When they did not, they were attacked by 'indignant citizens'. The police arrived. For once, the team of deputies acted in an unbiased way: they arrested some fifty strikers and some fifty indignant citizens.

It just so 'happened' that a campaigning journalist from back east witnessed the whole affray. He likewise reported the hearings before a local judge. The indignant citizens, finding they might be faced with prison sentences for causing bodily harm and inciting a riot, began to squawk: they wanted bail, they wanted a good lawyer. The crusading journalist ascertained without too much trouble that the lawyer who arrived hotfoot was hired by Galdeston Orchards, and that some of the indignant citizens weren't even local residents.

Friends began to distance themselves from Dick Galdeston. 'Look, pal,' they said, 'anybody can make a mistake, but to make it in public is bad business.'

'But it's worked before! They've never stayed out longer than three weeks – their strike fund always runs out by then.'

Not this time. And by the time Galdeston understood that the pickers were not going to accept sixteen cents, the peaches on a thousand acres of trees were falling to the ground, soft and brown and useless.

Something the same happened to the lettuce crop on Galdeston Products' land a month later. The foreman had the workforce summoned from a camp on the outskirts of Antioch, no trouble about rates, only too happy to take fifteen cents. Then on the morning they were to start, someone arrived from Martinez City with the news that the construction boss building the new aircraft factory in Old Diablo Valley was hiring diggers and drivers at vast wages, with long-term prospects.

The pickers loaded their families into their old trucks and took off. It took Galdeston Products almost a week to fetch in a new crew of pickers, by which time they were having to offer twenty-two cents and had lost a quarter of the harvest.

Galdeston began to have a name for bad luck. It almost seemed as if there was a jinx on him. He found it hard to hire transient workers. His permanent staff received better offers elsewhere. Newly-employed checkers let inferior fruit slip through to the canneries so that it was turned back after the first inspection at the cannery gates. His prune-plums were beaten to the market by another grower with new facilities and he had to accept ten cents less per basket. A transport depot, in which he'd invested heavily, was neglected in favour of a better depot opened by a new company at Stockton. Land he had bought in expectation of a projected dam was left useless on his hands when the dam was built elsewhere.

Now the aircraft and automobile factories were springing up all over western and southern California. Europe was shaken by recurrent crises caused by the actions of the dictators in Germany and Italy; the United States was going to supply the planes and trucks that would be needed if war actually broke out.

People who had come to California in desperation in the early days of the Depression found jobs now. Anyone who was able-bodied and could understand English found a welcome at the personnel offices. They became lathe-turners, machine-minders. They earned good money. They wanted somewhere decent to live.

Dick Galdeston watched the aircraft factory in Old Diablo Valley reach completion. Managers and design staff were already there, some of them living in trailers nearby, some in the town of Concord. When the factory hired men, they'd need a place to live. The aircraft company, mindful of its duty to its workers, was looking for a spread of land for a housing estate. Galdeston had a thousand acres of peach orchard which had brought him in a huge loss last year and which would make next to no profit this year if he had to pay the going rate to pickers now that the pickers could choose a factory job. The land was worth forty thousand dollars as fruit grove, close on a million for housing development if he could get it. Galdeston began to feel his luck had changed at last. He put out secret feelers to the aircraft factory's buying agents.

He was mistaken if he thought anything he did was a secret from Gregor McGarth.

Through a network of business contacts and willing helpers, Gregor knew almost everything Dick Galdeston did. He set about blocking the sale of Galveston Peach Orchard by the simple expedient of offering some land of his own in Old Diablo Valley – a smaller lot but much more reasonable in price per acre and with the benefit of good roads built by its previous owner for the transport of his fruit.

'I want you to put this through,' he told Rafael Mendoza, whose firm handled all his legal work now. 'I want you to act tough with Millan Aviation, but if there's anything they stick at, yield the point after a reasonable appearance of argument.'

'They want to bring the price down, of course, Señor McGarth.'

'Naturally. And we'll let them – I'd say a drop of one per cent would do it. We can let it be seen that we know they have other offers so we're willing to go down a little. But we know and they know they aren't going to get Galdeston down to anything like our selling price.'

'He may offer to sell part of his estate at a lower figure.'

'That's true, but I don't think so. Five hundred acres of old peach trees don't make

415

good business sense. He thinks he's going to sell the whole parcel and when he wakes up to the fact that he's been undercut, it'll be too late.'

'Señor – but would it not be better business to keep this piece of land for a better price? It will be needed by and by.'

'No, that's what I want *Galdeston* to do. The longer he has to keep unprofitable orchard in production the more it costs him. He either has to root out the trees and plant with something that markets easier, or sell – and though he may get more for it next year, he needs the money now.'

'Very well, Señor McGarth. I'll be in touch when we agree the final price.'

Gregor shook hands in the formal Spanish fashion and escorted Mendoza to the door of Montemoreno, where the Sunday conference had been taking place. As he returned to his study through the wide shady hall, Bess came through the French windows at the back, which led out to the garden and the pool.

'Gregor,' she said in a strange, quiet voice. 'May I speak to you a moment?'

'Certainly.' Her manner alarmed him. 'Is something wrong?'

His window was open to the warmth of

early September. From outside came the sound of nine-year-old Cory shouting with delight as he splashed in the pool with his friends, under the watchful eye of Rosita.

'Gregor, I have to apologise first. I overheard a lot of your conversation with Señor Mendoza.'

Gregor paused on his way to his familiar chair behind the desk.

'When I realised you were talking business I stopped. I didn't want to break in your conversation.' She coloured up, her fine skin showing pink under the freckles. 'I didn't intend to listen but by the time I realised what was being said I ... I found I wanted to know the rest.'

'It was a business matter, Bess.'

She stood across the desk from him, clenching and unclenching her hands. 'Do you think I'm a fool? I've taken messages for you, I've helped with your correspondence when you were busy – I've wondered before now, at some of the things I saw. But today I knew at last. It wasn't business, it was conspiracy.'

Gregor's mouth tightened. 'Bess, you don't understand–'

'Of course I understand!' she burst out. 'You've been plotting to ruin Richard Galdeston for over eighteen months now. And you've been succeeding. There's no basis for it in sound business, it's not business competition. You're targeting Galdeston for disaster–'

'There's a reason–'

'I know the reason. I can put two and two together, Greg. You never told me what the detective agency reported to you but when I saw what was happening here I went to O'Dowd. I let him suppose I came at your suggestion so he let me read the final report. I know,' she said, with pain and desolation, 'that Richard Galdeston was responsible for the death of my husband and your wife.'

'Then you understand what I'm doing! Why are you reacting like this, Bess? Don't you want him punished?'

Before she replied she waited a long moment, as if marshalling her thoughts. 'He's been punished,' she said. 'You've seen to that.'

'Not enough!' Gregor cried. 'Not enough! A few acres of land, a few thousand dollars – for two lives?'

'What will be enough?' she asked. 'When you've taken this chance away from him, what do you take next? The land itself? All his other business projects? His house and garden?'

'There's plenty left to take. Don't waste your pity on Dick Galdeston.'

'But what about his wife and children, Greg?' She made a little gesture of appeal. 'I know what it's like to lose my home – it's happened to me twice. I wouldn't wish it on anyone else.'

'Richard Galdeston has made provision for his wife and children in the event of his bankruptcy – you can be sure of that.'

'Is that what you're after? Driving him into bankruptcy?'

'Or as near to it as I can manage.'

'Oh, Greg! You're doing so much harm–'

'Of course I'm harming him!' It was a growl of exasperation. 'It's taken a year and half so far–'

'I didn't mean harm to Galdeston – I meant harm to yourself. Greg, you don't know how you've changed over these last months. I scarcely know you any more.'

'That's not true. It's just that you're seeing a side of me that you didn't know before. I was always a hard businessman before I left the financial world for the bureaucratic–'

'No, there's a difference. You don't listen to what I'm saying any more. You pretend you're interested, but your attention is only half with me – the rest is off somewhere, coldly calculating a man's ruin.'

Greg sat down in his desk chair so that, as always, his back was to the light. He found this position useful when interviewing others, but had never thought to use it for camouflage against Bess.

'I'm sorry if I've seemed impolite. It wasn't intended.'

'That's not what I mean and you know it!'

'Bess, I don't understand you. Don't you want him to pay – the man who killed your husband?' It was a brutal question, but he meant it brutally, to shock her out of her sentimental attitude.

She said: 'Greg, when the Depression first began to bite after the war, Neil took me on a tour of Craigallan properties in the farmlands. He was trying to save some of our tenant farmers who'd gone into debt with local banks. I remember we spent a long afternoon arguing with a particularly obtuse bank manager. When we got back to the hotel Neil said to me, "You know, Bess, money's just a tool. But in the hands of a stupid or a cruel man, it can become a weapon."'

He winced, covering it with a shrug as he

picked up a pencil to play with. 'And which am I? Stupid or cruel?'

'That you can even ask that question–!' To his astonishment her voice was full of tears. 'You must know that what you're doing is making you cruel.'

'I'm only doing what the law is too weak or too unwilling to do. I'm punishing a man who cost the lives of two people we loved, and of a poor migrant boy whose name we never learnt. It's not cruelty, it's justice.'

Bess turned as if to go, but then came back. 'You ought to be ashamed,' she said in a low, shuddering tone.

'What?' That completely astonished him. Her approval he had perhaps never expected, should she find out what he was doing: but this deep revulsion was something that almost shocked him.

'Last night we heard on the radio how the French and British Prime Ministers had declared war on Germany. You have a son one side of the hostilities, a niece the other. But all you can think of is your personal vendetta!'

'Bess, that's unfair! You know the cable and telephone lines are jammed up with diplomatic traffic. The minute I can get through to Switzerland I'll ask some friends in Zurich to contact Gina and see she gets out of Berlin. As to Lew…' He shook his head. 'Nothing's going to happen in the Pyrenees, Lew is safe enough.'

'All I know is that when I heard you talking to Mendoza, you were more concerned with the destruction of Richard Galdeston than the fact that the whole of Europe may go up in flames. You're obsessed with your own little war. You don't care that thousands, perhaps millions of lives are in danger. Nothing matters today except planning another step in the annihilation of Galdeston.'

He took refuge in cynicism. 'I notice your first thought is for those you love. Perhaps mine is for those I hate.'

Bess Craigallan stared at him. The look on her pale face was one of wonder and dismay, as if he were a frightening stranger. To his consternation, the tears welled up over the rims of her eyes and began to trickle down her cheeks. 'Cory thinks the world of you,' she said. 'He wants to grow up to be just like you.' She shook her head distractedly. 'I can't take the risk. It would break his heart if he looked up one day and saw you as you really are.'

'Bess—'

'I'm going away, Greg. I can't stay in this house if you go on with this wicked plan. It's warped you and it will warp Cory.'

'Bess, don't be silly–'

'I'm not being silly. I don't want my son to be infected with your sickness–'

'But where would go? This is your home, Bess!'

'I can go back to Chicago–'

'You can't do that to Cory! He loves it here–'

'So far,' she said, backing away, 'so far! But what if he finds out you're not the kind, indulgent uncle you appear, but a machine programmed for revenge? No, I'm leaving. I don't want to see all Cory's illusions shattered one day when he finds out what you've done.'

'No, Bess – wait–'

But she had whirled and, wrenching open the door, fled through it to the staircase and up to her room.

After the first shock of alarm, his reaction was anger. Women were so idiotic! Emotional... She would get over it. She was taking it too much to heart. After all, how did it really concern her? If she didn't want revenge, let her step aside. What *he* did was his own affair.

And as to packing up and leaving, that was nonsense. She couldn't go to Chicago. Her parents had almost no income, had no room to take her in. Of course Bess had a little money, from insurance, but she would be mad to try living on that, bringing up a boy like Cory.

Cory... She would think better of it for Cory's sake. He wouldn't want to leave Montemoreno if he were given any choice, not leave the school where he had friends and was doing so well. She might say she was leaving because of Cory but that was just self-justification. Typical woman's logic. She'd been shocked at what she discovered today and had flown into a fluster of reproach for which she had to find some reason, so she talked about Cory's welfare. But when she thought of it in the cold light of day she'd know that Gregor McGarth and his money could do far more for young Cory than a high-minded but penniless mother.

He was still angry at lunchtime, when he expected to sit down with Bess and her little boy. But they didn't appear. Rosita told him they'd accepted a spur-of-the-moment invitation from one of the mothers of the swimming party, to spend the afternoon at her house.

Late afternoon, Gregor at last got a line to Switzerland. He asked his friend to have someone in Berlin find Gina, and make funds available to get her on the first ship home to the U.S. After some thought, he sent a cable to Lewis in Biarritz: When there's unrest home's best stop. Contact Credit-Midi for funds stop. Hope see you soon stop. Father.

He wanted Bess to come home so he could tell her about it. But when she returned she went straight upstairs. Cory always had a light meal in the kitchen but on this evening a tray was taken up to him. The explanation was that he'd fallen from a swing at the Delacorts' home and was better off with an early bed.

Bess didn't come down to dinner. The maid said she had a headache.

The deferment of his news to her, about getting through to Europe, the frustration of having something to report that she'd approve of, made him irritable. He drank too much at dinner – a rare occurrence with Gregor McGarth. He listened to the radio, but the comedy show offended him. He remembered Bess's words: 'Europe may go up in flames... Thousands, perhaps millions of lives are in danger...'

He turned to a news channel and was rewarded with facts about Europe's first full day of hostilities. Air raid sirens had sounded in both London and Paris but no planes had come over. The German government was expressing shocked surprise at the declaration of war by Britain and France, but was driving into Poland with all the ferocity of its Panzer Brigades. Winston Churchill had been made First Lord of the Admiralty in Britain. The German navy had sunk the *Athenia*, a merchant ship, off Ireland.

The staccato delivery of the newsman made it all the more horrifying. He read it as if it were information about local traffic or the prices on the fruit market. But it was people's lives he was talking about.

Because he had drunk too much Gregor went to sleep quickly and slept heavily for the first few hours. But about three o'clock he was wakened by the sound of Cory crying.

He sat up in bed, listening. The boy was having a bad dream. He got out of bed and padded to the door of his room, but as he opened it he saw the light flick on in Cory's bedroom along the passage, heard the soothing murmur of Bess's voice.

He stood for a time at his door. He heard the child quieten. There was a long interval; Bess was sitting by the bedside until Cory fell asleep again, reassured.

Gregor put on his dressing gown. He went to his window. Reflected on the terrace below he could see the light from Cory's room, four doors along. He stood there watching, his mind ranging through a thousand thoughts, all his anger drained away in the stillness of the San Francisco night with its million stars.

It Bess went away, there would be no more moments like this. No more little anxieties about bad dreams and cut knees, no more running footsteps to greet him when he came home in the evening, no more childish chatter about schoolday achievement.

And no longer the quiet presence in his home – Bess, and her unobtrusive efficiency, her calmness, her good humour.

He couldn't imagine life without Bess and Cory. They had become part of his existence. Nothing was worth the loss of those two precious beings.

He gave a sudden laugh and said aloud in the darkness: 'I'm just not good at revenge!'

In his boyhood he had vowed to wreak

vengeance on Luisa Craigallan for her unkindness to his mother, for insults she had uttered. He had intended to oust her son Cornelius from his place in the family inheritance and be Robert Craigallan's heir. Yet in the end it had been he who went to the Philippines to rescue that same Cornelius Craigallan from guerrilla brigands. And it was he who had quietly provided funds for Luisa to end her days in comparative comfort.

In the same way, he had lost his grip on his plan to be revenged on Richard Galdeston. He had no doubt the man was guilty, and deserved to suffer. But not if he had to give up Bess and Cory to bring it about. That would be madness – a self-inflicted wound, compounding the damage Galdeston had done when he hired toughs to burn down the Regalo cabins.

He had harmed Galdeston, and had no regrets for what he had done. He didn't share Bess's view that he had been harming himself. Yet if that was her belief, and if the only way to keep her at Montemoreno was to go along with it, that was what he would do.

Galdeston would go untouched from now on. Gregor would withdraw from the contest to sell a development site to Millan Aircraft.

Ah no. Wait a minute. No need to be utterly *saintly* about it! He was in business, and had land to sell. He had as much right to offer it to Millan Aircraft as Dick Galdeston.

But he would instruct Mendoza tomorrow to offer it on equal terms, and then let the chips fall where they might. If he made the sale, so much the better.

He saw Cory's light go off and went to his door to call to Bess, to tell her his plan. He was a little too late. He saw her, ghostlike in her pale silk wrapper, flit through the doorway of her room. Her soft loose hair flared around her shoulders as she turned to close the door. He glimpsed a slender hand on the doorknob, then there came the click of its fastening.

He drew back. For a long moment he leaned against the jamb of his own doorway. Then, with a long indrawn breath, he went to sit on the side of his bed and stare at the shadowy pattern of the bedside rug.

He would tell Bess tomorrow that he was giving new instructions to Mendoza. He would say, I'll pay full attention when you talk to me.

Perhaps she'd been right. Only now, when he thought he might lose her, did he realise how much he had been taking her for granted.

## Chapter Fifteen

Gina Gramm was lying on her bed, recuperating after a frustrating day around the Ministries of Berlin. The phone rang. She picked it up without enthusiasm, sure it would be yet another injunction to read the notices put up every hour or so on the board by the lift on each floor. New regulations flowed from the bureaucrats now that the nation was actually at war.

'Mrs Gramm speaking.'

'Mrs Gramm? My name is Artur Froh, here on business on behalf of my bank, the Industriebank of Zurich. Your uncle Gregor McGarth asked me to get in touch with you.'

Gina sat up. 'Uncle Gregor did?'

'I wonder if we could meet, Mrs Gramm? I should like to have a chat.'

'About what?'

'We can discuss that when we see each other. Are you free this evening?'

'Well ... yes...'

'Perhaps we could have dinner?'

She hesitated. Here was a stranger, claiming acquaintanceship with Uncle Gregor – but this was a foreign city, a city at war. And she was an easy target for a confidence trickster, especially one who knew her to be the niece of a rich American. But when he suggested she should come to the Adlon Hotel, and ask for him at the desk, she knew she had no need to fear.

Artur Froh spent the evening trying to persuade her to leave. He expounded the problems of being a neutral in a capital city at war, and was not impressed when she explained she was looking for a friend who seemed to have gone missing.

'Dear lady, he is a German national, you tell me. He has probably gone to his family in the country or something of that kind. I advise you not to interfere – the present regime doesn't like interfering foreigners.'

Since he couldn't persuade her, he handed over a cheque which her uncle had sent so that she could settle her hotel bill and any other debts, then book a passage home. She thanked him for it, put it in her purse, and he could tell she had no intention of using it for the purpose intended.

The cheque from Uncle Greg solved some of her difficulties. It had dawned on her that a few marks quietly tucked into an apron pocket or laid in a hotel ledger could be very helpful. Her funds had not allowed her to use this ploy as often as she would have liked. Now she had plenty of money. She deposited the dollars in a nearby branch of the Morgan Overseas Bank then drew out a thousand Deutschemark. Thus armed, she resumed her quest.

But everybody was edgy. No one wanted to be seen in friendly conversation with a foreigner. At the end of the month everything got worse, if possible, when Germany concluded a friendship pact with its hated enemy, the Soviet Union.

Minor German officials were shocked, disheartened. How could they be in agreement with the Communists over anything, particularly the division of Poland, which everyone knew belonged by divine right to the Fatherland? Those same officials were frightened, too, when they remembered the uncomplimentary things they'd said in the past about Communists, who now suddenly were allies.

In amongst this, Gina tried to thread her way with her simple personal inquiry. Had Peter Brunnen entered the country? Had he come to Berlin? Had he registered at a Berlin hotel?

Had he seen Magda? And if so, where was she? Inquiries after Magda were always greeted with cold politeness. She had left the opera company, she had gone away, no, they had no forwarding address for her, they had no information on whether she had joined some other company, they had never heard her discuss her plans, they were sorry but they could not help.

She tried to contact Peter's parents. She remembered he'd said they had a small timber-selling business. She looked up the business directories and found a firm, in Katrinstrasse, close to the canal. She went there. The firm was no longer owned by Gebhardt Brunnen although they retained the name for convenience. When she asked for Mr Brunnen's private address she was greeted with great suspicion but in the end was given a village to the west, towards Rathenow.

She tried to telephone from her hotel. But either there really was no phone or the switchboard operator was unwilling to allow a foreigner to put through a call to an out-of-town number. A journey on a slow local train and a bus eventually got her to Schokental. Inquiry was greeted with surprised looks but she was pointed towards a steep-roofed little house in an alley off the village's main street.

'Frau Brunnen?' she asked the plump lady who opened the door.

'*Ja, gewiss,*' the lady said, as if in wonder that anyone in the village should doubt it. '*Wer sind Sie?*'

'Gina Gramm. Do you speak English?'

'*Englisch?*' Her little plump hands flew to her cheeks. '*Nein, nein, nein, ich spreche kein Englisch.*'

Gina groaned inwardly, but her halting German was sufficient to ask the all-important question. 'Is Peter here?'

'*Peter?*' Mrs Brunnen stared at her. 'What makes you ask that? Who are you?'

'I'm a friend – from America.'

'From America!' If anything, that alarmed Peter's mother even more. 'Peter was in America–'

'Yes, and then in London. He and I are friends.' She tapped herself on the chest. '*Freundin.*' She nodded with emphasis. 'Is Peter here?'

*'Nein, mein Sohn is nicht hier. Seit vielen Jahren'* He had gone away to San Francisco years ago. Since then, his parents had not seen him. His brother Franz was in the civil service, married, he had a son and a daughter. Peter had written earlier in the year to say he was coming on a visit but had never arrived. Franz said it was better that he should not – officials had come and lectured them all about Peter's duty to come home from wicked Hollywood but he had stayed away and, if they were honest, they had not tried to persuade him.

'You see, Frau Gramm,' Mrs Brunnen said over excellent cake and dreadful coffee in her gleaming kitchen, 'here we have had hard times. Peter was doing so well – why should we drag him home? But his refusal made the district officer very annoyed, and he was clearly only passing on what he'd been told by his superiors.'

'Did you make any inquiries when Peter didn't show up after saying he was coming?'

'No, no, why should we? We thought he had either changed his mind or had stayed in Berlin with that Magda.'

'That Magda'. It spoke volumes.

'He came to Germany, Mrs Brunnen. Whether he saw Magda I can't discover.

435

She's disappeared too.'

'Disappeared?' whispered the mother, her hands flying to her cheeks again in the familiar gesture of fear.

'I'm sorry – I didn't mean that. I mean, I can't seem to get in touch. I've been trying for weeks.'

'Perhaps she and Peter went away for a holiday together. There was talk of a divorce, you know. Perhaps Peter still wanted to persuade her out of it.' She was shaking her head in unwillingness over that.

'But such a long holiday, Frau Brunnen? Peter left England months ago and hasn't been in touch since. Magda hasn't appeared in an opera since February, though I can't find out if that's when she went away.'

'I don't understand any of this,' Mrs Brunnen said.

'Where is your husband? Could I speak to him?'

'Ach,' said Mrs Brunnen, with a shrug that set her ample bosom trembling, 'speak to him if you like. Go down to the river bank – he's fishing. But if you get any help from him, it will be a miracle. All he thinks about is fishing, beer and checkers. Why is it that retirement does that to a man? He was a bright, active fellow, my Gebhardt, until he sold the business...'

There was a knock on the door. Mrs Brunnen excused herself and toddled through the house to answer it. A conversation ensued, in Brandenburger dialect that Gina would have been unable to follow even if she could have heard it clearly. The door closed, Mrs Brunnen returned looking flushed and frightened.

'That was the village supervisor, Sergeant Mittlau. He'd heard I had a visitor, a stranger. Please, Mrs Gramm, I think you had better go now.'

Gina rose, startled by the apprehension in her hostess's eyes. 'But I'm only visiting the parents of a friend...?'

'You have an American accent so it was reported that you'd asked for our house. I told the sergeant you're the daughter of a schoolfriend of mine who emigrated. He's satisfied but you'd better leave. There's a bus back to Rathenow in ten minutes, and from there you can get a train back to Berlin.'

'But Mrs Brunnen, I don't see how it can be wrong or suspicious to be asking after your son...'

'Neither do I, neither do I,' Mrs Brunnen said, dashing at tears that brimmed at her eyes with a plump finger, 'yet it seems so. I don't understand the world these days. All I know is, it's best to be like my Gebhardt, interested in fishing and beer.'

She ushered Gina out and shook hands, saying loudly for the benefit of any listening neighbours, 'Give my regards to Klara when you get back to New York. Tell her I was very happy to meet her daughter.'

'Very well, Mrs Brunnen, I'll tell Mother.' She nodded in farewell and walked away. Although no one was about, and no one joined her at the bus stop, she felt she was under observation until she boarded the lumbering brown vehicle and was borne away to Rathenow.

That encounter scared her a little. For some days she did nothing much, except to look up telephone directories and year books. The big general post office had directories for all the villages surrounding Berlin and all the main German cities. She found there were many Ledermanns. She'd thought to contact Magda's relatives, but had never heard Peter mention which part of Berlin had been their home, nor what they did for a living.

On a cold grey November morning she went immediately after breakfast to a local office of the Ministry of Culture to ask whether Magda Ledermann had joined any other opera company. Although the official who took her inquiry was in civilian clothes, he wore a Nazi party badge in his lapel.

He grudgingly looked into the year books for the several civic opera companies. Magda's name didn't appear. Gina asked if there were other companies. He shrugged. 'Several.'

'Could you find me some information about the members of those companies?'

'Fräulein, I have better things to do than look up facts for you.'

She drew back, surprised. 'But I thought this was an information desk? That's what you're here for, isn't it – to answer inquiries?'

'Why do you want to know where this Fräulein Ledermann has gone? Are you another one of those "talent scouts" who try to tempt our German singers abroad?'

'I assure you–'

'Because if that's your game you won't succeed – no one can leave without permission and you won't get it these days.'

'I only wish to find Magda Ledermann for personal reasons–'

'She's a friend of yours?'

'Well, yes...'

'Friends with an American! It's not my business to help an American get in touch with a good German citizen.'

She couldn't understand his tone. He seemed to have a personal spite against her. She said in indignation, 'Your manners leave a lot to be desired, *mein Herr.*'

'Why should I waste good manners on you, American bitch?'

'You mean you only have a limited supply of good manners? But I don't need to ask. Thank you for your time, *Herr Auskunstoffizier!*'

'Go home and tell your Jew President Roosevelt that us Germans don't care what he does to help his cronies in England and France! We'll beat them, and then when we've finished with them we'll finish you Americans too!'

Gina went out as fast as she could, aware that something very bad must have happened to cause such an outburst. She bought a newspaper at the first kiosk, then went into a nearby café to puzzle over the headline in its curious Gothic print.

As far as she could make out, President Roosevelt had signed a bill annulling the Neutrality Act of 1937 so that Britain and

France could buy arms in the United States. It was more than an act to enable Allies to buy weapons, it was a gesture of friendship and support.

No wonder the little Nazi had been so angry with her!

She called in at the American Embassy to find out what the news might mean to visitors to Germany. 'Well, it doesn't help matters,' said the third undersecretary who was deputed to see her. 'I would recommend you to go home unless you have urgent business here in Germany.'

'Are you saying there will be actual danger?'

'Danger? No... But there may well be unpleasantness for a week or two.'

'I see. Thank you.' She rose to go.

'Say,' said the third undersecretary, 'could I ask what your business is in Berlin?'

'I'm not on business. I'm just trying to track down a friend of mine.'

'Are you with anyone? Friends? Relations?'

'No, I'm on my own at the Meierhof Hotel. Why?'

'We're just trying to keep tabs on our nationals – nothing official, just a good neighbour policy. My name's Frank Waller –

I wonder if we could have a drink together some time?'

Gina smiled. She recognised the ploy. 'That would be lovely, Mr Waller. Give me a ring some time. I generally stay around the hotel after dinner now the dark nights have come on.'

'I'll ring this evening if I may. We might go to a nightclub – do you like to dance?'

It was such a pleasant change from the weary trudging round offices, libraries, and government agencies that she took him up on the offer. For the next couple of weeks, since it was deemed politic to let the President's action fade a little, she allowed herself to spend some time with Frank Waller. He was a young-middle-aged diplomat, slight, fair, and more intelligent than he appeared.

When she confided the reason for her stay in Berlin, he was concerned. 'I shouldn't go on with this, if I were you. Peter Brunnen must mean a lot to you.'

'He does.' Gina thought to herself, suddenly, that this search for him was the one thing that seemed important.

'But there's something fishy about the disappearance of Magda Ledermann,' Frank went on. 'Drop it, Gina.'

'When you say "disappearance", do you

mean that? You think she has actually "disappeared"?'

'Well, it's a sure-fire cert she went very suddenly. And no one ever talks about her now.'

'So if Peter came asking for her, he might be in trouble?'

'I should imagine so.'

'Oh, Frank...'

'Honestly, Gina, this is an unhealthy business to be mixed up in. I should let it go.'

'But what you're saying is that you think something happened to Magda, and therefore something happened to Peter.'

'I didn't say that, Gina.'

She disregarded the denial. 'So there really is good reason to be worried about Peter.'

'There's reason to be worried about *you*. You could find yourself out of your depth.'

'I can't just back out now, Frank. Peter must be somewhere – and he may need help.'

Frank shook his head as if he doubted whether there was anything to be done. But finding that a gentleman in a black raincoat was paying a lot of attention to them from a table further back in the shadows of the nightclub, he got up and invited Gina to dance.

Christmas came. Presents and cards arrived from her friends, from her family in America. Her mother wrote from New York with some anxiety: 'I'd no idea you were going to stay so long. Don't you think you ought to come home?'

Perhaps she should. She'd been in Berlin four months and got nowhere. She began to look at the things she'd bought since coming here, in her mind choosing what to keep and what to throw away when she packed.

Her room phone rang. When she answered a beautiful deep bass voice said: 'Mrs Gramm?'

'Speaking.' She realised the English form of address had been used. 'Who is this?'

'Mrs Gramm, it is reasonable to believe that the switchboard operator has an adequate command of English. Let us therefore speak with some discernment, for as the poet Coleridge puts it, "He cannot choose but hear". Do you understand?'

'I do indeed,' she said, a little taken aback but not exactly surprised. She'd felt for some time that there was a listening presence on her telephone.

'I gather you are interested in a nightingale that has ceased to sing.'

A moment's rapid thought. Magda was a

singer. 'Intensely interested!'

'You are a bird fancier? I don't quite understand your interest.'

She sought about for a way to explain it. 'You heard this nightingale sing often?'

'Yes.'

'She used to sing alongside a fountain.' Peter's name, Brunnen, was the German for well or fountain; she emphasised the word.

'Ah. This little songster had a mate, I remember.'

'Yes, and that is why I was hoping to see her.'

'You realise, Mrs Gramm, there are no nightingales in Germany in December.'

She hesitated. 'I know that, of course. But they migrate to warmer climates, don't they? They can still be found?'

'Ah...' said the beautiful voice. After a long pause it continued: 'You know the phrase about men who lie abroad for the good of their country?'

That was the old joke about diplomats. 'Yes, I've heard it.'

'Have you any friends among them?'

'Acquaintances, perhaps.'

'There is a new production of *Un Ballo in Maschera* tomorrow night. Afterwards, a reception. Could you be included in the

445

party of your countrymen to attend it?'

'I could try.'

'I hope you succeed.'

'Why? Shall I meet you—?' But the phone at the end had gone dead.

## Chapter Sixteen

Frank Waller was delighted to include Gina in the party going to the Ministry of Culture reception. 'Even with a war on, there's so many events between Christmas and New Year, it's difficult to cover 'em all. Nice to have an extra player on the team.'

The reception was to be at the home of Baron von Jarneland, a large, ornate house in the Tiergartenstrasse. Gina had been uncertain whether her gown would be good enough and her doubt intensified when she stepped out of Frank's car. She was wearing one of the two evening dresses she'd brought with her, a simple but beautifully cut dinner dress of dark blue grosgrain.

The ground floor of the house was brilliantly lit once you got past the black-out screens in the marbled hall. Under a fine chandelier of Bohemian crystal, the room seemed full of officers in brown or black uniforms, Italians in tails and medal ribbons, Japanese in dinner suits. The big new Italian and Japanese embassies were just down the avenue.

Frank was greeted, Gina was introduced. Aristocratic names were mentioned, also titles from the academic world and from the ministries. Few of the women seemed to have names in their own right: it was 'Let me present you to Frau Professor Merker, allow me to introduce Minister Funk's daughter...'

With a shock of recognition, Gina saw a small man with a slight limp. Dr Goebbels, Minister for Propaganda. Now she thought of it, she'd heard he was interested in opera and the theatre. His wife was with him, her blonde hair flatly waved like patterns on enamel, overdressed in a concoction of frills at neck, waist and hem.

Gina moved through the crowd at Frank's elbow, accepting a glass of champagne, nibbling delicious little canapés. No matter that the German nation had been urged to choose guns rather than butter – there was no shortage of butter or cream in the food being handed around. Plenty of caviar, too –

but now the Russians were allies, presumably caviar would always be plentiful even in a war.

It was very late. The opera first night had ended about eleven-thirty, the reception had begun at twelve-thirty. One o'clock chimed sweetly on a French porcelain clock in the main salon, then the half hour. Gina was dying of fatigue, longing to go home and fall into bed. Yet she had been summoned here. Surely something was going to happen, some contact would be made?

She heard a voice she recognised. She turned quickly. A tall portly man was teasing a young girl, laughing as she blushed and giggled at his words. 'But of course! A good singer has to put on weight! If you take up opera, say goodbye to your sylph-like figure, Fräulein Launer.'

It was the voice on the phone. There was no mistaking that rich, deep basso.

Of course. He was a singer with Berlin Oper. She should have guessed.

Now her weariness left her. She tried to keep an eye on the singer. But he ignored her completely. She began to become impatient. Good God, if he wanted to tell her something, why didn't he make an opportunity to talk to her? In this crowd, it would be easy enough.

Yet perhaps not so easy. Everyone was watching everyone else. And Frank had warned her, not too seriously, to be careful what she said: 'There's probably a microphone in every floral arrangement.'

Nothing happened. People began to say farewells. Frank rejoined her from a group of men with whom he'd had a short, serious conversation. 'Time to go,' he said. 'Hope you haven't been too bored.'

'Oh, no, thank you,' she lied. 'I've enjoyed it.'

He beckoned to the maid in the hall, who went to fetch her short jacket of white fur – not quite ermine but not quite rabbit either. Frank helped her put it on, his car was waiting in the drive. She got in, he drove her to the Meierhof, kissed her a friendly goodnight, then she was in the lift going to her room, nearly dead on her feet.

It wasn't until next morning she found the note. It was pinned to the lining of the jacket she'd so carelessly thrown aside before falling into bed.

'Other birds are interesting. Ducks can be fed in the Tiergarten about three o'clock.'

After she had read it, she threw it down on

the dressing-table before going back to finish her morning coffee. She showered and dressed for the day. She picked up the scrap of paper, re-read the message, then crumpled it and threw it in the waste paper basket. She picked up her coat, bag and gloves and was at the door before a thought struck her.

Feeling an absolute fool, she retrieved the note from the basket, set light to it, let it burn to ash in the ashtray, then flushed the remains down the toilet. She even washed the ashtray before returning it to its position on the bedside table.

Too careful, perhaps... Yet last night's contact had been just as careful.

It was an achingly cold day when she walked into the Tiergarten just before three carrying a bag of buns she'd bought in Kurfurstendamm. Hoar frost still coated the paths and benches. Mallards stood forlorn on the pewter-coloured ice on the lake. Daylight had been reluctant to come to Berlin on this last day of December, and was leaving it early. The park was almost deserted, and no wonder.

What am I doing here, Gina asked herself. She was tense with expectation, though of what she couldn't say. She looked about in anxiety. There was a keeper stolidly picking up scraps of frozen paper with a pointed stick, a woman in a belted tweed coat furiously walking for the exercise, and in the distance among the lacework of winter trees a man throwing sticks for a big dog.

Gina took out one of the buns, tore it into pieces, and proceeded to feed the ducks. They, amazed at their luck, skittered towards her across the ice. Soon they were in a quacking crowd on the grass around her. She began to laugh. They really did sound like Donald Duck.

There was a yelping bark and the pounding of running paws on the hard ground. A voice shouted, 'Down, Macki, down! Come back, you fool!'

It was the voice on the telephone. As the ducks took off in low flight to escape the bouncing onslaught of the big Labrador, Gina looked round to find the portly man of last night approaching her, hat in hand, apologetic. 'I'm sorry, Fräulein, he's frightened away all your feathered friends. Just a minute, I'll put his lead on.' The Labrador sat down at his command and looked apologetic. His master clipped on the lead. 'Please recall the ducks to their dinner,' he went on, but in English now... 'I do like to

451

watch birds.'

'You're a bird fancier?' Gina asked.

'I prefer singing birds. Nightingales, for instance.'

She looked at him in a mixture of intense interest and apprehension. He was someone with whom she'd arranged a secret meeting. Why the secrecy? She was scared without knowing why.

He was tall, with a stomach as rotund as his voice. He had a bald head surrounded by a tonsure of iron grey hair. He now covered the bald patch with a little green hat with a feather in its hatband. He looked like an indulgent father taking out his little girl for a walk in the park.

'Please feed the ducks,' he urged. 'That's why you're in the park, remember?'

She obeyed at once, fingers fumbling because of the cold and the fright.

'We'll chat. You feed the ducks, I'll watch. You're looking for Magda Ledermann?'

'Yes.'

'But why?'

She dropped scraps of bread on the icy grass for the ducks. 'She's married to a friend of mine, Peter Brunnen. He came to look for her.'

'Did he?' He jerked in surprise and the

dog looked up at him, ready for action. 'No, sit, Macki.'

'You don't know about Peter?'

'No, which must mean he got stopped before he started asking questions at the Opera House. I wonder where he went first?'

'He'd have Magda's address. She had a flat, didn't she?'

'Hm...' He stamped his feet, to keep the circulation going. 'She was living in a villa on the Wannsee, a few miles outside Berlin.'

'But ... surely that was inconvenient if she was singing each night?'

'Not for Dr Goebbels.'

'What?'

'She was Dr Goebbels's mistress. The villa on the Wannsee is his. Very quiet and secluded in winter, when the weather makes it unlikely anyone will want to go boating and bathing.'

'Oh, good God! Peter had no idea of this, I'm sure!'

'I shouldn't think she would put that in any of her letters. If she did, the letters wouldn't get out of the country. Being the favourite of Dr Goebbels brings you a lot of advantages, but the right to privacy is not one of them.'

Gina found she had only one bun left. She

453

broke off smaller pieces, threw one to the anxious ducks. 'How do you know about this – that Magda and Dr Goebbels…?'

'Oh, it was common knowledge in the theatre world. Goebbels has a penchant for actresses and singers. And Magda was ambitious.'

She put out a hand as if to grasp his sleeve then remembered he was supposed to be a casual passer-by in the park.

'You speak of her in the past tense?'

'She's almost certainly dead. We've pieced together almost the whole story although we've no actual witness for the murder.'

Gina felt as if her whole body had turned to ice. She said after a moment, 'Could we sit down?'

'There's a bench a few yards off.' He led her to it, the Labrador padding at his heels. 'Sit, Macki. Close to the lady – warm her legs.' The dog flopped on the ground at her side and leaned comfortingly against her.

'Murdered?' she said through stiff lips.

'We have no eye witness to that. But we have a friend on the cleaning staff of the *Sicherheitsdienst* at Ploetzensee who told us she was taken down to the basement, never came back up again, and a body was burned in the furnace early the next morning.'

'It can't be!'

'There's little doubt.'

For a few minutes she sat, trying to regain control of her shivering body and her thought processes. Then she said, 'We? Who's "we"?'

'Mrs Gramm, you don't want names. You don't even want to go to the opera and find out who I am. The less you know the less you can be made to tell–'

'What! Me?'

'Do you imagine you're immune? My dear lady, this is Nazi Germany. No one is beyond the reach of the Gestapo.'

The Labrador, sensing her distress, leaned closer and put his head in her lap. Automatically she began to stroke him. It was comforting – warm and friendly in a hostile world.

'You feel bewildered. Perhaps a little background information will help. You must know that the Jews have been under persecution here for years. Some of us in the arts world felt it was cruelly unjust to colleagues who were talented and patriotic. We did what we could to help Jewish artistes get out of the country. Now that we're at war, our work is over, of course. But we haven't entirely disbanded. That's how we were able to get the message pinned in your wrap last night.'

'Please tell me what happened to Magda,' she said.

'She returned to Germany at the invitation of the Ministry of Culture and on the recommendation of some diplomat – we gather it might have been Ribbentrop.'

'I think that was Peter's impression.'

'She was given leading roles. She had a good voice, did quite well, but of course there are other singers with claims to the front rank. She was glad of Goebbels' interest, it was likely to help her career. Frau Goebbels, of course, wasn't pleased.'

'She knew?'

'Oh, it was no great secret. Frau Goebbels had been through all that before.'

'You're not saying that *she*–'

'Oh no, it was Little Josef himself who arranged her demise. You see, Magda was to sing Santuzza in *Cavalleria Rusticana*, and because Mrs Goebbels had heard about the new affair she came to the rehearsals. She took it upon herself to make a few suggestions to Magda about her interpretation. Magda lost her temper with her, told her not to interfere, and when Mrs Goebbels had marched out in indignation told the rest of the people present that she was damned if she was going to take orders about her singing from a horse-faced little nincompoop.'

Gina shook her head in dismay.

'Yes, it was tactless. Magda misread the situation. She imagined that because she had Little Josef's affections, she could lord it over his wife. You must remember, she had recently returned to this country, hadn't picked up all the nuances. We could have told her better, if she would have listened. Josef Goebbels likes his mistresses to know their place. His wife must always take precedence.'

'And for insulting his wife, Dr Goebbels had her killed?' Gina said in disbelief.

'Oh no. If Magda had had the sense to apologise at once, all might have been well.'

A dog-owner with a poodle came along the side of the lake. The poodle danced as far as it could towards the Labrador on the end of its lead. Its owner, a small, sharp-nosed lady, said in reproof: 'Now, Fritz!'

'A lively little fellow,' said the big man. 'Sit, Macki.'

'Too cold for me,' said the poodle-walker, and trotted on. As she went the big man said in conversational German, 'I call him

Macki, short for Macbeth – when he was a puppy he used to wake us up every half hour with his crying. "Macbeth doth murder sleep",' he ended, resorting to English again.

'You speak English marvellously well,' Gina said, glad for a moment's respite from the awful tale he was telling.

'Thank you. I didn't take up singing until my late twenties. I was reading English Literature at Oxford when the Great War prevented me from going on to my doctorate. After my stint in the army I couldn't settle down to the idea of being a professor.'

Macki, disturbed by the advent of the poodle, rose and lumbered a few paces towards the frozen pond. His master went with him, and Gina followed. The darkness was coming down fast now. They must soon leave, or make pretence of being a pair of lovers. But even then, the night-watch of the park would roust them out.

They began to stroll towards the gates. 'You can imagine,' he said, 'that Little Josef took Magda to task for her bad manners. This happened at a party given by some theatrical people. We had a friend among those present who tells us they spoke quietly together for a time, then grew more heated, and that it ended in a loud row and a slap in the face to Dr Goebbels. Our friend says she called him a conceited little ape. Then she marched out and was driven back to Wannsee, where she packed her things and left. The next we know, she's back at her apartment. She unpacks a few things, has a bath, and goes to bed. Then the Gestapo arrive and drag her away.'

'Oh, please,' gasped Gina, 'please don't tell me! It's so horrible.'

'Just as you wish. Briefly, she was taken to the barracks at Ploetzensee and killed.'

'But – just for slapping Goebbels face?'

'"Just"? My dear Mrs Gramm, people have died for merely failing to applaud after one of his speeches.'

'But how was it accounted for? She was supposed to sing Santuzza–'

'That's simple. When you receive a hint not to ask questions, you ask no questions. Unless you want to end up with your neck in a bowstring at Ploetzensee.'

'You mean ... she was strangled?'

'Almost certainly.'

'It's inhuman! It's utterly inhuman! Just for being a vain, ambitious singer? How can you bear to live in a country that allows a thing like that?'

'The answer is, we have no choice. The frontiers are closed.'

'But before – you could have left before.'

'Oh yes. Many of us did. I regret now that I delayed too long. I was to have gone to Cairo to sing in *Manon*, but the declaration of war put an end to that. Of course it's still possible to leave, if you can get a dozen permits or if you don't mind going as a penniless refugee. But I'm not a young man any longer, Mrs Gramm, and I have an ailing wife. And there are still one or two things I can do here in Germany that are useful.'

'You could find Peter! Could you ask your friends to find Peter? He came to Berlin, that's for sure. He has a German passport, he'd have no problems getting into the country and I'm sure he came straight to Berlin, because he was so worried about Magda.'

'With good reason, as it now proves,' said the singer drily.

'Could you find out what happened to him? He must have arrived here somewhere about the end of January or the beginning of February.'

'If he made any inquiries at the Opera House I haven't heard of them. By that time of course it was clearly understood that one didn't discuss Magda Ledermann. He probably met with a wall of silence.'

He fell silent. Gina's mind had been working overtime. 'If he ... if he looked like making a nuisance of himself, would anyone have taken steps to...?'

He took her hand, linked her arm through his, and pressed it against his loden coat. 'Take that thought to yourself, Mrs Gramm. You've been extremely persistent. You've attracted attention – mine, and probably others'. I decided to make contact with you for the very purpose of pointing out to you that you're putting yourself in great danger. You must accept the fact that Magda Ledermann is dead and if her husband came here demanding to know what happened to her, he may be dead too. You should leave, Mrs Gramm. At once.'

They had reached the road. Darkness had cloaked Berlin. The yellow buses trundled past, their headlights dimmed with blackout masking. People were beginning to hurry home from offices and factories, the pavements were crowded. On a busy corner the big man shook hands. 'Good evening, *gnädige Frau*,' he said in a genial, open tone. 'So glad to have had the pleasure of your company on my walk. Say goodbye, Macki.'

The dog obediently held up a paw. With her eyes suddenly full of silly tears, Gina took it and shook it. 'Goodbye, Macki,' she said. 'What a brave dog you are.'

She found a taxi to take her to Meierhof. She went straight to the bar, ordered a double brandy, and swallowed it almost in one gulp. It coursed through her frozen body, warming it, bringing it back to life. But nothing could cure the inner chill that this afternoon had brought to her.

She went to bed early, slept badly. Next day she felt quite unwell. She stayed close to the hotel, going out only to buy a paper. Frank Waller came by in the evening for a drink, leaving a little perturbed by her quietness. 'You coming down with the 'flu?'

'No, I'm all right.' She was on the verge of telling him she'd decided to go, was about to put her name on the waiting list for a trans-Atlantic passage, apply for an exit visa. But Frank spoke first.

'There's a party at the Embassy tomorrow night. How about coming along?'

'Oh, I don't think so, thanks.' She recalled the reception after the opera first night. Hours of boredom.

'Gee, that's a shame, there's a guy from

the German film industry coming, said he hoped to see you there.'

'Me?'

'Yeah, says he knew you in Hollywood – Schwab? Anton Schwab?'

She searched her memory. She couldn't recall ever meeting him. The name, she knew – he'd been a make-up artist, greatly respected. 'Anton Schwab wants to see me?'

'Yeah, honey. Say you'll come.'

'All right then, I will.'

It was her other evening gown, then, fancier than the dinner dress, sherry-coloured with a design of rhinestones at the deep neckline, and matching earrings. She examined herself in the mirror before she went down to her taxi. She was thinner, her face paler, but she still had good looks although her thirties were behind her now. But she had a feeling Anton Schwab didn't want to see her because of her good looks.

The party was elaborate, with a small band playing the Missouri Waltz and an enticing buffet. Gina went through the same long, slow process of meeting people who didn't interest her. Finally an attaché brought her to a group, and among the names was Anton Schwab.

He was a pudgy little man with a bushy

moustache. He smiled as he shook hands. 'Gee, it's nice to see you again, Mrs Gramm,' he said rather loudly. 'Remember that movie we worked on – when you tried to teach Albert Amozki to speak like a Boston aristocrat and I had to make him look seventy years old?'

She didn't remember anything of the sort but she smiled and said, 'Lovely to see you, Mr Schwab.'

'Oh, don't be formal – we used to be on first name terms.' He spoke English quickly and idiomatically but with a strong German accent. 'Come along, I'll get you a plate of goodies and we'll have a pow-wow about old times.'

She allowed him to lead her to the buffet in a side-room. They heaped food on plates, picked up a glass of wine, and headed for a corner of the entrance hall which allowed a certain amount of seclusion.

'One thing that's nice,' Schwab said through a mouthful of chicken a la king, 'if the Americans have hidden microphones, it doesn't matter what they pick up here.'

'What do you mean, Mr Schwab?'

'Anton, call me Anton. We're old friends, remember? It may not matter what the mikes pick up but there are guys here with eyes like hawks. Play it very friendly.'

She sipped wine, nodding and smiling as if he had told her some pleasant anecdote. 'What is this about?'

'Friends in the opera have let me know you're looking for a Viennese psychologist–'

'What?'

'Or is it a captain of hussars?'

'Oh! Yes – I am.' They were roles Peter had played.

'Our operatic friend told you he was probably dead. Well, he ain't. But God knows where he is.'

She knew she was going pale, and bent her head to hide it. When she looked up, her expression was determinedly bright. 'Do go on, Anton.'

'He got here beginning of February. I suppose it was to look for that damned wife of his. He used to talk to me about her when we'd share a bottle of Rhine wine.' He laughed loudly as if at his own joke, and Gina obediently did likewise. 'We were buddies, you know. But he had the sense not to accept this goddamned invitation to come home and be famous. I wish I'd stayed in Hollywood, Gina. But what the hell, here I am, and I have to make the best of it.'

'What happened to Peter?'

'He didn't get past first base. They recognised his name when he first came into the country, I think, and kept track of him. When he got to Berlin he booked into a hotel – mebbe he'd already reserved a room so they knew where to find him, I dunno. What I hear is, Gurbach wanted to make a film with Peter in a starring role – patriotic tale about a German naval officer giving up his sweet-heart to serve the Fatherland. So Gurbach went to see him the minute he unpacked.'

An elderly man happened along, examining the paintings on the walls of the entrance hall. He seemed particularly taken with the historical scene in the frame just above their heads.

'So after you left,' Gina said with a giggle, 'she kept coming to see me and calling me, asking if you had left any money for her. I said to her, "Maisie, I thought your feelings for Toni were on a higher plane–"'

The art-lover peered at the painting through his heavy glasses, sniffed, and moved off.

'He's a snoop,' said Schwab. 'But then so am I. When I get back to the studio tomorrow I'll have to report on who I saw and what was said. That's why I'm here, as far as the *Amt Abwehr* know.'

'And you're going to report what we're saying now?' she asked, a chill striking her.

'Oh, say, Gina... Don't be like that. I do what I have to to get by, but I'm not going to snitch on you or a buddy like Peter.'

'What happened to Peter?'

'He turned Gurbach down. That was a mistake because when he tried to leave the hotel he was stopped. They took him to the local police station and questioned him for hours.'

'But how dared they? He'd done nothing wrong—'

'Baby, he's German, and the way they look at it, he's got to do as he's told. Anyhow, so far as I can gather on the grapevine, they gave him a warning about his duty to the Fatherland, confiscated his passport, and kept him under detention at his hotel. Gurbach's secretary, who's a decent old bag, passed on the news to me. At that time they expected him to give in and take the role. I got word to him that he'd have to accept the part in the film or make himself scarce.'

'But what could they have done?'

'They could have put him away, lady. As an enemy of the state, as a non-contributing worker, as a subversive influence – you name it, they got it on the statute book.'

'So what did he do?'

'I've no idea. He's gone. All I know is, Gurbach's making the film with another guy in the lead, and they carried out a search for Peter over about three days, but they didn't find him.'

'He probably got away to Holland or Switzerland–'

'Not unless he got hold of a forged passport. They kept his, you remember. God knows what he's doing. He's a non-person now – no passport, no papers, no food coupons.'

'Have you tried to find him?'

Despite Schwab's warning that they must look as if they were gossiping and laughing, he gaped at her with horror. 'Are you crazy? It's all I can do to keep my head above water in this damn sea of troubles! When I heard the word from Bernhardt that you'd been looking for Peter, I thought I'd let you know the score, that's all.'

'Do you have any idea where he might be?'

'Not the slightest, and if I knew it would scare me. Gina, you've done all you can. Pack it in now and go home. This is no place for a nice American lady.'

She sighed and nodded. He had told her

all he could, and in any case it was time to move on to another conversational group if they were to avoid attention.

As Frank drove her home in the early hours of the morning he said, 'Did you enjoy meeting up with Schwab again?'

'Frank, it was extraordinary! He says Peter—'

'Don't tell me!' Frank said, taking one hand off the steering wheel to hold it up in admonition. 'The Embassy likes to invite people who used to live and work in the States, just to keep in touch in case anything might come of it. But it's all very innocent and informal and we want it to stay that way.'

'I see. All right.' So she had to keep to herself the feeling of relief and pleasure over Anton Schwab's news. Peter was alive. The lassitude and depression of the last two days were gone. She recognised them now for what they were – she had been mourning the death of a friend.

When she woke late the next morning she asked herself whether she should change her mind about queuing up for a passage to New York. But if she stayed, what could she do? Peter had gone into hiding. If she tried to find him, she might make matters worse.

She would leave Germany. But first she would go again to see his parents. She thought his mother would want to know that her son was back in his homeland, and had failed to contact them only because the authorities had prevented it.

She dressed in her plainest clothes – a thick tweed coat, winter boots, a headsquare tied under the chin. She didn't want to attract attention by any display of foreignness or money. The journey to Schokental was easier because this time she was familiar with it. She didn't have to ask the way to the house.

Mrs Brunnen swayed back from her door in alarm when she saw Gina. 'Mrs Gramm! What are you doing here?'

'I came to give you some news–'

'Go away! Go away! Questions were asked last time you came!'

'But Mrs Brunnen, it's about your son–!'

'Go away or I'll call Sergeant Mittlau! You'll get us into trouble! Go, go!'

Appalled, Gina backed away from the door. It slammed shut. There was something final about it.

After a moment's hesitation she turned to make her way to the main street. There was no bus until one o'clock. What was she to do? She'd freeze to death in this bitter cold if she stood at the bus stop for an hour and a half.

Perhaps there was a café. She might be able to get a cup of coffee. She began to make her way along the main street, but was struck by a thought.

Mrs Brunnen was in too much of a panic to hear what she had to say. But Peter had a father. What had his wife said about him? 'Go and find him down by the river.' Perhaps he was there now. Though it was a freezing winter day, fishermen never let that deter them.

It was easy to find the path to the riverbank – rivers are always at the bottom of any slope of the land. It was bordered by bare twigs of willow and alder. She saw a heron standing in silent watchfulness on the opposite bank. But by and by she glimpsed a little hut, scarcely more than four walls of woven willow and a turf roof. She could see, as she came closer along the path, that two men in heavy coats were sitting on stools by the bank, with fishing rods.

The one nearest her looked round as she approached, her feet squelching in the mud and thin ice of the puddles.

She began in rehearsed German: 'I wonder if you could tell me how to find Herr–'

She broke off. The man she was staring at was Peter.

### Chapter Seventeen

She was sitting on a canvas camp stool. Someone was holding a bakelite cup of hot liquid to her lips. 'Drink it, drink – you've had a shock.'

It was Peter's voice. She pushed aside the cup and said, 'What are you doing here?'

'What are *you* doing here! That's more to the point.'

She struggled to her feet. 'I came to give news about you to your mother–'

'Oh, *Himmel*!' Peter translated into German. The other man said in the same language, 'What did you tell her?'

'Nothing. She wouldn't speak to me.'

'*Gott sei dank*! My wife, Frau Gramm, is a very timid woman. It's better not to fluster her with knowledge she can't handle.'

'You mean, she doesn't know Peter is here?'

'No, when he turned up during May last

year looking the worse for wear, I decided the fewer people who knew, the better. Peter's brother Franz is like his mother, very nervous. We haven't told him either. When you came to see Mutti a few weeks ago, we were glad we'd kept everything from her – she was so upset by your visit it showed what she'd have been like if Peter had appeared.'

'I just can't seem to take it in. First I thought you were dead, then I thought you were missing – and yet here you are. Where have you *been*?'

'Oh, here and there – mostly there,' he said with some grimness. She could tell it was true. His face, always thin, was now gaunt under its careless dark beard. His hair was longer and more shaggy than she remembered. He was wearing a donkey jacket of rough navy cloth and a peaked cap. His bony hands were red and roughened with the cold. 'This is my father, Gina. He's kept me alive these past few months.'

'Only just alive.' He looked apologetically at her. 'I can only bring him the food Mutti gives me for a day's fishing, although I try to save scraps from other days. He slept here once or twice in the summer, in the hut–' He jerked a thumb over his shoulder. 'But

473

that wasn't safe because lovers sometimes use it, and now it's too cold.'

'Where *have* you been sleeping? You don't look well, Peter.'

'Never mind that. You ought not to be here—'

'Oh, nonsense. I want to help now I've found you. Tell me what I can do.'

'It's better not to get mixed up in this, Gina. I've no identity card, no papers, I'm dangerous to know. The Gestapo kept my passport. I got away with only what I stood up in, which was a Savile Row suit – I exchanged that as soon as I could for something less recognisably English.'

'What we need most,' his father said, refusing to let the opportunity slip, 'is money. Food's really quite scarce, and I can't give him much money because Mutti would notice.'

'Oh, money! I've got money!' she cried, opening her handbag to find her wallet. She pulled out a sheaf of notes. 'Here, take it.'

'But – there must be four hundred marks there—'

'I can get plenty more. You'll be able to buy food on the black market – there is one, isn't there?'

'Decidedly. In Berlin you can buy anything, if you have money.'

'Peter, if you could buy a work permit, everything would be a lot easier,' Gebhardt Brunnen suggested.

'That's true, but–'

'And if you're in Berlin, it would be easier for me to get money to you,' Gina added.

'I don't really want you involved, Gina. It's dangerous.'

'But I've been blundering about for months trying to find you, and nothing bad has happened to me. I think I'm regarded as just an eccentric American. Listen, when you've got your work permit, call me at the Meierhof–'

'Your telephone is probably tapped. I should think all aliens are under at least that much surveillance.'

'Yes, the man from the opera thought so. But we can use a simple code to arrange another meeting.'

'No, I don't think–'

'Peter, accept Gina's help,' his father urged. 'You can't keep turning up in Schokental. Someone's sure to notice you and report you.'

'I wonder no one's done so already,' Gina said. 'When you went missing, surely the police expected you to turn up here?'

'No doubt, but I didn't come here until almost three months after I went on the run. No one in the village knows what Gebhardt Brunnen's elder son looks like, so no one could really identify me. My parents only moved here after Father retired. I was brought up in Berlin. It's in Berlin that I feel really at home.'

'Well, if you can buy a work permit and some food coupons, you could probably get by in Berlin without too much trouble, until we think what else to do. Say you'll call me, Peter.'

Reluctantly he said, 'All right, I'll telephone to say your coat is ready for a fitting at such and such a time. That will mean I expect to see you at the time – where?'

'In the Tiergarten?' she said, remembering the dog walker. 'By the lake.'

'Now you must go. The bus goes through the village in about ten minutes.'

She hugged him hard, then held out her hand to his father. To her surprise he put a shopping basket in it. 'Townspeople often come to the country looking for little extras like eggs and game. This is your excuse if anyone looks at you.'

The basket contained two fish – barbel, though she didn't know it. Later, a lucky passer-by was happy to take them home from the Nordbahnhof where she ditched them.

'But how will you account for not having the basket when you get home?'

'I'll tell Mutti it fell in the river and drifted away while I was dozing. She'll think it quite typical.'

She was suddenly very sorry for him – an elderly man whose son was on the run and whose wife couldn't be trusted. She gave him a big hug too, then trudged off down the footpath carrying the basket.

When she met Peter two days later, he was wearing a decent secondhand suit and a raincoat. He smiled as she surveyed him. He looked altogether better, had had his beard trimmed and his hair cut. 'I'm supposed to be a draughtsman at Althof A.G.,' he explained. 'My name is now Otto Rethel, single, aged forty-one.' From then on they arranged to meet at a cinema not far from the lodgings he had taken in the Luisen-strasse. It was safe there, crowded, and suitable for a short murmured conversation in the back row. Sometimes, they would go to a café, other times they went for a walk through the dark streets.

On the first of those walks, she took his

arm through hers and pressed it protectively against her side. 'Peter, I have something very serious to tell you.'

'Oh?' She felt him give a jerk of alarm. 'What? Have the Gestapo been to see you–'

'No, it's not about me, Peter. It's about Magda.' She'd been dreading this moment. She was about to give him news that would grieve him, and he had enough to bear, an exile in his own homeland.

'You're going to tell me Magda is dead.'

'You know?'

They had slowed their pace. Now he walked on more briskly. 'Oh, they told me,' he said, very calm and practical. 'The first time they questioned me, at the police station. I told them I'd come to Germany only to find my wife – couldn't possibly report to UFA studios. They said, "Oh, if that's all that prevents you, forget it. She's where you won't find her". I was very stupid, still not frightened, you understand, so I said, "What does that mean?" The Gestapo man smiled – he thought I was a fool, and so I was, of course. He said, "Herr Brunnen, she's not even in the graveyard. Her ashes went into the Spree".'

Gina could think of nothing to say. She pressed his arm against her own body, hoping there was comfort in the contact.

Peter said: 'It's a terrible thing to have to say, but my only thought then was fear for myself. I didn't think of Magda. I look back now and I'm ashamed. But everything between Magda and me went wrong, I see that now. From the beginning, when I began to get offers of work as a singer and she did not... It spoiled our relationship. She couldn't help being envious. And that made me feel guilty – that I, who had less talent, should have a little success while she...'

'You're too hard on yourself, Peter!' Gina cried. 'Magda could have been glad for your success–'

'Well, so she could, if she had been a different girl. But you see, Gina, she was what she was and she has paid for it. Poor Magda.'

From his tone it was hard to tell what he was feeling. There was deep regret, and pity, but there was perhaps resignation too. Gina sighed within herself, but felt relief. She hadn't had to be the bearer of terrible news, she'd been spared that task. And Peter was already recovering from the sense of tragic waste. He had had to recover, because he needed his wits to save himself.

Now and again they were stopped by

police making spot checks on papers. After one of those Gina said, 'That stolen work permit isn't the solution. We've got to do something better.'

'The best solution is to get out of the country. But the Gestapo confiscated my passport.'

'The black market? Could you buy a passport on the black market?'

'You can buy anything on the black market,' he replied with bitterness, 'but the price is high.'

She called her Uncle Greg in San Francisco. 'Say, when are you coming home?' he demanded. 'You've been gone a long time! I thought you'd be back before this. Your letters don't say much?'

'I've met an old friend of ours, Uncle Greg. Remember that guy I used to teach English when I was working at the San Francisco Opera House?'

'What? I don't– Oh, you mean–'

'I've met up with him here in Berlin, Uncle Greg. It's a very sad story. He's as hard up as a hobo and the goon squad are after him.' There, she thought, if you're listening in and speak English, translate that!

'The goon squad... He ... er ... is in their

bad books?'

'Right! Can you send some lettuce to help him?'

'Of course. No problem.' Then, quickly, 'Are *you* in Dutch, Gina?'

'No, no, it's all aces showing at the moment, Uncle. Give my love to Bess and Cory.'

'I will. But look out for the Pinkerton men, my dear.'

'You bet. Goodbye.'

Two days later the Morgan Overseas Bank let her know a large sum had been transferred to her account.

She gave Peter the astronomical asking price for the false passport. The specified two weeks went by, then a third. 'I can't find the forger's contact-man anywhere,' Peter told her. 'Either he's made off with the money and it was a swindle, or he's been caught.'

'Oh, damn!' she groaned. 'Damn, damn, damn! It means going back to square one.'

'It means more than that. If he's been caught, he may have been made to talk. Or he may have given information about me for a reward.'

'We've got to try something else. Let me see what I can do, Peter.'

481

She went to the opera and had no difficulty identifying the man she had met in the Tiergarten as the bass playing the comic notary in *Don Pasquale*. She waited for him outside the stage door, and if the door-keeper thought it strange when she presented a bunch of tulips to a singer playing one of the minor roles, he shrugged it off.

There was no mistaking the panic in his eyes when he recognised her. He refused to hail a taxi. 'I always walk home,' he said, trying to disengage his arm.

'Then I'll walk with you. Please, I need your help.'

'I can do nothing. I told you that before.'

'But your group—'

'Our group is disbanded.'

'But the actual people must still exist. Would any of them know how to get hold of a forged passport?'

He jerked away from her. 'Certainly not! Formerly, every document we supplied to our emigrant colleagues was genuine. We got them by bribery but they were valid papers. I know nothing about forgery, nor do any of my friends.'

'I've found the man we were speaking of and—'

'Don't tell me any more. I don't want to

hear it. I'm sorry, Mrs Gramm, but I really can't help you. I don't have the contacts you need. Have you tried the black market?'

'Yes, but either we were swindled or something went wrong.'

'I think you'll find regulations are being tightened up. I advise you to be very, very careful. Goodnight Mrs Gramm.'

He was right about the increased regulations. Orders and controls were continually being published. As to the war, nothing much seemed to be happening. The Fatherland's armies had been victorious in Poland, the friendship with Russia was still in being, the craven British had tried unsuccessfully to cut off Germany's food supplies by means of a pact with the Balkan countries, the frivolous French were in disarray over a cabinet reshuffle.

And then, on the 9th April, Germany invaded Norway.

The blow was a stunning surprise. Berlin was in confusion. When British forces landed to counter-attack, a panicky gloom ensued, but cleared away when the British Navy had to evacuate in early May. Germany was *en fête* for the victory.

But new call-ups were announced. 'I'll be looking very conspicuous soon,' Peter said.

'They're getting towards my age group for able-bodied men.'

'We've *got* to get you out!'

In desperation, Gina asked Frank Waller to take her for a drive in the country and, in the safety of his car, explained Peter's plight.

'Ye gods!' he said. 'Do you know the risks you're running?'

'Never mind that, Frank. Do you know where we can buy him a forged passport?'

'If I did, I wouldn't tell you. Do you think the Gestapo isn't on the look-out for things like that?'

'But it's getting urgent. The longer he's on the run, the greater the danger of discovery. Tell me what to do, Frank!'

He drove fast down the Autobahn for a few miles then said, 'It's so simple, it's funny.'

'Simple?'

'Sure. All you have to do is marry the guy.'

'What!'

'The spouse of an American citizen becomes an American citizen. Once Peter's your husband, he's ninety per cent safe – even the most self-important brownshirt would hesitate before offending the United States Embassy.'

'Frank!' She clutched him thankfully, so

much so that he swerved out of his lane. Luckily no one else was coming up behind. 'Oh, thank you! How can we arrange it?'

'When are you seeing him again?'

'This evening.'

'Bring him to the Embassy with such identity papers as he has–'

'They're forged–'

'I don't want to hear that. I'll alert the documents clerk, they'll arrange for permits and visas. My advice to you is to go abroad on your honeymoon as quickly and un-ostentatiously as possible – because, Gina, I've been fending off inquiries about you from the Nazi authorities by saying you're my girl, and if you marry anyone they'll expect it to be *me*.'

When Peter heard the plan, he was indignant. 'I wouldn't dream of–'

'Now come on, Peter, don't be silly! All we have to do is say a few words in front of a preacher and you can be out of this accursed country in a few hours.'

'But good God, Gina! Do you *want* to be my wife?'

'That's no problem. We can be divorced as soon as we get to New York.'

In front of a Presbyterian minister at the American Embassy at eight o'clock that evening, Otto Rethel and Gina Gramm became husband and wife. There was a small wedding party afterwards at the Meierhof Hotel, in case any Nazi spies were taking an interest.

'Good luck, honey,' Frank said, kissing her with surprising fondness. 'Where you going for your honeymoon?'

'Paris, of course – where else?'

It was still possible for non-belligerent nationals to get out of Germany to France via neutral Belgium. On the eighth of May Gina and Peter took the night train. There was a tremendous amount of traffic on the railway between Berlin and the southern frontier. The passenger train was continually stopped and made to wait while freight trains went by. On the roads, too, hooded headlights could be glimpsed.

The three hundred and fifty mile journey to Brussels took almost twenty-four hours. Gina, exhausted by travel and the emotional suspense of the previous day, suggested they should stay a day or two in Brussels to recuperate and then book a passage on a Belgian ship bound for the United States. Peter, who had been very quiet ever since the marriage ceremony, agreed without demur.

They booked a double room in the Reine de Flandres. Stretched out with his arms behind his head in a single bed across a telephone table from his bride in another single bed, Peter Brunnen reflected that this was his second marriage. Like his first, it seemed likely to be somewhat less than romantic. He was grateful, of course, for the safety the marriage certificate guaranteed and for the courage she'd shown in looking for him for all those months. But gratitude wasn't the emotion he wanted to feel towards his wife, even a wife whom he would divorce in a few weeks.

He vowed not to be small-minded, but to be glad he had a friend like Gina Gramm.

They lay in the dark, each listening to the sounds of the other's breathing. It was Peter who drifted into sleep first.

Across the room Gina sighed to herself. This wasn't the kind of second marriage she'd envisaged for herself. But at least it insured Peter's safety.

Even that proved to be a misapprehension. When they woke next morning, it was to the news that Germany had invaded Holland and Belgium at dawn.

## Chapter Eighteen

Neither of them heard the weird keening of the air raid siren in the radiant dawn of the 10th May. They had fallen deeply asleep.

When the first explosions shook the hotel, they stirred and sat up. 'What's that?' Gina cried. 'Earthquake?' In San Francisco earth tremors sometimes occurred; that was her first waking thought.

She saw Peter in his pyjamas opening the shutter to look out. There was a shrilling of whistles, voices calling in French and Flemish. With the window closed, it was impossible to understand the words. She was asking, 'What are they calling?' when the words were drowned by a hideous whistling.

'Down!' cried Peter. Without stopping to ask what he meant, she threw herself down by the bed. A great blast of sound and sensation seemed to fill and empty her head. The room trembled and shook.

'Peter!'

He threw himself across the bed towards

her, crouched at her side with one arm about her as another bomb shrieked down. The whole building seemed to waver back and forth. The air reverberated with an enormous noise. Shock waves knocked from wall to wall. The windows shattered, the glass flying outwards.

'Get out of here!' Peter shouted. With one arm he hauled her to her feet and shoved her back, with the other he grabbed at their clothes, carelessly thrown over the back of a chair. 'Get dressed!'

She floundered across the floor and into the bathroom, which was windowless, being against the wall of the corridor. She turned the light switch, but no light came on. In the dark she pulled on the crumpled, travel-stained clothes she'd been so glad to shed the night before.

Outside the walls of the little bathroom the storm of noise and vibration was receding. She came out, tucking her blouse into her skirt, looking for shoes. Peter had on his trousers and shoes, was dragging his shirt over his head.

'Peter – it's an air raid–!'

He was turning to tell her to unlock the door and get out. Out of the corner of his eye he saw movement. He looked back.

The front wall of the building began very slowly to slide down like a roll shutter.

'My God!' She ran to him, pulled him away. Together they ran for the door. While she unlocked it he suddenly turned back, grabbed her handbag off the dressing-table, threw it to her, got his jacket from the back of the chair.

As she stood in the doorway she could feel the floor tilting downwards away from her towards the outside wall. 'Peter – quick–'

In two strides he was with her. They were in the corridor. They watched as the floor of their room slid downwards letting beds, tables, chairs, dressing-table, their suitcases, everything, cascade over the farther edge into the rubble in the street below. Finally only the dark red Brussels carpet was left, hanging out like a tongue in the morning light.

There were screams and cries from the rooms along the corridor. People in their night clothes ran for the stairs. Peter urged Gina along. The lift was hanging askew in the stairwell. They ran down the two flights to the ground floor. At the foot of the stairs they found piles of brickwork, and sheets of plaster from the ceiling. The chandelier lay across the reception desk. The clerk lay under it, his forehead pierced by a shard of crystal. A young page-boy was dragging in fury at a wedge of masonry that had been the hotel's entrance canopy. 'Alfred! Alfred!' But the doorman was already dead under nearly a ton of ornamental stone.

Scrabbling over the rubble, they came out into the Rue Brogniez. Already a fire engine was trying to make its way down the street to combat the blaze started by fractured gas mains and overturned cookers in the hotel's kitchens. The building next to the Reine de Flandres, an office block, was well alight. Men with armbands and little batons were directing the hotel guests and residents from bombed houses out of the way, so that the *pompiers* could get to work.

'What's happened?' Peter asked one of them. 'Why was there an air attack?'

The man replied in throaty Flemish. He was clearly swearing in rage and indignation. They could understand enough to catch the word 'Allemands'.

'But Belgium isn't at war—'

'Tell that to the damned Germans!'

Pushed and shoved by the police and the wardens, the crowd moved away, women sobbing, men growling in anger or exclaiming in horror. 'Where are we to go?

Our clothes, our money…'

'I'm sorry, *mesdames, messieurs,* this area is unsafe. You must move away.'

Peter automatically obeyed, taking Gina with him. They walked without purpose, tidying their hastily donned clothes.

'Welcome to Brussels,' he remarked.

'Can it be war?' Gina said, dazed. 'It can't be! We came through from Germany on the train last night…'

'I imagine we were on the last train to get over the frontier. That's what all the delay was about. That was what all those hooded lights were on the road – German troop transporters.'

'But they can't have! It would be madness!'

Peter made no reply. After a few moments he said, 'We're near the Gare du Midi. That's what the planes were aiming at, I suppose. Let's hope they didn't hit it – we ought to be able to get a cup of coffee there.'

'Oh, Lord yes… Do I need a cup of coffee!'

The station was booming with loud announcements on its Tannoy. Reservists were being called up, their numbers were being read out. Yet the place was buzzing

492

with life – almost all the neighbouring residents had come hurrying here in search of information.

The buffet was open, and not yet crowded. Peter bought two *cafes complets* which he brought to a table by the window. They could see the streets filling up with the Bruxellois rushing about in consternation. Cars and lorries began to roar along the road.

They sat in the buffet over their breakfast. They didn't yet know what had happened nor did they know what to do. They saw the morning rush-hour begin, bewildered men debating among themselves whether to catch local trains to their offices. Soldiers began to group, were called to order and marched out by a sergeant.

About nine o'clock the public address system ceased issuing orders for the reservists. A voice said, 'People of Belgium. Your government has just delivered the following protest to the German Ambassador. Although Germany has not declared war, the German army has just crossed the frontier of the kingdom of Belgium and has attacked the Belgium Army with considerable forces...'

A cry of horror and anger echoed up the

glass roof of the station. It blotted out the announcement for some sentences. 'As in 1914 … violation of undertakings… The German Reich will be considered responsible…'

Gina looked at Peter. She saw he had gone pale, though he had bent his head. She put out a hand and touched his. 'It's not your fault,' she whispered.

'But they're my people doing this!'

The reader finished the announcement, then began again at the beginning. He read the protest at intervals for the next half hour.

'What are we going to do?' Gina asked.

'My God, if it wasn't for me you wouldn't even *be* here!'

'Don't say things like that. No one could possibly have foreseen this.'

In that she was wrong. Frank Waller had foreseen it. Intelligence sources had warned that the German army was preparing an attack. But conventional wisdom had it that the Germans would subjugate first Holland, and then Belgium, and use those as a springboard for an attack on France. No one had foreseen that the High Command would order an attack simultaneously on the Dutch, Belgian and French borders.

After some discussion Gina and Peter decided to go to the American Embassy for advice. But when they got there they found it besieged. And it was easy to guess that many in the crowd were Jews in mortal terror of being once again under the power of the Nazis from whom they had already escaped once.

In face of their more desperate need, Gina was ashamed to claim priority because of her nationality. 'Let's go and find a hotel room so we can clean up,' she said. She rang her tongue over her teeth. 'And let's buy toothbrushes!'

Money was no problem. Peter's foresight in grabbing her handbag ensured they had funds and their passports. They found a taxi to take them to a hotel in the Place Rogier, where their lack of luggage was easily explained and presented no difficulty.

After freshening up, they went shopping. Gina bought a set of underwear to change into, a light blouse and skirt, and some walking shoes. Peter bought twill trousers and a knitted shirt. Combs, toothbrushes, a razor... It took up the rest of the morning, after which they had lunch and tried the Embassy once more.

As they walked towards the Rue de la

Science, they passed a radio-and-gramophone shop with its door wide open. A crowd was standing on the pavement to listen to the midday bulletin.

Parliament was to meet in the afternoon when a formal account of the early morning's happenings would be given. The German Ambassador had called on M. Spaak at eight-thirty with an absurd claim that the undeclared war had been to forestall an invasion by British forces. Fierce fighting was going on on the front at Eben Emanuel. Glider troops and parachute regiments of Germans were landing behind the defenders so as to attack from the rear. Citizens were to watch for infiltrators, report them to the police.

'It sounds like chaos,' muttered Gina.

Peter's reply was lost in the wailing of the air raid alert. They took shelter in the vaults of a wine merchant nearby. They emerged to walk only another few yards before the siren sounded again. The bombs seemed nearer the second time. 'Before they were trying for the aerodrome,' someone said. 'Now they're aiming for the Parliament building.'

At the Embassy the official advice was: if you have no business to keep you in Belgium, get out.

'What should we do? We were heading for Paris.'

'You'd better be quick, then, or the Germans may be there before you.'

'You're not serious!'

'Want to bet? The Belgians can't hold out – they're using bicycle brigades against armour! The Dutch are up against the ropes already, there are German naval forces in the island of Zeeland so Antwerp will be occupied tomorrow or next day.'

'But the French? The British?'

'The British haven't enough men on the Continent yet. As to the French...' The official shrugged. 'They don't want to fight.'

'That can't be true!'

'Just as you like. But our information is that they'll put up a token resistance and then give in. So if you're going to Paris, make it soon and don't stay long.'

This disheartening conversation sent them away in a mood of depression. 'What ought we to do, Peter?'

Peter was deep in thought. He took her into a bookshop in the Rue de la Regence where he bought a map. They went to a nearby café where, over English afternoon tea served by an impassive waiter, he studied it.

'It seems to me that it's no use heading for the ports hoping to get a ship. Nor is it good sense to head for Paris, if we were ever serious about that. I think we ought to make for Switzerland.'

'But ... what if the Nazis invade Switzerland?' Gina asked in a quavering tone. She was beginning to think they could do anything and succeed at it.

'Even the Nazis would think twice about invading the headquarters country of the Red Cross. Besides, I hear the Swiss have explosives planted to blow up every bridge and tunnel if an army crosses its borders.'

With a trembling hand Gina refilled her cup. 'So how do we get to Switzerland?' Her knowledge of geography was shaky.

'We'll have to head south as far as Chartres and then turn east. That means going via Paris if we go by train.'

'Oh, Peter...' She was thinking of the journey that had brought them to Belgium, and of the scenes in the Gare du Midi they had witnessed earlier.

'Well, we could hire a car–' He broke off, shaking his head. 'No one's going to hire out transport. The way things are going, they know they're unlikely to get it back.'

'We could buy one. I've got quite a lot of

cash – in dollars.'

'I don't think you should part with too much, Gina. It may be a long time before we reach a place where the banking system is working so you can get more.'

At the next table a thin-faced little lady leaned over. 'Excuse me, m'sieu, 'dame. I don't apologise for listening to what you've been saying. I always listen to English – it helps keep me in practice. May I introduce myself? Violette Lartaigne.'

'How do you do?' Gina said in astonishment.

'Madame, I am Jewish, a journalist, quite well-known for my articles against the Nazis. When they arrive – as they will, Liege can't hold out more than another day or so – I shall be put against a wall and shot. But I have a car. What I don't have is money.'

'And we have money, but no car. I see.'

'May we join forces? I too would like to reach Switzerland – or anywhere that is safe from the Nazis.'

Gina looked at Peter. He nodded. 'All right, it's a deal.'

They went with Mlle Lartaigne to her flat off the Rue Neuve. Her car proved to be a newish little Renault. Gina, formerly accustomed to American cars, accepted it without comment although Peter raised his eyebrows. It was a small conveyance for three people and some luggage on a hazardous journey across France to Switzerland.

They spent the night at their hotel, paid the bill, were collected by Violette at eight in the morning. They stopped in the market area to buy some necessities: soap and towels were provided by Violette but they needed food supplies, spare clothes. By nine-thirty they were on their way. They found they were in a press of traffic trying to get south while military vehicles commandeered the roads, moving north. Crossing the frontier control was no problem – they were waved aside and forward to allow a group of guns to pass, after which they simply drove on into France.

Violette, who was driving, turned onto a country road going east. The Renault bumped along on a poor road surface but was doing a reasonable twenty miles an hour against no opposition from other traffic.

'*Chut!*' cried little Violette. 'I was too pessimistic! Switzerland? Who wants to go to Switzerland? It's full of earnest clockmakers. *Mes amis*, let's go to Paris! There are far more openings for a journalist in Paris.'

Peter was against it, Gina was dubious. They argued. But as it was Violette's car and from Paris they could probably take a train to Switzerland – since, after all, things were more or less normal in France – they fell in with her wishes.

Paris was full of men in uniform and pretty girls quite unconcerned about the Germans. There had been no battles for months after the declaration of war: now the Germans were showing off their muscles by taking Holland and Belgium. But that would be the end of it. And, said the people in the bar of the Crillon, the war would soon be over. M. Bonnet would soon push M. Daladier from office, and then he would begin peace talks with the Germans.

'Peace talks?' Gina said in disbelief.

*'Pourquoi pas?* We're only in this stupid war because the British gave a guarantee to Poland. *Quelle sotise!* The real enemies of France are not the Germans but the Communists.'

'Well,' said Peter to Gina in private, 'if that's their view I think they're living in a fool's paradise.'

Events proved him right. The French radio announced that the Germans had taken Amiens. Three days later they were in Boulogne. 'When is this famous removal of Daladier supposed to take place?' Gina murmured. 'What about the supposed peace talks?'

'We oughtn't to hang about in Paris, Gina. It's a mistake. The Parisians can say what they like, but I don't think Hitler's going to talk peace until he's taken the city and driven down the Champs Elysées.'

They discussed and argued. Even if Hitler came, they ought still to be safe. They were American citizens. But she could see Peter was worried. Once Paris was under the control of the Nazis, papers would be examined very thoroughly. There was more than a chance that he would be pounced on by some film-going official who recognised his unmistakable voice.

'We'll go back to our original plan,' she said. 'I don't like Paris under these conditions, really. I'd like to see Switzerland.'

Violette Lartaigne was short of money so willingly sold the Renault to them. She was astonished at their decision to leave: 'The French will never let the Germans take Paris,' she declared.

It was the end of May. They set off eastwards once more. But now the roads were full of people coming south, people in cars, trucks, horse-drawn carts. Taking Violette's example they chose country roads, but now even these were busy. They continually had to stop to let troop columns go by. What amazed Gina was that troops seemed to be marching in all directions – east, west, north, and sometimes to her amazement even south. 'How can they fight the Germans if they go *south*?' she muttered. But Peter had no idea of the answer.

A week into June they had reached the little town of Chalons on the Marne, only some hundred and twenty miles from where they started. They were trapped in a horde of slow-moving traffic all trying to get away from the advancing Germans.

It was a very warm evening. A golden light lay over the fields. To get away from the slow procession on the chief road, Peter turned off at the entrance to the town. They found themselves approaching a big building with gates, outside which lorries and ambulances were lined up, blocking passage. Peter stopped.

'It's a hospital.' They had the car windows down for the fresh air. Now that he had cut the engine, they could hear the groans.

They looked at each other in horror. This

was the wounded from the war the Parisians had thought such a foolishness. Without a word they got out of the car, walked towards the gates of the hospital.

Stretchers were lined up in the vast courtyard, in uncountable numbers, perhaps as many as a thousand. Orderlies were picking up one or two, trotting forward under the direction of a surgeon in a bloodstained smock. Catching sight of Gina and Peter he called: 'If you're searching for a relative, we haven't had time to look at identity discs.'

The orderlies paused beside him. He stooped over the patient. A moment's examination then with a snort of irritated despair he waved them to put it aside. 'The man's dead, you idiots! Find a patient who's still alive and with a chance.'

Helplessly the bearers advanced on the rows of bodies. Some were tossing and moaning, some were lying only too still. They chose a stretcher and hefted it up.

'Don't hang around here,' the surgeon said sharply to Gina and Peter. 'It's not for civilians.'

'But where are the nurses – the ambulance men–'

He shrugged. 'The nurses are doing what they can inside. The ambulance men are trapped somewhere to the north.'

'Then who's doing anything for the wounded out here?'

'Who? No one, that's who.'

Gina walked forward. 'What would you like us to do?'

'You? Have you any medical training?'

'None at all. But at least I'm a pair of hands.' She glared at him.

Now, at last, he really saw her – a good-looking woman with a sensible pair of hazel eyes, looking at him with her chin jutting out. The man with her had a competent air. '*Très bien.* Go along the rows, put the blankets over the face of those who are already dead. Anyone with a wound to the belly, pull forward for urgent attention. Give sips of water to others if they are well enough to swallow but not much because, if we get to them soon for operation, they must have empty stomachs. Understood?'

'Yes, that's quite clear.'

From then on, all through the night, they toiled almost in silence. They began from opposite sides of the courtyard, working towards each other. Now and again they would call or signal, then they would lift the stretcher forward for the attention of the surgeons. Two other men in operating gowns appeared from time to time to check pulses, give injections. Sweating orderlies carried patients indoors.

About one in the morning another convoy of wounded arrived. These had to be laid outside on the roadway. Working by the light of a shaded torch, they had to be checked, sorted out into rows of hope or discard. Inside the hospital the medical staff were working by candle-light. The power station had been destroyed by enemy bombing on the previous day.

When daylight came, they were sent to rest by a sergeant of orderlies who was beyond being surprised at finding civilians helping. They found the Renault, shunted aside to allow ambulances to come in. They drove to the town, found an empty house, walked in, and fell on to the beds in two adjoining rooms.

An attack by fighter planes machine-gunning the main street woke them. It was about midday. The house was still empty – deserted, bread still standing on the table waiting to be cut, coffee cold in breakfast cups. Chalons had been abandoned by its inhabitants early the previous day.

They took turns to have a bath with the hot water from the ancient geyser in the bathroom. While Peter dressed, Gina found plentiful supplies of food – eggs, sausage, freshly ground coffee. They ate wolfishly: it was almost thirty-six hours since they'd had a meal.

When they returned to the hospital they found a different group of doctors on duty. 'Who the hell are you?' asked one.

'We were helping last night. We thought we might be needed again.'

'Have you had training – are you doctors?'

They shook their heads.

'Then how–'

'Emile,' intervened a younger man, 'if they really want to help, what we need is supplies.' He looked at Peter. 'Do you have transport? A car?'

'Yes, outside.'

'We need sterile supplies for the operating theatre. They come in sealed containers, they should have plenty at the *État-Major* which is at Rosnay. Will you go?'

'Of course.'

They got directions, found a deserted petrol pump in the village from which to refill, and set off. But en route they were forced off course to Guigny, a little rail depot town hemmed in by trees. There were empty factories and an abandoned railway siding, overhung by a pall of silence while the troops roared round it on the main road. While Peter waited for a break in the military traffic they found some food in, of all places, the deserted Mairie. They were eating it when the rumble of gunfire disturbed the uncanny stillness of the June afternoon.

At nightfall the traffic thinned, Peter got on the road again. But the sky was lit up by towns in flames to the west and the north. Vitry burned, and Ores. Rifle fire broke out in the woods to their left.

'We're cut off,' Peter said. 'I'm not sure where Rosnay is from here, and I don't think we can make it back to Chalons even if we get the supplies – I think the Germans are there now.'

So many pieces of terrible news had been thrown at her that Gina was past being surprised. 'We'll have to go south, then. There's nothing else to do.'

That night they found a deserted chateau off the road to their left. They pulled up in the courtyard, rang the bell in the porch. No one came. A dog trotted up, wagged his tail hopefully, but backed away when they tried to pat him.

Inside, everything was in perfect order except that there was no electricity. They had a meal from the items in the big refrigerator, remarking to each other that it was as well to eat them up as they'd undoubtedly perish in this heat. There was no hot water for baths but they washed and fell into bed, exhausted.

Some time after midnight they could hear the thunder of guns a few miles off. Gina got up from her bed, and looked out of the window. Flashes of light pinpointed the battle.

She went into the room Peter had taken. He was up, wearing a borrowed dressing gown over borrowed pyjamas. 'What do you think? Shall we move off?'

'I think we ought to. It sounds as if they might be here in a few hours.'

She went to him, leaned against him. 'Oh, Peter… It's all so awful…'

He put his arm about her. 'Don't despair. We must get to a place of safety some time if we just keep going.'

'I know, it's just that…' She held him close. 'I'm glad I've got you. It would be awful to be going through this on my own.'

'If you didn't "have" me you wouldn't be doing this at all.'

'But that doesn't matter. I just feel better, being with you.'

Somehow it seemed natural to move to the bed and lie on it together, arms about each other. And somehow it seemed equally natural to make love, finding in their sudden passion a moment when the miseries of a world gone mad were utterly forgotten.

Two hours later they were driving through the early morning darkness. They made fair headway until they got trapped by the great Paris-Lyons road. It was a moving mass of vehicles bumper to bumper: limousines, trucks, tiny Citroens, laundry vans, coal lorries, petrol tankers, Paris taxis, motorbikes.

It was impossible to cross it to head east. The only thing to do was drive parallel with it along country lanes in hopes that when they came to one of the great river bridges they could join a traffic stream going towards the Alps. They stopped overnight near Vesoul, and again at Tournus.

Movement was never easy but now at least the villages weren't deserted. Queues of cars could be seen at farmhouses with weary travellers bartering for food or a night's lodgings. After Tournus they ceased wasting dollars on hiring a room. They lay together in the warm, rose-scented night under trees or by a stream. In a strange way, they were happy. It seemed as if they had always been together.

On the fourteenth of June they heard that the Germans had marched into Paris. 'Oh, Violette...' murmured Peter.

They were washing in a little brook next morning in the countryside west of Lyons when Gina said suddenly: 'Why should we head for Switzerland? We're so far south now, Peter, we may as well go on.'

'Where? To the Pyrenees?'

'You can laugh. But I've got a cousin in Biarritz.'

'A cousin?'

'Yes, Lewis. You remember Lewis? He's there. And if anyone knows how to get us safely out of France, he does.'

## Chapter Nineteen

It took them two weeks to reach Biarritz. During that time it rained quite often, the Renault had a puncture and a leak in the radiator, and the news was unalterably bad. As they came through Biscarosse in Les Landes, they saw people in the *place* crowding round a newspaper.

'Hola!' Peter called. 'What's the news?'

An old man held out the newspaper, front page towards him. France had signed a peace treaty with Germany.

In Biarritz they didn't find Lewis by looking in any of the places frequented by the fashionable visitors, who were in any case making a hasty exodus. They enquired at the post office where they were informed that M McGarth had rooms with Pierre Delados, *'un vaut-rien'*, a ne'er-do-well.

'That figures,' sighed Gina.

It was a little stone cottage with white-washed walls out along the shore road, shaded by tall pines. When the said Pierre Delados opened the door and they announced themselves, he addressed a remark over his shoulder in an unknown patois.

Lewis appeared at his shoulder. 'God almighty!' he said. 'Gina! What the hell are you doing here?'

'Escaping from the Germans. How are you, Lew?'

'How d'you think? Angry, furious! Those damn fascist boot-lickers–'

'You remember Peter?' Gina intervened.

Pierre could provide a room for the night. They slept for fourteen hours then crawled out into the light of the July day to be greeted with the news that the British Navy had just sunk the French fleet in Oran harbour to prevent it being handed over to the Nazis.

'*Vive la marine Brittanique!*' roared Pierre, throwing a pair of fishing boots against the wall. '*A bas les traitres!*'

There were long queues at all the southern ports, of British trying to get home and scared nationals from other countries. There was no hope of booking passage on a ship. But by and by Pierre could arrange matters so that they could go on a fishing boat to Basque friends in San Sebastian.

'It will cost money, because *ces salauds de préfêture* have ordered no movement of French boats until further orders. But have patience.'

At the end of July, when the air war was moving to a climax over Britain, Pierre told them the Germans were bringing military advisers into almost all the French departments. 'But don't worry, the day after tomorrow we go to Spain.'

'I'm ready any time,' Peter remarked. 'How about you, Lew?'

'Me? What makes you ask that? *I'm* not going.'

'What do you mean? You can bet the Nazis won't let the Vichy government stay in control for long. You don't want to stay here under the Nazis?'

'I'm staying. There's work to be done here.'

'Lew!' Gina begged. Already there were rumours of resistance fighters forming bands in the *maquis*. 'You're not going to get involved in somebody else's war again?'

'It may be somebody else's to you. To me, it's my war,' he said, his dark Spanish face grim with long-suppressed anger. 'I'm staying.'

Nothing they could say would alter his intention. Anxious and unwilling, Gina said goodbye to him. She and Peter were put ashore in San Sebastian in the pre-dawn darkness. Pierre led them from the quay in the town, greeting fishermen on their way to their boats for the morning's fishing.

In the main square he left them. 'All you have to do now is go to the American consul. He'll give you any necessary permits to stay in Spain. You may have to wait to get to New York but all you need now is patience.'

'Thank you, Pierre. You've been a good friend.'

He embraced them both. Then he cleared

his throat. 'Madame?'

'Yes?'

'The little Renault car… You will be sending for it?'

'Not at all.' She never wanted to see the mean-spirited little beast again. 'Have you any use for it?'

'Oh, madame, it would be such a blessing to us in our little pursuits – you understand?'

So when Gina and Peter eventually set sail in the Maria de Cielo, it was with the knowledge that the car which had carried them out of the reach of the Nazis was still doing its work.

Gina's mother was on the docks at New York to greet them. Suddenly, introducing Peter, Gina felt her easiness with him evaporate. Now they were in America, it would be the end of their marriage of convenience.

'My God, what a fright you've had us in!' said Ellie-Rose. 'We didn't know where you were for weeks! And married!' She wrung Peter's hand. 'We've never met, but I remember you in the movies. Congratulations – I hope you'll be very happy.'

They had a room in the Waldorf, arranged by Uncle Greg, who rang that evening to ask how they were. He had clearly been very worried, and still was. 'Are you sure Lew can't be talked into coming home? I hope he's not going to do something silly, Gina.'

Privately, she was afraid that was just what he would do. But aloud she said, 'He has to follow his conscience, Uncle Greg.'

'You'll come home now, won't you?'

'Home?'

'To San Francisco. That's your home, isn't it?'

'I suppose it is.'

'Please come,' Greg said. 'I'd like you here for the wedding.'

'What wedding?'

'Bess and I are getting married.'

'Uncle Greg! Oh, that's great! I don't know what to say! It's just the best news I've had in weeks! Tell Bess—'

'Tell her yourself. She's standing by waiting to speak to you.'

Bess came on the line, to congratulate Gina on her marriage and speak smilingly of her own. When she put down the phone Gina was thoughtful. Were she and Peter destined to stay married much longer? That had been their bargain, a divorce, and she didn't want him to feel that just because they'd become lovers, it necessarily meant they had to stay man and wife.

When she told her mother she would be going to San Francisco soon, Ellie-Rose replied, 'That's what I expected. Peter will be taking up his film career again, won't he?'

'That remains to be seen. Bert Kolin is negotiating for him. He's been away from the screen quite some time – it doesn't help.'

'Would the pair of you ever think of settling in New York, perhaps? I'd like that. Now that your brother Bobby is heading for Harvard, it would be nice to have a daughter close by.'

'Mother!' Gina exclaimed. 'What Peter does won't concern *me*! We only got married so he could be a U.S. citizen. He still takes it for granted we'll be divorced just as soon as possible.'

Ellie-Rose gasped at her daughter. 'But that ... that's terribly ungrateful.'

'Nothing of the kind. We agreed on it before we left Berlin.'

'Yes, but you're in love with him, I can see you are. He may want a divorce, but *you* don't.'

'Don't be absurd. I wouldn't dream of tying up Peter in a marriage that he never really wanted.'

Ellie-Rose was incensed. She took Peter

into her husband's poky little office next time they visited her apartment in Brooklyn to say with hauteur, 'I quite appreciate that you and my daughter made a bargain to stay married until you were safe in the United States, but I think it would only be polite not to be in a hurry to divorce.'

'Divorce?' Peter echoed, sitting up straight in John Martin's typing chair. 'Who's talking about divorce?'

'You are.' Ellie-Rose looked at him. 'Aren't you?'

'Not I,' he said with emphasis. A shadow passed over his lean face. 'I thought, in fact... But perhaps I was wrong.'

'What did you think? What?'

'I thought we'd decided not to break up our marriage.'

'That's not what Gina says. She thinks you expect a divorce as soon as decently possible.'

'But that – well, that's only if *she* does.'

Ellie-Rose began to laugh. 'Then I can safely tell you – she does not.'

Peter, however, didn't laugh. He thought about it then said, 'I must speak to her.'

'Yes, you must.'

'At once.'

'Quite,' said Ellie-Rose. She went into the

kitchen, pottered about with the preparations for the dinner they were to share, called her husband John to help her, and thus in typically matchmaking fashion left the half-married Brunnens alone to talk over their problem.

It was more difficult for Peter than any scene he would ever play.

'I must know,' Peter said, 'whether you love me. I love you, but that mustn't make you feel tied to me.'

Gina frowned in surprise. 'What makes you say all this all of a sudden?'

'Your mother says you think you should start divorce proceedings.'

'Well... That was the agreement.'

He reached out for her. 'That was before I began to be in love with you.'

She took refuge in frivolity. 'And when was that, pray tell?'

'I'm not sure. I think it was in that hotel room in Brussels that first night, I suddenly knew I wanted you beside me.'

'Oh, why didn't you *say* something, Peter?' She looked at him, tears brimming in her dark eyes, still as beautiful as the day he had first seen her, in the San Francisco Opera House.

'I'm saying it now. You still haven't

answered my question.'

'What was the question?'

'Whether you want to stay married.'

Gina leaned towards him and buried her face in his shoulder. 'If this is a belated proposal, the answer is, yes.'

It was spring when they set off for San Francisco by car, enjoying the slow progress across the country. Bess and Greg were to be married in April. The newspapers were already running little paragraphs: 'McGarth Enjoying Double Blessing – Oil Bonanza and Wedding Bells.' Clare was coming home from Hawaii for the ceremony, bringing her little daughter Estelle. Ellie-Rose and John would follow later by train. Curt was to be present, but had promised not to bring his latest lady-love, a wealthy divorcée from Milwaukee.

'We're so lucky,' Gina sighed, leaning her head against her husband's shoulder as their Cadillac, a wedding present from Greg, ate up the miles. 'All of Europe's in a mess, but we've got peace – and Roosevelt for a third term as President.'

Luckily she couldn't see into the future. The Japanese attack on Pearl Harbor was still nine months away. For the moment she and all who were dear to her were in the

Promised Land, that 'good ground' where the seed can grow and flourish.

She had happiness for the present. Few can hope for more.

The publishers hope that this book has given you enjoyable reading. Large Print Books are especially designed to be as easy to see and hold as possible. If you wish a complete list of our books please ask at your local library or write directly to:

**Magna Large Print Books**
Magna House, Long Preston,
Skipton, North Yorkshire.
BD23 4ND

This Large Print Book, for people
who cannot read normal print,
is published under the auspices of

## THE ULVERSCROFT FOUNDATION

## Other MAGNA Titles
## In Large Print

**ANNE BAKER**
Merseyside Girls

**JESSICA BLAIR**
The Long Way Home

**W. J. BURLEY**
The House Of Care

**MEG HUTCHINSON**
No Place For A Woman

**JOAN JONKER**
Many A Tear Has To Fall

**LYNDA PAGE**
All Or Nothing

**NICHOLAS RHEA**
Constable Over The Bridge

**MARGARET THORNTON**
Beyond The Sunset